HIGH FANTASY

Here in worlds of the absurd, the impossible, and the exquisite—where beauty walks with illusion and radiance sweeps the sky—you may wander into the Red-Peach-Blossom-Inlet, charmed home of divine rapture and immortality, or climb the staircase fashioned of silver and crystal to gaze into the glass of supreme moments.

You will meet the Chinese fisherman who leaves his hook unbaited so no fish will disturb his meditation; experience the land of the Kith of Elf-Folk, where the soulless Wild Things can only be seen at night when their headlamps are lit; and follow Nerryn on her perilous quest to free a frozen kingdom from a mountain goddess' spell.

This companion volume to THE FANTASTIC IMAGINATION, presents the works of sixteen authors in realms of myth fantasy, fairy tale, and heroic adventure—from George Mac Donald's "The Golden Key" (1867) to Vera Chapman's "Crusader Damosel" (1977)—a century of stories by the finest writers of high fantasy.

Other Avon books by
Robert H. Boyer
and
Kenneth J. Zahorski

THE FANTASTIC IMAGINATION   32326 $2.25

The Fantastic Imagination II

An Anthology of High Fantasy

Edited by
**ROBERT H. BOYER &
KENNETH J. ZAHORSKI**

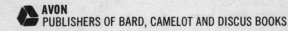

AVON
PUBLISHERS OF BARD, CAMELOT AND DISCUS BOOKS

FANTASTIC IMAGINATION II is an original publication of Avon Books. This work has never before appeared in book form.

Cover illustration by Elizabeth Malczynski.

AVON BOOKS
A division of
The Hearst Corporation
959 Eighth Avenue
New York, New York 10019

First Avon Printing, December, 1978

AVON TRADEMARK REG. U.S. PAT. OFF. AND IN
OTHER COUNTRIES, MARCA REGISTRADA, HECHO EN
U.S.A.

Printed in the U.S.A.

ACKNOWLEDGMENTS

George Mac Donald, "The Golden Key." Reprinted from Glenn Edward Sadler, ed., *The Gifts of the Child Christ: Fairy Tales and Stories for the Childlike.* Vol. I. (Grand Rapids, Michigan: William Eerdmans Publishing Co., 1973). Used by permission of the William Eerdmans Publishing Co.

Barry Pain, "The Glass of Supreme Moments." Reprinted from *Stories and Interludes* (Harper, 1892), by permission of Harper & Row, Publishers, Inc.

Frank R. Stockton, "Old Pipes and the Dryad," in *The Storyteller's Pack* (New York: Charles Scribner's Sons, 1968). Reprinted by permission of Charles Scribner's Sons.

Lord Dunsany, "The Kith of the Elf-folk," in *The Sword of Welleran and Other Tales of Enchantment* (New York: The Devin-Adair Co., 1954). Reprinted by permission of The Devin-Adair Co., Old Greenwich, Conn. Copyright © 1954 by Lord Dunsany.

Kenneth Morris, "Red-Peach-Blossom Inlet." Reprinted from *The Secret Mountain and Other Tales* (London: Faber & Gwyer, 1926).

Selma Lagerlöf, "The Legend of the Christmas Rose," in *Sweden's Best Stories: An Introduction to Swedish Fiction* (New York: W. W. Norton Company, Inc. Reprint of 1928 Edition). Translated by Charles Wharton Stork. Edited by Hanna Astrup Larsen. Reprinted by permission of the American Scandinavian Foundation, 127 East 73 Street, New York, N.Y. 10021.

Evangeline Walton, "Above Ker-Is." Printed by permission of Harold Ober Associates, Inc., 40 East 49th Street, New York, N.Y. 10017. Copyright © 1978 by Evangeline Walton.

Eric Linklater, "The Abominable Imprecation," in *God Likes Them Plain: Short Stories* (London: Jonathan Cape, Ltd., 1935). Reprinted by permission of Jonathan Cape, Ltd., 30 Bedford Square, London, WC I; reprinted by permission of A. D. Peters & Co., Ltd., London.

C. L. Moore, "Jirel Meets Magic," in *Shambleau and Others* (New York: Gnome Press, 1953). Copyright © 1953 by C. L. Moore, reprinted by permission of Harold Matson Co., Inc., New York.

David H. Keller, "The Thirty and One," in *Life Everlasting and Other Tales of Science, Fantasy, and Horror* (Westport, Conn.: Hyperion Press, 1974). Reprinted by permission of Hyperion Press, Inc.

Ursula K. Le Guin, "April in Paris," in *The Wind's Twelve Quarters* (New York: Harper & Row, 1975). Copyright © 1962, 1975 by Ursula K. Le Guin; reprinted by permission of the author and the author's agent, Virginia Kidd.

Joan Aiken, "A Harp of Fishbones," from the book *Not What You Expected*. Copyright © 1974 by Joan Aiken. Reprinted by permission of Doubleday & Company, Inc. Also reprinted by permission of Brandt & Brandt, New York; Jonathan Cape, London; and A. M. Heath & Co., Ltd., Authors' Agents, London.

Lloyd Alexander, "The Smith, the Weaver, and the Harper," in *The Foundling and Other Tales of Prydain* (New York: Holt, Rinehart and Winston, 1973). Copyright © 1973 by Lloyd Alexander. Reprinted by permission of Holt, Rinehart and Winston, Publishers.

Patricia A. McKillip, Chapters 2 and 3 from *The Throme of the Erril of Sherill* (New York: Atheneum Publishers, 1973). Copyright © 1973 by Patricia A. McKillip from *The Throme of the Erril of Sherill*. Used by permission of Atheneum Publishers.

Sylvia Townsend Warner, "Elphenor and Weasel," in

Acknowledgments

Kingdoms of Elfin (New York: The Viking Press, 1977). Copyright © 1974 by Sylvia Townsend Warner. Originally appeared in *The New Yorker*. Reprinted by permission of The Viking Press.

Vera Chapman, "Crusader Damosel." Copyright © 1978 by Vera Chapman. Printed by permission of Vera Chapman.

CONTENTS

PREFACE

We are pleased to express our gratitude to those who, in various ways, shared with us the excitement and the labors involved in compiling this anthology: to Marianne Miller, our research assistant, and to Mark Allen, our former assistant, whose advice we continue to solicit; to Peggy Schlapman, who is a combination proofreader, typist, and gracious lady; to the staff of the Saint Norbert College Library, in particular Don Pieters and Lory Wieseckel; to the staff of the Brown County Library, especially Louanne Crowder, Head, Young Adult Department, for her support and encouragement; to Grace Knoche, Leader, The Theosophical Society–International, for researching material on Kenneth Morris; to Jessica Kemball-Cooke for her constructive criticism and, especially, for introducing us to the work of Vera Chapman; to Donald B. King, Dean of Saint Norbert College, for his personal interest in this project; and to Marijean and Barb, our wives and our muses.

INTRODUCTION

This anthology is a companion volume to *The Fantastic Imagination: An Anthology of High Fantasy*. Like its predecessor, which we can now refer to as Volume I, Volume II consists solely of works of high fantasy, that is, of stories which take place in or border on a magical or supernatural other world, places like Joiry and Prydain. Until the appearance of Volume I, just about a year ago, there simply were no collections devoted exclusively to this type of fantasy, and, happily, it appears that one such volume is not enough to satisfy readers. Certainly no one volume, however representative, could present the substantial number of high quality fantasy writers who deserve inclusion, a number that is steadily growing with the appearance of new writers and the rediscovery of older, hitherto neglected ones. This present work is, then, a response to the favorable critical and popular reception given to Volume I by both the academic community and the general public. Of the sixteen authors presented here, only six appear in Volume I. Two of the stories have never before been published.

The definition of high fantasy presented here, while substantially the same as in Volume I, has been refined with the help of criticism from reviewers and from students. It is best to begin defining high fantasy by differentiating the kinds of tales that are not high fantasy from those that are. Typically, animal fables like "The Fox and the Crow," folk tales of the Paul Bunyan variety, farcical stories like those hilarious exaggerations of G. K. Chesterton or James Thurber, and tales of the macabre with their ghosts or zombies are not high fantasy. High fantasy consists, rather, of fairy tales such as "Gawain and the Green Knight" or Joan Aiken's "A

Harp of Fishbones" and myth-based tales such as the four branches of the *Maginogion* or Evangeline Walton's "Above Ker-Is."

The fairy tale and the myth-based tale are both set, entirely or in part, in a secondary world—that of faërie or the otherworld where gods and men mingle. Magic is the prime ingredient in the one, while the supernatural feats of the gods or their agents predominate in the other. As J.R.R. Tolkien has pointed out in his now-classic essay, "On Fairy-Stories," the two types of high fantasy are closely related. Fairy tales, which Tolkien dubs "low myth," are descended from myth proper, or "high myth." The difference is revealed simply by asking the question, "Are the gods still in evidence?" as in Walton's "Above Ker-Is" or Alexander's "The Smith, the Weaver, and the Harper," or have they been replaced by magicians in various guises, as in Keller's "The Thirty and One," or McKillip's "The Throme of the Erril of Sherill." In some cases, the gods are not far from faërie. Thus, one can perceive vestiges of Pan in the protagonist of Stockton's "Old Pipes and the Dryad" or of Artemis and Medusa in the two sisters in Linklater's "The Abominable Imprecation."

But if folk tales, animal fables, hyperbolic farces, and macabre stories are not high fantasy, what are they? To the extent that they include rationally inexplicable events, happenings that are impossible by human standards, they are fantasy and may be classified as low fantasy. The distinction between high and low fantasy is thus not a qualitative one. Low fantasy is simply much closer to reality as we know it, including the fables where animals are simply masks for human personaltiy types. High fantasy provides a greater distance from our normal reality, taking us to—or near—much more distant realms, like the Red-Peach-Blossom Inlet or the Kingdom of Everywhere, where the impossible is the norm.

High fantasy has a number of other unique characteristics that accompany—indeed are integral to—its otherworld setting and causality. The characters in high fantasy often are imposing figures who, with unearthly powers, inspire wonder or fear, or often both: dragon kings, elves, dryads, demon princesses. High fantasy deals prominently with archetypal figures, motifs, and themes such as the temptress, death and renewal, and the spiritual quest, with its demands for courage and self-lessness. And, finally, the style of high fantasy is a fit-tingly elevated one, characteristically working through imagery and metaphor to evoke its imaginary worlds. The singular effect of the other-world setting, the impos-ing characters, the intuitively recognizable archetypes, and the elevated style through which these come alive has best been described by Tolkien as one of "awe and wonder."

"Awe and wonder" indeed describes the principal ef-fect the stories in this anthology have. Three of the stories—those by Lloyd Alexander, Kenneth Morris, and Evangeline Walton—are myth fantasy. The rest are fairy tales, but, as mentioned before, several of them con-tain echoes of their mythic origins. Two of the tales differ from the others and serve nicely to illustrate that our definition of high fantasy, while necessarily limiting, is not a Procrustean bed. Selma Lagerlöf's "The Legend of the Christmas Rose" clearly contains a secondary world, the transformed Garden of Göinge Forest. The power that effects the transformation of the Garden is what makes the story different. The power emanates from the Christ Child as the celebration of Christmas approaches. The renewal of the forest is a manifestation of one of the great mysteries of Christian myth, behind which one senses the presence of the still older nature myths of northern Europe. The other somewhat atypical story is "April in Paris," by Ursula K. Le Guin. In this story, the power of magic—it draws largely from the power of human longing—is operative, but the setting makes the story different. After all, the scene never shifts from Paris. There is a secondary world, however: the small space circum-scribed by the pentagram, which transcends the limita-tions of time.

As in our first volume, the designation as high fantasy has been the primary criterion used in the selection of stories. It has not, however, been the sole one.

To begin with, we have tried to include a wide variety of fantasy authors, whose work covers a considerable period of time. More than a century of literary endeavor in the area of fantasy literature is represented here. The oldest piece is George Mac Donald's "The Golden Key," which was first collected in *Dealings With Fairies* (1867), and the most recent is Vera Chapman's "Crusader Damosel" (1977), which was written expressly for this volume. Within this broad time frame we have not only selected writers who have become permanent fixtures in the field but relative newcomers as well. MacDonald and Dunsany certainly belong in the first category, while Le Guin, Chapman, and McKillip are in the early stages of their careers as fantasists.

We have also included as many selections as possible of relatively inaccessible stories and stories that, for one reason or another, have been neglected. We first heard of Kenneth Morris, for instance, when reading Ursula Le Guin's fine essay on fantasy stylists, "From Elfland to Poughkeepsie," where she recommends his work and describes him as one of the "master stylists" of fantasy literature. And, indeed, he is. His works are extremely difficult to find, so we are pleased to give you a taste of his fantasy in the form of the delightful story, "Red-Peach-Blossom Inlet." We think you will want to seek out more of his works. Barry Pain is another fantasist who deserves rereading and reevaluation. Although he has been receiving more attention in the past few years, his fantasy tales are still relatively unknown, especially in America. Eric Linklater is quite popular in England, as our recent exploration of several London bookshops revealed, but very little attention has been paid to him on this side of the Atlantic. He is a wonderfully witty and meticulous literary craftsman who seems destined to assume a prominent position in the history of twentieth-century fantasy. Vera Chapman is still another English writer who is making her presence felt in the realm of fantasy. Well into her seventies, she has just launched what promises to be a brilliant career as a fantasist. Within the past two years she has published four full-length fantasy works and has others scheduled for publication in the near future. And even though Sylvia Townsend Warner has been a published writer for more than fifty years, she has just recently begun devoting her full literary energies to the world of faërie, in her Broceliande series of fantasy stories.

Two of the works in this volume are making their publication debuts: Vera Chapman's "Crusader Damosel" and Evangeline Walton's "Above Ker-Is." Both works are important additions to the twentieth-century repertory of fantasy literature.

Perhaps the most important requirement for inclusion in this anthology has been that the stories be good literature. As in our first volume, we have selected only stories that are effective both as literature and as fantasy. While it may be possible for a story to be of poor quality as literature and yet successful as fantasy, we have avoided choosing such. In short, our goal has been to include only those works which will hold up under the careful scrutiny of the discerning reader.

One of the most delightful discoveries we have made on our many travels through the realms of high fantasy is the rich diversity that exists within this genre. In both Volumes I and II we have attempted to take full advantage of this diversity by including stories that display a wide variety of settings, characters, themes, and styles.

Since the author of high fantasy is literally, as Tolkien so aptly put it, a "sub-creator" of other worlds, the settings in this genre are characteristically unique and memorable. Some of our selections, including Linklater's "The Abominable Imprecation," Aiken's "A Harp of Fishbones," and McKillip's "The Throme of the Erril of Sherill," are set entirely in secondary worlds. But others, like Lagerlöf's "The Legend of the Christmas Rose," Lord Dunsany's "The Kith of the Elf-folk," and Le Guin's "April in Paris" display a deft juxtaposition of scenes from both the primary and secondary worlds—a juxtaposition carefully calculated to set both in bold relief. Often, the exotic magic portals that allow us to enter the secondary worlds are as intriguing as the worlds themselves. In Pain's "The Glass of Supreme Moments," for instance, we follow a mysterious, veiled lady up a magnificent staircase "fashioned of silver and crystal," into the world beyond. There are, indeed, many brave new worlds to be explored in high fantasy.

Inhabiting these diverse worlds are a variety of unusual characters who are sure to appeal to many different tastes and interests. Readers with a philosophical bent will especially enjoy the adventures of Morris's Wang-Tao-Chen, a deeply contemplative fisherman who contentedly floats on the calm surface of Lake Tao-ting day after day with a bare hook hanging over the side of his small fishing boat—a hook deliberately kept unbaited to prevent hungry fish from disturbing his meditations. For those more interested in action than in meditation, there is C. L. Moore's Jirel, a fiery "warrior lady" who handles a sword as well as any man, and Aiken's Nerryn, a determined and courageous young girl who engages in a perilous quest to free a frozen kingdom from a mountain goddess's spell. Even Death is given a distinct personality in high fantasy. In Pain's "Supreme Moments," Death takes the unlikely form of a beautiful young woman with ". . . passionate eyes that make men forget honor, and reason, and everything." A more conventional personification of Death, however, is found in Alexander's "The Smith, the Weaver, and the Harper." But not all the characters in high fantasy are so unusual and exotic. Indeed, Professor Barry Pennywither of Le Guin's "April in Paris" is almost painfully mundane. But even this scholarly drudge takes on new life and dynamism when he encounters the magic of Jean Lenoir, a medieval Parisian living in a world centuries removed from Pennywither's own dreary environment.

Most of the archetypal themes and motifs characteristic of high fantasy can be found in this volume, but the reader may be surprised to discover a number of others more commonly associated with mainstream literature. Sylvia Townsend Warner's "Elphenor and Weasel," for example, poignantly illustrates the theme of prejudice by showing that it exists not only in the primary world, but in the secondary world of faërie as well. Similar in message is Chapman's "Crusader Damosel," where the protagonist, Adela, painfully discovers the irrationality and futility of the brutal warfare being waged between Christian and Muslim. Although written more than seventy-five years ago, Lord Dunsany's "Elf-folk" contains a highly contemporary statement on the ugliness of environment and the sterility of spirit and character that often accompany technological progress and industrialization. Of the more conventional high-fantasy motifs, that of the quest is probably the most prominent. The quests, however, are not all the same. For example, in Mac Donald's "The Golden Key," the search of Mossy and Tangle is clearly a spiritual one. So, too, is the quest of Abbot Hans ("Christmas Rose"), and that of the little "Wild Thing" who longs for a soul in "Elf-folk." The quest of the Cnite Caerles for the "dark, haunting, lovely" Throme of the Erril of Sherill has a more romantic motivation, however, as does Lady Angelica's in Keller's "The Thirty and One." Also noteworthy is the archetypal theme of the transforming power of love, vividly illustrated in both Chapman's "Crusader Damosel" and Warner's "Elphenor and Weasel."

From the rich tapestry of vivid imagery and metaphorical expression in "The Throme of the Erril of Sherill" to the classic economy and simplicity of "The Thirty and One," the reader will encounter a wide variety of stylistic approaches in this anthology. Some writers, like Pain and Le Guin, create an intriguing, and rather unique, stylistic effect through a judicious blending of colloquial and elevated diction. Just as distinctive, though, is the style of Sylvia Townsend Warner, replete with sophisticated, urbane wit and razor-sharp satire. Readers who have not yet had the pleasure of reading a Kenneth Morris work will be delighted with his rich verbal portraits. It is not difficult to understand why Le Guin singles him out as one of the finest prose stylists of the century.

People like to speculate on the reasons for the continuing interest in high fantasy, an interest shared by increasing numbers of academicians and critics as well as the general public. Whatever the reasons, the interest is there and so are the writers—good ones—and publishers of fantasy. The past few years have seen the appearance of outstanding works like Susan Cooper's *The Grey King* (1976), the fifth in her *Dark Is Rising* series; Patricia McKillip's *The Riddle Master of Hed* (1976), the first book in a projected trilogy; Joy Chant's new work, *The Grey Mane of Morning* (1977); and Terry Brook's voluminous *Sword of Shannara* (1977). And 1977 will, of course, be remembered as the year in which Tolkien's *Silmarillion* made its long-awaited appearance. Fittingly, it was also the year in which another posthumous volume appeared, *The Dark Tower and Other Stories,* by Tolkien's colleague and friend C. S. Lewis.

Some interesting trends in the high fantasy field are emerging. A large number of the contemporary fantasists are women, as the names above—as well as in this collection—show. Recently, too, more Americans have entered the field, writers of high caliber like Le Guin, McKillip, Alexander, and Peter Beagle. From the critics the plea for the future is for fantasy to develop a greater complexity, to go beyond its traditional black and white polarity of good versus evil. Whether this plea underestimates traditional fantasy or not is debatable; what is certain, however, is that such criticism, which calls for an expansion of traditional boundaries, both reflects and increases the strength of the genre in question. Whatever direction fantasy takes, however, the best of it will continue to enable its readers to retreat to a secondary world, there to regain a sense of "awe and wonder" and a fresh perspective on their primary world. This, along with a number of pleasurable hours, is what we hope *The Fantastic Imagination,* Volume II, will bring to the reader.

GEORGE MAC DONALD
(1824–1905)

George Mac Donald, Scottish clergyman, poet, novelist, and writer of fairytales, was born in Huntly, Aberdeenshire, the son of a farmer. After attending Aberdeen University (1840–45), where he took prizes in chemistry and natural philosophy, he prepared for the ministry at Independent College, Highbury. His studies completed, he assumed his duties as Congregationalist pastor at Arundel, England, in 1850. Because of illness and theological disagreements with his congregation, however, he left his post after only three years and devoted the rest of his life to writing. Although constantly plagued with poor health, Mac Donald led a full, vigorous, and rewarding life. He established friendships with literary luminaries such as Ruskin, Carlyle, Tennyson, Arnold, and Morris; he conducted a remarkably popular and successful lecture tour of the United States in 1872; and, for many years, he served as a dedicated and enthusiastic lay preacher of the Anglican Church. He was probably most content and happy, however, when reading one of his fairy stories to his adoring family of eleven children. He died at Ashtead, Surrey, on September 18, 1905.

Mac Donald's long and prolific literary career began in 1855 with the publication of a lengthy dramatic poem entitled *Within and Without*. Although he wrote and published other poems, his real success came as a writer of fiction. Especially popular during his lifetime were novels like *David Elginbrod* (1863), *Alec Forbes* (1865), and *Robert Falconer* (1868), which accurately depicted Scottish life in Aberdeenshire countryside.

Mac Donald is probably now best remembered, though, for his two adult romances, *Phantastes* (1858) and *Lilith* (1895), and for his delightful children's books *At the*

Back of the North Wind (1871), *The Princess and the Goblin* (1872), and *The Princess and Curdie* (1882). It was fantasy classics such as these, along with his collections of sermons and theological treatises, that so impressed and influenced C. S. Lewis that he pronounced Mac Donald one of his chief literary mentors. Indeed, Mac Donald's works continue to exert a strong influence on many of today's fantasy authors.

"The Golden Key," one of Mac Donald's most beautiful, touching, and meaningful stories, defies precise categorization. There is no doubt about its being high fantasy, with its magic, secondary world, and archetypal motifs— but neither this label, nor any other, can do complete justice to this intriguing admixture of fairytale, Christian allegory, and Carrollesque surrealism. (As a close friend of Charles L. Dodgson, it was Mac Donald who, after reading *Alice's Adventures in Wonderland* to his children, persuaded the young Oxford don to have the work published.) Although not devoid of the delicious humor, subtle irony, and satirical wit so characteristic of his lighter fairytales, this story is definitely more serious and substantive than most of the others. In "The Golden Key," which is strongly informed with Mac Donald's distinct brand of Christian allegory, the magic of fairyland quickly gives way to a more profound mystery—the miracle of spiritual rebirth.

As for style, the Mac Donald hallmarks are all here: spontaneity, beautiful imagery (it's difficult to forget the "beautiful forms slowly ascending" the arch of the magnificent rainbow), a compassionate and meaningful treatment of character, and a skilled handling of narrative and point of view. The seeming casualness and charming informality of Mac Donald's polished prose style often mask the meticulous craftsmanship of this accomplished storyteller, who wrote not only for children, "but for the childlike, whether of five, or fifty, or seventy-five."

⋖ The Golden Key ⋗

George Mac Donald

There was a boy who used to sit in the twilight and listen to his great-aunt's stories.

She told him that if he could reach the place where the end of the rainbow stands he would find there a golden key.

"And what is the key for?" the boy would ask. "What is it the key of? What will it open?"

"That nobody knows," his aunt would reply. "He has to find that out."

"I suppose, being gold," the boy once said, thoughtfully, "that I could get a good deal of money for it if I sold it."

"Better never find it than sell it," returned his aunt.

And then the boy went to bed and dreamed about the golden key.

Now all that his great-aunt told the boy about the golden key would have been nonsense, had it not been that their little house stood on the borders of Fairyland. For it is perfectly well known that out of Fairyland nobody ever can find where the rainbow stands. The creature takes such good care of its golden key, always flitting from place to place, lest any one should find it! But in Fairyland it is quite different. Things that look real in this country look very thin indeed in Fairyland, while some of the things that here cannot stand still for a moment, will not move there. So it was not in the least absurd of the old lady to tell her nephew such things about the golden key.

"Did you ever know anybody to find it?" he asked, one evening.

"Yes. Your father, I believe, found it."

"And what did he do with it, can you tell me?"

"He never told me."

"What was it like?"

"He never showed it to me."

"How does a new key come there always?"

"I don't know. There it is."

"Perhaps it is the rainbow's egg."

"Perhaps it is. You will be a happy boy if you find the nest."

"Perhaps it comes tumbling down the rainbow from the sky."

"Perhaps it does."

One evening, in summer, he went into his own room, and stood at the lattice-window, and gazed into the forest which fringed the outskirts of Fairyland. It came close up to his great-aunt's garden, and, indeed, sent some straggling trees into it. The forest lay to the east, and the sun, which was setting behind the cottage, looked straight into the dark wood with his level red eye. The trees were all old, and had few branches below, so that the sun could see a great way into the forest; and the boy, being keen-sighted, could see almost as far as the sun. The trunks stood like rows of red columns in the shine of the red sun, and he could see down aisle after aisle in the vanishing distance. And as he gazed into the forest he began to feel as if the trees were all waiting for him, and had something they could not go on with till he came to them. But he was hungry, and wanted his supper. So he lingered.

Suddenly, far among the trees, as far as the sun could shine, he saw a glorious thing. It was the end of a rainbow, large and brilliant. He could count all the seven colours, and could see shade after shade beyond the violet; while before the red stood a colour more gorgeous and mysterious still. It was a colour he had never seen before. Only the spring of the rainbow-arch was visible. He could see nothing of it above the trees.

"The golden key!" he said to himself, and darted out of the house, and into the wood.

He had not gone far before the sun set. But the rainbow only glowed the brighter. For the rainbow of Fairyland is not dependent upon the sun as ours is. The trees welcomed him. The bushes made way for him. The rainbow grew larger and brighter; and at length he found himself within two trees of it.

It was a grand sight, burning away there in silence, with its gorgeous, its lovely, its delicate colours, each distinct, all combining. He could now see a great deal more of it. It rose high into the blue heavens, but bent so little that he could not tell how high the crown of the arch must reach. It was still only a small portion of a huge bow.

He stood gazing at it till he forgot himself with delight—even forgot the key which he had come to seek. And as he stood it grew more wonderful still. For in each of the colours, which was as large as the column of a church, he could faintly see beautiful forms slowly ascending as if by the steps of a winding stair. The forms appeared irregularly—now one, now many, now several, now none—men and women and children—all different, all beautiful.

He drew nearer to the rainbow. It vanished. He started back a step in dismay. It was there again, as beautiful as ever. So he contented himself with standing as near it as he might, and watching the forms that ascended the glorious colours towards the unknown height of the arch, which did not end abruptly, but faded away in the blue air, so gradually that he could not say where it ceased.

When the thought of the golden key returned, the boy very wisely proceeded to mark out in his mind the space covered by the foundation of the rainbow, in order that he might know where to search, should the rainbow disappear. It was based chiefly upon a bed of moss.

Meantime it had grown quite dark in the wood. The rainbow alone was visible by its own light. But the moment the moon rose the rainbow vanished. Nor could any change of place restore the vision to the boy's eyes. So he threw himself down upon the mossy bed, to wait till the sunlight would give him a chance of finding the key. There he fell fast asleep.

When he woke in the morning, the sun was looking straight into his eyes. He turned away from it, and the same moment saw a brilliant little thing lying on the moss within a foot of his face. It was the golden key. The pipe of it was of plain gold, as bright as gold could be. The handle was curiously wrought and set with sapphires. In a terror of delight he put out his hand and took it, and had it.

He lay for a while, turning it over and over, feeding his eyes upon its beauty. Then he jumped to his feet, remembering that the pretty thing was of no use to him yet. Where was the lock to which the key belonged? It must be somewhere, for how could anybody be so silly as to make a key for which there was no lock? Where should he go to look for it? He gazed about him, up into the air, down to the earth, but saw no keyhole in the clouds, in the grass, or in the trees.

Just as he began to grow disconsolate, however, he saw something glimmering in the wood. It was a mere glimmer that he saw, but he took it for a glimmer of rainbow, and went towards it.—And now I will go back to the borders of the forest.

Not far from the house where the boy had lived, there was another house, the owner of which was a merchant, who was much away from home. He had lost his wife some years before, and had only one child, a little girl, whom he left to the charge of two servants, who were very idle and careless. So she was neglected and left untidy, and was sometimes ill-used besides.

Now it is well known that the little creatures commonly called fairies, though there are many different kinds of fairies in Fairyland, have an exceeding dislike to untidiness. Indeed, they are quite spiteful to slovenly people. Being used to all the lovely ways of the trees and flowers, and to the neatness of the birds and all woodland creatures, it makes them feel miserable, even in their deep woods and on their grassy carpets, to think that within the same moonlight lies a dirty, uncomfortable, slovenly house. And this makes them angry with the people who live in it, and they would gladly drive them out of the world if they could. They want the whole earth nice and clean. So they pinch the maids black and blue, and play them all manner of uncomfortable tricks.

But this house was quite a shame, and the fairies in

the forest could not endure it. They tried everything on
the maids without effect, and at last resolved upon making a clean riddance, beginning with the child. They
ought to have known that it was not her fault, but they
have little principle and much mischief in them, and they
thought that if they got rid of her the maids would be
sure to be turned away.

So one evening, the poor little girl having been put
to bed early, before the sun was down, the servants
went off to the village, locking the door behind them. The
child did not know she was alone, and lay contentedly
looking out of her window towards the forest, of which,
however, she could not see much, because of the ivy and
other creeping plants which had straggled across her window. All at once she saw an ape making faces at her
out of the mirror, and the heads carved upon a great old
wardrobe grinning fearfully. Then two old spider-legged
chairs came forward into the middle of the room, and
began to dance a queer, old-fashioned dance. This set her
laughing, and she forgot the ape and the grinning
heads. So the fairies saw they had made a mistake, and
sent the chairs back to their places. But they knew that
she had been reading the story of Silverhair all day. So
the next moment she heard the voices of the three bears
upon the stair, big voice, middle voice, and little voice,
and she heard their soft, heavy tread, as if they had
had stockings over their boots, coming nearer and nearer
to the door of her room, till she could bear it no longer.
She did just as Silverhair did, and as the fairies wanted
her to do: she darted to the window, pulled it open, got
upon the ivy, and so scrambled to the ground. She then
fled to the forest as fast she she could run.

Now, although she did not know it, this was the very
best way she could have gone; for nothing is ever so
mischievous in its own place as it is out of it; and,
besides, these mischievous creatures were only the children of Fairyland, as it were, and there are many
other beings there as well; and if a wanderer gets in
among them, the good ones will always help him more
than the evil ones will be able to hurt him.

The sun was now set, and the darkness coming on, but
the child thought of no danger but the bears behind her.

If she had looked round, however, she would have seen that she was followed by a very different creature from a bear. It was a curious creature, made like a fish, but covered, instead of scales, with feathers of all colours, sparkling like those of a humming-bird. It had fins, not wings, and swam through the air as a fish does through the water. Its head was like the head of a small owl.

After running a long way, and as the last of the light was disappearing, she passed under a tree with drooping branches. It dropped its branches to the ground all about her, and caught her as in a trap. She struggled to get out, but the branches pressed her closer and closer to the trunk. She was in great terror and distress, when the air-fish, swimming into the thicket of branches, began tearing them with its beak. They loosened their hold at once, and the creature went on attacking them, till at length they let the child go. Then the air-fish came from behind her, and swam on in front, glittering and sparkling all lovely colours; and she followed.

It led her gently along till all at once it swam in at a cottage-door. The child followed still. There was a bright fire in the middle of the floor, upon which stood a pot without a lid, full of water that boiled and bubbled furiously. The air-fish swam straight to the pot and into the boiling water, where it lay quiet. A beautiful woman rose from the opposite side of the fire and came to meet the girl. She took her up in her arms, and said,—

"Ah, you are come at last! I have been looking for you a long time."

She sat down with her on her lap, and there the girl sat staring at her. She had never seen anything so beautiful. She was tall and strong, with white arms and neck, and a delicate flush on her face. The child could not tell what was the colour of her hair, but could not help thinking it had a tinge of dark green. She had not one ornament upon her, but she looked as if she had just put off quantities of diamonds and emeralds. Yet here she was in the simplest, poorest little cottage, where she was evidently at home. She was dressed in shining green.

The girl looked at the lady, and the lady looked at the girl.

"What is your name?" asked the lady.

"The servants always called me Tangle."

"Ah, that was because your hair was so untidy. But that was their fault, the naughty women! Still it is a pretty name, and I will call you Tangle too. You must not mind me asking you questions, for you may ask me the same questions, every one of them, and any others that you like. How old are you?"

"Ten," answered Tangle.

"You don't look like it," said the lady.

"How old are you, please?" returned Tangle.

"Thousands of years old," answered the lady.

"You don't look like it," said Tangle.

"Don't I? I think I do. Don't you see how beautiful I am?"

And her great blue eyes looked down on the little Tangle, as if all the stars in the sky were melted in them to make their brightness.

"Ah! but," said Tangle, "when people live long they grow old. At least I always thought so."

"I have no time to grow old," said the lady. "I am too busy for that. It is very idle to grow old.—But I cannot have my little girl so untidy. Do you know I can't find a clean spot on your face to kiss?"

"Perhaps," suggested Tangle, feeling ashamed, but not too much so to say a word for herself—"perhaps that is because the tree made me cry so."

"My poor darling!" said the lady, looking now as if the moon were melted in her eyes, and kissing her little face, dirty as it was, "the naughty tree must suffer for making a girl cry."

"And what is your name, please?" asked Tangle.

"Grandmother," answered the lady.

"Is it really?"

"Yes, indeed. I never tell stories, even in fun."

"How good of you!"

"I couldn't if I tried. It would come true if I said it, and then I should be punished enough."

And she smiled like the sun through a summer-shower.

"But now," she went on, "I must get you washed and dressed, and then we shall have some supper."

"Oh! I had supper long ago," said Tangle.

"Yes, indeed you had," answered the lady—"three

years ago. You don't know that it is three years since
you ran away from the bears. You are thirteen and more
now."

Tangle could only stare. She felt quite sure it was
true.

"You will not be afraid of anything I do with you—
will you?" said the lady.

"I will try very hard not to be; but I can't be certain,
you know," replied Tangle.

"I like your saying so, and I shall be quite satisfied,"
answered the lady.

She took off the girl's night-gown, rose with her in her
arms, and going to the wall of the cottage, opened a door.
Then Tangle saw a deep tank, the sides of which were
filled with green plants, which had flowers of all colours.
There was a roof over it like the roof of the cottage. It
was filled with beautiful clear water, in which swam a
multitude of such fishes as the one that had led her to
the cottage. It was the light their colours gave that
showed the place in which they were.

The lady spoke some words Tangle could not understand, and threw her into the tank.

The fishes came crowding about her. Two or three of
them got under her head and kept it up. The rest of
them rubbed themselves all over her, and with their wet
feathers washed her quite clean. Then the lady, who had
been looking on all the time, spoke again; whereupon
some thirty or forty of the fishes rose out of the
water underneath Tangle, and so bore her up to the
arms the lady held out to her. She carried her back
to the fire, and, having dried her well, opened a chest,
and taking out the finest linen garments, smelling of grass
and lavender, put them upon her, and over all a green
dress, just like her own, shining like hers, and soft like
hers, and going into just such lovely folds from the waist,
where it was tied with a brown cord, to her bare feet.

"Won't you give me a pair of shoes too, Grandmother?"
said Tangle.

"No, my dear; no shoes. Look here. I wear no shoes."

So saying, she lifted her dress a little, and there were
the loveliest white feet, but no shoes. Then Tangle was
content to go without shoes too. And the lady sat down

with her again, and combed her hair, and brushed it, and
then left it to dry while she got the supper.

First she got bread out of one hole in the wall; then
milk out of another; then several kinds of fruit out of a
third; and then she went to the pot on the fire, and took
out the fish, now nicely cooked, and, as soon as she had
pulled off its feathered skin, ready to be eaten.

"But," exclaimed Tangle. And she stared at the fish,
and could say no more.

"I know what you mean," returned the lady. "You do
not like to eat the messenger that brought you home. But
it is the kindest return you can make. The creature was
afraid to go until it saw me put the pot on, and heard
me promise it should be boiled the moment it returned
with you. Then it darted out of the door at once. You
saw it go into the pot of itself the moment it entered,
did you not?"

"I did," answered Tangle, "and I thought it very
strange; but then I saw you, and forgot all about the
fish."

"In Fairyland," resumed the lady, as they sat down to
the table, "the ambition of the animals is to be eaten by
the people; for that is their highest end in that condition.
But they are not therefore destroyed. Out of that pot
comes something more than the dead fish, you will see."

Tangle now remarked that the lid was on the pot. But
the lady took no further notice of it till they had eaten
the fish, which Tangle found nicer than any fish she had
ever tasted before. It was as white as snow, and as delicate as cream. And the moment she had swallowed a
mouthful of it, a change she could not describe began to
take place in her. She heard a murmuring all about her,
which became more and more articulate, and at length,
as she went on eating, grew intelligible. By the time she
had finished her share, the sounds of all the animals in
the forest came crowding through the door to her ears;
for the door still stood wide open, though it was pitch
dark outside; and they were no longer sounds only; they
were speech, and speech that she could understand. She
could tell what the insects in the cottage were saying to
each other too. She had even a suspicion that the trees
and flowers all about the cottage were holding midnight

communications with each other; but what they said she could not hear.

As soon as the fish was eaten, the lady went to the fire and took the lid off the pot. A lovely creature in human shape, with large white wings, rose out of it, and flew round and round the roof of the cottage; then dropped, fluttering, and nestled in the lap of the lady. She spoke to it some strange words, carried it to the door, and threw it out into the darkness. Tangle heard the flapping of its wings die away in the distance.

"Now have we done the fish any harm?" she said, returning.

"No," answered Tangle, "I do not think we have. I should not mind eating one every day."

"They must wait their time, like you and me too, my little Tangle."

And she smiled a smile which the sadness in it made more lovely.

"But," she continued, "I think we may have one for supper tomorrow."

So saying she went to the door of the tank, and spoke; and now Tangle understood her perfectly.

"I want one of you," she said,—"the wisest."

Thereupon the fishes got together in the middle of the tank, with their heads forming a circle above the water, and their tails a larger circle beneath it. They were holding a council, in which their relative wisdom should be determined. At length one of them flew up into the lady's hand, looking lively and ready.

"You know where the rainbow stands?" she asked.

"Yes, Mother, quite well," answered the fish.

"Bring home a young man you will find there, who does not know where to go."

The fish was out of the door in a moment. Then the lady told Tangle it was time to go to bed; and, opening another door in the side of the cottage, showed her a little arbour, cool and green, with a bed of purple heath growing in it, upon which she threw a large wrapper made of the feathered skins of the wise fishes, shining gorgeous in the firelight. Tangle was soon lost in the strangest, loveliest dreams. And the beautiful lady was in every one of her dreams.

In the morning she awoke to the rustling of leaves over her head, and the sound of running water. But, to her surprise, she could find no door—nothing but the moss-grown wall of the cottage. So she crept through an opening in the arbour, and stood in the forest. Then she bathed in a stream that ran merrily through the trees, and felt happier; for having once been in her grandmother's pond, she must be clean and tidy ever after; and, having put on her green dress, felt like a lady.

She spent that day in the wood, listening to the birds and beasts and creeping things. She understood all that they said, though she could not repeat a word of it; and every kind had a different language, while there was a common though more limited understanding between all the inhabitants of the forest. She saw nothing of the beautiful lady, but she felt that she was near her all the time; and she took care not to go out of sight of the cottage. It was round, like a snow-hut or a wigwam; and she could see neither door nor window in it. The fact was, it had no windows; and though it was full of doors, they all opened from the inside, and could not even be seen from the outside.

She was standing at the foot of a tree in the twilight, listening to a quarrel between a mole and a squirrel, in which the mole told the squirrel that the tail was the best of him, and the squirrel called the mole Spade-fists, when, the darkness having deepened around her, she became aware of something shining in her face, and looking round, saw that the door of the cottage was open, and the red light of the fire flowing from it like a river through the darkness. She left Mole and Squirrel to settle matters as they might, and darted off to the cottage. Entering, she found the pot boiling on the fire, and the grand, lovely lady sitting on the other side of it.

"I've been watching you all day," said the lady. "You shall have something to eat by-and-by, but we must wait till our supper comes home."

She took Tangle on her knee, and began to sing to her—such songs as made her wish she could listen to them for ever. But at length in rushed the shining fish, and snuggled down in the pot. It was followed by a youth who had outgrown his worn garments. His face was ruddy with health, and in his hand he carried a little jewel, which sparkled in the firelight.

The first words the lady said were,—

"What is that in your hand, Mossy?"

Now Mossy was the name his companions had given him, because he had a favourite stone covered with moss, on which he used to sit whole days reading; and they said the moss had begun to grow upon him too.

Mossy held out his hand. The moment the lady saw that it was the golden key, she rose from her chair, kissed Mossy on the forehead, made him sit down on her seat, and stood before him like a servant. Mossy could not bear this, and rose at once. But the lady begged him, with tears in her beautiful eyes, to sit, and let her wait on him.

"But you are a great, splendid, beautiful lady," said Mossy.

"Yes, I am. But I work all day long—that is my pleasure; and you will have to leave me so soon!"

"How do you know that, if you please, madam?" asked Mossy.

"Because you have got the golden key."

"But I don't know what it is for. I can't find the key-hole. Will you tell me what to do?"

"You must look for the keyhole. That is your work. I cannot help you. I can only tell you that if you look for it you will find it."

"What kind of box will it open? What is there inside?"

"I do not know. I dream about it, but I know nothing."

"Must I go at once?"

"You may stop here to-night, and have some of my supper. But you must go in the morning. All I can do for you is to give you clothes. Here is a girl called Tangle, whom you must take with you."

"That *will* be nice," said Mossy.

"No, no!" said Tangle. "I don't want to leave you, please, Grandmother."

"You must go with him, Tangle. I am sorry to lose you, but it will be the best thing for you. Even the fishes, you see, have to go into the pot, and then out into the dark. If you fall in with the Old Man of the Sea, mind you ask him whether he has not got some more fishes ready for me. My tank is getting thin."

So saying, she took the fish from the pot, and put the lid on as before. They sat down and ate the fish, and then the winged creature rose from the pot, circled the roof, and settled on the lady's lap. She talked to it, carried it to the door, and threw it out into the dark. They heard the flap of its wings die away in the distance.

The lady then showed Mossy into just such another chamber as that of Tangle; and in the morning he found a suit of clothes laid beside him. He looked very handsome in them. But the wearer of Grandmother's clothes never thinks about how he or she looks, but thinks always how handsome other people are.

Tangle was very unwilling to go.

"Why should I leave you? I don't know the young man," she said to the lady.

"I am never allowed to keep my children long. You need not go with him except if you please, but you must go some day; and I should like you to go with him, for he has the golden key. No girl need be afraid to go with a youth that has the golden key. You will take care of her, Mossy, will you not?"

"That I will," said Mossy.

And Tangle cast a glance at him, and thought she should like to go with him.

"And," said the lady, "if you should lose each other as you go through the—the—I never can remember the name of that country,—do not be afraid, but go on and on."

She kissed Tangle on the mouth and Mossy on the forehead, led them to the door, and waved her hand eastward. Mossy and Tangle took each other's hand and walked away into the depth of the forest. In his right hand Mossy held the golden key.

They wandered thus a long way, with endless amusement from the talk of the animals. They soon learned enough of their language to ask them necessary questions. The squirrels were always friendly, and gave them nuts out of their own hoards; but the bees were selfish and rude, justifying themselves on the ground that Tangle and Mossy were not subjects of their queen, and charity must begin at home, though indeed they had not one drone in their poorhouse at the time. Even the blinking moles would fetch them an earth-nut or a truffle now and then, talking as if their mouths, as well as their eyes and ears, were full of cotton wool, or their own velvety fur. By the time they got out of the forest they were very fond of each other, and Tangle was not in the least sorry that her grandmother had sent her away with Mossy.

At length the trees grew smaller, and stood farther apart, and the ground began to rise, and it got more and more steep, till the trees were all left behind, and the two were climbing a narrow path with rocks on each side. Suddenly they came upon a rude doorway, by which they entered a narrow gallery cut in the rock. It grew darker and darker, till it was pitch-dark, and they had to feel their way. At length the light began to return, and at last they came out upon a narrow path on the face of a lofty precipice. This path went winding down the rock to a wide plain, circular in shape, and surrounded on all sides by mountains. Those opposite to them were a great way off, and towered to an awful height, shooting up sharp, blue, ice-enamelled pinnacles. An utter silence reigned where they stood. Not even the sound of water reached them.

Looking down, they could not tell whether the valley below was a grassy plain or a great still lake. They had never seen any space look like it. The way to it was difficult and dangerous, but down the narrow path they went, and reached the bottom in safety. They found it composed of smooth, light-coloured sandstone, undulating in parts, but mostly level. It was no wonder to them now that they had not been able to tell what it was, for this surface was everywhere crowded with shadows. It was a sea of shadows. The mass was chiefly made up of the shadows of leaves innumerable, of all lovely and imaginative forms, waving to and fro, floating and quivering in the breath of a breeze whose motion was unfelt, whose sound was unheard. No forests clothed the mountainsides, no trees were anywhere to be seen, and yet the shadows of the leaves, branches, and stems of all various trees covered the valley as far as their eyes could reach. They soon spied the shadows of flowers mingled with those of the leaves, and now and then the shadow of a bird with open beak, and throat distended with song. At times would appear the forms of strange, graceful creatures, running up and down the shadow-boles and along the branches, to disappear in the wind-tossed foliage. As they walked they waded knee-deep in the lovely lake. For the shadows were not merely lying on the surface of the ground, but heaped up above it like substantial forms of darkness, as if they had been cast upon a thousand different planes of the air. Tangle and Mossy often lifted their heads and gazed upwards to descry whence the shadows came; but they could see nothing more than a bright mist spread above them, higher than the tops of the mountains, which stood clear against it. No forests, no leaves, no birds were visible.

After a while, they reached more open spaces, where the shadows were thinner; and came even to portions over which shadows only flitted, leaving them clear for such as might follow. Now a wonderful form, half bird-like half human, would float across on outspread sailing pinions. Anon an exquisite shadow group of gambolling children would be followed by the loveliest female form, and that again by the grand stride of a Titanic shape, each disappearing in the surrounding press of shadowy foliage. Sometimes a profile of unspeakable beauty or grandeur would appear for a moment and vanish. Sometimes they seemed lovers that passed linked arm in arm, sometimes father and son, sometimes brothers in loving contest, sometimes sisters entwined in gracefullest community of complex form. Sometimes wild horses would tear across, free, or bestrode by noble shadows of ruling men. But some of the things which pleased them most they never knew how to describe.

About the middle of the plain they sat down to rest in the heart of a heap of shadows. After sitting for a while, each, looking up, saw the other in tears: they were each longing after the country whence the shadows fell.

"We *must* find the country from which the shadows come," said Mossy.

"We must, dear Mossy," responded Tangle. "What if your golden key should be the key to *it?*"

"Ah! that would be grand," returned Mossy.—"But

we must rest here for a little, and then we shall be able to cross the plain before night."

So he lay down on the ground, and about him on every side, and over his head, was the constant play of the wonderful shadows. He could look through them, and see the one behind the other, till they mixed in a mass of darkness. Tangle, too, lay admiring, and wondering, and longing after the country whence the shadows came. When they were rested they rose and pursued their journey.

How long they were in crossing this plain I cannot tell; but before night Mossy's hair was streaked with grey, and Tangle had got wrinkles on her forehead.

As evening drew on, the shadows fell deeper and rose higher. At length they reached a place where they rose above their heads, and made all dark around them. Then they took hold of each other's hand, and walked on in silence and in some dismay. They felt the gathering darkness, and something strangely solemn besides, and the beauty of the shadows ceased to delight them. All at once Tangle found that she had not a hold of Mossy's hand, though when she lost it she could not tell.

"Mossy, Mossy!" she cried aloud in terror.

But no Mossy replied.

A moment after, the shadows sank to her feet, and down under her feet, and the mountains rose before her. She turned towards the gloomy region she had left, and called once more upon Mossy. There the gloom lay tossing and heaving, a dark, stormy, foamless sea of shadows, but no Mossy rose out of it, or came climbing up the hill on which she stood. She threw herself down and wept in despair.

Suddenly she remembered that the beautiful lady had told them, if they lost each other in a country of which she could not remember the name, they were not to be afraid, but to go straight on.

"And besides," she said to herself, "Mossy has the golden key, and so no harm will come to him, I do believe."

She rose from the ground, and went on.

Before long she arrived at a precipice, in the face of which a stair was cut. When she had ascended half-way, the stair ceased, and the path led straight into the mountain. She was afraid to enter, and turning again towards the stair, grew giddy at the sight of the depth beneath her, and was forced to throw herself down in the mouth of the cave.

When she opened her eyes, she saw a beautiful little creature with wings standing beside her, waiting.

"I know you," said Tangle. "You are my fish."

"Yes. But I am a fish no longer. I am an aëranth now."

"What is that?" asked Tangle.

"What you see I am," answered the shape. "And I am come to lead you through the mountain."

"Oh! thank you, dear fish—aëranth, I mean," returned Tangle, rising.

Thereupon the aëranth took to his wings, and flew on through the long, narrow passage, reminding Tangle very much of the way he had swum on before when he was a fish. And the moment his white wings moved, they began to throw off a continuous shower of sparks of all colours, which lighted up the passage before them.—All at once he vanished, and Tangle heard a low, sweet sound, quite different from the rush and crackle of his wings. Before her was an open arch, and through it came light, mixed with the sound of sea-waves.

She hurried out, and fell, tired and happy, upon the yellow sand of the shore. There she lay, half asleep with weariness and rest, listening to the low plash and retreat of the tiny waves, which seemed ever enticing the land to leave off being land, and become sea. And as she lay, her eyes were fixed upon the foot of a great rainbow standing far away against the sky on the other side of the sea. At length she fell fast asleep.

When she awoke, she saw an old man with long white hair down to his shoulders, leaning upon a stick covered with green buds, and so bending over her.

"What do you want here, beautiful woman?" he said.

"Am I beautiful? I am so glad!" answered Tangle, rising. "My grandmother is beautiful."

"Yes. But what do you want?" he repeated, kindly.

"I think I want you. Are not you the Old Man of the Sea?"

"I am."

"Then Grandmother says, have you any more fishes ready for her?"

"We will go and see, my dear," answered the old man, speaking yet more kindly than before. "And I can do something for you, can I not?"

"Yes—show me the way up to the country from which the shadows fall," said Tangle.

For there she hoped to find Mossy again.

"Ah! indeed, that would be worth doing," said the old man. "But I cannot, for I do not know the way myself. But I will send you to the Old Man of the Earth. Perhaps he can tell you. He is much older than I am."

Leaning on his staff, he conducted her along the shore to a steep rock that looked like a petrified ship turned upside down. The door of it was the rudder of a great vessel, ages ago at the bottom of the sea. Immediately within the door was a stair in the rock, down which the old man went, and Tangle followed. At the bottom the old man had his house, and there he lived.

As soon as she entered it, Tangle heard a strange noise, unlike anything she had ever heard before. She soon found that it was the fishes talking. She tried to understand what they said; but their speech was so old-fashioned, and rude, and undefined, that she could not make much of it.

"I will go and see about those fishes for my daughter," said the Old Man of the Sea.

And moving a slide in the wall of his house, he first looked out, and then tapped upon a thick piece of crystal that filled the round opening. Tangle came up behind him, and peeping through the window into the heart of the great deep green ocean, saw the most curious creatures, some very ugly, all very odd, and with especially queer mouths, swimming about everywhere, above and below, but all coming towards the window in answer to the tap of the Old Man of the Sea. Only a few could get their mouths against the glass; but those who were floating miles away yet turned their heads towards it. The Old Man looked through the whole flock carefully for some minutes, and then turning to Tangle, said,—

"I am sorry I have not got one ready yet. I want more

time than she does. But I will send some as soon as I can."

He then shut the slide.

Presently a great noise arose in the sea. The Old Man opened the slide again, and tapped on the glass, whereupon the fishes were all as still as asleep.

"They were only talking about you," he said. "And they do speak such nonsense!—To-morrow," he continued, "I must show you the way to the Old Man of the Earth. He lives a long way from here."

"Do let me go at once," said Tangle.

"No. That is not possible. You must come this way first."

He led her to a hole in the wall, which she had not observed before. It was covered with the green leaves and white blossoms of a creeping plant.

"Only white-blossoming plants can grow under the sea," said the Old Man. "In there you will find a bath, in which you must lie till I call you."

Tangle went in, and found a smaller room or cave, in the further corner of which was a great basin hollowed out of rock, and half-full of the clearest sea-water. Little streams were constantly running into it from cracks in the wall of the cavern. It was polished quite smooth inside, and had a carpet of yellow sand in the bottom of it. Large green leaves and white flowers of various plants crowded up and over it, draping and covering it almost entirely.

No sooner was she undressed and lying in the bath, than she began to feel as if the water were sinking into her, and she were receiving all the good of sleep without undergoing its forgetfulness. She felt the good coming all the time. And she grew happier and more hopeful than she had been since she lost Mossy. But she could not help thinking how very sad it was for a poor old man to live there all alone, and have to take care of a whole seaful of stupid and riotous fishes.

After about an hour, as she thought, she heard his voice calling her, and rose out of the bath. All the fatigue and aching of her long journey had vanished. She was as whole, and strong, and well as if she had slept for seven days.

Returning to the opening that led into the other part of

the house, she started back with amazement, for through it she saw the form of a grand man, with a majestic and beautiful face, waiting for her.

"Come," he said; "I see you are ready."

She entered with reverence.

"Where is the Old Man of the Sea?" she asked, humbly.

"There is no one here but me," he answered, smiling. "Some people call me the Old Man of the Sea. Others have another name for me, and are terribly frightened when they meet me taking a walk by the shore. Therefore I avoid being seen by them, for they are so afraid, that they never see what I really am. You see me now.— But I must show you the way to the Old Man of the Earth."

He led her into the cave where the bath was, and there she saw, in the opposite corner, a second opening in the rock.

"Go down that stair, and it will bring you to him," said the Old Man of the Sea.

With humble thanks Tangle took her leave. She went down the winding-stair, till she began to fear there was no end to it. Still down and down it went, rough and broken, with springs of water bursting out of the rocks and running down the steps beside her. It was quite dark about her, and yet she could see. For after being in that bath, people's eyes always give out a light they can see by. There were no creeping things in the way. All was safe and pleasant, though so dark and damp and deep.

At last there was not one step more, and she found herself in a glimmering cave. On a stone in the middle of it sat a figure with its back towards her—the figure of an old man bent double with age. From behind she could see his white beard spread out on the rocky floor in front of him. He did not move as she entered, so she passed round that she might stand before him and speak to him.

The moment she looked in his face, she saw that he was a youth of marvellous beauty. He sat entranced with the delight of what he beheld in a mirror of something like silver, which lay on the floor at his feet, and which from behind she had taken for his white beard. He sat on, heedless of her presence, pale with the joy of his vision.

She stood and watched him. At length, all trembling, she spoke. But her voice made no sound. Yet the youth lifted up his head. He showed no surprise, however, at seeing her—only smiled a welcome.

"Are you the Old Man of the Earth?" Tangle had said.

And the youth answered, and Tangle heard him, though not with her ears:—

"I am. What can I do for you?"

"Tell me the way to the country whence the shadows fall."

"Ah! that I do not know. I only dream about it myself. I see its shadows sometimes in my mirror: the way to it I do not know. But I think the Old Man of the Fire must know. He is much older than I am. He is the oldest man of all."

"Where does he live?"

"I will show you the way to his place. I never saw him myself."

So saying, the young man rose, and then stood for a while gazing at Tangle.

"I wish I could see that country too," he said. "But I must mind my work."

He led her to the side of the cave, and told her to lay her ear against the wall.

"What do you hear?" he asked.

"I hear," answered Tangle, "the sound of a great water running inside the rock."

"That river runs down to the dwelling of the oldest man of all—the Old Man of the Fire. I wish I could go to see him. But I must mind my work. That river is the only way to him."

Then the Old Man of the Earth stooped over the floor of the cave, raised a huge stone from it, and left it leaning. It disclosed a great hole that went plumb-down.

"That is the way," he said.

"But there are no stairs."

"You must throw yourself in. There is no other way."

She turned and looked him full in the face—stood so for a whole minute, as she thought: it was a whole year—then threw herself headlong into the hole.

When she came to herself, she found herself gliding

down fast and deep. Her head was under water, but that did not signify, for, when she thought about it, she could not remember that she had breathed once since her bath in the cave of the Old Man of the Sea. When she lifted up her head a sudden and fierce heat struck her, and she sank it again instantly, and went sweeping on.

Gradually the stream grew shallower. At length she could hardly keep her head under. Then the water could carry her no farther. She rose from the channel, and went step for step down the burning descent. The water ceased altogether. The heat was terrible. She felt scorched to the bone, but it did not touch her strength. It grew hotter and hotter. She said, "I can bear it no longer." Yet she went on.

At the long last, the stair ended at a rude archway in an all but glowing rock. Through this archway Tangle fell exhausted into a cool mossy cave. The floor and walls were covered with moss—green, soft, and damp. A little stream spouted from a rent in the rock and fell into a basin of moss. She plunged her face into it and drank. Then she lifted her head and looked around. Then she rose and looked again. She saw no one in the cave. But the moment she stood upright she had a marvellous sense that she was in the secret of the earth and all its ways. Everything she had seen, or learned from books; all that her grandmother had said or sung to her; all the talk of the beasts, birds, and fishes; all that happened to her on her journey with Mossy, and since then in the heart of the earth with the Old man and the Older man—all was plain: she understood it all, and saw that everything meant the same thing, though she could not have put it into words again.

The next moment she descried, in a corner of the cave, a little naked child, sitting on the moss. He was playing with balls of various colours and sizes, which he disposed in strange figures upon the floor beside him. And now Tangle felt that there was something in her knowledge which was not in her understanding. For she knew there must be an infinite meaning in the change and sequence and individual forms of the figures into which the child arranged the balls, as well as in the varied harmonies of

their colours, but what it all meant she could not tell.*
He went on busily, tireless, playing his solitary game,
without looking up, or seeming to know that there was a
stranger in his deep-withdrawn cell. Diligently as a lace-
maker shifts her bobbins, he shifted and arranged his
balls. Flashes of meaning would now pass from them to
Tangle, and now again all would be not merely obscure,
but utterly dark. She stood looking for a long time, for
there was fascination in the sight; and the longer she
looked the more an indescribable vague intelligence went
on rousing itself in her mind. For seven years she had
stood there watching the naked child with his coloured
balls, and it seemed to her like seven hours, when all
at once the shape the balls took, she knew not why, reminded her of the Valley of Shadows, and she spoke:

"Where is the Old Man of the Fire?" she said.

"Here I am," answered the child, rising and leaving his
balls on the moss. "What can I do for you?"

There was such an awfulness of absolute repose on the
face of the child that Tangle stood dumb before him. He
had no smile, but the love in his large gray eyes was deep
as the centre. And with the repose there lay on his face a
shimmer as of moonlight, which seemed as if any moment
it might break into such a ravishing smile as would cause
the beholder to weep himself to death. But the smile
never came, and the moonlight lay there unbroken. For
the heart of the child was too deep for any smile to reach
from it to his face.

"Are you the oldest man of all?" Tangle at length,
although filled with awe, ventured to ask.

"Yes, I am. I am very, very old. I am able to help
you, I know. I can help everybody."

And the child drew near and looked up in her face so
that she burst into tears.

"Can you tell me the way to the country the shadows
fall from?" she sobbed.

"Yes. I know the way quite well. I go there myself
sometimes. But you could not go my way; you are not old
enough. I will show you how you can go."

* I think I must be indebted to Novalis for these geometrical
figures.

"Do not send me out into the great heat again," prayed Tangle.

"I will not," answered the child.

And he reached up, and put his little cool hand on her heart.

"Now," he said, "you can go. The fire will not burn you. Come."

He led her from the cave, and following him through another archway, she found herself in a vast desert of sand and rock. The sky of it was of rock, lowering over them like solid thunderclouds; and the whole place was so hot that she saw, in bright rivulets, the yellow gold and white silver and red copper trickling molten from the rocks. But the heat never came near her.

When they had gone some distance, the child turned up a great stone, and took something like an egg from under it. He next drew a long curved line in the sand with his finger, and laid the egg in it. He then spoke something Tangle could not understand. The egg broke, a small snake came out, and, lying in the line in the sand, grew and grew till he filled it. The moment he was thus full-grown, he began to glide away, undulating like a sea-wave.

"Follow that serpent," said the child. "He will lead you the right way."

Tangle followed the serpent. But she could not go far without looking back at the marvellous Child. He stood alone in the midst of the glowing desert, beside a fountain of red flame that had burst forth at his feet, his naked whiteness glimmering a pale rosy red in the torrid fire. There he stood, looking after her, till, from the lengthening distance, she could see him no more. The serpent went on, turning neither to the right nor left.

Meantime Mossy had got out of the lake of shadows, and, following his mournful, lonely way, had reached the sea-shore. It was a dark, stormy evening. The sun had set. The wind was blowing from the sea. The waves had surrounded the rock within which lay the Old Man's house. A deep water rolled between it and the shore, upon which a majestic figure was walking alone.

Mossy went up to him and said,—

"Will you tell me where to find the Old Man of the Sea?"

"I am the Old Man of the Sea," the figure answered.

"I see a strong kingly man of middle age," returned Mossy.

Then the Old Man looked at him more intently, and said,—

"Your sight, young man, is better than that of most who take this way. The night is stormy: come to my house and tell me what I can do for you."

Mossy followed him. The waves flew from before the footsteps of the Old Man of the Sea, and Mossy followed upon dry sand.

When they had reached the cave, they sat down and gazed at each other.

Now Mossy was an old man by this time. He looked much older than the Old Man of the Sea, and his feet were very weary.

After looking at him for a moment, the Old Man took him by the hand and led him into his inner cave. There he helped him to undress, and laid him in the bath. And he saw that one of his hands Mossy did not open.

"What have you in that hand?" he asked.

Mossy opened his hand, and there lay the golden key.

"Ah!" said the Old Man, "that accounts for your knowing me. And I know the way you have to go."

"I want to find the country whence the shadows fall," said Mossy.

"I dare say you do. So do I. But meantime, one thing is certain.—What is the key for, do you think?"

"For a keyhole somewhere. But I don't know why I keep it. I never could find the keyhole. And I have lived a good while, I believe," said Mossy, sadly. "I'm not sure that I'm not old. I know my feet ache."

"Do they?" said the Old Man, as if he really meant to ask the question; and Mossy, who was still lying in the bath, watched his feet for a moment before he replied.

"No, they do not," he answered. "Perhaps I am not old either."

"Get up and look at yourself in the water."

He rose and looked at himself in the water, and there was not a gray hair on his head or a wrinkle on his skin.

"You have tasted of death now," said the Old Man. "Is it good?"

"It is good," said Mossy. "It is better than life."

"No," said the Old Man; "it is only more life.—Your feet will make no holes in the water now."

"What do you mean?"

"I will show you that presently."

They returned to the outer cave, and sat and talked together for a long time. At length the Old Man of the Sea rose, and said to Mossy,—

"Follow me."

He led him up the stair again, and opened another door. They stood on the level of the raging sea, looking towards the east. Across the waste of waters, against the bosom of a fierce black cloud, stood the foot of a rainbow, glowing in the dark.

"This indeed is my way," said Mossy, as soon as he saw the rainbow, and stepped out upon the sea. His feet made no holes in the water. He fought the wind, and clomb the waves, and went on towards the rainbow.

The storm died away. A lovely day and a lovelier night followed. A cool wind blew over the wide plain of the quiet ocean. And still Mossy journeyed eastward. But the rainbow had vanished with the storm.

Day after day he held on, and he thought he had no guide. He did not see how a shining fish under the waters directed his steps. He crossed the sea, and came to a great precipice of rock, up which he could discover but one path. Nor did this lead him farther than half-way up the rock, where it ended on a platform. Here he stood and pondered.—It could not be that the way stopped here, else what was the path for? It was a rough path, not very plain, yet certainly a path.—He examined the face of the rock. It was smooth as glass. But as his eyes kept roving hopelessly over it, something glittered, and he caught sight of a row of small sapphires. They bordered a little hole in the rock.

"The keyhole!" he cried.

He tried the key. It fitted. It turned. A great clang and clash, as of iron bolts on huge brazen caldrons, echoed thunderously within. He drew out the key. The rock in front of him began to fall. He retreated from it as far as the breadth of the platform would allow. A great slab fell at his feet. In front was still the solid rock, with this one slab fallen forward out of it. But the moment he stepped upon it, a second fell, just short of the edge of the first, making the next step of a stair, which thus kept dropping itself before him as he ascended into the heart of the precipice. It led him into a hall fit for such an approach—irregular and rude in formation, but floor, sides, pillars, and vaulted roof, all one mass of shining stones of every colour that light can show. In the centre stood seven columns, ranged from red to violet. And on the pedestal of one of them sat a woman, motionless, with her face bowed upon her knees. Seven years had she sat there waiting. She lifted her head as Mossy drew near. It was Tangle. Her hair had grown to her feet, and was rippled like the windless sea on broad sands. Her face was beautiful, like her grandmother's, and as still and peaceful as that of the Old Man of the Fire. Her form was tall and noble. Yet Mossy knew her at once.

"How beautiful you are, Tangle!" he said, in delight and astonishment.

"Am I?" she returned. "Oh, I have waited for you so long! But you, you are like the Old Man of the Sea. No. You are like the Old Man of the Earth. No, no. You are like the oldest man of all. You are like them all. And yet you are my own old Mossy! How did you come here? What did you do after I lost you? Did you find the keyhole? Have you got the key still?"

She had a hundred questions to ask him, and he a hundred more to ask her. They told each other all their adventures, and were as happy as man and woman could be. For they were younger and better, and stronger and wiser, than they had ever been before.

It began to grow dark. And they wanted more than ever to reach the country whence the shadows fall. So they looked about them for a way out of the cave. The door by which Mossy entered had closed again, and there was half a mile of rock between them and the sea. Neither could Tangle find the opening in the floor by which the serpent had led her thither. They searched till it grew so dark that they could see nothing, and gave it up.

After a while, however, the cave began to glimmer

again. The light came from the moon, but it did not look like moonlight, for it gleamed through those seven pillars in the middle, and filled the place with all colours. And now Mossy saw that there was a pillar beside the red one, which he had not observed before. And it was of the same new colour that he had seen in the rainbow when he saw it first in the fairy forest. And on it he saw a sparkle of blue. It was the sapphires round the keyhole.

He took his key. It turned in the lock to the sounds of Aeolian music. A door opened upon slow hinges, and disclosed a winding stair within. The key vanished from his fingers. Tangle went up. Mossy followed. The door closed behind them. They climbed out of the earth; and, still climbing, rose above it. They were in the rainbow. Far abroad, over ocean and land, they could see through its transparent walls the earth beneath their feet. Stairs beside stairs wound up together, and beautiful beings of all ages climbed along with them.

They knew that they were going up to the country whence the shadows fall.

And by this time I think they must have got there.

BARRY ERIC ODELL PAIN
(1865–1928)

Barry Pain, English humorist, parodist, and short-story writer, was born in Cambridge, the son of a linen draper. After receiving his education at Sedbergh School (1879–83), and Corpus Christi College, Cambridge, he spent four years as an army tutor at Guildford. Pain then went to London, where he embarked on a career as journalist, first getting work on the *Daily Chronicle* and *Black and White,* and then, in 1897, succeeding Jerome K. Jerome as editor of *To-Day.* His career as journalist and freelance writer was interrupted by his service during World War I in the antiaircraft section of the Royal Naval Volunteer Reserve. He died at Watford, Hertfordshire, on May 5, 1928, at the age of sixty-four.

Pain's interest in writing was lifelong. While at Sedbergh he was editor of the school magazine, and during his stay at Cambridge he not only edited the *Grata,* but regularly contributed to it. As a matter of fact, his third book, *In a Canadian Canoe* (1891), was a collection of his contributions to this publication. After leaving the university he began contributing regularly to *Punch, Cornhill Magazine,* and other periodicals. A number of his books were published during this time, including *Graeme and Cyril* (1893), *Playthings and Parodies* (1896), and *Stories and Interludes* (1898), but his first real literary success was not until *Eliza* (1900), a comedy of manners that proved popular enough to call for four sequels. Also extremely popular were his parodies *Another Englishwoman's Love Letters* (1901), *Madge Askinforit* (a parody of the Margot Asquith diaries that was very popular with American audiences; 1920), and *If Summer Don't* (1922).

Currently, there are some healthy signs that this once very popular but now rather neglected author is making a comeback. But whereas during his lifetime he was read primarily for his skills as a humorist and parodist, he is now being looked to by many twentieth-century readers for his highly polished, psychologically oriented short stories. Good collections of his serious short stories are *Stories in Grey* (1912) and *Collected Tales* (1916). In addition to short stories, parodies, and humorous sketches, Pain published a number of crime stories (e.g., his *Constantine Dix* tales); some ghost stories; a critical study of literary craftmanship, *The Short Story* (1915); and some extremely fine and poignant fantasies, bearing memorable titles like "The Celestial Grocery" and "The Moon-Slave." Other significant works include *Nothing Serious* (1901), *Wilhelmina in London* (1906), *Mrs. Murphy* (1913), *Edwards* (1915), and *Confessions of Alphonse* (1917).

The quality of "The Glass of Supreme Moments" makes it clear why there has been a renewal of interest in Pain's fiction. Part of Pain's literary genius was his remarkable ability to juxtapose the realistic with the fantastic in such a way as to enable both elements to profit from the contact. In "Glass," for example, the fantastic staircase "fashioned of silver and crystal" takes on an even more exotic character when introduced immediately after the depressing description of Lucas Morne's drab college room, with its dirty tea cups, cold toast, and stale aroma of Latakia.

But this high fantasy exhibits other unique features, as well. It is rare to find stories of this type infused with such deep psychological insight and with the kind of whimsy and sardonic wit so characteristic of Pain. A good example of the latter occurs when Lucas views the race between Blake and himself in the magical "glass of supreme moments." He begins thinking of how helpful it would be in "betting on a race," but then stops short when he realizes that under the present extraordinary circumstances his thoughts were "becoming a little inappropriate."

All in all, this is a good story, well told. The descriptions are full of rich and memorable imagery (the fabulous staircase; the mysterious, veiled lady; the glass of

supreme moments and the room in which it is housed);
the atmosphere of mystery and suspense is deftly created
and nicely sustained; the central device (the glass of supreme moments) is ingeniously handled; the narrative
thread is strong; the character delineation is solid and believable; and there is more than ample thematic substance. Clearly, this story constitutes one of Pain's
supreme literary moments.

❦ The Glass of Supreme Moments ❧

Barry Pain

Lucas Morne sat in his college rooms, when the winter afternoon met the evening, depressed and dull. There were various reasons for his depression. He was beginning to be a little nervous about his health. A week before he had run second in a mile race, the finish of which had been a terrible struggle; ever since then any violent exertion or excitement had brought on symptoms which were painful, and to one who had always been strong, astonishing. He had felt them early that afternoon, on coming from the river. Besides, he was discontented with himself. He had had several men in his rooms that afternoon, who were better than he was, men who had enthusiasms and had found them satisfying. Lucas had a moderate devotion to athletics, but no great enthusiasm. Neither had he the finer perceptions. Neither was he a scholar. He was just an ordinary man.

His visitors had drunk his tea, talked of their own enthusiasms, and were gone. Nothing is so unclean as a used tea-cup; nothing is so cold as toast which has once been hot, and the concrete expression of dejection is crumbs. Even Lucas Morne, who had not the finer perceptions, was dimly conscious that his room had become horrible, and now flung open the window. One of the men—a large, clumsy man—had been smoking mitigated Latakia; and Latakia has a way of rolling itself all round the atmosphere and kicking. Lucas seated himself in his easiest chair.

His rooms were near the chapel, and he could hear the organ. The music and the soft fall of the darkness were soothing; he could hardly see the used tea-cups now; the

42

light from the gas-lamp outside came just a little way into the room, shyly and obliquely.

Well, he had not noticed it before, but the fireplace had become a staircase. He felt too lazy to wonder much at this. He would, he thought, have the things all altered back again on the morrow. It would be worth while to sell the staircase, seeing that its steps were fashioned of silver and crystal. Unfortunately he could not see how much there was of it, or whither it led. The first five steps were clear enough; he felt convinced that the workmanship of them was Japanese. But the rest of the staircase was hidden from his sight by a gray veil of mist. He found himself a little angry, in a severe and strictly logical way, that in these days of boasted science he would not prevent a piece of fog, measuring ten feet by seven, from coming in at an open window and sitting down on a staircase which had only just begun to exist, and blotting out all but five steps of it in its very earliest moments. He allowed that it was a beautiful mist; its color changed slowly from gray to rose, and then back again from rose to gray; fire-flies of silver and gold shot through it at intervals; but it was a nuisance, because he wanted to see the rest of the staircase, and it prevented him. Every moment the desire to see more grew stronger. At last he determined to shake off his laziness, and go up the staircase and through the mist into the something beyond. He felt sure that the something beyond would be beautiful—sure with the certainty which has nothing to do with logical conviction.

It seemed to him that it was with an effort that he brought himself to rise from the chair and walk to the foot of that lovely staircase. He hesitated there for a moment or two, and as he did so he heard the sound of footsteps, high up, far away, yet coming nearer and nearer, with light music in the sound of them. Someone was coming down the staircase. He listened eagerly and excitedly. Then through the gray mist came a gray-robed figure.

It was the figure of a woman—young, with wonderful grace in her movements. Her face was veiled, and all that could be seen of her as she pased on the fifth step was the soft, dark hair that reached to her waist, and her arms —white wonders of beauty. The rest was hidden by the gray veil, and the long gray robe, that left, however, their suggestion of classical grace and slenderness. Lucas Morne stood looking at her tremulously. He felt sure, too, that she was looking at him, and that she could see through the folds of the thin gray veil that hid her face. She was the first to speak. Her voice in its gentleness and delicacy was like the voice of a child; it was only afterward that he heard in it the under-thrill which told of more than childhood.

"Why have you not come? I have been waiting for you, you know, up there. And this is the only time," she added.

"I am very sorry," he stammered. "You see—I never knew the staircase was there until to-day. In fact—it seems very stupid of me—but I always thought it was a fireplace. I must have been dreaming, of course. And then this afternoon I thought, or dreamed, that a lot of men came in to see me. Perhaps they really did come; and we got talking, you know—"

"Yes," she said, with the gentlest possible interruption. "I *do* know. There was one man, Fynsale, large, ugly, clumsy, a year your senior. He sat in that chair over there, and sulked and smoked Latakia. I rather like the smell of Latakia. He especially loves to write or to say some good thing; and at times he can do it. Therefore, you envy him. Then there was Blake. Blake is an athlete, like yourself, but is just a little more successful. Yes, I know you are good, but Blake is very good. You were tried for the 'Varsity—Blake was selected. He and Fynsale both have delight in ability, and you envy both. There was that dissenting little Paul Reece. He is not exactly in your set, but you were at school with him, and so you tolerate him. How good he is, for all his insignificance and social defects! Blake knows that, and kept a guard on his talk this afternoon. He would not offend Paul Reece for worlds. Paul's belief gives him earnestness, his earnestness leads him to self-sacrifice, and self-sacrifice is deep delight to him. You have more ability than Paul Reece, but you cannot reach that kind of enthusiastic happiness, and therefore you envy him. I could say similar things of the other men. It was because they made you vaguely dissatisfied with yourself that they bored you. You take pleasure —a certain pleasure—in athletics, and that pleasure would become an enthusiastic delight if you were a little better at them. Some men could get the enthusiastic delight out of as much as you can do, but your temperament is different. I know you well. You are not easily satisfied. You are not clever, but you are—" She paused.

"What am I?" he asked eagerly. He felt sure that it would be something good, and he was not less vain than other men.

"I do not think I will say—not now."

"But who are you?" His diffidence and stammering had vanished beneath her calm, quiet talk. "You must let me at least ask that. Who are you?"

"I am a woman, but not an earth-woman. And the chief difference between us is that I know nearly all the things you do not know, and you do not know nearly all the things that I know. Sometimes I forget your ignorance —do not be angry for a word; there is no other for it, and it is not your fault. I forgot it just now when I asked you why you had not come to me up the staircase of silver and crystal, through the gray veil where the fire-flies live, and into that quiet room beyond. This is the only time; tomorrow it will not be possible. And I have—" Once more she paused. There was a charm for Lucas Morne in the things which she did not say. "Your room is dark," she continued, "and I can hardly see you."

"I will light the lamp," said Lucas hurriedly, "and— and won't you let me get you some tea?" He saw, as soon as he had said it, how unspeakably ludicrous this proffer of hospitality was. He almost fancied a smile, a moment's shimmer of little white teeth, beneath the long gray veil. "Or shall I come now—at once?" he added.

"Come now; I will show you the mirror."

"What is that?"

"You will understand when you see it. It is the glass of supreme moments."

She looked graceful, and she suggested the most perfect beauty as she stood there, a slight figure against the background of gray mist, which had grown luminous as the room below grew darker. Lucas Morne went carefully up the five steps, and together they passed through the gray, misty curtain. He was wondering what the face was like which was hidden beneath that veil; would it be possible to induce her to remove the veil? He might, perhaps, lead the conversation thither—delicately and subtly.

"A cousin of mine," he began, "who has travelled a good deal, once told me that the women of the East—"

"Yes," she said, and her voice and way were so gentle that it hardly seemed like an interruption; "and so do I."

He felt very much anticipated; for a moment he was driven back into the shy and stammering state. There were only a few more steps now, and then they entered through a rosy curtain into a room, which he supposed to be "that quiet room beyond," of which she had spoken.

It was a large room, square in shape. The floor was covered with black and white tiles, with the exception of a small square space in the centre, which looked like silver, and over which a ripple seemed occasionally to pass. She pointed it out to him. "That," she said, "is the glass of supreme moments." There were no windows, and the soft light that filled the room seemed to come from that liquid silver mirror in the centre of the floor. The walls, which were lofty, were hung with curtains of different colors, all subdued, dreamy, reposeful. These colors were repeated in the painting of the ceiling. In a recess at the further end of the room there were seats, low seats on which one could sleep. There was a faint smell of syringa in the air, making it heavy and drowsy. Now and then one heard faintly, as if afar off, the great music of an organ. Could it, he found himself wondering, be the organ of the college chapel? It was restful and pleasant to hear. She drew him to one of the seats in the recess, and once more pointed to the mirror.

"All the ecstasy in the world lies reflected there. The supreme moments of each man's life—the scene, the spoken words—all lie there. Past and present, and future —all are there."

"Shall I be able to see them?"

"If you will."

"And how?"

"Bend over the mirror, and say the name of the man or woman into whose life you wish to see. You only have to want it, and it will appear before your eyes. But there are some lives which have no supreme moments."

"Commonplace lives?"

"Yes."

Lucas Morne walked to the edge of the mirror and knelt down, looking into it. The ripple passed to and fro over the surface. For a moment he hesitated, doubting for whom he should ask; and then he said in a low voice: "Are there supreme moments in the life of Blake— Vincent Blake, the athlete?" The surface of the mirror suddenly grew still, and in it rose what seemed a living picture.

He could see once more the mile race in which he had been defeated by Blake. It was the third and last lap; and he himself was leading by some twenty yards, for Blake was waiting. There was a vast crowd of spectators, and he could hear every now and then the dull sound of their voices. He saw Vincent Blake slightly quicken his pace and marked his own plucky attempt to answer it; he saw, too, that he had very little left in him. Gradually Blake drew up, until a hundred yards from the finish there were not more than five yards between the two runners. Then he noticed his own fresh attempt. There were some fifty yards of desperate fighting, in which neither seemed to gain or lose an inch on the other. The voices of the excited crowd rose to a roar. And then—then Blake had it his own way. He saw himself passed a yard from the tape.

"Blake has always just beaten me," he said savagely as he turned from the mirror.

He went back to his seat. "Tell me," he said; "does that picture really represent the supreme moments of Blake's life?"

"Yes," answered the veiled woman, "he will have nothing quite like the ecstasy which he felt at winning that race. He will marry, and have children, and his married life will be happy, but the happiness will not be so intense. There is an emotion-meter outside this room, you know, which measures such things."

"Now if one wanted to bet on a race," he began. Then he stopped short. He had none of the finer perceptions, but it did not take these to show him that he was becoming a little inappropriate. "I will look again at the mirror," he added after a pause. "I am afraid, though, that all this will make me more discontented with myself."

Once more he looked into the glass of supreme moments. He murmured the name of Paul Reece, the good little dissenter, his old school-fellow. It was not in the power of accomplishment that Paul Reece excelled Lucas Morne, but only in the goodness and spirituality of his nature. As he looked, once more a picture formed on the surface of the mirror. It was a picture of the future.

It was a sombre picture of the interior of a church. Through the open door one saw the snow falling slowly into the dusk of a winter afternoon. Within, before the richly decorated altar, flickered the little ruby flames of hanging lamps. On the walls, dim in the dying light, were painted the stations of the Cross. The fragrance of the incense smoke still lingered in the air. He could see but one figure, bowed, black-robed, before the altar. "And is this Paul Reece—who was a dissenter?" he asked himself, knowing that it was he. Someone was seated at the organ, and the cry of the music was full of appeal, and yet full of peace: *Agnus Dei, qui tollis peccata mundi!*

Then the picture died away, and once more the little ripple moved to and fro over the surface of the liquid silver mirror. Lucas went back again to his place. The veiled woman was leaning backward, her small white hands linked together. She did not speak, but he was sure that she was looking at him—looking at him intently. Slowly it came to him that there was in this woman a subtle, mastering attraction which he had never known before. And side by side with this thought there still remained the feeling which had filled him as he witnessed the supreme moments of Paul Reece, a paradoxical feelin which was half restlessness and half peace.

"I do not know if I envy Paul," he said, "but if so, it is not the envy which hurts. I shall never be like him. I can't feel as he does. It's not in me. But this picture did not make me angry as the other did." He looked steadfastly at the graceful, veiled figure, and added in a lower tone: "When I spoke of the travels of my cousin a little while ago—over Palestine and Turkey, and thereabouts, you know—I had meant to lead up to a question, as you saw. I had meant to ask you if you would put away your veil and let me see your face. And there are many things which I want to know about you. May I not stay here by your side and talk?"

"Soon, very soon, I will talk with you, and after that you will see me. What do you think, then, of the glass of supreme moments?"

"It is wonderful. I only feared the sight of exquisite happiness in others would make me more discontented. At first you seemed to think that I was too dissatisfied."

"Do not be deceived. Do not think that these supreme moments are everything; for that life is easiest which is gentle, level, placid, and has no supreme moments. There is a picture in the life of your friend Fynsale which I wish you to see. Look at it in the mirror; then I will tell you something."

Lucas did as he was bidden. The mirror showed him a wretched, dingy room—sitting-room and bedroom combined—in a lodging house. At a little rickety table, pushed in front of a very small fire, Fynsale sat writing by lamp-light. The lamp was out of order apparently. The combined smell of lamp and Latakia was poignant. There was a pile of manuscripts before him, and on the top of it he was placing the sheet he had just written. Then he rose from his chair, folded his arms on the mantel-piece, and bent down, with his head on his hands, looking into the fire. It was an uncouth attitude of which, Lucas remembered, Fynsale had been particularly fond when he was at college.

When the picture had passed, Lucas looked round, and saw that the veiled woman had left the recess and was now standing by his side. "I do not understand this," he said. "How can those be the supreme moments in Fynsale's life? He looked poor and shabby, and the room was positively wretched. Where does the ecstasy come in?"

"He has just finished his novel; and he is quite madly in love with it. Some of it is very good, and some of it— from merely physical reasons—is very bad; he was half-starved when he was writing it, and it is not possible to write very well when one is half-starved. But he loves it. I am speaking of all this as if, like the picture of it, it were present; although, of course, it has not happened yet. But I will tell you more. I will show you, in this case at least, what these moments of ecstasy are worth. Some of

Fynsale's book, I have said, is very good, and some of it is very bad; but none of it is what people want. He will take it to publisher after publisher, and they will refuse it. After three years it will at last be published, and it will not succeed in the least. And all through these years of failure he will recall from time to time the splendid joy he felt at finishing that book, and how glad he was that he had made it. The thought of that past ecstasy will make the torture all the worse."

"Perhaps, then, after all I should be glad that I am commonplace?"

"It does not always follow, though, that the commonplace people have commonplace lives. There have been men who have been so ordinary that it hurt one to have anything to do with them, and yet the gods have made them come into poetry."

Once more Lucas fancied that a smile with magic in it might be fluttering under that gray veil. Every moment the fascination of this woman, whose face he had not seen, and with whom he had spoken for so short a time, grew stronger on him. He did not know from whence it came, whether it lay in the grace of her figure and her movements, or in the beauty of her long, dark hair, or in the music of her voice, or in that subtle, indefinable way in which she seemed to show him that she cared for him deeply. The room itself, quiet, mystical, restful, dedicated to the ecstasy of the world, had its effect upon his senses. More than ever before he felt himself impressed, tremulous with emotion. He knew that she saw how, in spite of himself, the look of adoration would come into his eyes.

And suddenly she, whom but a moment before he had imagined to be smiling at her own light thoughts, seemed swayed by a more serious impulse.

"You must be comforted, though, and be angry with yourself no longer. For you are *not* commonplace, because you know that you *are* commonplace. It is something to have wanted the right things, although the gods have given you no power to attain them, nor even the wit and words to make your want eloquent." Her voice was deeper, touched with the under-thrill.

"This," he said, "is the second time you have spoken of the gods—and yet we are in the nineteenth century."

"Are we?" I am very old and very young. Time is nothing to me; it does not change me. Yesterday in Italy each grave and stream spoke of divinity. *'Non omnis moriar,'* sang one in confidence, *'Non omnis moriar!'* I heard his voice, and now he is passed and gone from the world."

"We read him still," said Lucas Morne, with a little pride. He was not intending to take the classical tripos, but he had with the help of a translation read that ode from which she was quoting. She did not heed his interruption in the least. She went on speaking:

"And to-day in England there is but little which is sacred; yet here, too, my work is seen; and here, too, as they die, they cry, 'I shall not die, but live!'"

"You will think me stupid," said Lucas Morne, a little bewildered, "but I really do not understand you, I do not follow you."

"That is because you do not know who I am. Before the end of to-day I think we shall understand each other well."

There was a moment's pause, and then Lucas Morne spoke again:

"You have told me that even in the lives of commonplace people there are sometimes supreme moments. I had scarcely hoped for them and you have bidden me not to desire them. Shall I—even I—know what ecstasy means?"

"Yes, yes; I think so."

"Then let me see it, as I saw the rest pictured in the mirror." He spoke with some hesitation, his eyes fixed on the tiled floor of the room.

"That need not be," she answered, and she hardly seemed to have perfect control over the tones of her voice now. "That need not be, Lucas Morne, for the supreme moments of your life are here, here and now."

He looked up, suddenly and excitedly. She had flung back the gray veil over her long, dark hair, and stood revealed before him, looking ardently into his eyes. Her face was paler than that of average beauty; the lips, shapely and scarlet, were just parted; but the eyes gave the most wonderful charm. They were like flames at midnight—not the soft, gray eyes that make men better, but the passionate eyes that make men forget honor, and reason, and everything. She stretched out both hands toward him, impulsively, appealingly. He grasped them in his own. His own hands were hot, burning; every nerve in them tingled with excitement. For a moment he held her at arm's-length, looking at her, and said nothing. At last he found words:

"I knew that you would be like this. I think that I have loved you all my life. I wish that I might be with you forever."

There was a strange expression on her face. She did not speak, but she drew him nearer to her.

"Tell me your name," he said.

"Yesterday, where that poet lived—that confident poet—they called me Libitina; and here to-day, they call me Death. My name matters not, if you love me. For to you alone have I come thus. For the rest, I have done my work unseen. Only in this hour—only in this hour—was it possible."

He had hardly heeded what she said. He bent down over her face.

"Stay!" she said in a hurried whisper; "if you kiss me you will die."

He smiled triumphantly. "But I shall die kissing you," he said. And so their lips met. Her lips were scarlet, but they were icy cold.

FRANK R. STOCKTON

(1834–1902)

Frank Stockton was born in Philadelphia into a family that traced its paternal ancestry back to mid-seventeenth-century English settlers who were prominent in the affairs of New Jersey. One of his direct ancestors was a signer of the Declaration of Independence. His father wanted him to become a doctor, but young Stockton, who had already won prizes for his writing while a student at Central High School in Philadelphia, inclined towards a more artistic or creative career. After graduation he became a wood engraver. He seems to have been modestly successful, sufficiently so to enable him to marry Marian Edward Tuttle of Virginia in 1860. His inventiveness led to his taking out a patent for an engraving tool in 1866. He gave up engraving, however, sometime around 1866 to devote himself to writing and to editorial work. *Ting-a-Ling* (1870) is his first collection of children's fairy tales. He continued to work as an assistant editor for several children's magazines, to which he frequently contributed stories as well, until 1881, when he became a full-time writer.

It was the enormous success of his farcical novel *Rudder Grange* (1879) that enabled him to write full time. He became one of the most popular of the American humorists of the 1880s, during which time he wrote principally, though not exclusively, for adults. His other most notable and successful farcical novel was *The Casting Away of Mrs. Lecks and Mrs. Aleshine* (1886). His fantasies, however, remained in the form of short stories, some of the more important ones appearing in *The Floating Prince and Other Fairy Tales* (1881) and *The*

Bee Man of Orn and Other Fanciful Tales (1887). With the exception of his "The Lady or the Tiger?" (1882), unquestionably the most widely known of his works, time has proven his children's fantasies, stories such as "The Griffin and the Minor Canon," "The Bee Man of Orn," and "The Accommodating Circumstance," to be his most durable writing.

According to all the accounts of people who knew him, Frank Stockton was a man of gentleness and unvarying good humor. These are traits one notices immediately in "Old Pipes and the Dryad." We are introduced to the childlike innocent, Old Pipes, in an idyllic pastoral setting, and we would resent the note of conflict that the lazy, scheming echo dwarf introduces if the dwarf were not also a delightfully comical character. The old dwarf, like both the sprightly Dryad and Old Pipes, also illustrates the important point that all creatures must follow the natural laws that govern them. Nor does Stockton exempt himself from the laws that govern his craft. The story is told in a folk-tale style whose simplicity veils a painstaking craftsmanship that the careful reader will notice in Stockton's attention to detail and inner consistency.

❧ Old Pipes and the Dryad ❧

Frank Stockton

A mountain brook ran through a little village. Over the
brook there was a narrow bridge, and from the bridge a
footpath led out from the village and up the hillside to the
cottage of Old Pipes and his mother. For many, many
years Old Pipes had been employed by the villagers to
pipe the cattle down from the hills. Every afternoon, an
hour before sunset, he would sit on a rock in front of his
cottage and play on his pipes. Then all the flocks and
herds that were grazing on the mountains would hear him,
wherever they might happen to be, and would come down
to the village—the cows by the easiest paths, the sheep by
those not quite so easy, and the goats by the steep and
rocky ways that were hardest of all.

But now, for a year or more, Old Pipes had not piped
the cattle home. It is true that every afternoon he sat upon
the rock and played upon his familiar instrument; but
the cattle did not hear him. He had grown old, and his
breath was feeble. The echoes of his cheerful notes,
which used to come from the rocky hill on the other side
of the valley, were heard no more; and twenty yards from
Old Pipes one could scarcely tell what tune he was playing. He had become somewhat deaf and did not know
that the sound of his pipes was so thin and weak
that the cattle did not hear him. The cows, the sheep, and
the goats came down every afternoon as before, but this
was because two boys and a girl were sent up after them.
The villagers did not wish the good old man to know that
his piping was no longer of any use, so they paid him his
little salary every month and said nothing about the two
boys and the girl.

Old Pipes's mother was, of course, a great deal older than he was and as deaf as a gate—posts, latch, hinges, and all—and she never knew that the sound of her son's pipe did not spread over all the mountainside and echo back strong and clear from the opposite hills. She was very fond of Old Pipes and proud of his piping; and as he was so much younger than she was, she never thought of him as being very old. She cooked for him and made his bed and mended his clothes; and they lived very comfortably on his little salary.

One afternoon, at the end of the month, when Old Pipes had finished his piping, he took his stout staff and went down the hill to the village to receive the money for his month's work. The path seemed a great deal steeper and more difficult than it used to be; and Old Pipes thought that it must have been washed by the rains and greatly damaged. He remembered it as a path that was quite easy to traverse either up or down. But Old Pipes had been a very active man, and as his mother was so much older than he was, he never thought of himself as aged and infirm.

When the Chief Villager had paid him and he had talked a little with some of his friends, Old Pipes started to go home. But when he had crossed the bridge over the brook and gone a short distance up the hillside, he became very tired and sat down upon a stone. He had not been sitting there half a minute when along came two boys and a girl.

"Children," said Old Pipes, "I'm very tired tonight, and I don't believe I can climb up this steep path to my home. I think I shall have to ask you to help me."

"We will do that," said the boys and the girl, quite cheerfully; and one boy took him by the right hand and the other by the left, while the girl pushed him in the back. In this way he went up the hill quite easily and soon reached his cottage door. Old Pipes gave each of the three children a copper coin, and then they sat down for a few minutes' rest before starting back to the village.

"I'm sorry that I tired you so much," said Old Pipes.

"Oh, that would not have tired us," said one of the boys, "if we had not been so far today after the cows, the sheep, and the goats. They rambled high up on the mountain, and we never before had such a time in finding them."

"Had to go after the cows, the sheeps, and the goats!" exclaimed Old Pipes. "What do you mean by that?"

The girl, who stood behind the old man, shook her head, put her hand on her mouth, and made all sorts of signs to the boy to stop talking on this subject; but he did not notice her and promptly answered Old Pipes.

"Why, you see, good sir," said he, "that as the cattle can't hear your pipes now, somebody has to go after them every evening to drive them down from the mountain, and the Chief Villager has hired us three to do it. Generally it is not very hard work, but tonight the cattle had wandered far."

"How long have you been doing this?" asked the old man.

The girl shook her head and clapped her hand on her mouth more vigorously than before, but the boy went on.

"I think it is about a year now," he said, "since the people first felt sure that the cattle could not hear your pipes; and from that time we've been driving them down. But we are rested now and will go home. Good night, sir."

The three children then went down the hill, the girl scolding the boy all the way home. Old Pipes stood silent a few moments, and then he went into his cottage.

"Mother," he shouted, "did you hear what those children said?"

"Children!" exclaimed the old woman. "I did not hear them. I did not know there were any children here."

Then Old Pipes told his mother, shouting very loudly to make her hear, how the two boys and the girl had helped him up the hill and what he had heard about his piping and the cattle.

"They can't hear you?" cried his mother. "Why, what's the matter with the cattle?"

"Ah, me!" said Old Pipes. "I don't believe there's anything the matter with the cattle. It must be with me and my pipes that there is something the matter. But one thing is certain: if I do not earn the wages the Chief Villager pays me, I shall not take them. I shall go straight down to the village and give back the money I received today."

"Nonsense!" cried his mother. "I'm sure you've piped as well as you could, and no more can be expected. And what are we to do without the money?"

"I don't know," said Old Pipes; "but I'm going down to the village to pay it back."

The sun had now set, but the moon was shining very brightly on the hillside, and Old Pipes could see his way very well. He did not take the same path by which he had gone before, but followed another, which led among the trees upon the hillside, and although longer, was not so steep.

When he had gone about halfway, the old man sat down to rest, leaning his back against a great oak tree. As he did so, he heard a sound like knocking inside the tree, and then a voice distinctly said, "Let me out! Let me out!"

Old Pipes instantly forgot that he was tired and sprang to his feet. "This must be a dryad tree!" he exclaimed. "If it is, I'll let her out."

Old Pipes had never, to his knowledge, seen a dryad tree, but he knew there were such trees on the hillsides and the mountains and that dryads lived in them. He knew, too, that in the summertime, on those days when the moon rose before the sun went down, a dryad could come out of her tree if anyone could find the key which locked her in and turn it. Old Pipes closely examined the trunk of the tree, which stood in the full moonlight. "If I see that key," he said, "I shall surely turn it." Before long, he perceived a piece of bark standing out from the tree, which appeared to him very much like the handle of a key. He took hold of it and found he could turn it quite around. As he did so, a large part of the side of the tree was pushed open, and a beautiful dryad stepped quickly out.

For a moment she stood motionless, gazing on the scene before her—the tranquil valley, the hills, the forest, and the mountainside, all lying in the soft, clear light of the moon. "Oh, lovely! lovely!" she exclaimed. "How long it is since I have seen anything like this!" And then, turning to Old Pipes, she said, "How good of you to let me out! I am so happy and so thankful that I must kiss you, you dear old man!" And she threw her arms around the neck of Old Pipes and kissed him on both cheeks. "You don't know," she then went on to say, "how doleful it is to be shut up so long in a tree. I don't mind it in the winter, for then I am glad to be sheltered, but in summer it is a rueful thing not to be able to see all the beauties of the world. And it's ever so long since I've been let out. People so seldom come this way; and when they do come at the right time they either don't hear me, or they are frightened and run away. But you, you dear old man, you were not frightened, and you looked and looked for the key, and you let me out, and now I shall not have to go back till winter has come and the air grows cold. Oh, it is glorious! What can I do for you, to show you how grateful I am?"

"I am very glad," said Old Pipes, "that I let you out, since I see that it makes you so happy; but I must admit that I tried to find the key because I had a great desire to see a dryad. But if you wish to do something for me, you can, if you happen to be going down toward the village."

"To the village!" exclaimed the Dryad. "I will go anywhere for you, my kind old benefactor."

"Well, then," said Old Pipes, "I wish you would take this little bag of money to the Chief Villager and tell him that Old Pipes cannot receive pay for the services which he does not perform. It is now more than a year that I have not been able to make the cattle hear me when I piped to call them home. I did not know this until tonight; but now that I know it, I cannot keep the money, and so I send it back." And handing the little bag to the Dryad, he bade her good night and turned toward his cottage.

"Good night," said the Dryad. "And I thank you over and over and over again, you good old man!"

Old Pipes walked toward his home, very glad to be saved the fatigue of going all the way down to the village and back again. "To be sure," he said to himself, "this path does not seem at all steep, and I can walk along it very easily; but it would have tired me dreadfully to come up all the way from the village, especially as I could not have expected those children to help me again." When he reached home, his mother was surprised to see him returning so soon.

"What!" she exclaimed. "Have you already come back?

What did the Chief Villager say? Did he take the money?"

Old Pipes was just about to tell her that he had sent the money to the village by a dryad when he suddenly reflected that his mother would be sure to disapprove such a proceeding, and so he merely said he had sent it by a person whom he had met.

"And how do you know that the person will ever take it to the Chief Villager?" cried his mother. "You will lose it, and the villagers will never get it. Oh, Pipes! Pipes! When will you be old enough to have ordinary common sense?"

Old Pipes considered that as he was already seventy years of age he could scarcely expect to grow any wiser, but he made no remark on this subject; and saying that he doubted not that the money would go safely to its destination, he sat down to his supper. His mother scolded him roundly, but he did not mind it; and after supper he went out and sat on a rustic chair in front of the cottage to look at the moonlit village and to wonder whether or not the Chief Villager really received the money. While he was doing these two things, he went fast asleep.

When Old Pipes left the Dryad, she did not go down to the village with the little bag of money. She held it in her hand and thought about what she had heard. "This is a good and honest old man," she said; "and it is a shame that he should lose this money. He looked as if he needed it, and I don't believe the people in the village will take it from one who has served them so long. Often, when in my tree, have I heard the sweet notes of his pipes. I am going to take the money back to him." She did not start immediately, because there were so many beautiful things to look at; but after a while she went up to the cottage, and finding Old Pipes asleep in his chair, she slipped the little bag into his coat pocket and silently sped away.

The next day Old Pipes told his mother that he would go up the mountain and cut some wood. He had a right to get wood from the mountain, but for a long time he had been content to pick up the dead branches which lay about his cottage. Today, however, he felt so strong and vigorous that he thought he would go and cut some fuel that would be better than this. He worked all the morning, and when he came back he did not feel at all tired, and he had a very good appetite for his dinner.

Now, Old Pipes knew a good deal about dryads, but there was one thing which, although he had heard, he had forgotten. This was that a kiss from a dryad made a person ten years younger. The people of the village knew this, and they were very careful not to let any child of ten years or younger go into the woods where the dryads were supposed to be; for if they should chance to be kissed by one of these tree nymphs, they would be set back so far that they would cease to exist. A story was told in the village that a very bad boy of eleven once ran away into the woods and had an adventure of this kind; and when his mother found him, he was a little baby of one year old. Taking advantage of her opportunity, she brought him up more carefully than she had done before, and he grew to be a very good boy indeed.

Now, Old Pipes had been kissed twice by the Dryad, once on each cheek, and he therefore felt as vigorous and active as when he was a hale man of fifty. His mother noticed how much work he was doing and told him that he need not try in that way to make up for the loss of his piping wages; for he would only tire himself out and get sick. But her son answered that he had not felt so well for years and that he was quite able to work. In the course of the afternoon Old Pipes, for the first time that day, put his hand in his coat pocket, and there, to his amazement, he found the little bag of money. "Well, well!" he exclaimed, "I am stupid, indeed! I really thought that I had seen a dryad; but when I sat down by that big oak tree, I must have gone to sleep and dreamed it all; and then I came home thinking I had given the money to a dryad, when it was in my pocket all the time. But the Chief Villager shall have the money. I shall not take it to him today, but tomorrow I wish to go the village to see some of my old friends; and then I shall give up the money."

Toward the close of the afternoon Old Pipes, as had been his custom for so many years, took his pipes from the shelf on which they lay and went out to the rock in front of the cottage.

"What are you going to do?" cried his mother. "If you will not consent to be paid, why do you pipe?"

"I am going to pipe for my own pleasure," said her son. "I am used to it, and I do not wish to give it up. It does not matter now whether the cattle hear me or not, and I am sure that my piping will injure no one."

When the good man began to play upon his favorite instrument, he was astonished at the sound that came from it. The beautiful notes of the pipes sounded clear and strong down into the valley and spread over the hills and up the sides of the mountain beyond, while, after a little interval, an echo came back from the rocky hill on the other side of the valley.

"Ha ha!" he cried. "What has happened to my pipes? They must have been stopped up of late, but now they are as clear and good as ever."

Again the merry notes went sounding far and wide. The cattle on the mountain heard them, and those that were old enough remembered how these notes had called them from their pastures every evening, and so they started down the mountainside, the others following.

The merry notes were heard in the village below, and the people were much astonished thereby. "Why, who can be blowing the pipes of Old Pipes?" they said. But as they were all very busy, no one went up to see. One thing, however, was plain enough: the cattle were coming down the mountain. And so the two boys and the girl did not have to go after them and had an hour for play, for which they were very glad.

The next morning Old Pipes started down to the village with his money, and on the way he met the Dryad. "Oh, ho!" he cried. "Is that you? Why, I thought my letting you out of the tree was nothing but a dream."

"A dream!" cried the Dryad. "If you only knew how happy you have made me, you would not think it merely a dream. And has it not benefited you? Do you not feel happier? Yesterday I heard you playing beautifully on your pipes."

"Yes, yes," cried he. "I did not understand it before, but I see it all now. I have really grown younger. I thank you, I thank you, good Dryad, from the bottom of my heart. It was the finding of the money in my pocket that made me think it was a dream."

"Oh, I put it in when you were asleep," she said, laughing, "because I thought you ought to keep it. Good-bye, kind, honest man. May you live long and be as happy as I am now."

Old Pipes was greatly delighted when he understood that he was really a younger man; but that made no difference about the money, and he kept on his way to the village. As soon as he reached it, he was eagerly questioned as to who had been playing his pipes the evening before, and when the people heard that it was himself, they were very much surprised. Thereupon, Old Pipes told what had happened to him, and then there was greater wonder, with hearty congratulations and handshakes; for Old Pipes was liked by everyone. The Chief Villager refused to take his money, and although Old Pipes said that he had not earned it, everyone present insisted that, as he would now play on his pipes as before, he should lose nothing because for a time he was unable to perform his duty.

So Old Pipes was obliged to keep his money, and after an hour or two spent in conversation with his friends, he returned to his cottage.

There was one individual, however, who was not at all pleased with what had happened to Old Pipes. This was an echo-dwarf who lived on the hills on the other side of the valley, and whose duty it was to echo back the notes of the pipes whenever they could be heard. There were a great many other echo-dwarfs on these hills, some of whom echoed back the songs of maidens, some the shouts of children, and others the music that was often heard in the village. But there was only one who could send back the strong notes of the pipes of Old Pipes, and this had been his sole duty for many years. But when the old man grew feeble and the notes of his pipes could not be heard on the opposite hills, this echo-dwarf had nothing to do, and he spent his time in delightful idleness; and he slept so much and grew so fat that it made his companions laugh to see him walk.

On the afternoon on which, after so long an interval, the sound of the pipes was heard on the echo hills, this dwarf was fast asleep behind a rock. As soon as the first notes reached them, some of his companions ran to wake him. Rolling to his feet, he echoed back the merry tune of Old Pipes. Naturally, he was very much annoyed and indignant at being thus obliged to give up his life of comfortable leisure, and he hoped very much that this pipe-playing would not occur again. The next afternoon he was awake and listening, and, sure enough, at the usual hour, along came the notes of the pipes as clear and strong as they ever had been; and he was obliged to work as long as Old Pipes played. The echo-dwarf was very angry. He had supposed, of course, that the pipe-playing had ceased forever, and he felt that he had a right to be indignant at being thus deceived. He was so much disturbed that he made up his mind to go and try to find out whether this was to be a temporary matter or not. He had plenty of time, as the pipes were played but once a day, and he set off early in the morning for the hill on which Old Pipes lived. It was hard work for the fat little fellow, and when he had crossed the valley and had gone some distance into the woods on the hillside, he stopped to rest, and in a few minutes the Dryad came tripping along.

"Ho, ho!" exclaimed the dwarf. "What are you doing here, and how did you get out of your tree?"

"Doing!" cried the Dryad. "I am being happy; that's what I am doing. And I was let out of my tree by the good old man who plays the pipes to call the cattle down from the mountain. And it makes me happier to think that I have been of service to him. I gave him two kisses of gratitude, and now he is young enough to play his pipes as well as ever."

The echo-dwarf stepped forward, his face pale with passion. "Am I to believe," he said, "that you are the cause of this great evil that has come upon me and that you are the wicked creature who has again started this old man upon his career of pipe-playing? What have I ever done to you that you should have condemned me for years and years to echo back the notes of those wretched pipes?"

At this the Dryad laughed loudly.

"What a funny little fellow you are." she said. "Anyone would think you had been condemned to toil from morning till night; while what you really have to do is merely to imitate for half an hour every day the merry notes of Old Pipes's piping. Fie upon you, Echo-dwarf! You are lazy and selfish; and that is what is the matter with you. Instead of grumbling at being obliged to do a little wholesome work, which is less, I am sure, than that of any other echo-dwarf upon the rocky hillside, you should rejoice at the good fortune of the old man who has regained so much of his strength and vigor. Go home and learn to be just and generous; and then perhaps you may be happy. Good-bye."

"Insolent creature!" shouted the dwarf, as he shook his fat little fist at her. "I'll make you suffer for this. You shall find out what it is to heap injury and insult upon one like me and to snatch from him the repose that he has earned by long years of toil." And shaking his head savagely, he hurried back to the rocky hillside.

Every afternoon the merry notes of the pipes of Old Pipes sounded down into the valley and over the hills and up the mountainside; and every afternoon, when he had echoed them back, the little dwarf grew more and more angry with the Dryad. Each day, from early morning till it was time for him to go back to his duties upon the rocky hillside, he searched the woods for her. He intended, if he met her, to pretend to be very sorry for what he had said, and he thought he might be able to play a trick upon her which would avenge him well. One day, while thus wandering among the trees, he met Old Pipes. The Echo-dwarf did not generally care to see or speak to ordinary people; but now he was so anxious to find the object of his search that he stopped and asked Old Pipes if he had seen the Dryad. The piper had not noticed the little fellow, and he looked down on him with some surprise.

"No," he said, "I have not seen her, and I have been looking everywhere for her."

"You!" cried the dwarf. "What do you wish with her?"

Old Pipes then sat down on a stone, so that he should be nearer the ear of his small companion, and he told what the Dryad had done for him.

When the Echo-dwarf heard that this was the man whose pipes he was obliged to echo back every day, he would have slain him on the spot had he been able; but as he was not able, he merely ground his teeth and listened to the rest of the story.

"I am looking for the Dryad now," Old Pipes continued, "on account of my aged mother. When I was old myself, I did not notice how very old my mother was; but now it shocks me to see how feeble and decrepit her years have caused her to become; and I am looking for the Dryad to ask her to make my mother younger, as she made me."

The eyes of the Echo-dwarf glistened. Here was a man who might help him in his plans.

"Your idea is a good one," he said to Old Pipes, "and it does you honor. But you should know that a dryad can make no person younger but one who lets her out of her tree. However, you can manage the affair very easily. All you need do is to find the Dryad, tell her what you want, and request her to step into her tree and be shut up for a short time. Then you will go and bring your mother to the tree; she will open it, and everything will be as you wish. Is not this a good plan?"

"Excellent!" cried Old Pipes; "and I will go instantly and search more diligently for the Dryad."

"Take me with you," said the Echo-dwarf. "You can easily carry me on your strong shoulders; and I shall be glad to help you in any way that I can."

"Now, then," said the little fellow to himself, as Old Pipes carried him rapidly along, "if he persuades the Dryad to get into a tree—and she is quite foolish enough to do it—and then goes away to bring his mother, I shall take a stone or a club, and I will break off the key to that tree, so that nobody can ever turn it again. Then Mistress Dryad will see what she has brought upon herself by her behavior to me."

Before long they came to the great oak tree in which the Dryad had lived, and at a distance they saw that beautiful creature herself coming toward them.

"How excellently well everything happens!" said the dwarf. "Put me down, and I will go. Your business with the Dryad is more important than mine; and you need not say anything about my having suggested your plan to you. I am willing that you should have all the credit of it yourself."

Old Pipes put the Echo-dwarf upon the ground, but

the little rogue did not go away. He concealed himself between some low, mossy rocks, and he was so much of their color that you would not have noticed him if you had been looking straight at him.

When the Dryad came up, Old Pipes lost no time in telling her about his mother and what he wished her to do. At first the Dryad answered nothing but stood looking very sadly at Old Pipes.

"Do you really wish me to go into my tree again?" she said. "I should dreadfully dislike to do it, for I don't know what might happen. It is not at all necessary, for I could make your mother younger at any time if she would give me the opportunity. I had already thought of making you still happier in this way; and several times I have waited about your cottage, hoping to meet your aged mother, but she never comes outside, and you know a dryad cannot enter a house. I cannot imagine what put this idea into your head. Did you think of it yourself?"

"No, I cannot say that I did," answered Old Pipes. "A little dwarf whom I met in the woods proposed it to me."

"Oh!" cried the Dryad. "Now I see through it all. It is the scheme of that vile Echo-dwarf—your enemy and mine. Where is he? I should like to see him."

"I think he has gone away," said Old Pipes.

"No, he has not," said the Dryad, whose quick eyes perceived the Echo-dwarf among the rocks. "There he is. Seize him and drag him out, I beg of you."

Old Pipes perceived the dwarf as soon as he was pointed out to him, and running to the rocks, he caught the little fellow by the arm and pulled him out.

"Now, then," cried the Dryad, who had opened the door of the great oak, "just stick him in there, and we will shut him up. Then I shall be safe from his mischief for the rest of the time I am free."

Old Pipes thrust the Echo-dwarf into the tree; the Dryad pushed the door shut; there was a clicking sound of bark and wood, and no one would have noticed that the big oak had ever had an opening in it.

"There," said the Dryad; "now we need not be afraid of him. And I assure you, my good piper, that I shall be very glad to make your mother younger as soon as I can. Will you not ask her to come out and meet me?"

"Of course I will," cried Old Pipes; "and I will do it without delay."

And then, the Dryad by his side, he hurried to his cottage. But when he mentioned the matter to his mother, the old woman became very angry indeed. She did not believe in dryads; and if they really did exist, she knew they must be witches and sorceresses, and she would have nothing to do with them. If her son had ever allowed himself to be kissed by one of them, he ought to be ashamed of himself. As to its doing him the least bit of good, she did not believe a word of it. He felt better than he used to feel, but that was very common. She had sometimes felt that way herself, and she forbade him ever to mention a dryad to her again.

That afternoon Old Pipes, feeling very sad that his plan in regard to his mother had failed, sat down upon the rock and played upon his pipes. The pleasant sounds went down the valley and up the hills and mountain, but to the great surprise of some persons who happened to notice the fact, the notes were not echoed back from the rocky hillside but from the woods on the side of the valley on which Old Pipes lived. The next day many of the villagers stopped in their work to listen to the echo of the pipes coming from the woods. The sound was not as clear and strong as it used to be when it was sent back from the rocky hillside, but it certainly came from among the trees. Such a thing as an echo changing its place in this way had never been heard of before, and nobody was able to explain how it could have happened. Old Pipes, however, knew very well that the sound came from the Echo-dwarf shut up in the great oak tree. The sides of the tree were thin, and the sound of the pipes could be heard through them, and the dwarf was obliged by the laws of his being to echo back those notes whenever they came to him. But Old Pipes thought he might get the Dryad in trouble if he let anyone know that the Echo-dwarf was shut up in the tree, and so he wisely said nothing about it.

One day the two boys and the girl who had helped Old Pipes up the hill were playing in the woods. Stopping near the great oak tree, they heard a sound of knocking within it, and then a voice plainly said, "Let me out! Let me out!"

For a moment the children stood still in astonishment, and then one of the boys exclaimed, "Oh, it is a dryad, like the one Old Pipes found! Let's let her out!"

"What are you thinking of?" cried the girl. "I am the oldest of all, and I am only thirteen. Do you wish to be turned into crawling babies? Run! Run! Run!"

And the two boys and the girl dashed down into the valley as fast as their legs could carry them. There was no desire in their youthful hearts to be made younger than they were. And for fear that their parents might think it well that they should commence their careers anew, they never said a word about finding the dryad tree.

As the summer days went on, Old Pipes's mother grew feebler and feebler. One day when her son was away—for he now frequently went into the woods to hunt or fish or down into the valley to work—she arose from her knitting to prepare the simple dinner. But she felt so weak and tired that she was not able to do the work to which she had been so long accustomed. "Alas! Alas!" she said. "The time has come when I am too old to work. My son will have to hire someone to come here and cook his meals, make his bed, and mend his clothes. Alas! Alas! I had hoped that as long as I lived I should be able to do these things. But it is not so. I have grown utterly worthless, and someone else must prepare the dinner for my son. I wonder where he is." And tottering to the door, she went outside to look for him. She did not feel able to stand, and reaching the rustic chair, she sank into it, quite exhausted, and soon fell asleep.

The Dryad, who had often come to the cottage to see if she could find an opportunity of carrying out Old Pipes's affectionate design, now happened by; and seeing that the much desired occasion had come, she stepped up quietly behind the old woman and gently kissed her on each cheek and then as quietly disappeared.

In a few minutes the mother of Old Pipes awoke, and looking up at the sun, she exclaimed, "Why, it is almost dinner time! My son will be here directly, and I am not ready for him." And rising to her feet, she hurried into the house, made the fire, set the meat and vegetables to cook, laid the cloth; and by the time her son arrived, the meal was on the table.

"How a little sleep does refresh one," she said to herself as she was bustling about. She was a woman of very vigorous constitution and at seventy had been a great deal stronger and more active than her son was at that age. The moment Old Pipes saw his mother, he knew that the Dryad had been there; but, while he felt as happy as a king, he was too wise to say anything about her.

"It is astonishing how well I feel today," said his mother; "and either my hearing has improved or you speak much more plainly than you have done of late."

The summer days went on and passed away, the leaves were falling from the trees, and the air was becoming cold.

"Nature has ceased to be lovely," said the Dryad, "and the night winds chill me. It is time for me to go back into my comfortable quarters in the great oak. But first I must pay another visit to the cottage of Old Pipes."

She found the piper and his mother sitting side by side on the rock in front of the door. The cattle were not to go to the mountain any more that season, and he was piping them down for the last time. Loud and merrily sounded the pipes of Old Pipes, and down the mountainside came the cattle—the cows by the easiest paths, the sheep by those not quite so easy, and the goats by the most difficult ones among the rocks—while from the great oak tree were heard the echoes of the cheerful music.

"How happy they look, sitting there together," said the Dryad; "and I don't believe it will do them a bit of harm to be still younger." And moving quietly up behind them, she first kissed Old Pipes on his cheek and then his mother.

Old Pipes, who had stopped playing, knew what it was, but he did not move, and said nothing. His mother, thinking that her son had kissed her, turned to him with a smile and kissed him in return. And then she arose and went into the cottage, a vigorous woman of sixty, followed by her son, erect and happy and twenty years younger than herself.

The Dryad sped away to the woods, shrugging her shoulders as she felt the cool evening wind.

When she reached the great oak, she turned the key and opened the door. "Come out," she said to the Echodwarf, who sat blinking within. "Winter is coming on, and I want the comfortable shelter of my tree for myself. The cattle have come down from the mountain for the last time this year, the pipes will no longer sound, and you can go to your rocks and have a holiday until next spring."

Upon hearing these words, the dwarf skipped quickly out, and the Dryad entered the tree and pulled the door shut after her. "Now, then," she said to herself, "he can break off the key if he likes. It does not matter to me. Another will grow out next spring. And although the good piper made me no promise, I know that when the warm days arrive next year, he will come and let me out again."

The Echo-dwarf did not stop to break the key of the tree. He was too happy to be released to think of anything else, and he hastened as fast as he could to his home on the rocky hillside.

The Dryad was not mistaken when she trusted in the piper. When the warm days came again, he went to the oak tree to let her out. But to his sorrow and surprise he found the great tree lying upon the ground. A winter storm had blown it down, and it lay with its trunk shattered and split. And what became of the Dryad, no one ever knew.

LORD DUNSANY
(1878–1957)

Lord Dunsany has the distinction of being one of the finest and most influential fantasy writers of the past century and a half. Many have tried to match his prodigious imaginative powers and to imitate his lyrical prose style, but few have succeeded. Born Edward John Moreton Drax Plunkett in London, on July 24, 1878, he became the eighteenth Baron Dunsany when his father, an Irish nobleman, died in 1899. Educated at Cheam School, Eton, and Sandhurst, Dunsany served as an officer in the Coldstream Guards in the Boer War, and as a captain in the Royal Iniskilling Fusiliers during World War I. He was wounded in the Easter Rebellion of 1916. During World War II, Dunsany held the chair of Byron Professor of English Literature at the University of Athens and was there when Nazi troops invaded and captured the city. He subsequently disappeared for some time, finally arriving in Dublin in 1942 but refusing to explain what had happened during his disappearance.

Dunsany was a handsome, robust, and athletic man who loved to play sports, hunt, and travel. He crisscrossed America on several reading tours, and spent a good deal of time hunting lions on safari in Africa. In addition, he immensely enjoyed playing chess and was considered a master at the game. It is difficult to understand how Dunsany could do all the things he did and still find the time to write more than sixty books. His dynamic and fascinating life is chronicled in rich detail in a series of memoirs: *Patches of Sunlight* (1938), *While the Sirens Slept* (1944), and *The Sirens Wake* (1945). He died in Dublin on October 25, 1957.

Although Dunsany's first published work was a collection of short stories entitled *The Gods of Pegana* (1905), it was the drama that first brought him widespread recognition and critical acclaim as a literary artist. In 1909, at the request of W. B. Yeats, Dunsany wrote a play, *The Glittering Gate,* for production at the famed Abbey Theatre. A solid success, this drama was followed by a number of others, including *The Gods of the Mountain* (1911), *The Laughter of the Gods* (1916), *If* (1921), and *Alexander* (1925). Many commentators consider his *A Night at an Inn* (1916) to be one of the best one-act plays ever written. Besides his many plays, Dunsany published several excellent novels, such as *The Charwoman's Shadow* (1926), *The Blessing of Pan* (1927), and *The Curse of the Wise Woman* (1933), winner of the Irish Academy's Harmsworth Prize. Perhaps his best work in this genre, however, is his fantasy masterpiece, *The King of Elfland's Daughter* (1924), which tells of the bittersweet love affair between Alveric, Prince of the Vale of Erl, and the beautiful Elf-Princess, Lirazel. In addition to his plays and novels, Lord Dunsany published collections of verse (e.g., *Fifty Poems,* 1929; *Mirage Water,* 1938), numerous essays, and seven volumes of short stories, including *Time and the Gods* (1906), *The Sword of Welleran* (1908), and *Fifty-one Tales* (1915). Disdaining the inventions and luxuries of the mechanized age in which he lived, Dunsany wrote most of his works with a quill pen and rarely changed a word once it was put down on paper.

Lord Dunsany wrote many exquisite fantasies, but none with more grace and feeling than this charming tale of the Wild Thing who desired a soul. "The Kith of the Elf-folk" truly represents Dunsany at his finest, for not only does the story exhibit his characteristic elegance of phrase, rich imagery, and fertile imagination, but also his ability to forcefully articulate a thematic idea. At the very heart of this narrative is Dunsany's fervent belief that man can experience the good life only if he learns to appreciate, protect, and live in harmony with nature. There is a clear and vivid dichotomy in this story. On the one hand, there is the pristine beauty of the unspoiled Marshlands, epitomized by the wonderful freedom of the Wild Things and the "wild rejoicing of the wings of the waterfowl." On the other, there is the depressing ugliness of the "great manufacturing city of the Midlands" where there is "nothing . . . good for a soul to see"; "a sullen city under a murky sky." Like so many other fantasists (Tolkien and Garner, for example), Dunsany had a deep love and respect for nature and recognized its vital importance in man's life.

Although many of Dunsany's stories exhibit a biblical influence, "The Kith of the Elf-folk" is especially rich in the biblical cadences Dunsany loved so well. Lines such as "And the light of the candles shone on the curate's fair hair, and his voice went ringing down the aisle, and Mary Jane rejoiced that he was there," help provide the proper tone and atmosphere to this essentially serious story about the longings of the soul.

❧ The Kith of the Elf-folk ❧

Lord Dunsany

The north wind was blowing, and red and golden the last days of Autumn were streaming hence. Solemn and cold over the marshes arose the evening.

It became very still.

Then the last pigeon went home to the trees on the dry land in the distance, whose shapes already had taken upon themselves a mystery in the haze.

Then all was still again.

As the light faded and the haze deepened, mystery crept nearer from every side.

Then the green plover came in crying, and all alighted. And again it became still, save when one of the plover arose and flew a little way uttering the cry of the waste. And hushed and silent became the earth, expecting the first star. Then the duck came in, and the widgeon, company by company: and all the light of day faded out of the sky saving one red band of light. Across the light appeared, black and huge, the wings of a flock of geese beating up wind to the marshes. These too went down among the rushes.

Then the stars appeared and shone in the stillness, and there was silence in the great spaces of the night.

Suddenly the bells of the cathedral in the marshes broke out, calling to evensong.

Eight centuries ago on the edge of the marsh men had built the huge cathedral, or it may have been seven centuries ago, or perhaps nine; it was all one to the Wild Things.

So evensong was held, and candles lighted, and the lights through the windows shone red and green in the water, and the sound of the organ went roaring over the the marshes. But from the deep and perilous places, edged with bright mosses, the Wild Things came leaping up to dance on the reflection of the stars, and over their heads as they danced the marsh-lights rose and fell.

The Wild Things are somewhat human in appearance, only all brown of skin and barely two feet high. Their ears are pointed like the squirrel's, only far larger, and they leap to prodigious heights. They live all day under deep pools in the loneliest marshes, but at night they come up and dance. Each Wild Thing has over its head a marsh-light, which moves as the Wild Thing moves; they have no souls, and cannot die, and are of the kith of the Elf-folk.

All night they dance over the marshes, treading upon the reflection of the stars (for the bare surface of the water will not hold them by itself); but when the stars begin to pale, they sink down one by one into the pools of their home. Or if they tarry longer, sitting upon the rushes, their bodies fade from view as the marsh-fires pale in the light, and by daylight none may see the Wild Things of the kith of the Elf-folk. Neither may any see them even at night unless they were born, as I was, in the hour of dusk, just at the moment when the first star appears.

Now, on the night that I tell of, a little Wild Thing had gone drifting over the waste, till it came right up to the walls of the cathedral and danced upon the images of the coloured saints as they lay in the water among the reflection of the stars. And as it leaped in its fantastic dance, it saw through the painted windows to where the people prayed, and heard the organ roaring over the marshes. The sound of the organ roared over the marshes, but the song and prayers of the people streamed up from the cathedral's highest tower like thin gold chains, and reached to Paradise, and up and down them went the angels from Paradise to the people, and from the people to Paradise again.

Then something akin to discontent troubled the Wild Thing for the first time since the making of the marshes; and the soft grey ooze and the chill of the deep water seemed to be not enough, nor the first arrival from north-wards of the tumultuous geese, nor the wild rejoicing of the wings of the wildfowl when every feather sings, nor the wonder of the calm ice that comes when the snipe depart and beards the rushes with frost and clothes the hushed waste with a mysterious haze where the sun goes red and low, nor even the dance of the Wild Things in the marvellous night; and the little Wild Thing longed to have a soul, and to go and worship God.

And when evensong was over and the lights were out, it went back crying to its kith.

But on the next night, as soon as the images of the stars appeared in the water, it went leaping away from star to star to the farthest edge of the marshlands, where a great wood grew where dwelt the Oldest of Wild Things.

And it found the Oldest of Wild Things sitting under a tree, sheltering itself from the moon.

And the little Wild Thing said: "I want to have a soul to worship God, and to know the meaning of music, and to see the inner beauty of the marshlands and to imagine Paradise."

And the Oldest of the Wild Things said to it: "What have we to do with God? We are only Wild Things, and of the Kith of the Elf-folk."

But it only answered, "I want to have a soul."

Then the Oldest of the Wild Things said: "I have no soul to give you; but if you got a soul, one day you would have to die, and if you knew the meaning of music you would learn the meaning of sorrow, and it is better to be a Wild Thing and not to die."

So it went weeping away.

But they that were kin to the Elf-folk were sorry for the little Wild Thing; and though the Wild Things cannot sorrow long, having no souls to sorrow with, yet they felt for awhile a soreness where their souls should be, when they saw the grief of their comrade.

So the kith of the Elf-folk went abroad by night to make a soul for the little Wild Thing. And they went over the marshes till they came to the high fields among the flowers and grasses. And there they gathered a large piece of gossamer that the spider had laid by twilight; and the dew was on it.

Into this dew had shone all the lights of the long banks of the ribbed sky, as all the colours changed in the restful spaces of evening. And over it the marvellous night had gleamed with all its stars.

Then the Wild Things went with their dew-bespangled gossamer down to the edge of their home. And there they gathered a piece of the grey mist that lies by night over the marshlands. And into it they put the melody of the waste that is borne up and down the marshes in the evening on the wings of the golden plover. And they put into it too the mournful song that the reeds are compelled to sing before the presence of the arrogant North Wind. Then each of the Wild Things gave some treasured memory of the old marshes, "For we can spare it," they said. And to all this they added a few images of the stars that they gathered out of the water. Still the soul that the kith of the Elf-folk were making had no life.

Then they put into it the low voices of two lovers that went walking in the night, wandering late alone. And after that they waited for the dawn. And the queenly dawn appeared, and the marsh-lights of the Wild Things paled in the glare, and their bodies faded from view; and still they waited by the marsh's edge. And to them waiting came over field and marsh, from the ground and out of the sky, the myriad song of the birds.

This too the Wild Things put into the piece of haze that they had gathered in the marshlands, and wrapped it all up in their dew-bespangled gossamer. Then the soul lived.

And there it lay in the hands of the Wild Things no larger than a hedgehog; and wonderful lights were in it, green and blue; and they changed ceaselessly, going round and round, and in the grey midst of it was a purple flare.

And the next night they came to the little Wild Thing and showed her the gleaming soul. And they said to her: "If you must have a soul and go and worship God, and become a mortal and die, place this to your left breast a little above the heart, and it will enter and you will become a human. But if you take it you can never be rid of it to become immortal again unless you pluck it out and give it to another; and *we* will not take it, and most of the humans have a soul already. And if you cannot find a human without a soul you will one day die, and your soul cannot go to Paradise, because it was only made in the marshes."

Far away the little Wild Thing saw the cathedral windows alight for evensong, and the song of the people mounting up to Paradise, and all the angels going up and down. So it bid farewell with tears and thanks to the Wild Things of the kith of Elf-folk, and went leaping away towards the green dry land, holding the soul in its hands.

And the Wild Things were sorry that it had gone, but could not be sorry long, because they had no souls.

At the marsh's edge the little Wild Thing gazed for some moments over the water to where the marsh-fires were leaping up and down, and then pressed the soul against its left breast a little above the heart.

Instantly it became a young and beautiful woman, who was cold and frightened. She clad herself somehow with bundles of reeds, and went towards the lights of a house that stood close by. And she pushed open the door and entered, and found a farmer and a farmer's wife sitting over their supper.

And the farmer's wife took the little Wild Thing with the soul of the marshes up to her room, and clothed her and braided her hair, and brought her down again, and gave her the first food that she had ever eaten. Then the farmer's wife asked many questions.

"Where have you come from?" she said.

"Over the marshes."

"From what direction?" said the farmer's wife.

"South," said the little Wild Thing with the new soul.

"But none can come over the marshes from the south," said the farmer's wife.

"No, they can't do that," said the farmer.

"I lived in the marshes."

"Who are you?" asked the farmer's wife.

"I am a Wild Thing, and have found a soul in the marshes, and we are kin to the Elf-folk."

Talking it over afterwards, the farmer and his wife agreed that she must be a gipsy who had been lost, and that she was queer with hunger and exposure.

So that night the little Wild Thing slept in the farmer's house, but her new soul stayed awake the whole night long dreaming of the beauty of the marshes.

As soon as dawn came over the waste and shone on the farmer's house, she looked from the window towards the glittering waters, and saw the inner beauty of the marsh. For the Wild Things only love the marsh and know its haunts, but now she perceived the mystery of its distances and the glamour of its perilous pools, with their fair and deadly mosses, and felt the marvel of the North Wind who comes dominant out of unknown icy lands, and the wonder of that ebb and flow of life when the wildfowl whirl in at evening to the marshlands and at dawn pass out to sea. And she knew that over her head above the farmer's house stretched wide Paradise, where perhaps God was now imagining a sunrise while angels played low on lutes, and the sun came rising up on the world below to gladden fields and marsh.

And all that heaven thought, the marsh thought too; for the blue of the marsh was as the blue of heaven, and the great cloud shapes in heaven became the shapes in the marsh, and through each ran momentary rivers of purple, errant between banks of gold. And the stalwart army of reeds appeared out of the gloom with all their pennons waving as far as the eye could see. And from another window she saw the vast cathedral gathering its ponderous strength together, and lifting it up in towers out of the marshlands.

She said, "I will never, never leave the marsh."

An hour later she dressed with great difficulty and went down to eat the second meal of her life. The farmer and his wife were kindly folk, and taught her how to eat.

"I suppose the gipsies don't have knives and forks," one said to the other afterwards.

After breakfast the farmer went and saw the Dean, who lived near his cathedral, and presently returned and brought back to the Dean's house the little Wild Thing with the new soul.

"This is the lady," said the farmer. "This is Dean Murnith." Then he went away.

"Ah," said the Dean, "I understand you were lost the other night in the marshes. It was a terrible night to be lost in the marshes."

"I love the marshes," said the little Wild Thing with the new soul.

"Indeed! How old are you?" said the Dean.

"I don't know," she answered.

"You must know about how old you are," he said.

"Oh, about ninety," she said, "or more."

"Ninety years!" exclaimed the Dean.

"No, ninety centuries," she said; "I am as old as the marshes."

Then she told her story—how she had longed to be a human and go and worship God, and have a soul and see the beauty of the world, and how all the Wild Things had made her a soul of gossamer and mist and music and strange memories.

"But if this is true," said Dean Murnith, "this is very wrong. God cannot have intended you to have a soul.

"What is your name?"

"I have no name," she answered.

"We must find a Christian name and a surname for you. What would you like to be called?"

"Song of the Rushes," she said.

"That won't do at all," said the Dean.

"Then I would like to be called Terrible North Wind, or Star in the Waters," she said.

"No, no, no," said Dean Murnith; "that is quite impossible. We could call you Miss Rush if you like. How would Mary Rush do? Perhaps you had better have another name—say Mary Jane Rush."

So the little Wild Thing with the soul of the marshes took the names that were offered her, and became Mary Jane Rush.

"And we must find something for you to do," said Dean Murnith. "Meanwhile we can give you a room here."

"I don't want to do anything," replied Mary Jane; "I want to worship God in the cathedral and live beside the marshes."

Then Mrs. Murnith came in, and for the rest of that day Mary Jane stayed at the house of the Dean.

And there with her new soul she perceived the beauty of the world; for it came grey and level out of misty distances, and widened into grassy fields and ploughlands right up to the edge of an old gabled town; and solitary in the fields far off an ancient windmill stood, and his honest handmade sails went round and round in the free East

Anglian winds. Close by, the gabled houses leaned out over the streets, planted fair upon sturdy timbers that grew in the olden time, all glorying among themselves upon their beauty. And out of them, buttress by buttress, growing and going upwards, aspiring tower by tower, rose the cathedral.

And she saw the people moving in the streets all leisurely and slow, and unseen among them, whispering to each other, unheard by living men and concerned only with bygone things, drifted the ghosts of very long ago. And wherever the streets ran eastwards, wherever were gaps in the houses, always there broke into view the sight of the great marshes, like to some bar of music weird and strange that haunts a melody, arising again and again, played on the violin by one musician only, who plays no other bar, and he is swart and lank about the hair and boarded about the lips, and his moustache droops long and low, and no one knows the land from which he comes.

All these were good things for a new soul to see.

Then the sun set over green fields and ploughland, and the night came up. One by one the merry lights of cheery lamp-lit windows took their stations in the solemn night.

Then the bells rang, far up in a cathedral tower, and their melody fell on the roofs of the old houses and poured over their eaves until the streets were full, and then flooded away over green fields and plough, till it came to the sturdy mill and brought the miller trudging to evensong, and far away eastwards and seawards the sound rang out over the remoter marshes. And it was all as yesterday to the old ghosts in the streets.

Then the Dean's wife took Mary Jane to evening service, and she saw three hundred candles filling all the aisle with light. But sturdy pillars stood there in unlit vastnesses; great colonnades going away into the gloom, where evening and morning, year in year out, they did their work in the dark, holding the cathedral roof aloft. And it was stiller than the marshes are still when the ice has come and the wind that brought it has fallen.

Suddenly into this stillness rushed the sound of the organ, roaring, and presently the people prayed and sang.

No longer could Mary Jane see their prayers ascending like thin gold chains, for that was but an elfin fancy, but she imagined clear in her new soul the seraphs passing in the ways of Paradise, and the angels changing guard to watch the World by night.

When the Dean had finished service, a young curate, Mr. Millings, went up into the pulpit.

He spoke of Abana and Pharpar, rivers of Damascus: and Mary Jane was glad that there were rivers having such names, and heard with wonder of Nineveh, that great city, and many things strange and new.

And the light of the candles shone on the curate's fair hair, and his voice went ringing down the aisle, and Mary Jane rejoiced that he was there.

But when his voice stopped she felt a sudden loneliness, such as she had not felt since the making of the marshes; for the Wild Things never are lonely and never unhappy, but dance all night on the reflection of the stars, and, having no souls, desire nothing more.

After the collection was made, before any one moved to go, Mary Jane walked up the aisle to Mr. Millings.

"I love you," she said.

Nobody sympathised with Mary Jane.

"So unfortunate for Mr. Millings," everyone said; "such a promising young man."

Mary Jane was sent away to a great manufacturing city of the Midlands, where work had been found for her in a cloth factory. And there was nothing in that town that was good for a soul to see. For it did not know that beauty was to be desired; so it made many things by machinery, and became hurried in all its ways, and boasted its superiority over other cities and became richer and richer, and there was none to pity it.

In this city Mary Jane had had lodgings found for her near the factory.

At six o'clock on those November mornings, about the time that, far away from the city, the wildfowl rose up out of the calm marshes and passed to the troubled spaces of the sea, at six o'clock the factory uttered a prolonged howl and gathered the workers together, and there they worked, saving two hours for food, the whole of the daylit hours and into the dark till the bells tolled six again.

There Mary Jane worked with other girls in a long

dreary room, where giants sat pounding wool into a long thread-like strip with iron, rasping hands. And all day long they roared as they sat at their soulless work. But the work of Mary Jane was not with these, only their roar was ever in her ears as their clattering iron limbs went to and fro.

Her work was to tend a creature smaller, but infinitely more cunning.

It took the strip of wool that the giants had threshed, and whirled it round and round until it had twisted it into hard thin thread. Then it would make a clutch with fingers of steel at the thread that it had gathered, and waddle away about five yards and come back with more.

It had mastered all the subtlety of skilled workers, and had gradually displaced them; one thing only it could not do, it was unable to pick up the ends if a piece of the thread broke, in order to tie them together again. For this a human soul was required, and it was Mary Jane's business to pick up broken ends; and the moment she placed them together the busy soulless creature tied them for itself.

All here was ugly; even the green wool as it whirled round and round was neither the green of the grass nor yet the green of the rushes, but a sorry muddy green that befitted a sullen city under a murky sky.

When she looked out over the roofs of the town, there too was ugliness; and well the houses knew it, for with hideous stucco they aped in grotesque mimicry the pillars and temples of old Greece, pretending to one another to be that which they were not. And emerging from these houses and going in, and seeing the pretence of paint and stucco year after year until it all peeled away, the souls of the poor owners of those houses sought to be other souls until they grew weary of it.

At evening Mary Jane went back to her lodgings. Only then, after the dark had fallen, could the soul of Mary Jane perceive any beauty in that city, when the lamps were lit here and there a star shone through the smoke. Then she would have gone abroad and beheld the night, but this the old woman to whom she was confided would not let her do. And the days multiplied themselves by seven and became weeks, and the weeks passed by, and all days were the same. And all the while the soul of Mary Jane was crying for beautiful things, and found not one, saving on Sundays, when she went to church, and left it to find the city greyer than before.

One day she decided that it was better to be a wild thing in the lovely marshes, than to have a soul that cried for beautiful things and found not one. From that day she determined to be rid of her soul, so she told her story to one of the factory girls, and said to her:

"The other girls are poorly clad and they do soulless work; surely some of them have no souls and would take mine."

But the factory girl said to her: "All the poor have souls. It is all they have."

Then Mary Jane watched the rich whenever she saw them, and vainly sought for some one without a soul.

One day at the hour when the machines rested and the human beings that tended them rested too, the wind being at that time from the direction of the marshlands, the soul of Mary Jane lamented bitterly. Then, as she stood outside the factory gates, the soul irresistibly compelled her to sing, and a wild song came from her lips, hymning the marshlands. And into her song came crying her yearning for home and for the sound of the shout of the North Wind, masterful and proud, with his lovely lady the Snow; and she sang of tales that the rushes murmured to one another, tales that the teal knew and the watchful heron. And over the crowded streets her song went crying away, the song of waste places and of wild free lands, full of wonder and magic, for she had in her elf-made soul the song of the birds and the roar of the organ in the marshes.

At this moment Signor Thompsoni, the well-known English tenor, happened to go by with a friend. They stopped and listened; every one stopped and listened.

"There has been nothing like this in Europe in my time," said Signor Thompsoni.

So a change came into the life of Mary Jane.

People were written to, and finally it was arranged that she should take a leading part in the Covent Garden Opera in a few weeks.

So she went to London to learn.

London and singing lessons were better than the City of the Midlands and those terrible machines. Yet still Mary Jane was not free to go and live as she liked by the edge of the marshlands, and she was still determined to be rid of her soul, but could find no one that had not a soul of their own.

One day she was told that the English people would not listen to her as Miss Rush, and was asked what more suitable name she would like to be called by.

"I would like to be called Terrible North Wind," said Mary Jane, "or Song of the Rushes."

When she was told that this was impossible and Signorina Maria Russiano was suggested, she acquiesced at once, as she had acquiesced when they took her away from her curate; she knew nothing of the ways of humans.

At last the day of the Opera came round, and it was a cold day of the winter.

And Signorina Russiano appeared on the stage before a crowded house.

And Signorina Russiano sang.

And into the song went all the longing of her soul, the soul that could not go to Paradise, but could only worship God and know the meaning of music, and the longing pervaded that Italian song as the infinite mystery of the hills is borne along the sound of distant sheep-bells. Then in the souls that were in that crowded house arose little memories of a great while since that were quite quite dead, and lived awhile again during that marvellous song.

And a strange chill went into the blood of all that listened, as though they stood on the border of bleak marshes and the North Wind blew.

And some it moved to sorrow and some to regret, and some to an unearthly joy. Then suddenly the song went wailing away, like the winds of the winter from the marshlands when Spring appears from the South.

So it ended. And a great silence fell foglike over all that house, breaking in upon the end of a chatty conversation that a lady was enjoying with a friend.

In the dead hush Signorina Russiano rushed from the stage; she appeared again running among the audience, and dashed up to the lady.

"Take my soul," she said; "it is a beautiful soul. It can worship God, and knows the meaning of music and can imagine Paradise. And if you go to the marshlands with it you will see beauiful things; there is an old town there built of lovely timbers, with ghosts in its streets."

The lady stared. Every one was standing up. "See," said Signorina Russiano, "it is a beautiful soul."

And she clutched at her left breast a little above the heart, and there was the soul shining in her hand, with the green and blue lights going round and round and the purple flare in the midst.

"Take it," she said, "and you will love all that is beautiful, and know the four winds, each one by his name, and the songs of the birds at dawn. I do not want it, because I am not free. Put it to your left breast a little above the heart."

Still everybody was standing up, and the lady felt uncomfortable.

"Please offer it to some one else," she said.

"But they all have souls already," said Signorina Russiano.

And everybody went on standing up. And the lady took the soul in her hand.

"Perhaps it is lucky," she said.

She felt that she wanted to pray.

She half-closed her eyes, and said, "Unberufen." Then she put the soul to her left breast a little above the heart, and hoped that the people would sit down and the singer go away.

Instantly a heap of clothes collapsed before her. For a moment, in the shadow among the seats, those who were born in the dusk hour might have seen a little brown thing leaping free from the clothes; then it sprang into the bright light of the hall, and became invisible to any human eye.

It dashed about for a little, then found the door, and presently was in the lamplit streets.

To those that were born in the dusk hour it might have been seen leaping rapidly wherever the streets ran northwards and eastwards, disappearing from human sight as it passed under the lamps, and appearing again beyond them with a marsh-light over its head.

Once a dog perceived it and gave chase, and was left far behind.

The cats of London, who are all born in the dusk hour, howled fearfully as it went by.

Presently it came to the meaner streets, where the houses are smaller. Then it went due northeastwards, leaping from roof to roof. And so in a few minutes it came to more open spaces, and then to the desolate lands, where market gardens grow, which are neither town nor country. Till at last the good black trees came into view, with their demoniac shapes in the night, and the grass was cold and wet, and the night-mist floated over it. And a great white owl came by, going up and down in the dark. And at all these things the little Wild Thing rejoiced elvishly.

And it left London far behind it, reddening the sky, and could distinguish no longer its unlovely roar, but heard again the noises of the night.

And now it would come through a hamlet glowing and comfortable in the night; and now to the dark, wet, open fields again; and many an owl it overtook as they drifted through the night, a people friendly to the Elf-folk. Sometimes it crossed wide rivers, leaping from star to star; and, choosing its way as it went, to avoid the hard rough roads, came before midnight to the East Anglian lands.

And it heard there the shout of the North Wind, who was dominant and angry, as he drove southwards his adventurous geese; while the rushes bent before him chaunting plaintively and low, like enslaved rowers of some fabulous trireme, bending and swinging under blows of the lash, and singing all the while a doleful song.

And it felt the good dank air that clothes by night the broad East Anglian lands, and came again to some old perilous pool where the soft green mosses grew, and there plunged downward and downward into the near dark water, till it felt the homely ooze once more coming up between its toes. Thence, out of the lovely chill that is in the heart of the ooze, it arose renewed and rejoicing to dance upon the image of the stars.

I chanced to stand that night by the marsh's edge, forgetting in my mind the affairs of men; and I saw the marshfires come leaping up from all the perilous places. And they came up by flocks the whole night long to the number of a great multitude, and danced away together over the marshes.

And I believe that there was a great rejoicing all that night among the kith of the Elf-folk.

KENNETH VENNOR MORRIS

(1879–1937)

Kenneth Morris is one of the finest but least known of the writers of contemporary fantasy. We are indebted to Ursula K. Le Guin for bringing him to our attention. In her essay on style, "From Elfland to Poughkeepsie," Le Guin includes him as one of three "master stylists" of modern fantasy, along with E. R. Eddison and J. R. R. Tolkien. She refers to Morris's *The Book of the Three Dragons* (1930) as "a singularly fine example of the recreation of a work magnificent in its own right (the *Mabinogion*)—a literary event rather rare except in fantasy, where its frequency is perhaps proof, if one were needed, of the ever-renewed vitality of myth." Le Guin strongly recommends Morris, but warns that the prospective reader will have to search for him on the dusty back shelves, and usually in the section devoted to outdated children's works. Only a small portion of *Three Dragons,* Morris's last published book, has been reproduced for a wider audience, in Lin Carter's adult fantasy series. Nor, surprisingly, can one find Morris listed in any of the standard biographical references devoted to adult or children's authors. We are grateful to The Theosophical Society–International, in which Morris was active most of his life, for the following information. We hope that this information, and more importantly, the story that follows, will bring Morris some measure of the attention he deserves.

Kenneth Morris was born in Potamman, South Wales, on July 31, 1879. His family was modestly wealthy, thanks to his grandfather. The family suffered a series of misfortunes, however: Morris's father died in 1884, his grandfather in 1885, and shortly afterwards the family business was ruined by the American Tariff Law. When the family moved to London in 1885 or 1886, Morris enrolled in Christ's Hospital, a school that had been attended by such luminaries as Coleridge, Lamb, and Leigh Hunt. He left school at the age of sixteen and, in 1896, spent some time with a group of writers in Dublin. There he formed close ties with the poet and short-story writer A.E. (George Russell). He also joined the Theosophical Society, an organization that profoundly influenced his life. By 1899 he was back in Wales, contributing prose and poetry to the magazine published by the Theosophical Society in Cardiff. In 1908 he came to the United States, where he became professor of literature and history at the Theosophical University in Point Loma, California. He remained in that position, teaching and writing, until he returned to Wales in 1930. He published the monthly magazine *Y Fforum Theosophaid* from 1930 until his death on April 21, 1937.

The twenty-two years that Morris spent in the United States seem to have been his most productive in terms of his writing. While teaching at Point Loma, he also wrote a good deal, including works of history, literary criticism, poetry, and fiction. In his myth-based fiction, Morris blends his two great loves, theosophy and Wales. His first book, *The Fates of the Princes of Dyfed* (1913), is a close retelling of parts of the *Mabinogion*, the medieval compendium of Welsh mythology. In *The Secret Mountain and Other Tales* (1926), his second major publication, Morris expanded his interest in myth to include tales from a number of other countries. A.E., who reviewed the collection for the April 23, 1927, edition of *The Irish Statesman of Dublin*, admired Morris's ability to capture the authentic spirit of various mythologies, including those of India and China. A.E. also compared Morris's tales favorably with those of Dunsany for their inventiveness and convincing other-world settings. But Morris's stories have, according to A.E., a more "mystical character," being the product of "long mystical meditation." *Three Dragons*, Morris's third and last major fiction publication, is a continuation of his 1913 rendering of the *Mabinogion*. Morris also applied his genius to New-World myth in an unpublished story about ancient Mexico, *The Chalchuhuite Dragon.*

Morris's theosophy instilled in the man and his work a catholicity of outlook that was at the same time profound and penetrating. His writings thus attain to the sort of universality that Morris saw as the proper aim of fantasy. He defines the function of romance as "proclaiming indestructable truth in terms of the imagination; using the symbols provided by the poetic or creative imagination to show forth those truths which are permanent, because they lie at the heart of life, not on its surface; and which belong to all ages, because all eternity is the birthday of the soul" (quoted in *The San Diego Union,* May 15, 1927).

"Red-Peach-Blossom Inlet" is a myth fantasy, with Chinese Taoism as its source. Lao-tse the Master, whom Wang Tao-chen meets in the story, was the founder of Taoism in the seventh century B.C. But, as in any good fantasy of this type, both the myth and its expression are universal. Recognizable archetypes such as the quest, the crossing of the waters, the garden, and the tree of knowledge and immortality underly the story. The style fits the contents. In this respect "Red-Peach-Blossom Inlet" sets a standard that few stories by other writers will be able to match. The inlet is a paradise of sight, smell, and taste delights, all of which are vividly conveyed by Morris's sensuous imagery. The archetypes and imagery, however, are not the only memorable aspects of the tale. Its conclusion will linger in the memory, causing the reader to reflect for some time on the meaning of Wang Tao-chen's fate.

◄§ Red-Peach-Blossom Inlet §►

Kenneth Morris

Wang Tao-chen loved the ancients: that was why he was a fisherman. Modernity you might call irremediable: it was best left alone. But far out in the middle lake, when the distances were all a blue haze and the world a sapphirean vacuity, one might breathe the atmosphere of ancient peace and give oneself to the pursuit of immortality. By study of the Classics, by rest of the senses, and by cultivating a mood of universal benevolence, Wang Tao-chen proposed to become superior to time and change: a Sennin—an adept, immortal.

He had long since put away the desire for an official career. If, thought he, one could see a way, by taking office, to reform the administration, the case would be different. One would pass one's examinations, accept a prefecture, climb the ladder of promotion, and put one's learning and character to use. One would establish peace, of course; and presently, perhaps, achieve rewelding into one the many kingdoms into which the empire of Han had split. But unfortunately there were but two roads to success: force and fraud. And, paradoxically, they both always led to failure. As soon as you had cheated or thumped your way into office, you were marked as the prey of all other cheaters and thumpers; and had but to wait a year or two for the most expert of them to have you out, handed over to the Board of Punishments, and perchance shortened of stature by a head. The disadvantages of such a career outweighed its temptations; and Wang Tao-chen had decided it was not for him.

So he refrained from politics altogether, and transplanted his ambitions into more secret fields. Inactive, he would do well by his age; unstriving, he would attain possession of Tao. He would be peaceful in a world disposed to violence; honest where all were cheats; serene and unambitious in an age of fussy ambition. Let the spoils of office go to inferior men; for him the blue calmness of the lake, the blue emptiness above: the place that his soul should reflect and rival, and the untroubled noiseless place that reflected and rivalled heaven.—Where, too, one might go through the day unreminded that that unintelligent Li Kuang-ming, one's neighbour, had already obtained his prefecture, and was making a good thing of it; or that Fan Kao-sheng, the flashy and ostentatious, had won his *chin shih* degree, and was spoken well of by the undiscerning on all sides. Let *him* examine either of them in the Classics! . . .

Certainly there was no better occupation for the meditative than fishing. One suffered no interruption—except when the fish bit. He tolerated this vile habit of theirs for a year or two; and brought home a good catch to his wife of an evening, until such time as he had shaken off— as it seemed to him—earthly ambitions and desires. Then, when he could hear of Li's and Fan's successes with equanimity, and his own mind had grown one-pointed towards wisdom, he turned from books to pure contemplation, and became impatient even of the attentions of the fish. He would emulate the sages of old: in this respect a very simple matter. One had but to bend one's hook straight before casting it, and everything with fins and scales in Lake Tao-ting might wait its turn to nibble, yet shake down none of the fruits of serenity from the branches of his mind. It was an ingenious plan, and worked excellently.

You may ask, What would his wife say?—he, fortunately, had little need to consider that. He was lucky, he reflected, in the possession of such a spouse as Pu-hsi; who, though she might not tread with him his elected path, stood sentry at the hither end of it, so to say, without complaint or fuss. A meek little woman, lazily minded yet withal capable domestically, she gave him no trouble in the world; and received in return unthinking confidence and complete dependence in all material things—as you might say, a magnanimous marital affection. His home in the fishing village was a thing not to be dispensed with, certainly; nor yet much to be dwelt upon in the mind by one who sought immortality. No doubt Pu-hsi felt for him the great love and reverence which were a husband's due, and would not presume to question his actions.

True, she had once, soon after their marriage, mildly urged him to follow the course of nature and take his examinations; but a little eloquence had silenced her. In this matter of the fish, he would let it dawn on her in her own time that there would be no more, either to cook or to sell. Having realized the fact she would, of course, dutifully exert herself the more to make things go as they should. There would be neither inconvenience nor disturbance, at home.

Which things happened. One night, however, she examined his tackle and discovered the unbent hook; and meditated over it for months. Then a great desire for fish came over her; and she rose up while he slept and bent the hook back to its proper shape with care, and baited it; and went to sleep again, hoping for the best.

Wang Tao-chen never noticed it; perhaps because, as he was gathering up his tackle to set out, a neighbour came to the door and borrowed a net from him, promising to return it that same evening. It was an interruption which Wang resented inwardly; and the resentment made him careless, I suppose. He was far out on the lake, and had thrown his line, before composure quite came back to him; and it had hardly come when there was a bite to frighten it away again,—and such a bite as might not be ignored. Away went the fish, and Wang Tao-chen after it: speeding over the water so swiftly that he had no thought even to drop the rod. Away and away, breathless, until noon; then suddenly the boat stopped and the line hung loose. He drew it in, and found the baited hook untouched; and fell to pondering on the meaning of it all. . . .

He had come into a region unknown to him, lovelier than any he had visited before. He had left the middle lake far behind, and was in the shadow of lofty hills. The water, all rippleless, mirrored the beauty of the mountains; and inshore, here reeds greener than jade, there hibiscus splendid with bloom. High up among the pines a little blue-tiled temple glowed in the magical air. Above the bluff yonder, over whose steep sheer face little pinetrees hung jutting half-way between earth and heaven, delicate feathers of cloud, bright as polished silver, floated in a sky bluer than glazed porcelain. From the woods on the hillsides came birdsong strangely and magically sweet. Wang Tao-chen, listening, felt a quickening of the life within him: the rising of a calm sacred quality of life, as if he had breathed airs laden with immortality from the Garden of Siwangmu in the western world. Shore and water seemed bathed in a light at once more vivid and more tranquil than any that shone in familiar regions.

Quickening influences in the place stirred him to curiosity, to action; and he took his oar and began to row. He passed round the bluff and into the bay beyond; and as he went, felt himself drawing nearer to the heart of beauty and holiness. A high pine-clad island stood in the mouth of the bay; so that, unless close in shore, you might easily pass the latter undiscovered. Within—between the island and the hills, the whole being of him rose up into poetry and peace. The air he breathed was keenness of delight, keenness of perception. The pines on the high hills on either side blushed into deep and exquisite green. Blue long-tailed birds like fiery jewels flitted among the trees and out from the boscage over the bay; the water, clear as a diamond, glassed the wizardry of the hills and pines and the sweet sky with its drifting delicacy of cloudlets; glassed, too, the wonder of the lower slopes where, and in the valley-bottom, glowed an innumerable multitude of peachtrees, red-blossomed, and now all lovely like soft clouds of sunset with bloom.

He rowed shoreward, and on under the shadow of the faery peach-trees, and came into a narrow inlet, deepwatered, that seemed the path for him into bliss and the secret places of wonder. The petals fell about him in a slow roseate rain; even in midstream, looking upward, one could see but inches and glimpses of interstitial blueness. He went on until a winding of the inlet brought him into the open valley: to a thinning of the trees,—a house beside the water,—and then another and another: into the midst of a scattered village and among a mild, august and kindly people, unlike, in fashion of garb and speech, any whom he had seen—any, he would have said, that had lived among the Hills of Han[1] these many hundred years. They had an air of radiant placidity, passionless joy and benevolence, lofty and calm thought. They appeared to have expected his coming: greeted him majestically, but with affability; showed him, presently, a house in which, they said, he might live as long as he chose. They had no news, he found, of the doings in any of the contemporary kingdoms, and were not interested; they were without politics entirely; wars nor rumours of wars disturbed them. Here, thought Wang, he would abide for ever; such things were not be be found elsewhere. In this lofty peace he would grow wise: would blossom, naturally as a flower, but into immortality. They let fall, while talking to him, sentences strangely illuminating—yet strangely tantalizing too, as it seemed to him: one felt stupendous wisdom concealed—saw a gleam of it, or as it were a corner trailing away; and missed the satisfaction of its wholeness. This in itself was supreme incitement; in time one would learn and penetrate all. Of course he would remain with them forever; he would supply them with fish in gratitude for their hospitality. Falling asleep that night, he knew that none of his days had been flawless until that day—until the latter part of it, at least. . . .

The bloom fell from the trees; the young fruit formed, and slowly ripened in a sunlight more caressing than any in the world of men. With their ripening, the air of the valley became more wonderful, more quickening and inspiring daily. When the first dark blush appeared on the yellow-green of the peaches, Wang Tao-chen walked weightless, breathed joy, was as one who had heard tidings glorious and never expected. Transcendent thoughts had been rising in him continually since first he came into the valley; now, his mind became like clear night-skies among the stars of which luminous dragons sail always, liquid, gleaming, light-shedding, beautiful. By his door grew a tree whose writhing branches overhung a pool of golden carp; as he came out one morning, he saw the first of the ripe peaches drop shining from its bough, and fall into the

[1] i.e. in China.

water; diffusing the sweetness of its scent on the diamond light of the young day. Silently worshipping heaven, he picked up the floating peach, and raised it to his mouth. As he did so he heard the leisurely tread of oxhoofs on the road above: it would be his neighbour So-and-so, who rode his ox down to drink at the inlet at that time each morning. (Strange that he should have learnt none of the names of the villagers; that he should never, until now, have thought of them as bearing names.) As the taste of the peach fell on his palate, he looked up, and saw the Ox-rider . . . and fell down and made obeisance; for it was Laotse the Master, who had ridden his ox out of the world, and into the Western Heaven, some seven or eight hundred years before.

Forthwith and thenceforward the place was all new to him, and a thousand times more wonderful. What had seemed to him cottages were lovely pagodas of jade and porcelain, the sunlight reflected from their glaze of transparent azure or orange or vermilion, of luminous yellow or purple or green. Through the shining skies of noon or evening you might often see lordly dragons floating: golden and gleaming dragons; or that shed a violet luminance from their wings; or whose hue was the essence from which blue heaven drew its blueness; or white dragons whose passing was like the shooting of a star. As for his neighbours, he knew them now for the Mighty of old time: the men made one with Tao, who soared upon the Lonely Crane; the men who had eaten the Peaches of Immortality. There dwelt the founders of dynasties vanished millennia since: Men-Dragons and Divine Rulers: the Heaven-Kings and the Earth-Kings and the Man-Kings: all the figures who emerge in dim radiance out of the golden haze on the horizon of Chinese prehistory, and shine there quaintly wonderful. Their bodies emitted a heavenly light; the tones of their voices were an exquisite music; for their amusement they would harden snow into silver, or change the nature of the cinnabar until it became yellow gold. And sometimes they would bridle the flying dragon, and visit the Fortunate Isles of the Morning; and sometimes they would mount upon the hoary crane, and soaring through the empyrean, come into the Enchanted Gardens of the West: where Siwangmu is Queen of the

Evening, and whence her birds of azure plumage fly and sing unseen over the world, and their singing is the love, the peace, and the immortal thoughts of mankind. Visibly those wonder-birds flew through Red-Peach-Blossom Inlet Valley; and lighted down there; and were fed with celestial food by the villagers, that their beneficent power might be increased when they went forth among men.

Seven years Wang Tao-chen dwelt there: enjoying the divine companionship of the sages, hearing the divine philosophy from their lips: until his mind became clarified to the clear brightness of the diamond; and his perceptions serenely overspread the past, the present and the future; and his thoughts, even the most commonplace of them, were more luminously lovely than the inspirations of the supreme poets. Then one morning while he was fishing his boat drifted out into the bay, and beyond the island into the open lake.

And he fell to comparing his life in the valley with his life as it might be in the outer world. Among mortals, he considered, with the knowledge he had won, he would be as a herdsman with his herd. He might reach any pinnacle of power; he might reunite the world, and inaugurate an age more glorious than that of Han. . . . But here among these Mighty and Wise Ones, he would always be.— Well; was it not true that they must look down on him? He remembered Pu-hsi, the forgotten during all these years; and thought how astounded she would be,—how she would worship him more than ever, returning, so changed, after so long an absence. It would be nothing to row across the lake and see; and return the next day—or when the world of men bored him. He landed at the familiar quay in the evening, and went up with his catch to his house.

But Pu-hsi showed no surprise at seeing him, nor any rapturous satisfaction until she saw the fish. It was a cold shock to him; but he hid his feelings. To his question as to how she had employed her time during his absence, she answered that the day had been as other days. There was embarrassment, even guilt, in her voice, if he had noticed it. "The day?" said he; "the seven years!" —and her embarrassment was covered away with surprise and uncomprehension. But here the neighbour came to the door, "to return the net," he said, "that he had borrowed in the morning";—the net Wang Tao-chen had lent him before he went away. And to impart a piece of gossip, it seemed: "I hear," said he, "that Ping Yang-hsi and Po Lo-hsien are setting forth for the provincial capital to-morrow, to take their examination." Wang Tao-chen gasped. "They should have passed," he began; and bit off the sentence there, leaving "seven years ago" unsaid. Here were mysteries indeed.

He made cautious inquiries as to the events of this year and last; and the answers still further set his head spinning. He had only been away a day: everything confirmed that. Had he dreamed the whole seven years then? By all the glory of which they were compact; by the immortal energy he felt in his spirit and veins; *no!* He would prove their truth to himself; and he would prove himself to the world! He announced that he too would take the examination.

He did; and left all competitors to marvel: passed so brilliantly that all Tsin was talking about it; and returned to find that his wife had fled with a lover. That was not likely to trouble him much: he had lived forgetting her for seven years. But she, at least, should repent: she should learn what a Great One she had deserted. Without delay he took examination after examination; and before the year was out was hailed as the most brilliant of rising stars. Promotion followed promotion, till the Son of Heaven called him to be prime minister. At every success he laughed to himself: he was proving to himself that he had lived with the Immortals. His fame spread through all the kingdoms of China; he was courted by the emissaries of many powerful kings. Yet nothing would content him: he must prove his grand memory still further; so he went feeding his ambition with greater and greater triumphs. Heading the army, he inflicted disaster upon the Huns, and imposed his will on the west and north. The time was almost at hand, people said, when the Black-haired people should be one again, under the founder of a new and most mighty dynasty.

And still he was dissatisfied: he found no companionship in his greatness: no one whom he loved or trusted, none to give him trust or love. His emperor was but a

puppet in his hands, down to whose level he must painfully diminish his inward stature; his wife—the emperor's
daughter—flattered and feared, and withal despised him.
The world sang his praises and plotted his downfall busily;
he discovered the plots, punished the plotters, and filled
the world with his splendid activities. And all the while
a voice was crying in his heart: *In Red-Peach-Blossom-
Inlet Valley you had peace, companionship, joy!*

Twenty years yassed, and his star still rose: it was
whispered that he was certainly no common mortal, but
a genie, or a *sennin,* possessor of Tao. For he grew no
older as the years went by, but still had the semblance of
young manhood, as on the day he returned from the
Valley. And now the Son of Heaven was dying, and
there was no heir to the throne but a sickly and vicious
boy; and it was thought everywhere that the great Wang
Tao-chen would assume the Yellow. The dynasty had
exhausted the mandate of heaven.

It was night; and he sat alone; and home sickness
weighed upon his soul. He had just dismissed the great
court functionaries, the ministers and ambassadors, who
had come to offer him the throne. The people were everywhere crying out for reunion, an end of dissensions, and
the revival of the ancient glories of Han: and who but
Wang Tao-chen could bring these things to pass? He
had dismissed the courtiers, promising an answer in the
morning. He knew that not one of them had spoken from
his heart sincerely, nor voiced his own desire; but had
come deeming it politic to anticipate the inevitable. For
alas! in all the world there was none who was his
equal. . . . Of these that had pressed upon him sover-
eignty especially, there was none to whom he could
speak his mind—none with the greatness to understand.
He saw polite enmity and fear under their bland expres-
sions, and heard it beneath their courtly phrases of flat-
tery. To be Son of Heaven—among such courtiers as
these!

But in Red-Peach-Blossom-Inlet Valley one might talk
daily with the Old Philosopher and with Such-a-One [2];

---

[2] Laotse and Confucius.

with the Duke of Chow and with Muh Wang and Tang the Completer; with the Royal Lady of the West; with Yao, Shun and Ta Yü themselves, those stainless Sovereigns of the Golden Age;—ah! with Fu-hsi the Man-Dragon Emperor and his seven Dragon Ministers; with the August Monarchs of the three August Periods of the world-dawn: the Heaven-Kings and the Earth-Kings and the Man-Kings. . . .

He did off his robes of state, and donned an old fisherman's costume which he had never had the heart to part with; and slipped away from his palace and from the capital; and set his face westward towards the shores of Lake Tao-ting. He would get a boat, and put off on the lake, and come to Red-Peach-Blossom-Inlet Valley again; and consult with Fu-hsi and the Yellow Emperor as to this wearing of the Yellow Robe,—as to whether it was Their will that he, the incompetent Wang Tao-chen, should dare to mount Their throne. But when he had come to his native village, and bought a boat and fishing-tackle, and put forth on the lake in the early morning, his purpose had changed: never, never, never would he leave the company of the Immortals again. Let kinghood go where it would; he would dwell with the Mighty and Wise of old time, humbly glad to be the least of their servants. He had won a name for himself in history; *They* would not wholly look down on him now. And he knew that his life in that bliss would be forever: he had eaten of the Peaches of Immortality, and could not die. He wept at the blue lonely beauty of the middle lake when he came to it; he was so near now to all that he desired. . . .

In due time he came to the far shore; and to one bluff after another that he thought he recognized; but rounding it, found no island, no bay, no glazed-tile roofed temples, no grove of red-bloomed peaches. The place must be farther on . . . and farther on. . . . Sometimes there would be an island, but not *the* island; sometimes a bay, but not *the* bay; sometimes an island and a bay that would pass, and even peach-trees; but there was no inlet running in beneath the trees, with quiet waters lovely with a rain of petals—least of all that old divine red rain. Then he remembered the great fish that had drawn him into that sacred vicinity; and threw his line, fixing his hopes on that . . . fixing his desperate hopes on that.

All of which happened some sixteen hundred years ago. Yet still sometimes, they say, the fishermen on Lake Tao-ting, in the shadowy hours of evening, or when night has overtaken them far out on the waters, will hear a whisper near at hand: a whisper out of vacuity, from no boat visible: a breathless despairing whisper: *It was here . . . surely it must have been here! . . . No, no; it was yonder!* And sometimes it is given to some few of them to see an old, crazy boat, mouldering away —one would say the merest skeleton or ghost of a boat dead ages since, but still by some magic kept floating; and in it a man dressed in the rags of an ancient costume, on whose still young face is to be seen unearthly longing and immortal sadness, and an unutterable despair that persists in hoping. His line is thrown; he goes by swiftly, straining terrible eyes on the water, and whispering always: *It was here; surely it was here. . . . No, no; it was yonder . . . it must have been yonder. . . .*

SELMA LAGERLÖF

(1858–1940)

(Translated By Charles Wharton Stork)

Selma Ottiliana Lovisa Lagerlöf is one of the most eminent names in Scandinavian literature, ranking in importance with writers like Henrik Ibsen and August Strindberg. Her fiction, for children and adults, has been translated into at least thirty languages, and it brought her national and international recognition during the early part of this century. She received an honorary Doctor of Philosophy degree from Uppsala University in 1904. Then, in 1909, she became the first woman ever to win the Nobel Prize in Literature. A few years later, in 1914, she became the first woman to be admitted to the Swedish Academy. Her seventieth birthday was the occasion for a national holiday in Sweden; at that time she received numerous awards, including the diploma of the French Legion of Honor and the Danish Distinguished Service Medal. The latter award was particularly significant: Lagerlöf's fiction for younger people had become second in popularity only to that of Hans Christian Andersen.

Lagerlöf owes a great deal of her success and popularity to her early childhood. She spent this childhood, as well as the majority of her eighty-one years, on a one hundred and forty acre farm named Mårbacka in the county of Värmland in southern Sweden. In "The Story of a Story," her slightly fictionalized account of the genesis of her first novel, she says of her early environment, "they seemed to have a greater love for books and reading there than elsewhere, and an air of restfulness and peace always pervaded it." Her love of reading and listening to stories became in fact her "keenest enjoyment," since, because of chronically poor health, she couldn't romp and play with her numerous brothers, sisters, and cousins. The stories she listened to so avidly were about the "many legends and traditions" which "hovered about the farm" and about the rugged lands and dense forests of the Värmland province.

Lagerlöf immortalized the Mårbacka farmhouse as the setting for *Gösta Berling,* the first and best known of her novels, which was published in part in 1891 and in completed form in 1894. The book became an instant success and after 1895 helped to free her from her teaching duties. She had been teaching in a school in Skåne, in the far southern portion of Sweden, since 1885. She then travelled to Italy, Palestine, and the Orient, all of which became scenes for her fiction. But her most successful writings remained those about Swedish country gentry and peasants, works like her volume of short stories, *From a Swedish Homestead* (1899), or her novel *The Emperor of Portugallia* (1914), which are set in the rural lands and deep, legend-laden forests of Värmland. This is also the setting for her children's stories *The Adventures of Nils* (1906–07).

Perhaps the outstanding trait of Lagerlöf's writing is her descriptive style, which is rich in imagery and suggestive comparisons. This style is the more remarkable for coming into being during the reign in Northern literature of an austere realism. In fact, Lagerlöf admired this literature and at first tried to apply its style to her subjects. In her fictionalized account of herself she describes the conflict: "Although her brain was filled to overflowing with stories of ghosts and mad love, of wondrously beautiful women and adventure-loving cavaliers, she tried to write about it all in calm, realistic prose." She recognized the impossibility of this and made the rather courageous decision to turn away from the prevailing fashion and to gamble with a more colorful and emotional style. Her success enabled her to write about real subjects, but subjects about whom a magical past still lingered and could at any moment come to the fore.

It is the evocative style that more than anything else makes "The Legend of the Christmas Rose" a successful story and an admirable example of high fantasy. In the pages that describe the transformation of the desolate waste of Göinge Forest into a Christmas garden, it is the style that creates this secondary world by flooding all of our senses and convincing us of the genuine beauty and goodness of nature; it is the style that enables us to sense what the pre-Fall garden of the Bible must have been like. The story, however, also expresses the dark note of human cynicism and lack of trust that sully this innocence and for which we all, like the monk, must do penance. Fortunately, there are those who, like Abbot Hans and Robber Mother, with their childlike simplicity, remind us—often at their own peril—of a lost but not irretrievable rose of innocence.

⊰ The Legend of the Christmas Rose ⊱

Selma Lagerlöf

(Translated By Charles Wharton Stork)

Robber Mother, who lived in the robbers' cave in Göinge
Forest, went down to the village one day on a begging
tour. Father Robber himself was an outlawed man, and
dared not leave the forest; he could only plunder way-
farers who ventured within the borders of the wood. But
in those days travellers were not very plentiful in northern
Skåne, and if the husband had had a few weeks of bad
luck, the wife would take to the road. Her five children
in their ragged buckskin tunics and birch-bark shoes—
each child with a bag on his back as long as himself—
always accompanied her. When Robber Mother stepped
inside the door of a cottage, nobody dared refuse her
anything she demanded—for she was not above coming
back in the night and setting fire to a house where she
had not been well received. Robber Mother and her brats
were worse than a pack of wolves, and many a man felt
tempted to run a spear through them. But everyone knew,
of course, that the husband was back in the forest, and
that he would take revenge, were anything to happen to
his wife or his children.

Now that Robber Mother went from place to place
begging, she appeared one day at Övid, which was then
a monastery. She rang the bell and asked for food. The
watchman opened a small wicket in the gate and handed
her out six round loaves of bread, one for herself and
one for each of the five children. While the mother stood
quietly at the gate, the youngsters were running about.
And now one of them came and pulled at her skirt,
which meant that he had found something which she
should come and see, and she went at once.

The monastery was enclosed by a high, strong wall, and the youngster had discovered a narrow back gate that stood ajar. Robber Mother pushed the gate wide-open and walked in, as was her custom, without asking leave.

Övid Monastery was under the priorship of Abbot Hans, who was a collector of herbs. Just inside the cloister wall he had planted a little herb garden, and it was into this the woman had forced her way.

Robber Mother was so astonished at first that she paused for a moment and only looked. It was high summer, and the Abbot's garden was so full of bright flowers that her eyes were fairly dazzled by all the reds, blues, and yellows. But a smile of satisfaction overspread her features, as she walked down the narrow path between the many flower-beds.

A friar was at work in the garden, pulling up weeds. It was he who had left the gate half-open, that he might throw the couch grass and pigweed on the rubbish heap outside. When he saw Robber Mother in the garden and all her youngsters, he ran over to her and ordered her out. The beggar woman walked right on, now glancing at the stiff white lilies that spread before her feet, now at the climbing ivy that covered the cloister wall —and took no notice of the friar. He, thinking that she had not understood him, was about to take her by the arm and turn her round toward the gate when she gave him a look that made him draw back. She had been walking quite bent under the weight of her beggar's pack, but now she drew herself up to her full height, and said:

"I am Robber Mother of Göinge Forest, so touch me if you dare!"

It was obvious that she was as sure of being left in peace as if she had announced that she was the Queen of Denmark. All the same the friar dared to disturb her, though now that he knew who she was he tried to reason with her.

"You must know, Robber Mother, that this is a monastery, and that no woman is allowed within these walls. If you do not go away, the monks will be angry at me for leaving the gate open, and perhaps they may drive me out of the cloister and the garden."

But such prayers were wasted on Robber Mother. She continued her stroll among the flower-beds, looking at the hyssop with its magenta flowers, and at the honeysuckles with their rich clusters of deep orange.

The friar then saw nothing for it but to run to the cloister and call for help. He came back directly with two stalwart monks. Robber Mother realized that now they meant business! She planted her feet firmly in the path and began to shout in a strident voice all the awful things she would do to the monastery if she were not allowed to remain in the garden as long as she wished. The monks did not appear to be alarmed by her threats; they thought only of getting her out.

Of a sudden Robber Mother, with a wild shriek, threw herself upon the monks, clawing and biting at them. And so did all her children. The men soon found that she was too much for them, and went back for reinforcements.

They were running through the passage leading into the cloister, when they met Abbot Hans, hurrying out to see who was raising all this racket in the garden. They had to tell him that Robber Mother of Göinge Forest was in the garden, that they had not been able to drive her out and must call for assistance.

Abbot Hans rebuked the men for resorting to force and forbade their calling for help. He sent the two monks back to their work, and although he himself was a frail old man, he took with him only the friar.

When he came out, Robber Mother was still walking about among the flower-beds, and he could not help regarding her with admiration and wonder. He was quite certain that she had never seen an herb garden before, yet she sauntered leisurely between the many beds, each of which had its own species of rare plant, and looked at them as if they were old acquaintances; at some she smiled, at others she shook her head.

Now the Abbot loved his garden as much as he could love anything that was earthly and perishable. Savage and terrible as the intruder looked, he could not help liking her for having fought with three monks for the privilege of viewing his garden in peace. He went up to

her and asked her meekly whether she was pleased with
the garden.

Robber Mother turned upon Abbot Hans defiantly,
expecting to be trapped and overpowered; but when she
saw his white hair and frail, bent form, she answered
quietly:

"I thought at first that I had never seen a more beautiful garden, but now I see that it can't be compared
with the one I know."

Abbot Hans had expected quite a different answer.
So, when Robber Mother declared she had seen a garden
more beautiful than his, it brought a faint flush to his
wizened cheek. The friar, who was standing close by,
began to admonish the woman.

"This is Abbot Hans," he said, "who has collected
from far and near, with the utmost care and diligence,
the herbs you see in his garden. We all know there is not
a finer garden to be found in all Skåneland, and it is not
for you who live in the wild forest the whole year round
to pass judgment on his work."

"I've no wish to set myself up as a judge of either
him or you," said Robber Mother. "I am only saying that
if you could see the garden I'm thinking of, you'd up-
root all the flowers planted here and cast them out as
weeds."

The Abbot's assistant was hardly less proud of the
flowers than the Abbot himself, and he said with a scornful laugh:

"It must be a grand garden you have made for yourself among the pines of Göinge Forest! I'll wager my
soul's salvation that you have never been inside the walls
of an herb garden before."

Robber Mother went crimson with wrath to think that
her word was doubted. "It may be true," she said, "that
until to-day I was never inside the walls of an herb garden. But you monks, who are holy men, must know that
every year on Christmas Eve the Göinge Forest is transformed into a pleasure garden, to celebrate the birth
night of our Lord. We who live in the forest have witnessed this miracle every year. And in that garden I
have seen flowers so lovely that I did not dare so much
as to put out a hand to pluck them."

The friar wanted to retort, but Abbot Hans motioned to him to keep silent. For, from his early childhood, the Abbot had heard tell how on every Christmas Eve the forest clothed itself in festal verdure. He had always longed to see it, but had never had the pleasure. And now he begged Robber Mother fervently to let him come up to the robbers' cave on Christmas Eve. If she would only send one of her children to show him the way, he would ride thither alone, and he would never betray her or hers. On the contrary, he would reward them to the full extent of his power.

Robber Mother refused at first, for she was thinking of Robber Father and the harm that might befall him were she to permit Abbot Hans to visit their cave; but her desire to prove to the monk that the garden she knew was more beautiful than his prevailed, and she finally assented.

"But you cannot take with you more than one person, and you are not to waylay us or trap us, on your word as a holy man."

Abbot Hans gave his word, and Robber Mother went her way. The Abbot then commanded the friar not to reveal to a living soul that which had just been arranged. He was afraid that his monks, if they heard of it, would never allow a man so advanced in years to ride up to the robbers' cave.

Nor did the Abbot himself intend to speak of his project to any one. But it so happened that Archbishop Absalon of Lund came one day to Övid and stayed over night. While Abbot Hans was showing the Bishop his garden, he got to thinking of Robber Mother's visit, and the friar, who was at work in the garden, heard the Abbot tell the Bishop about Robber Father, who for many years had been an outlaw in the forest, and ask him for a letter of ransom for the man, that he might again lead an honest life in common with others. "As things are now," said the Abbot, "his children are growing up to be a worse menace than the Father himself, and you will soon have a whole band of robbers to deal with up in the forest."

Archbishop Absalon replied that he could not think of letting the wicked robber run loose on the countryside among honest folk; it was best for all that he stayed in his forest.

Then Abbot Hans waxed zealous, and told the bishop about Göinge Forest, how every year at Christmastide it arrayed itself in summer bloom around the robbers' cave. "If these outlaws are not too wicked to have revealed to them the glory of God, surely they cannot be too bad for the grace of mortals."

The Archbishop knew how to answer the Abbot. "This much I can promise you, Abbot Hans," he said with a smile, "any day that you send me a blossom from the Christmas garden at Göinge Forest, I will give you letters of ransom for all the robbers you may choose to plead for."

The friar understood that Archbishop Absalon no more believed this story of Robber Mother's than he himself did. But Abbot Hans had no such thought; he thanked the Archbishop for his kind promise, and said that he would surely send him the flower.

It was Christmas Eve, and Abbot Hans was on his way to Göinge Forest. Before him ran one of Robber Mother's wild youngsters, and behind him rode the friar who had talked with Robber Mother in the herb garden.

Abbot Hans had looked forward to this journey with longing, and was very happy now that it had come about. With the friar, however, it was quite a different matter. He loved Abbot Hans devotedly and would have been loath to let another attend and guard him; but he did not think they would see any Christmas garden. To his mind, the whole thing was a snare, cunningly laid by Robber Mother, to get Abbot Hans into the clutches of her husband.

As the Abbot rode northward toward the forest, he saw everywhere preparations for the celebration of Christmas. On every farm fires were burning in the bath-house to warm it for the afternoon bathing. Great quantities of bread and meat were being carried from the larders to the houses, and from the byres came the men with big sheaves of straw to be strewn over the floors. At each little church along the way the priest, with the help of his sexton, was decorating his sanctuary. And when he came to the road leading to Bossjö Cloister he saw the poor of the parish coming with armfuls of bread and with long candles which they had received at the cloister gate.

The sight of all these Christmas preparations made the Abbot the more eager to reach the forest; for he was thinking of the festival in store for him, which was so much greater than any that others would be permitted to enjoy.

But the friar fretted and complained, as he saw how at every lowly cabin they were preparing to celebrate Christmas. He became more and more apprehensive of danger, and begged and implored Abbot Hans to turn back, and not throw himself into the hands of the robber.

Abbot Hans rode on, paying no heed to the friar's lamentations. The open country was at last behind him, and he rode into a wild and desolate region, where the road was only a rocky, burr-grown path, with neither bridge nor plank to help them over brook and river. The farther they rode, the colder it grew, and after a while they came upon snow-covered ground.

It was a long and hazardous ride. They climbed steep, slippery by-paths, crossed marshes and swamps, and pushed their way through windfalls and brambles. Just as daylight was waning, the robber boy led them across a woodland meadow, skirted by tall fir trees and denuded leaf trees. Just beyond the meadow rose a mountain wall, in which there was a door made of thick pine boards.

Abbot Hans, understanding that they had arrived, dismounted. As the child opened the heavy door for him, he found himself looking into a poor mountain grotto with only bare stone walls. Robber Mother was sitting by a log fire that burned in the middle of the floor. Along the walls were beds of spruce-fir and moss, and on one of the beds lay Robber Father, asleep.

"Come in, you out there!" Robber Mother shouted without rising. "And fetch the horses in with you, so they won't freeze to death in the cold night air."

Abbot Hans bravely walked into the cave, the friar following. Here were wretchedness and poverty! Nothing had been done to celebrate Christmas. Robber Mother had neither brewed nor baked. Nor had she washed or scoured. The children sprawled on the bare floor around a kettle, from which they were eating. The only fare provided them was a thin water-gruel.

Robber Mother now said in a tone as haughty and dictatorial as that of any well-to-do peasant woman:

"Sit down by the fire and warm yourself, Abbot Hans. If you've any food with you, eat; for the food we prepare in the forest I don't think you'd care to taste. And if you feel tired after your long ride, you can lie down on one of these beds, and rest. There's no fear of your over-sleeping, for I'm sitting here by the fire, keeping watch. I'll wake you in time to see what you've come here to see."

Abbot Hans opened his food bag, but he was too fatigued to eat, and as soon as he had stretched out on the bed, he fell asleep.

The friar had also been given a bed to rest on. But he thought he had better keep an eye on Father Robber, lest he should jump up and try to bind Abbot Hans. However, he too was so exhausted that after a little he dropped into a doze.

When he awoke, Abbot Hans was sitting by the fire, talking with Robber Mother. The outlaw, a tall, thin man, with a sluggish and gloomy appearance, also sat by the fire. He had his back turned toward the Abbot as if he were not listening to the conversation.

Abbot Hans was telling Robber Mother about all the Christmas preparations he had seen on the journey, and reminding her of jolly feasts and Christmas games in which she had participated in her youth, when she lived at peace with mankind.

"I am sorry for your children," he said, "who can never run on the village street in fantastic array, or tumble about in the Christmas straw."

Robber Mother at first made short, gruff replies; but after a little she became rather subdued, and listened intently. Suddenly Robber Father turned round and shook his clenched fist in the Abbot's face.

"You miserable monk!" he cried. "Did you come here to lure away my wife and children? Don't you know that I'm an outlawed man, and cannot leave the forest?"

Abbot Hans, unafraid, looked him straight in the eyes.

"I propose to obtain a letter of ransom for you from Archbishop Absalon," he said.

Whereupon the outlaw and his wife burst out laughing. They knew well enough the kind of mercy a forest robber could expect from Bishop Absalon!

"Oh," said Robber Father, "if I get a letter of ransom from Absalon, I'll promise never again to steal so much as a goose."

The friar was indignant at their daring to laugh at Abbot Hans. Otherwise he was well pleased. Never had he seen the Abbot sitting more tranquil and meek with his own monks at Övid than he now sat with these robber folk.

Of a sudden, Robber Mother arose. "You sit here talking, Abbot Hans," she said, "so that we are forgetting to look at the forest. I can hear, even in this cave, that the Christmas bells are ringing."

And now they all jumped up and ran out. It was still black night in the forest and raw winter weather. They saw nothing, but they heard a distant chime, borne hither on a light south wind.

"How can this bell-ringing ever awaken the sleeping forest?" Abbot Hans wondered. For now, as he stood outside in the dark of winter, it seemed far less likely to him that a summer garden could bloom here than it had seemed before.

The chimes had pealed but a few seconds, when a wave of light broke upon the forest; it was gone in a moment, and then suddenly returned. Now it came floating through the dark trees like a luminous mist, and the night was merged in a faint daybreak.

Abbot Hans noted that the snow had disappeared from the ground, as if some one had removed a carpet, and that the earth was turning green. The ferns shot up through the soil, their fronds curling like a bishop's staff; the heather growing on the hill and the bog-myrtle rooted in the marsh quickly put on fresh green. The moss-tufts expanded and rose, and the spring flowers came out with swelling buds, which already had a touch of color.

Abbot Hans' heart beat fast at the first signs of the awakening of the forest. "Shall I, old man that I am, behold so great a miracle?" he mused, the tears springing to his eyes.

Then it grew so hazy that he feared the night darkness would again prevail; but immediately there came a new rush of light, which brought with it the murmur of brooks and the roar of water-falls. And now the trees put out their leaves so rapidly it looked as if millions of green butterflies had flown up and settled on the branches. It was not only trees and plants that had awakened, but grossbeaks hopped from branch to branch and woodpeckers hammered on the boughs till the splinters flew about them. A flock of starlings on the wing alighted in a spruce top to rest, and every time the birds moved, the bright red tips of their feathers glittered like precious jewels.

It darkened again for a moment, and again came a new light-wave. A warm, fresh south wind came up and scattered over the forest meadow all the little seeds brought from southern lands by birds and ships and winds. These seeds took root and sprouted the moment they touched the earth.

The next warm wave ripened the blueberries and whortleberries. Cranes and wild geese came shrieking their calls; bulfinches began building their nests, and squirrels played in the trees.

Everything went so swiftly now that Abbot Hans had no time to meditate on the wonder of the miracle that was taking place. He could only use his eyes and ears.

The wave of light that now came rolling in brought the scent of newly plowed fields, and from far, far away were heard the voices of milkmaids coaxing their cows, and the tinkle of sheep bells. Pine trees and spruce trees were so thickly laden with small red cones they shone like crimson mantles. The berries on the juniper changed their color every second, and wood-flowers covered the ground till it was all white, blue, and yellow.

Abbot Hans bent down, broke off a wild-strawberry blossom, and as he straightened his body, the berry ripened in his hand. The mother fox came out of her lair with a big litter of black-legged young. She went over to Robber Mother and scratched at her skirt.

Robber Mother leant down to her and praised her babies. The horned owl, who had just started out on his nightly hunt, blinded by the light, flew back to his ravine to perch until dark. The cock cuckoo crowed, and the hen cuckoo, with an egg in her bill, stole up into the nest of another bird.

Robber Mother's children sent up twittering cries of delight as they ate their fill of berries from the bushes, where they hung large as pine cones. One of the children played with a litter of baby hares; another raced with some young crows that had ventured down from the nest before their wings were quite ready for flying; a third picked up an adder from the ground and wound it round his neck and arm.

Robber Father stood out in the marsh eating cloudberries. When he looked up he saw a big black bear at his side. He broke off a willow twig and switched the bear on the nose.

"You keep to your own ground," he said; "this is my turf." The huge bear then turned and lumbered off in another direction.

And all the while new waves of light and warmth kept coming. The chatter of ducks could be heard from the wood-pond. Golden pollen from rye fields filled the air; and now came butterflies so big they looked like flying lilies. The beehive in a hollow oak was so full of honey, it oozed out and dripped down the stem. All the plants which had come up from seeds blown hither from foreign lands suddenly burst into bloom. The most gorgeous roses clambered up the side of the mountain in a race with the blackberry vines, and down in the meadow bloomed flowers large as a human face.

Abbot Hans thought of the flower he was to pluck for Archbishop Absalon, but each flower that came out was more beautiful than the last, and he wanted to pick for the Bishop the most beautiful flower in the garden.

Wave upon wave of light rolled in, until the sky became so dazzlingly bright that it fairly glittered. All the life and beauty and joy of summer smiled on Abbot Hans. He felt that the earth could hold no greater bliss than that which welled about him.

"I do not know what new glories another wave may bring," he said.

But there came more and more light; and now it seemed to Abbot Hans that it brought with it something from an infinite distance. He felt himself being enwrapped, as it were, by an atmosphere superterrestrial, and, trembling with awe, he awaited the approaching glories of Heaven.

There was a hush, a stillness in the forest. The birds were silent, the young foxes played no more, and the flowers stopped growing. The glory now drawing nigh was such as to make the heart stand still and the soul long to rise to the Eternal. From far, far away came faint strains of harp music and celestial song.

Abbot Hans folded his hands and went down upon his knees. His face shone with bliss. Never had he dreamed that in this life he was to taste the joys of Heaven and hear the angels sing Christmas carols!

But close by stood the friar who had come with the Abbot, and in his mind dark thoughts arose. "This cannot be a true miracle," he thought, "since it is revealed to criminals. It can never have come from God, but must have been sent hither by Satan. The powers of evil are bewitching us and compelling us to see that which has no existence."

Angel harps and angel voices sounded in the distance; but the friar believed that the spirits of Hell were approaching. "They would charm and seduce us," he sighed, "and we shall be bound and sold into perdition."

The angel hosts were now so near that Abbot Hans could see their shining forms through the trees. The friar saw them too, but he thought that behind all this wondrous beauty lay something malevolent. To him, it was the Devil who worked these wonders on the night of our Saviour's birth. He thought it was done only in order to delude poor human beings the more effectually and lay a snare for them.

All this time the birds had been circling round the head of Abbot Hans, and had let him take them in his hands. But the birds and animals were afraid of the friar; no bird perched on his shoulder, no snake played at his feet. There was a little forest dove who, seeing the angels draw near, took courage and flew down to the friar's shoulder and laid her head against his cheek. The friar, thinking the Adversary himself had come right upon him, to tempt and corrupt him, struck at the dove and cried in a loud voice, that reverberated through the whole forest:

"Get thee back to Hell, whence thou art come!"

Just then the angels were so near that the motion of their great wings fanned the face of Abbot Hans, and he bowed his head to the earth in reverent salutation. But the moment the friar uttered those words the singing stopped, and the holy visitors turned and fled. At the same time, the light and the warmth departed in unspeakable terror of the darkness and cold in a human heart. Black night descended upon the earth; the frost came, the plants shrivelled, the animals ran to cover, the roar of the rapids was hushed, the leaves fell off the trees with a rustling noise that sounded like a shower of rain.

Abbot Hans felt his heart—which had just been so full of bliss—contract with insufferable agony.

"I can never get over this," he thought, "that the angels of Heaven had been so near and were driven away; that they wanted to sing Christmas carols for me, and were put to flight!" He remembered the flower he had promised Bishop Absalon, and in the last moment he fumbled among the leaves and moss for a blossom. But he could feel the ground freezing beneath his fingers and the snow that came gliding over the earth. His heart gave him still further trouble; he tried to rise, and fell prostrate on the ground.

When the robber folk and the friar had groped their way, in utter darkness, back to the cave, they missed Abbot Hans. They snatched brands from the fire and went out to search for him. . . . And they found him lying dead upon a blanket of snow.

The friar wept and wailed—for he knew that he had killed Abbot Hans by dashing from his lips the cup of happiness which he had been thirsting to drain to its last drop.

When Abbot Hans had been carried back to Övid the monks who took charge of his body noticed that the right hand was locked tightly around something which must have been grasped at the moment of death. And when they finally got the hand open they found that that which had been held in so firm a grip was a pair of white root-bulbs, which had been pulled up from the moss.

The friar who had accompanied Abbot Hans to the forest took the bulbs and planted them in the Abbot's garden. He nursed and guarded them the whole year, hoping to see a flower come up from them. He waited in vain through the spring, the summer, and the autumn; and when winter set in and all the leaves and flowers were dead, he ceased caring for them.

But when Christmas Eve came again it brought Abbot Hans so vividly before his mind that he went out into the garden to think of him. When he came to the spot where he had planted the bare root-bulbs, he saw that from them had sprung flourishing green stalks which bore beautiful flowers, with silvery white petals.

He called out all the monks at Övid, and when they beheld the plant that bloomed on Christmas Eve, when all the other plants were dead, they knew that this flower had indeed been plucked by Abbot Hans in the Christmas Garden at Göinge Forest.

The friar then asked for permission to take a few flowers to Archbishop Absalon. When he appeared before the Archbishop and gave him the flowers, he said:

"Abbot Hans sends you these; they are the flowers he promised to pluck for you in the Christmas Garden of Göinge Forest."

And when Archbishop Absalon saw the flowers which had sprung from the earth in darkest winter, and heard the message, he went pale as if he had met a ghost. He sat silent for a long moment, whereupon he said:

"Abbot Hans has faithfully kept his word, and I shall keep mine." He ordered a letter of ransom to be drawn up for the robber who had been outlawed and compelled to live in the forest from the days of his youth. He entrusted the letter to the friar, who left at once for the forest.

When the friar stepped into the robbers' cave on Christmas Day, Robber Father came toward him with axe uplifted.

"I'd like to hack you monks to pieces, many as you are!" he said. "It must be your fault that the forest was not dressed last night in Christmas bloom."

"The fault is mine alone," the friar replied, "and I am ready to die for it; but first I must deliver a message from Abbot Hans." He drew forth the Archbishop's letter and told the outlaw that he was now a free man.

"Hereafter," he said, "you and your children shall play in the Christmas straw and celebrate your Christmas among men, as Abbot Hans wished to have you."

The robber stood there pale and speechless, but Robber Mother answered in his name:

"Abbot Hans has kept his promise, and Robber Father will keep his."

When the robber and his family left their cave, the friar moved into it; and there he lived all alone, in the solitude of the forest, in penance and prayer.

But Göinge Forest never again celebrated the natal hour of our Saviour, and of all its glory there remains today only the flower which Abbot Hans plucked. It has been named the Christmas Rose. And every year at Yuletide it sends up from the mold its green stalks and white blossoms, as if it could never forget that it once grew in the great Christmas Garden.

EVANGELINE WALTON ENSLEY
(1907–   )

Evangeline Walton Ensley's ". . . three books (*The Island of the Mighty, The Children of Llyr,* and *The Song
of Rhiannon*), together with C. S. Lewis's *Out of the
Silent Planet, Perelandra,* and *That Hideous Strength* and
T. H. White's *The Once and Future King,* are not only
the best fantasies of the twentieth century. They are also
great works of fiction." So writes Patrick Merla in " 'What
Is Real?' Asked the Rabbit One Day," an important fea-
ture article on fantasy literature that appeared in *Satur-
day Review* (4 Nov. 1972, pp. 43–50). Merla's assess-
ment of Evangeline Walton Ensley's superlative achieve-
ment as a writer of fantasy is typical of the high praise
currently being lavished upon this remarkably adroit
storyteller and superb prose stylist. But although Ensley
(Walton is a family name she uses as her pseudonym) is
now widely recognized as one of this century's finest fantasists, surprisingly little has been published about her life
and writings. Much of the biographical information included here, as a matter of fact, has been gleaned from
correspondence and telephone conversations with Ensley,
and from two newspaper interviews she has most graciously sent to us (J. C. Martin, *The Arizona Daily Star,*
May 16, 1977; and Dan Pavillard, "Fantastic Author
Escapes on the Typewriter," *Tuscon Daily Citizen,* Dec.
2, 1972).

Born in Indianapolis on November 24, 1907, Evangeline Ensley quickly revealed her literary bent. At the
tender age of six she began composing stories that her
mother recorded and later sent (when Evangeline was
eight) to an Indianapolis publisher, who praised the

works but deemed them not quite ready for publication. Because of her frail health (she suffered from pneumonia nearly every winter), the youthful writer was unable to attend school. Consequently, her entire education was received at home under the careful tutelage of a great-aunt. As eager to read as to write, Evangeline Ensley took full advantage of the many fine books which filled her home. She had many favorites, including L. Frank Baum's Oz books, Lord Dunsany's tales of glamour and adventure, and John Cowper Powys's collections of verse, but she was especially fond of, and influenced by, the Irish poet and story writer James Stephens, whom she still regards as her literary mentor.

The work destined to have the single greatest impact upon her literary career, however, was that magnificent collection of eleven medieval Welsh tales known as the *Mabinogion*. It was her reading of this rich repository of Celtic myth and legend that inspired the writing, in 1936, of *The Virgin and the Swine*, a beautiful retelling of the fourth "branch" of the *Mabinogion*. Although the book received deserved critical acclaim, its sales were not substantial enough to prevent it from soon going out of print. For nearly thirty-five years the work was known to only a small coterie of dedicated readers. Paul Spencer brought the novel to the attention of Lin Carter, who reissued the book as part of the Ballantine Adult Fantasy series under the new title *The Island of the Mighty* (1970). Reader response to the newly reissued novel was enthusiastic and Ensley was soon under contract. She then proceeded to practice her literary magic with the other three branches of the *Mabinogion* by retelling their tales in *The Children of Llyr* (1971), *The Song of Rhiannon* (1973), and *Prince of Annwn* (1974). Other works by Ensley include *Witch House* (1945), the first volume in the Library of Arkham House Novels of Fantasy and Terror; *The Cross and the Sword* (1956), an historical fiction published in England under the title *Son of Darkness;* an unpublished novel, *The Prince of Air;* an unpublished "poem-play"; and a number of critical essays.

In a recent letter, Ensley says, "At present I'm engaged in re-writing a Theseus trilogy which I had all ready to send out just when Mary Renault's *The King Must Die*

(1958) was published. I hope to goodness the new slant given Theseus's affairs by the Santorini eruption business will finally enable me to re-launch this project, which has always been very dear to my heart." We too hope for such a prompt relaunching, since we are sure that her dedicated research, which includes four trips to Greece and the island of Crete in the past decade, and her proven ability to effectively treat mythical materials will result in a superlative, and unique, treatment of the Theseus story. Ensley currently lives in a small bungalow with a mountain view in Tucson, her home for the past thirty-one years.

"Above Ker-Is" is published for the first time in this volume. Written by Ensley when she was twenty years old, the story was packed away with other papers for approximately a half-century. In the spring of 1977, we wrote to Ensley, inquiring if she had any short fantasy fiction that might be appropriate for our sequel to *The Fantastic Imagination*. Much to our delight, she graciously offered to search through her papers for a story or two she thought might be in hiding there. "Above Ker-Is" is the happy consequence of her search. A powerful story which was inspired by Anatole Le Braz's *Les Pays des Pardons*, "Ker-Is" provides further evidence of Ensley's lifelong interest in Celtic myth and folklore. Few readers will be satisfied with a single perusal of "Ker-Is." Its author handles the device of literary ambiguity in such a masterful fashion that a series of unanswered questions will haunt the reader long after he or she has turned the last page of this tale. Who, or what, was Alise-Guenn? Even the normally confident narrator, Jean Rosel, seems to be unsure after listening to the anguished confessions of Guennole Kerival. We are grateful to Ensley for having given us the opportunity to figure so prominently in the debut of "Above Ker-Is." It has remained in hiding long enough.

⋅§ Above Ker-Is §⋅

Evangeline Walton

In my will I have left instructions that at my death the envelope containing these papers shall be burned unopened. Otherwise to write them would have violated the secrets of the confessional. And this is the strangest confession to which I, Jean Rosel, a parish priest of Douarnenez, have eve⁻ listened; one shrouded in uncanny, fabulous dreams of an earlier day, even though part of it is as simple if also as old as flesh.

It was the time of the *pardon* at La Palude, the greatest of our Breton festivals, and all day pilgrims had been passing on their way to the blessed St. Anne. The sick going to pray for healing, fishermen going to give thanks for preservation from their great enemy, the sea. Late that afternoon he knocked at my garden gate, a tall gaunt man in whose dark face a tremendous vitality warred oddly with asceticism. We talked of common things at first, of the *pardon* and the pilgrims.

"They come as their ancestors came, Father, when Heol was still worshipped on Menez Bre. Now they come to pray to the blessed grandmother of Jesus; then they paid homage to Another, older and more terrible. Her whose laughter fishermen still think they heard, down in the deep."

"It is a blessing," I said, "that the worship of the gentle mother of Mary has replaced that of cruel elemental forces."

"It was not only storm-tossed waves they feared and worshipped, Father. There was *Another*."

He was leaning forward, and his eyes were wide and bright, even glassy. He pointed to the great nearby Bay

126

of Douarnenez, beneath whose blue waters, the peasants say, now lies King Gralon's palace of cedar, silvery and gold. There, by St. Guennole's command, the King stayed the flood by casting in his daughter, despite her tears and terror. A grim tale, perhaps a twisted reminiscence of human sacrifice, and my guest's mouth was grim.

"She made a full meal there, Father. But she wanted more."

Somewhat startled, I said: "The sunken city of Ys may well be an old wives' tale."

His voice changed suddenly. "Will you hear my confession, Father?"

Until then we had been only two gentlemen talking together. I was startled again, I do not know quite why, but I agreed, as was my duty.

He said slowly: "My family has owned land near here for centuries. The Kerivals. You have heard of Guennole Kerival, Father?"

I had. As a divinity student of great promise, but one who had never taken his vows. He had disappeared instead, leaving vague and scandalous rumors behind. I said only, "Yes. I have heard of him."

"As a great sinner?" He smiled rather wryly. "I never have been sure how great my sin was, but tonight I am going to find out. That is why I came here—I may not be able to come to any priest again."

I felt suddenly uneasy. Twilight was coming; the sky was pale blue, mottled with great splashes of gold, but a faint shadow already lay upon the earth. There was a stillness like the stealthy quiet of gathering forces.

"Self-murder? Surely you would not dare that crime against yourself, my son?"

He laughed. "When I stand in guilt before the Highest, it will not be for my own death. Yet the man I might have been died long ago; these many years I have been his ghost. But who killed him—myself or another—that is what I must find out tonight."

He looked down at his hands, where they lay open on his knees. Long hands, sinewy and powerful; their strength could have thrown an ox, yet once he had been famed for his brilliance, for his learning. . . .

"You know that I was trained to be a priest, Father.

It was my lifelong dream, and my mother's. She thought me as handsome and clever as my name-saint, and my father's opposition completed the parallel. When he died it seemed that heaven had opened the way for us. I was free to seek that holiness on which my mind had been set from infancy."

"My son, did you never think of the dangers of presumption?"

"Maybe so. I have come to think, of late years, that it was my nature to carry things too far. . . . But right or wrong, St. Guennole was always before me, my hero and model, he who likewise had forsworn all the good things of the world and even ignored his own father's wishes, in that search for holiness. He had been beautiful, yet no earthly love had stayed him. He had been good, yet terrible in his goodness; unafraid, in his own complete sanctity, to punish, taking in his hands that vengeance which is God's." For a little while he was silent, brooding. "Before I went away to study I quarrelled about him—my saint—with Alise-Guenn, the flax-spinner's daughter. My mother said that Alise-Guenn had the modern irreverence for all holy things, but I think it may have been only that then as always Alise-Guenn was a law unto herself. And who has a right to be that?" His strong hands clenched.

" 'I do not like your St. Guennole,' she told me that day. 'He was a bad man.'

" 'For saying that you should have fear—and shame too, Alise-Guenn!' I said angrily. 'St. Guennole was a holy man. One of the blessed saints.'

"She smiled at me with her blue-green eyes that seemed all green then, and there was more mockery than usual in her twisted coral mouth, though her smiles always mocked. 'Murderers are considered bad,' she said, 'and St. Guennole made King Gralon drown the Princess Ahes. Gralon's own daughter. That wasn't holy. It was murder.'

"I drew away from her, saying stiffly: "You had better ask God to forgive you, Alise-Guenn. The Princess was a demon; she had to die.'

" 'Why? She only stole the silver key to open the gate for her lover! It was by accident that she opened the dikes and submerged Ker-Is. I don't care! It was ugly—ugly—for her own father to kill her! And for your saint to make him do it. Doing ugly things can't be holy.'

"She threw back her hair and faced me. She was not yet twelve then, but already the boys were watching her. Her mother too used to watch her, with the air of a fat, comfortable barnyard hen who has hatched out a swan. Or something stranger. . . . People said that the flax-spinner, being long barren, had finally supplicated that famous dark stone, the Groach H'ouard, with heathenish and never-to-be-told-of rites, as our childless and mis-guided Breton women have done for ages. If so, Alise-Guenn was no right human child; the One who answers such prayers cannot be God. And she did have a strange-ness about her. To look at her was to think of legendary fairy women born and reborn in human shape, with Oeil-en-Lune, to fulfill some mysterious pagan destiny. Such beauty fascinates, even though it is not of God.

"I said sternly: 'You're blaspheming, Alise-Guenn.' But she only laughed at me."

" 'I'm glad—glad—that she's still alive down there in the water! Even if she does kill sailors with her singing and her kisses. Being murdered didn't make an end of her. Nothing can stop her now. Your St. Guennole can't; the Virgin herself can't. She said so.'

" 'That's only a legend,' I answered roughly, 'a silly, blasphemous legend. There's nothing God and his saints and the Virgin can't stop. Probably St. Guennole never had any princess drowned at all, but if he did he was *right*. Whatever a saint does is right, because he is a saint. If we question that, it's sacrilege, and the devil is working in us. You're as bad as a heretic, Alise-Guenn; you ask the same kind of wicked questions they do.'

"She stared at me, and her eyes were like two great emeralds, two stone-hard, mocking emeralds. 'I don't think a little exercise would hurt your head, Guennole. Are you never going to think a thought your name-saint or somebody else hasn't already thought—one of your own?'

"I wanted to seize her and shake her, but somehow I was afraid of contact with her flesh. Though I wanted to touch it—to feel the warm firmness, the rose-petal softness of it. To bruise it. . . . I said still more sternly: 'If you're going to do nothing but blaspheme, Alise-Guenn, I'll go!'

" 'If you're going to do nothing but preach, as if you'd already taken orders, you'd better go, Guennole. I didn't come out here to go to church.'

"I turned my back upon her and she added: 'I think it's really rather nice of the princess to kiss the sailors. The storms would come and drown them anyway.'

"Without more words I left her, but as I walked off through the twilight her voice pursued me with the Princess Ahes's siren song, its eerie wailing sweetness mingling with the murmur of the sea:

'Ahes breman Mary Morgan,
E skeud an cabr, d'an noz, a gan.'*

"I left for the city without seeing her again, and the next few years were filled with study. With unswerving, dedicated labor. In my mind I always saw myself as one of the faithful few, a white-robed figure walking steadfastly upon the heights, above the masses **who** lived joyously and naturally, like the beasts. I despised their weakness. Love was an uncleanness of the flesh, incompatible with purity. And the more I withstood the flesh, the fiercer my ambition—that is, my yearning for holiness—grew. All earthly fires fused into that one magnificent dream of spiritual glory: God—and myself serving Him, not failing Him like all those others. . . . Egotism, you say? No, no, the thirst for holiness!

"Then my mother fell ill, and I was forced to return home.

"That was in the spring, a spring of endless, neverpausing rain. The gray mist and the cruel monotonous patter of the raindrops seemed to fill the universe; one wondered that earth and sky did not melt together into one great gray cloud. . . . I was of no real help to my mother. All she wanted of me was to have me there to smile at whenever she did wake from her continual, weak dozing. If I could have talked to her of God's goodness, read aloud to her from pious works, it would

* See Anatole Le Braz's *Les Pays des Pardons*.

have been different. My idleness irked me; I grew restless, strained. . . .

"I asked our housekeeper about Alise-Guenn. She said that all the young men of the parish were mad about the girl, who smiled on each and laughed at them all. 'Like a cat with a pack of mice,' she said and sniffed.

" 'But she is going to marry young François Kerbastiou now; her own aunt stopped by and told me that it is settled at last.' My mother woke unexpectedly and said, 'So you need not worry about her, Guennole.'

"Instead of relief I felt a hot sick dismay. Something so like jealousy that I was horrified and astonished. . . .

A few days later a *pardon* was held. The weather suddenly cleared and my mother urged me to go. And I told myself that a strong man did not need to avoid temptation. I came after Vespers, when the young men were wrestling and running races before the girls grouped near the old church. One stood near the yellow bonfire, and her hair gleamed with a strange, greenish light. Can it be natural for gold hair to shine like that under some lights?

" 'Alise-Guenn!' Somehow I found myself beside her, holding her hands. She drew back, out of the circle of the firelight, and her low laugh had a note of crooning sweetness, of elemental power.

" 'So you have not forgotten old friends—monsieur?'

" 'Not 'monsieur' to you, Alise-Guenn.'

"Then I was silent, regretting my impulsive words, awkwardly groping for safer ones. Her hands were cool and slim, yet I dropped them as if they had been hot. Yet I walked on with her, into the shadow of the trees. One, gnarled and low-trunked, made a natural seat, which she took. In the dusk her face was like a silver flame, and her eyes were blue-green, unfathomable shadows of beauty. She seemed one with some great harmony that held all the vastness of the moonlit woods and the far-off, gently murmuring sea.

"I had to say something; I said: 'You and François should have waited until I was ordained. Then I could have married you.'

"She laughed. She laughed until she rocked back and forth and would have fallen from the tree if I had not caught her. The feel of her body shocked me like electricity, and I tried to draw away, but the fair shining head lay back on my shoulder. She smiled up into my eyes.

" 'So they have been telling you that too? Well, if I am ever married, you will marry me, Guennole Kerival.'

"The rest of the evening I kept a distance between myself and her, but I could still feel her, feel that strange, half-delightful, half-dreadful tingling her body had sent through mine. As though in some subtle sense she still lay there, invincible and inescapable, in my arms.

"I got little rest that night. Time after time I woke, jerking myself up out of troubled dreams. Then at last I found myself walking towards the bay. I thought, 'I will bathe there; then perhaps I can sleep.'

"But I could not find the bay. The beach had vanished. Instead there was solid land, crowned by the white walls of a great city.

"The city of Ker-Is—Ker-Ahes—in all its lost splendors!

"For a moment I stopped, thinking that I had gone mad. Then I went on, as it seemed predestined that I should go on. I walked between the great gates, down the streets of wonder that legend had preserved and deified, past pale palaces whose contents not even legend remembers. I saw a church, and I told myself that all must be well. Surely the swimmer who old tales foretell had found sunken Ys and rung its church bells, so bringing it up again out of the sea.

"But I heard no church-bells, and in that gleaming place I felt nothing Christian. But I never thought of turning back. Neither did I choose my way; I only followed it as steel follows the magnet. . . . The smell of the sea was in my nostrils, and also the smell of cedar.

"And then, round a bend in the way, I saw it—King Gralon's palace of cedar, silver, and gold. Gorgeous as though sun and moon had fused together to form that wonder, their radiance dimmed by the lovely soft colors of countless twilights, until it was bearable to human sight. The silver doors were shut, but as I looked they opened, with a movement that had the irresistible, effortless softness of waves. The space within was like a pit of magic dusk, a dusk which filled me with the fear that a poor swimmer feels for deep waters. But like the magnet-drawn I could neither stop nor turn back. . . .

"I stood in a great shining chamber, and in the center of it was a couch, and on the couch *she* sat. She wore only a wave, and it foamed white against the more rosy white of her breast and shoulders. Her hands were held out to me, and she was smiling, an irresistible, beckoning smile. And I knew that wherever the sea was, waves were rising around us, a flood that could not be escaped. I cried out like a drowning man, yet in delight as well as horror:

" 'Ahes . . . Ahes . . . Alise-Guenn!'

"Later, much later, I woke alone in my own bed, and the moonlight was falling, in a pale pure pool, upon the rug.

"I did not stay long in Brittany after that. My mother was mending slightly, and she herself was the first to say that I should go back to my neglected studies. All my pride and hopes had come to this: that I ached to flee from the scene of my humiliation and sickening shame. . . .

"I made confession. I flung myself into study and prayer; I filled my mind with high, safe things. Yet always she hovered at the back of it, a lovely, evil shadow waiting to enter. Alise-Guenn, who had roused the defiling urges of my flesh. . . .

"Then my mother grew worse. I had to return to Brittany. I am not sure why I thought I had to ask about Alise-Guenn.

"She had grown cold toward François Kerbastiou. There was no real proof, my housekeeper admitted, that she ever had made him any promise. But François, wild with anger and grief, had followed her one day when she had walked upon the cliffs, and she had returned alone. Later, when his body was washed up by the sea, his mother had accused her of murder. Nobody really believed that the girl had actually pushed her lover over the cliff, but many felt that she had driven him to suicide. She was no better than an outcast now; her own mother had died, and it was said that in her last days few words had passed between mother and daughter. I saw how well-deserved Alise-Guenn's lot must be, but I also felt unwilling doubt and pity. The memory of her, gay and unafraid, cried out against this utter defeat.

"Late in the autumn my mother died. I mourned for her; it was the breaking of the oldest, completest tie, but it was also the breaking of a chain. Now I could escape. Yet on the night of her funeral I could not rest. Striving with some trouble I could not or would not put a name to, I paced the cliff paths. Until I heard a voice behind me.

" 'Monsieur—Guennole—'

"I wheeled sharply. In the intense stillness I had heard nothing, only the lapping of the waves, but she was there, her black dress one with the dark, her face a shining pallor.

"I could not speak. I felt my whole being tensing for our final struggle, and she came nearer.

" 'Say whatever you really believe, Guennole.'

"Somehow I found my voice. 'I have heard ugly things of you. What is the truth, Alise-Guenn?'

" 'It is hard to say.' For a moment she was silent, then her emerald eyes met mine squarely. 'Ugly things—do you think I would do them, when I hate ugliness more than anything in the world? More than what you call sin?' She stopped and drew a deep breath. 'I will be honest. I made a mistake. I only smiled at François Kerbastiou as I smiled at all the others, but I should have stopped smiling at him. For he was one who could believe what he wanted to believe.' "

" 'Your smiles, Alise-Guenn!' I said bitterly . . . 'What are they?' "

" 'They are half friendliness, at least.' The shining gaze did not waver; it grasped me as a magnet grasps. 'And the other half—well, it has always been as if something greater than myself bade me do it—as if I had to follow some old, old law. . . . But I did not want François Kerbastiou to follow me up here that day. I told him that his love would pass, and it would have—it was of that kind, a feverish thing. But he was like a little boy, he could not bear to give up what he wanted. He seized me. I pushed him back,—and he slipped. . . .'

"Her shoulders shook, as water ripples, and she was crying. Never, even in our childhood, had I seen her cry. She put her hands to hide the shining tears.

" 'Do you think it was sweet to see him fall? That it is a sweet sight to remember? . . . And now no woman speaks a friendly word to me, and no man, except for one reason. . . . But I will not abase myself. I will not try to explain to people who think only of themselves and little things. But you too know what it is to dream. That is why I care, Guennole; why I have always cared.'

"I believed her then. I thought I knew that she was honest, and that I understood her for the first time. Pagan or not, there was nothing dark or weak in her. She was like a strong wine, but so she had been made. All the depths and the heights were in her, and yet she was neither too high nor too low.

"In a great rush of tenderness and pity I put my arms about her. What I felt seemed beautiful and holy. 'Don't cry, Alise-Guenn. Sweetheart—love—'

"She put her arms round me. I felt her breasts, and the old fire ran through me. I knew then what I had done. . . .

"I flung her from me, but she did not fall. It was I who staggered back. She was still there before me, a figure of eerie glamorous beauty gleaming there.

" 'So that is all you can see in me—evil and temptation.' Back into the liquid silver of her voice had come the mockery, hard and bitter now. 'You have spoilt both the man and the priest, Guennole Kerival.'

"I wanted to run away, but I could not. My body was hot and quivering: one awful ache of longing. She moved forward, and it seemed to me that her moving was like the rising of the sea, resistless, beautiful. Like Ahes rising from her waters; from those waves that are said to form a bed for her and the man who dies beneath her kiss. . . .

" 'But you will always want me, even if you cannot love me.' Her laugh cut like a silver whip.

"I was between her and the path. She put her hand on my arm to push me aside. If she had not—if she had not —I seized her then. She cried out once, but in my ears a louder voice was ringing—St. Guennole's command to Gralon long ago. It gave me strength—and as I lifted her, held her above the sea that roared far below us, I cried out myself: 'St. Guennole was right! St. Guennole was right!' "

He hid his face in his hands. My garden was very still. The tide was coming in.

"No one ever guessed. She was never—found." He lifted his face, and its weary hopelessness dispelled my horror. "That is significant, surely, Father? On our coast the bodies of the drowned are always found. I think it significant, too, that François Kerbastiou died by drowning. The fate of all her victims, through all the ages. Is she not said to be many times reborn? Maybe she herself does not always know, maybe sometimes she shares some of the feelings of other women. Once she was born as that princess who destroyed her own city, and again as—"

"My son, do not delude yourself." I spoke sternly. "You murdered a woman. There is no Ahes."

"The Father of the early Church believed that the pagan gods were demons!" he flashed back at me, his jaw setting. But instantly he grew quiet. "Forgive me, Father. To you, I know, it must seem a delusion. I myself do not wholly believe. For the deed did not free me. I could not take my vows. All these years I have wandered—wondered, until I was almost worn out with wondering: Was it—or was it not—murder?"

I was silent; I had already given him my answer. Perhaps, in a little while, he could bring himself to face it.

He said, still quietly: "For years I have hidden inland, Father, but tonight I am going out to sea. If she does not come, I will admit my delusion, I will give myself up to the law. If she comes, it will be enough to know that I am not a common murderer. I *must* know."

Perhaps I did not act wisely then. I was taken by surprise, stunned by the horror and strangeness of it all. I did insist upon accompanying him. He agreed to that readily, saying: "She will not harm you, Father. Her quarrel is with me."

We set off in the twilight, with my good Yann Bergat, in his fishing-boat. The gold splashes in the sky were growing paler and smaller, like a fading halo, and the sea sung about our bows with a mocking yet crooning sound, exquisitely sweet. The sound was like a woman's laugh, I thought, amused by my overwrung folly, and like a cat's contented purring. It was strangely soothing. I found myself very weary, and lay down in the thwarts. Kerival sat up very straight, his fixed, unhappy eyes staring out to sea. . . .

A great slap of water in my face woke me. I called out and pulled myself up into a sitting position. Luckily, we were not far from shore, but the sky had darkened. Wind and waves were roaring. I looked around and then called again, sharply: "Yann! Where is Monsieur Kerival?"

He crossed himself. "St. Anne knows. He was at the far end of the boat, and my back was turned. But when this storm came up all of a sudden and I looked around, he was not there. I could see nothing on the water. Nothing anywhere. . . ."

ERIC LINKLATER
(1899–1974)

Eric Linklater, like his somewhat older countrymen Lord Dunsany and John Buchan, fits the mold of the English gentleman: sophisticated, educated, and widely traveled yet deeply rooted in his native soil. Linklater was born in Dounby on the Orkney Islands, Scotland. While the relative isolation of northern Scotland remained his focal point, he ventured forth on numerous occasions to sample life elsewhere, and to write about it.

His first adventure took him to France in World War I as an enlistee in the Black Watch. After the war, and after recovering from his wounds, he went to the University of Aberdeen, where he earned a master's degree in literature. His next journey took him to Bombay, where he held a post as an assistant editor of *The Times of India*. He returned to Scotland and in 1927 became a lecturer at the University of Aberdeen. He next spent two years, 1928–30, in the United States on a Commonwealth Fellowship to Cornell and the University of California. But since he had decided to be a writer, he spent more time seeing the country than studying. When he returned to Scotland, he was indeed able to support himself as a writer. He married Marjorie MacIntyre in 1933 and the couple had two daughters. World War II drew him forth once again. He was a major in the Royal Engineers, defending the British fleet at Scapa Flow, and later he served as a military historian with British troops in Italy. Home once again from the wars, he served as rector of the University of Aberdeen from 1945 to 1948. In 1951 he traveled to the Pacific, to Shanghai and Japan.

Linklater's many travels, as well as his Orkney home,

furnished a prodigious amount of material for his equally prodigious literary output. The last volume of his three-volume autobiography, *Fanfare for a Tin Hat* (1970), lists sixty-one book-length works. These include novels; children's books; collections of short stories; plays; historical, biographical, and autobiographical works; and collections of essays. His second book, *Juan in America* (1931), is a thinly veiled autobiographical account of his coast-to-coast travels in the United States. It remains, in the eyes of many, one of his best works. Another book that received notice in this country is *The Wind in the Moon*, which won the Carnegie Award as the best children's book of 1944. His 1946 novel, *Private Angelo*, was later made into a movie starring Peter Ustinov. Nonetheless, he now appears to be relatively unknown to American readers. While his books, both hard- and softcover, are readily available on English bookshelves, he has, unfortunately, received scant critical or popular attention in the United States in recent years.

Characteristic of Linklater's writing are his madcap wit and exuberance. These qualities are nicely balanced by a polished style and a gentle but firm advocacy of responsible conduct. His fantasy stories, which exhibit this blend of humor and seriousness, are consequently reminiscent of the fantasies of his fellow Scotsman George Mac Donald, although Linklater tips the scales a bit more towards humor and moralizes much less explicitly or religiously than does Mac Donald.

"The Abominable Imprecation" is one of Linklater's most successful fantasies. On the level of plot, it is an engaging tale of adventure and romance, with punishments and rewards meted out, appropriate to the participants' conduct. The descriptive style is elegant and vivid, creating numerous memorable and moving scenes. Yet the work bristles with humor, stemming largely from incongruities. One of these is, of course, the situation in which Perigot finds himself as a result of the story's central device, the abominable imprecation. Another incongruity is the style of the dialogue. Kings and queens, heroes and nymphs, all speak, for the most part, in a most comically commonplace fashion. There is yet another dimension to the story: its erotic overtones (the curse) and undertones (the sickle and the flute). Such erotic elements are relatively rare in high fantasy, but rather frequent in Linklater's case, making it quite clear that while his stories are by no means offensive to children, many of them are written primarily with adults in mind.

The Abominable Imprecation

Eric Linklater

Unlike so many musicians, Perigot was handsome. His eyes were blue and his hair was black. A lock of it fell with engaging disorder over his broad forehead. Even while he played upon his pipe, his upper lip, pursed for its melodious task, retained a whimsical fascination, and when he put down his reed and yawned, he showed white teeth that looked the whiter for his brown skin, and the arms he stretched were long and muscular.

The river-nymph, Cleophantis, hiding in a clump of yellow irises, felt her natural shyness conquered by a much stronger force, and first cutting, with a silver sickle she carried, a few of the tall flowers to supplement her exiguous costume, emerged from her shelter and walked towards him. Her voice was a little uncertain with mingled excitement and shame, and as she spoke a blush played prettily on her pale cheeks.

"I don't want you to think that I am one of those impressionable creatures who lose their heads on every possible occasion," she said, "but really, I've never heard anything so lovely as that last little dancing tune. Of course it's impertinent of me to speak like this to an utter stranger, and quite unforgivable to ask him a favour, but you would make me so happy if you were to play it again!"

Perigot, at first, was amused rather than surprised by her appearance and ingenuous request; for his playing had often attracted, from their river-homes or dark-blossoming corners of the wood, nymphs and dryads whose fervent admiration of his skill upon the pipe had invariably been succeeded by a declaration of their tenderness towards himself. To begin with he had been flattered by their addresses, but after some dozen encounters he had discovered an unsubstantial airy monotony in their company. They were agreeable to look at, they pattered a few pretty sentences, but they had no personality and their charm was vapid and standardized; so Perigot had long since ceased to be impressed by the undines, sylphs, and hamadryads, errant glimpses of whom threw so many of his contemporaries, less gifted than himself, into a perfect fever of desire. Now, thinking that here was only another of that kind, he was not very interested by the nymph's appearance, but before she had finished speaking he perceived in her something different, a quality that made her far superior to the trivial sprites of his previous acquaintance, and hurriedly rising he led her, with pleasant words of welcome, to a cushion of comfortable green turf.

Putting down her silver sickle and discreetly arranging her bunch of flags and yellow irises, she smiled and said, "My name is Cleophantis, and I am, so far as we know, the youngest daughter of the Moon King."

Perigot played his dancing tune, and all the birds within hearing flew near to listen, while a brock came out of the wood with a small deer following it, and from the riverbank tumbled a sleek family of otters.

"That was beautiful," said Cleophantis when he had finished. "Oh, so beautiful! I could sit and listen to you for ever."

Her voice and eyes, however, betrayed a regard for Perigot greater than that for his music, which Perigot quite clearly recognized; for though he was not conceited he was intelligent. Generally, when he noticed this transference of interest in his audience, he was displeased and bored, for he knew how readily a nymph was taken by mere outward appearance, and as an artist he was depressed to find that his music had never more than a minor appeal for women. But now he was delighted to see the brightness of Cleophantis' eyes, their bashful veiling by long lashes, and to note the tremor in her voice. He sat down beside her.

"Your father won't be up for hours yet," he said, and kissed her with a warmth of which she, in the coolness of her river, had never dreamed.

She sprang from him, dropping her flags and flowers, red as a lily-pool at sunset, and Perigot, laughing and eager, pursued her. He caught her easily, but when he found her shyness was real, and not assumed, he became gentle and courteous with her, though her beauty, of which he became ever more sensible, constantly tempted him into little sallies of ardour. These Cleophantis rebuked with increasing distress, for she had fallen deeply in love with the handsome shepherd, and only her early training in the chaste schoolroom of the osier beds prevented her from yielding to the persuasion which intermittently escaped his disciplined politeness. At last she said she would have to go, and nothing Perigot could say would make her tarry longer, for she was afraid of the awful lengths to which love might lead her.

"But you will come back?" said Perigot, pleading.

"Perhaps," said Cleophantis, and meant, "You know I will!"

"And you will not always keep me at arm's length, or even a finger-breadth away?"

"I am going to speak to my elder sister about you," answered Cleophantis, and though Perigot groaned, for he thought this was an ill omen for love, Cleophantis continued, "She is extraordinarily wise, and I have the greatest respect for her opinion. It is true that she has never had a lover, but in spite of that she is very broadminded. Oh, Perigot, if she says we are right to love, how happy I shall be!"

"You will come to-morrow?" said Perigot.

"At noon," said Cleophantis, "and for a pledge that I shall return, keep this sickle. Its blade is silver from the Mountains of the Moon, forged with the last heat of the moon, and tempered in its coldest stream. No man or beast can resist its edge, and the handle is an emerald that will keep its owner always in health."

While Perigot was examining the sickle, Cleophantis, fearing her resolution would fail, ran to the edge of the nearby stream. She stood for a moment on the bank, looked back, and whispered, "Perigot, my heart!" But Perigot's head was still bent over the flashing blade, and so she stepped unseen into the welcoming river. When Perigot looked up she had gone.

The sun was low and he realized that it was time to go home, so he whistled to the sheep-dogs that were lying far afield, guarding the fringes of the flock, and they gathered the sheep before them while Perigot, thrusting the sickle under his belt, played on his pipe the merriest song the meadows had ever heard, and strode briskly towards the hill on the far side of which stood his father's house. It seemed to him that the quicker he walked the sooner tomorrow would come, and with it Cleophantis—if her sister let her; and his tune grew so glad and so exciting that the lambs capered madly, and the old ewes were puzzled, and the half-grown rams leapt like mountain goats as they followed him over the hill.

Perigot's mother sighed when he came in to supper, for she at once perceived he was in love again, and she was always nervous when her sons were in that state of mind; but his father, a heartless and wealthy man who owned several thousand sheep, two rich valleys, and much hill-land, asked in a gruff voice if the flock was safe, and finding it was told Perigot to keep quiet while he ate, for only children or idiots, he said, must sing with their mouths full of porridge.

In the morning Perigot rose early and was about to lead his flock back to the river-pasture when a man who looked like a Saracen or an Indian, and who had been lounging by the sheepfold, stopped him and said, "I've heard tell you know a good fighting-cock when you see one, sir?"

Now Perigot was a sportsman, and though till that moment his thoughts had all been of Cleophantis, as soon as the Indian spoke of fighting-cocks a picture rushed into his mind of brave birds tussling in the air—bronze feathers gleaming, spurs clashing—and eagerly he asked, "Have you any to sell or match with mine?"

"Better birds than any in your country," said the Indian.

"I doubt that," answered Perigot, "but I'll have a look at them." And he called Thenot, his younger brother, a freckled boy with a snub nose, and told him to take the sheep to the river-field, and he would follow by-and-by.

So fine were the Indian's birds, and such a heroic main was fought, that the sun was overhead before Perigot remembered his tryst with Cleophantis. Then, in a kind of panic, he threw some silver coins to the Indian and began to run, as fast as he could, up the steep path that led over the hill to the riverside grazing. He knew that he would be late, and though he tried to comfort himself with the thought that a little waiting never did any girl harm, he could not convince himself, for Cleophantis was the Moon King's daughter, and very different from any other nymph or forest-girl he had ever seen.

It was a full hour past noon when he reached the flock, and immediately his young brother called to him in a strange sobbing voice. Thenot's freckled face was tear-stained, and in great distress he gasped, "She's dead, Perigot, she's dead! Oh, why didn't you come in time? She waited for you a little while, walking to and fro, and then she sat down, for she felt weak, and still you did not come, and presently she fainted. I rubbed her hands, but they were so delicate I could not rub them hard. Once she opened her eyes and asked, 'Do you see him coming?' And then she said, 'My heart is breaking,' and she died. Oh, Perigot, she was lovely! Why did you not come in time?"

Perigot, numb with remorse, looked down at her where she lay like a plucked lily on the grass. He could not speak, and his brain was too cold even to frame a proper thought. He just stood and looked at her, and knew that he had never seen such loveliness alive. Suddenly Thenot gave a frightened cry and ran away. Perigot looked up and saw, coming to him from the stream, a tall and dreadful nymph with a black river-squall blowing about her, bending the grass and flowers and chilling the summer air.

"Murderer!" she said. "Killer of my sister!" She raised a wet arm round which a water-snake was twisted. The river-squall howled at her back, and Perigot, shivering with cold, fell to his knees beside the dead girl.

"I never dreamt that such a thing could happen," he cried. "Truly I loved her, and truly I hurried to be in time!"

"Murderer and liar!" said the elder sister in a terrible voice. "An unkind thought could bruise her skin, you must have known that such neglect as yours would kill her. But I'm not easily hurt, and I'm not easily swayed by

a handsome face and soft words. Be quiet, murderer, and
hear your punishment. Oh, my sister, he who killed you
will suffer more than you and ten thousand times as
long!"

For a moment the squall was silent, and the dreadful
nymph, whose face seemed to Perigot like broken water
in its darkness, said in a clear hard voice, "The curse of
Shepherd Alken be on you!"

Then the storm howled again, and under its wings the
nymph took up her dead sister and carried her, over the
broken flowers and bent grasses, back to the dark and
sullen stream.

For more than a week Perigot lived in utter misery. His
pipe was silent and his flock untended. Wolves stole a
lamb or two, and he never heard the woeful bleating of
the ewes. But his father, counting the sheep and finding
several missing, rated his son with harsh and brutal words.

"You're the fool of the family," he shouted. "You've
wasted your time cock-fighting and playing that idiot pipe
of yours, and now you blubber for a week because a
worthless undine jilts you. I'm ashamed and sick of the
sight of you!"

"Then let me go away from here," said Perigot. "I'm
tired of keeping your silly sheep. I must do something
braver than that, something dangerous and great, to justify
my wretched life and perhaps forget, in peril of my own
death, the death of Cleophantis."

"H'mph!" said his father. "If you mean what you say—
but I doubt it—you'd better go to Gargaphie. The King's
in a pretty pickle, and shouting east and west for help."

"No, no!" cried Perigot's mother, "not there, he'd be
killed as all the other young men have been killed, and
to no purpose at all. You mustn't go there, Perigot!"

"Tell me what is happening in Gargaphie," said Perigot.

"Oh, the usual thing," said his father, that heartless
man. "A dragon has gone off with the King's daughter,
and killed a dozen young fools who've tried to rescue her.
Do you fancy dragon-baiting? She's a well-made girl, I
believe, and I suppose you could marry her if you got her
away. That's the orthodox reward, isn't it?"

"I shall never marry," said Perigot bitterly. But the
thought of so desperate an adventure made him resolute

to go to Gargaphie, and when he remembered the sickle that Cleophantis had given him he felt confident of his ability to slay the monster who had stolen the King's daughter; though so far he had never seen a dragon and had only a very vague idea of what one looked like.

His mother wept when he told her of his determination, but finding his intention fixed she made such preparation for his journey as seemed suitable. Perigot polished his magic sickle with a woollen cloth and felt happier than he had been since Cleophantis died. Only the memory of her sister's curse hung like a little cloud over his mind. He had told no one about it. He had, indeed, tried to forget it, and in his preoccupation with grief almost succeeded. But now, for the first time admitting his anxiety, he thought it advisable to discover all he could about the malediction with which he had been saddled.

His old nurse Dorcas was an aged woman with a great reputation for wisdom, and Perigot, on the evening before his journey to Gargaphie, went to the fireside-corner where she sat spinning, and said in a conversational way, "Tell me, Dorcas, have you ever heard of a shepherd called Alken?"

"Indeed and I have, Master Perigot," she answered, very glad of the opportunity to talk and show off her knowledge. "And a wicked old man he was, and hated everybody, and what with sitting by himself for days on end, and talking to serpents and owls and mandrakes, he invented the most horrible curse in the world, partly to punish his poor wife, who was almost as nasty as he was, and partly out of pure spite against all humanity."

"What was the curse?" asked Perigot.

"Well, it was like this," said Dorcas, putting aside her wheel and sucking her old gums. "Shepherd Alken used to think a lot about the misery of his life, and indeed he'd hardships enough, what with sitting all day in the hot sun, and little to drink, while he watched his sheep; and lambing them while the snow was on the ground, and that's hard work; and always the danger of wolves; and knowing he'd be poor to the end of his days. But all he thought about his misery was little to what his wife said about hers, for she'd had eleven children, and those who didn't die brought shame and disgrace to her; and to keep her house clean was heart-breaking, for the fire smoked and the roof leaked and the hens came in through the broken door, so to tell the truth she had something to talk about. But the shepherd hated her for it, and thought his own life was far, far worse. So he made up a curse that turned her into a man, and he sent her out to keep the sheep while he sat at home. And he had the satisfaction of hearing her grumble louder than ever, for she could stand neither the heat nor the cold, and she was terribly frightened of wolves. But though it pleased him to hear her complaining so, he wasn't comfortable at all, for there was no one to cook his supper, and the hens made the floor like a midden, and if there was no smoke in the house that was because the fire was always out. So he thought he would use another kind of curse on himself, and turn himself into a woman, and then housework would come easy and natural to him. Well, he spoke the words, and the very next morning he was a woman. But somehow he didn't like it, and every day he liked it less, and when, old though he was, he found himself in the family way, as they call it, he nearly went off his head altogether. So it seemed to him that if there was one thing harder than being a man it was being a woman; and the way his wife grumbled showed him that the only thing worse than a woman's life was a man's life. And then he thought that if he could put two curses into one handy-like little sentence he could do a lot of harm in the world with it, and that's what he wanted. Well, he talked to his friends the Owl and the Serpent and the Mandrake, and they helped him, and by-and-by he had it, and the first use he made of it was in his own house, and he and his wife changed places once again, and she bore her twelfth child and died of it. But the curse became famous, and wicked folk who know the way of it use it a lot, just saying 'The curse of Shepherd Alken be on you,' and that signifies 'If you're a man, become a woman. If you're a woman, become a man.' And that's enough to spread misery wherever it goes, as you'll learn, Master Perigot, when you're a little older—though there's nothing but good fortune I wish you, as you know.'

Perigot listened to this story with growing consternation,

for he remembered that lately his voice had assumed, once or twice, a curious treble tone, and before he went to bed that night he examined himself anxiously to see if there were any further signs that the malediction was working. He discovered nothing, however, except a little plumpness about his chest, and even that he was not very sure of. The next morning he set off for Gargaphie.

He travelled for a week, and came by degrees to country more mountainous and savage than any he had seen before. In Gargaphie itself there were everywhere signs of grief and mourning faces, for the Princess Amoret had been popular as well as beautiful, and the thought of her durance in the dragon's cave caused great distress to young and old. As soon as Perigot made known his mission he was taken to the King, whose gloom visibly lightened when he heard Perigot's stout assertion of his intention to slay the monster and rescue its poor prisoner. But he was a fair-minded man, and he thought it his duty to warn Perigot of the danger he was about to face.

"That wretched dragon has already killed twelve brave young men, all apt in war," he said.

"I am not afraid," answered Perigot, and the King, seeing his bold attitude, his broad shoulders, and the stern light in his blue eyes, felt there was at least a possibility of his success.

"I have promised my daughter's hand to her rescuer," he said, "and though of course I speak with a father's partiality, I think I may say without fear of contradiction that she is the most beautiful girl in all Gargaphie."

"I shall never marry," said Perigot in a grim way, "and I undertake this adventure without any hope of personal gain."

"I can show you a picture of her, if you don't believe me," said the King, a little testily; but the Queen interrupted him, and said to Perigot, "Your attitude, sir, is a noble example to us all," while to the King she whispered rapidly, "Don't argue! Can't you see that he has had an unfortunate love affair, and will fight all the better for it, being careless of his life?" So the King, who appreciated his wife's good sense, said nothing more except to call very loudly for dinner, which had been put back because of Perigot's arrival.

In the morning the King and his courtiers led Perigot to a high rock from which he could see the dragon's den, and there they waited while he went forward alone, for such fear had the monster spread that none dared go within a mile of the waterfall behind which it lived. But Perigot, feeling perfectly confident, climbed down to the torrent-bed, and thence by a narrow path got to the dragon's lair. Lightly he sprang to a rock that the waterfall sprinkled with its high white splashing, and there, first easing the sickle in his belt, he sat down and began to play upon his pipe. First, in a whimsical mood, he played a serenade, but that had no effect, so he began a little taunting air, full of a gay defiance, with shrill notes in it that suggested a small boy being impudent to his elder brother. And presently, through the rushing veil of the waterfall, Perigot saw two huge and shining eyes.

The dragon poked its head out, and when it snorted the waterfall divided and was blown to left and right in large white fans of mist. Perigot now played an inviting tune called *Tumble in the Hay,* and the dragon, amazed by his fearlessness and somewhat attracted by the melody, pushed farther through the waterfall, that now spread like a snowy cape about its shoulders. Its colour was a changing green, on which the sun glittered wildly, and its eyes were like enormous emeralds. Perigot was dazzled by them, and had he not been aware how exceptionally well he was playing, he would have been frightened. As it was, he changed his tune again, with a flourish of sharp leaping notes, and what he played now was an irresistible ribald air called *Down, Wantons, Down.*

The dragon, surprised, then tickled, then captured by delight, opened its enormous mouth and roared with joy. It plunged into the pool in front of the waterfall, and Perigot was soaked to the skin with the splash it made. But he continued to play, and the dragon rolled and floundered in its bath, and what with the sunlight on the waterfall, and the sun shining on its glimmering hide, it seemed as though someone were throwing great handfuls of diamonds, emeralds, and opals into the pool.

Perigot finished the ribald song and slid cunningly into a tune so honey-sweet, so whispering of drowsy passion, that one thought of nightingales, and white roses heavy with dew, and young love breathless and faint for love. The dragon stopped its whale-like gambols, and sighed luxuriously. It rolled over on to its back, and a dreamy look clouded its emerald eyes. It sighed again, like far-off thunder, and came closer to the rock on which Perigot sat. His pipe sang more sweetly still. A kind of foolish smile twisted the dragon's horrible mouth, and its eyes half-closed. Its head was touching the rock.

Sudden as lightning Perigot drew his moon-made sickle, and slashed fiercely at the monster's thick green throat. The blade went through its tough hide, through muscle and bone, as easily as an ordinary sickle goes through grass; and torrents of black blood stained the pool that the dragon's death-struggle made stormier than a tempest-twisted sea. When the headless body at last was still, and blackness lay like a film on the water, Perigot, first cleaning his sickle, climbed by a way he had discovered through the waterfall and into the cave behind it. There he found the Princess Amoret, tied to a rock but apparently unharmed.

He cut her loose and helped her out of the greenish cave that was full of the noise of falling water. She looked at the dead monster, turned away with a shudder, and still for a minute or two did not speak.

Then she said, "How can I express my gratitude? For words are such little things, mere symbols of conventional emotion that time has defaced. I need new words to thank you, but, alas, I am not a poet and can make none. You are an artist, though—I heard your music—and know how I feel."

"I am only too happy to have been of service to you," said Perigot a little stiffly.

The Princess suddenly knelt and embraced his knees. "You have rid me of the most horrible fear in the world," she said, and when she looked up her eyes were clouded with tears, and her face was radiant with happiness because her life had been saved, and because her rescuer was so handsome, and so gifted a musician.

The path was narrow, and as the Princess was weary from long restraint, and as Perigot found that he could talk to her more easily and with more pleasure than to any girl he had ever met before, they took a long time to return to the rock on which the King and his courtiers waited so anxiously—for at that great distance they had been unable to perceive how the battle went. The King's joy at seeing his daughter again was overwhelming, but when he had satisfied himself that she was unhurt, and embraced her a score of times, and blessed all heaven for her deliverance, he remembered the necessity of thanking her rescuer, and did so very heartily.

"And you thought you wouldn't want to marry her, eh?" he said. "Well, haven't you changed your mind by this time?"

As it happened, Perigot had; and no one who realized the excitement of his battle with the dragon, or observed the beauty of Princess Amoret, accused him of undue fickleness for so quickly forgetting his determination to respect in lifelong celibacy the memory of poor Cleophantis. Nor was he embarrassed by the reminder of what he had said, on the previous evening, about his views on marriage. He merely remarked, with some dignity, "I had no wish to force my attentions on the Princess until I had ascertained the possibility of their welcome."

The courtiers were all impressed by this evidence of a noble temper, and Amoret immediately cried, "Father, let there be no hesitation or pretence about this. We love each other, and we were made for each other!"

"That's the way to speak!" said the King. "There's nothing like honesty, and we'll have a wedding after all. I like weddings."

The Queen, a tolerant and kindly woman, was made so happy by Amoret's return that she hardly cared whom her daughter married, if the match were dictated by love; and thereupon the King, in great spirits, declared that Perigot should wed her that night—"If it's quite convenient for you, my dear?" he added.

"Quite convenient," said Amoret, "and, indeed just what I wish myself."

Preparations for a feast were speedily made, and with much ceremony the marriage took place. At a late hour Perigot and his bride retired to their chamber.

For an hour or two Perigot had been feeling his clothes uncommonly tight about his chest and hips, but he imagined the discomfort was due to somewhat excessive eating and drinking. When he undressed, however, he discovered to his horror that the nymph's curse had taken effect, and he had become, for all practical purposes, a woman.

The shock almost unnerved him, but with a great effort he retained his self-control. His predicament was appalling. Not only was he madly in love with Amoret, but Amoret was madly in love with him. She approached him with endearing words, and when Perigot offered her a slight and distant embrace, which was all he dared to offer for fear of revealing his shameful secret, she accepted it with really pitiful disappointment. He stood for a long time looking out of the window, while Amoret sat on the edge of her bed and wondered why Perigot had turned so cold or if this was all that marriage meant. She could not believe that its mystery cloaked precisely nothing.

After an agonized vigil of the dark sky, Perigot remembered his pipe. He took it from the chimney-piece where he had laid it, and played a gentle phrase or two.

"You must be tired, my dear," he said. "Let me play you to sleep."

Amoret turned her face from him, and wept quietly into her pillow. In a little while, however, Perigot's sweet and mournful lullaby soothed her brain, and drove consciousness away, and presently she slept. Perigot lay awake till morning, so bitter were all his thoughts, and before the sun was up he dressed himself and went out, and left Amoret still dreaming.

The day was embarrassing to them both, for in Gargaphie weddings occasioned a certain jocularity that often made ordinary brides and bridegrooms feel uncomfortable. But no wedded couple had ever been in the curious plight of Amoret and Perigot, and their distress at the customary witticisms was so marked as to make even the wits doubtful of their taste. And the day's embarrassments naturally increased as darkness fell, for Amoret was full of doubt and more affectionate than ever, and Perigot was doubly miserable. That night it took him at least an hour, and he needed every bit of his skill upon the pipe, to play his bride asleep.

This wretched state of affairs continued for several days, until the Queen, seeing how unhappy and even ill her daughter looked, talked seriously to her for a long time, and at last elicited some part of the facts.

"But my poor dear!" she said in amazement.

"I assure you that what I say is true," sobbed Amoret. "Every night he plays his pipe until I fall asleep. Sometimes I wonder if he is a man at all."

"The King must be told immediately," said the Queen with decision, and straightaway went to look for her husband, in spite of Amoret's protests, who still loved Perigot dearly and feared that her father would do him harm.

The King, though normally a genial man, lost his temper completely when he heard what the Queen had to say.

"I suspected something of the sort!" he roared. "Did you hear his voice last night? Squeaking like a girl! The insolent impostor! I'll wring his neck with my own hands, I'll drop him over the battlements, I'll hound him out of Gargaphie!"

"There must be no scandal," said the Queen, quietly but firmly. "Not for Perigot's sake, but for Amoret's. The girl has suffered enough without being made the subject of national gossip. I admit it would be a good thing to get rid of Perigot, but it must be done discreetly. I'm sure that you can think of some clever plan to remove him quietly and without fear of unpleasant comment."

"There's something in what you say," admitted the King, "and as for plans, my head is full of them. It always is, and that's why Gargaphie is a happy and prosperous country. Now what about sending Perigot off to retrieve the golden apples that my great-grandfather lost? He'd never come back from that errand alive."

"You'll never persuade him to start on it," objected the Queen.

"Nonsense," said the King. "All that's needed is a little tact and diplomacy. Just you see."

As soon as the Queen had gone he sent his personal herald to look for Perigot, and when the young man appeared, greeted him in a serious and a friendly way.

"Perigot," he said, "there is a stain on the escutcheon of my house which I think you are the very man to erase. In my great-grandfather's time we had, among our family treasures, three golden apples that were said to confer upon their owners health, wealth, and happiness. Whether or not that was so, they were at least intrinsically valuable, and as objects of art, I believe, incomparable. Unhappily, in an affair that did credit to neither side, they were stolen by the Cloud King and taken by him to his favourite castle, which, as probably you are aware, is seven days' march to the north of Gargaphie. On several occasions enterprising young men have endeavoured to retrieve these apples, but every one of them, I am sorry to say, has perished at the hands, or in the teeth, of a curious monster, half-human and half-dog, that the Cloud King retains as a kind of seneschal or warder. You, however, who kill dragons with such ease, would probably make short work of the Hound-man, and if you can bring back those apples I shall seriously consider making you my heir. I don't want to press you, of course . . ."

"There's no need to," said Perigot, "for I'll go very willingly. When can I start?"

The King was a little astonished by his eagerness to undertake so perilous an expedition, but as he did not want to give Perigot an opportunity to change his mind, he said, as though thinking about it very carefully, "Well, there's a full moon to-night, and if you're really in a hurry you could start at once. I'll give you a guide for the first part of your journey, and after that anyone will tell you your way."

So Perigot said good-bye to Amoret and set out on his desperate enterprise. His hope was partly to forget in danger the embarrassment of his married life, and partly to give healing time a chance to restore him to his normal shape. For the curse, he thought, might be a passing or permanent one.

For seven days he marched through wild and desolate country, where the clouds hung ever closer on towering black mountains, and the crying of eagles came hoarsely through the mist. It was a cold and friendless land, and no sign of his returning manhood, except his intrepid spirit, came to comfort him. On the eighth day he reached the Cloud King's castle, and over it, to his surprise, the sky was clear. The castle was empty and deserted except for the great grey Hound-man lying at the gate.

When Perigot appeared the Hound-man rose and growled, and the brindled hair on its neck bristled terribly.

Perigot took out his pipe and began to play the first tune that came into his mind. The Hound-man lifted his head and howled most dismally. Perigot played something else, and the Hound-man bayed like a pack of hunting-dogs. Clearly music would have no effect on him. So Perigot, putting away his pipe, drew his moon-made sickle and warily advanced.

Showing great fangs like icicles, the Hound-man leapt to kill him, but Perigot neatly evaded its rush and cut off its right arm. Foaming at the mouth the brute again attacked him, but this time Perigot with great skill lopped off both its legs, and the Hound-man fell to the ground and lay dying. Its eyes began to glaze, but the wickedness in its heart still lived, and out of its great throat came a growling voice that said, "The curse of Shepherd Alken be on you!"

"What did you say?" demanded Perigot excitedly.

"The curse of Shepherd Alken on you!" repeated the Hound-man. "If you are a man become a woman, if you are a woman become a man!" And died in that instant.

Perigot was so excited that he almost forgot his errand, but just as he was turning back to Gargaphie he remembered that he had come to look for some golden apples, and breaking into the castle speedily found them in the Cloud King's bedroom. He put them into a satchel he had brought for the purpose, and then, wasting no more time, he began to run southwards down the path he had lately climbed so grimly. He made such speed—for his clothes no longer felt tight about the chest—that he reached Gargaphie on the evening of the fourth day, just at the time when everybody was getting ready to go to bed.

The King was astounded to see him, and despite his pleasure in regaining the golden apples that his great-grand-father had lost, found it difficult to infuse his welcome with any cordiality. But Perigot paid little attention to the King. Amoret, he was told, had taken her candle a few minutes earlier and already retired to her chamber.

She, poor girl, was delighted by his return, for she loved him though he had deceived her, and she had feared he was dead. But after they had embraced each other once or twice she remembered her former disappointment, and a little bitterly she said, "Where is your pipe, Perigot? Aren't you going to play me to sleep?"

"That for my pipe!" said Perigot, and threw it out of the window.

"Perigot!" she said.

"Amoret!" he answered, in a deep manly voice that made her heart flutter strangely.

The following morning it was Amoret who rose first, and left Perigot sleeping. At her chamber door the King and Queen were waiting for her.

"Well, my dear," said the King, "I'm afraid that my attempt to get rid of your so-called husband has failed, well-thought-out though it was. But don't worry. I've plenty more plans in my head, and when he's out of the way we'll get you a proper man."

"A proper man!" said Amoret, laughing happily. "Oh, my dear father and my very dear mother, he's the most wonderful man in the whole wide world. I wouldn't change him for all the husbands in Gargaphie."

CATHERINE LUCILLE MOORE
(1911–   )

In 1934 the fantasy story "The Black God's Kiss" appeared in the October issue of *Weird Tales,* written by one C. L. Moore. In itself this was not so unusual, since that author had already become a popular writer with her first publication, "Shambleau" (1933), and three other stories, all published in *Weird Tales* and featuring the space-cowboy-hero Northwest Smith and his interplanetary adventures. What was unusual about "The Black God's Kiss" was that it introduced Jirel of Joiry as protagonist, a heroine in the speculative-fiction field, a literature notorious for its male chauvinism. What is equally significant is that the many readers—and possibly the publisher as well—who welcomed the creator of Northwest Smith and Jirel of Joiry had unknowingly admitted a woman (Moore used her initials) into the male-dominated field of the sf and fantasy pulp magazines. Some years later, Sam Moskowitz was to say of Moore that she became the most important woman writer in the field of speculative fiction since Mary Shelley. It is certainly true that she became one of the freshest, most original and effective contributors to the popular sf and fantasy magazines of the 1930s and 1940s.

C. L. Moore was born and raised in Indianapolis. She was chronically ill throughout her teens and as a consequence spent a great deal of time dreaming up and writing stories. She read widely also, including Greek mythology (Shambleau is a Medusa figure), the Oz books, and the works of Edgar Rice Burroughs. Apparently having conquered her illness, she entered the University of Indiana, where she enjoyed an active social life. She was, however, forced to leave college after a year and a half because of the Depression and take a secretarial job in an Indianapolis bank. This was unfortunate for her, but a boon to sf and fantasy readers, because it was at this time that she began writing "Shambleau," while practicing her typing. After its publication she contributed frequently to such magazines as *Weird Tales* and *Astounding Science Fiction*. Her most popular stories, however, were those that featured Northwest Smith (sf) or Jirel of Joiry (fantasy).

In 1940 she married the promising sf writer Henry Kuttner, with whom she had already collaborated in producing several works, using a variety of pen names. The fruitful collaboration continued for the eighteen years of their marriage, but, unfortunately, Moore wrote fewer and fewer stories by herself. Nonetheless, some of those she did write are now regarded as her best work. These stories, such as "No Woman Born" (1944), which presents an early bionic woman, continued to demonstrate the sort of bold creativity that earlier had led her to introduce a female protagonist into speculative fiction.

After her husband died in 1958, Moore devoted herself to writing scripts for television and to teaching writing at the University of Southern California. She had finished her own interrupted undergraduate education there in 1956; she later received her M.A. from UCLA. She remarried in 1964 to Thomas Reggie. She had previously decided to stop writing. In fact she had written no new sf or fantasy stories in more than twenty years. Yet her stories, both sf and fantasy, remain popular and, fortunately, continue to appear in collections and anthologies.

"Jirel Meets Magic" is a classic of sword-and-sorcery fantasy. It presents a full measure of rousing combat at the outset with the warrior-queen Jirel leading the men of her medieval kingdom of Joiry against the treacherous wizard-prince Giraud. After these initial bloody hackings, however, the tempo evens off and the focus shifts to an abundance of magic, as Jirel passes through an enchanted casement into an eerie fairyland to seek her revenge. The plot then becomes mainly an emotional and psychological conflict between Jirel and the fairy queen Jarisme.

The resolution to the conflict may seem a bit too simple, ultimately, but one hardly notices this. The fascinating magical appurtenances and the strangeness of this secondary world absorb the reader's attention. There is a kaleidoscopic procession of sensuous imagery. And there is the ingeniously handled image of the door, as one observes or passes through a succession of otherworld portals until arriving with Jirel at the entrance to the domain of the no-God. As Jirel—and Jarisme—discover, it is tempting fate to tamper with this entryway.

Jirel Meets Magic

C. L. Moore

Over Guischard's fallen drawbridge thundered Joiry's warrior lady, sword swinging, voice shouting hoarsely inside her helmet. The scarlet plume of her crest rippled in the wind. Straight into the massed defenders at the gate she plunged, careering through them by the very impetuosity of the charge, the weight of her mighty warhorse opening up a gap for the men at her heels to widen. For a while there was tumult unspeakable there under the archway, the yells of fighters and the clang of mail on mail and the screams of stricken men. Jirel of Joiry was a shouting battle-machine from which Guischard's men reeled in bloody confusion as she whirled and slashed and slew in the narrow confines of the gateway, her great stallion's iron hoofs weapons as potent as her own whistling blade.

In her full armor she was impregnable to the men on foot, and the horse's armor protected him from their vengeful blades, so that alone, almost, she might have won the gateway. By sheer weight and impetuosity she carried the battle through the defenders under the arch. They gave way before the mighty war-horse and his screaming rider. Jirel's swinging sword and the stallion's trampling feet cleared a path for Joiry's men to follow, and at last into Guischard's court poured the steel-clad hordes of Guischard's conquerors.

Jirel's eyes were yellow with blood-lust behind the helmet bars, and her voice echoed savagely from the steel cage that confined it, "Giraud! Bring me Giraud! A gold piece to the man who brings me the wizard Giraud!"

She waited impatiently in the courtyard, reining her

162

excited charger in mincing circles over the flags, unable to dismount alone in her heavy armor and disdainful of the threats of possible arbalesters in the arrow-slits that looked down upon her from Guischard's frowning gray walls. A crossbow shaft was the only thing she had to fear in her impregnable mail.

She waited in mounting impatience, a formidable figure in her bloody armor, the great sword lying across her saddlebow and her eager, angry voice echoing hoarsely from the helmet, "Giraud! Make haste, you varlets! Bring me Giraud!

There was such bloodthirsty impatience in that hollowly booming voice that the men who were returning from searching the castle hung back as they crossed the court toward their lady in reluctant twos and threes, failure eloquent upon their faces.

"What!" screamed Jirel furiously. "You, Giles! Have you brought me Giraud? Watkin! Where is that wizard Giraud? Answer me, I say!"

"We've scoured the castle, my lady," said one of the men fearfully as the angry voice paused. "The wizard is gone."

"Now God defend me!" groaned Joiry's lady. "God help a poor woman served by fools! Did you search among the slain?"

"We searched everywhere, Lady Jirel. Giraud has escaped us."

Jirel called again upon her Maker in a voice that was blasphemy in itself.

"Help me down, then, you hell-spawned knaves," she grated. "I'll find him myself. He must be here!"

With difficulty they got her off the sidling horse. It took two men to handle her, and a third to steady the charger. All the while they struggled with straps and buckles she cursed them hollowly, emerging limb by limb from the casing of steel and swearing with a soldier's fluency as the armor came away. Presently she stood free on the bloody flagstones, a slim, straight lady, keen as a blade, her red hair a flame to match the flame of her yellow eyes. Under the armor she wore a tunic of link-mail from the Holy Land, supple as silk and almost as light, and a doeskin shirt to protect the milky whiteness of her skin.

She was a creature of the wildest paradox, this warrior lady of Joiry, hot as a red coal, chill as steel, satiny of body and iron of soul. The set of her chin was firm, but her mouth betrayed a tenderness she would have died before admitting. But she was raging now.

"Follow me, then, fools!" she shouted. "I'll find that God-cursed wizard and split his head with this sword if it takes me until the day I die. I swear it. I'll teach him what it costs to ambush Joiry men. By heaven, he'll pay with his life for my ten who fell at Massy Ford last week. The foul spell-brewer! He'll learn what it means to defy Joiry!"

Breathing threats and curses, she strode across the court, her men following reluctantly at her heels and casting nervous glances upward at the gray towers of Guischard. It had always borne a bad name, this ominous castle of the wizard Giraud, a place where queer things happened, which no man entered uninvited and whence no prisoner had ever escaped, though the screams of torture echoed often from its walls. Jirel's men would have followed her straight through the gates of hell, but they stormed Guischard at her heels with terror in their hearts and no hope of conquest.

She alone seemed not to know fear of the dark sorceror. Perhaps it was because she had known things so dreadful that mortal perils held no terror for her—there were whispers at Joiry of their lady, and of things that had happened there which no man dared think on. But when Guischard fell, and the wizard's defenders fled before Jirel's mighty steed and the onrush of Joiry's men, they had plucked up heart, thinking that perhaps the ominous tales of Giraud had been gossip only, since the castle fell as any ordinary lord's castle might fall. But now—there were whispers again, and nervous glances over the shoulder, and men huddled together as they re-entered Guischard at their lady's hurrying heels. A castle from which a wizard might vanish into thin air, with all the exits watched, must be a haunted place, better burned and forgotten. They followed Jirel reluctantly, half ashamed but fearful.

In Jirel's stormy heart there was no room for terror as she plunged into the gloom of the archway that opened upon Guischard's great central hall. Anger that the man might have escaped her was a torch to light the way, and she paused in the door with eager anticipation, sweeping the corpse-strewn hall at a glance, searching for some clue to explain how her quarry had disappeared.

"He can't have escaped," she told herself confidently. "There's no way out. He *must* be here somewhere." And she stepped into the hall, turning over the bodies she passed with a careless foot to make sure that death had not robbed her of vengeance.

An hour later, as they searched the last tower, she was still telling herself that the wizard could not have gone without her knowledge. She had taken special pains about that. There was a secret passage to the river, but she had had that watched. And an underwater door opened into the moat, but he could not have gone that way without meeting her men. Secret paths and open, she had found them all and posted a guard at each, and Giraud had not left the castle by any door that led out. She climbed the stairs of the last tower wearily, her confidence shaken.

An iron-barred oaken door closed the top of the steps, and Jirel drew back as her men lifted the heavy crosspieces and opened it for her. It had not been barred from within. She stepped into the little round room inside, hope fading completely as she saw that it too was empty, save for the body of a page-boy lying on the uncarpeted floor. Blood had made a congealing pool about him, and as Jirel looked she saw something which roused her flagging hopes. Feet had trodden in that blood, not the mailed feet of armed men, but the tread of shapeless cloth shoes such as surely none but Giraud would have worn when the castle was besieged and falling, and every man's help needed. Those bloody tracks led straight across the room toward the wall, and in that wall—a window.

Jirel stared. To her a window was a narrow slit deep in stone, made for the shooting of arrows, and never covered save in the coldest weather. But this window was broad and low, and instead of the usual animal pelt for hangings a curtain of purple velvet had been drawn back to disclose shutters carved out of something that might have been ivory had any beast alive been huge enough to yield such great unbroken sheets of whiteness. The shutters were unlatched, swinging slightly ajar, and upon them Jirel saw the smear of bloody fingers.

With a little triumphant cry she sprang forward. Here, then, was the secret way Giraud had gone. What lay beyond the window she could not guess. Perhaps an unsuspected passage, or a hidden room. Laughing exultantly, she swung open the ivory shutters.

There was a gasp from the men behind her. She did not hear it. She stood quite still, staring with incredulous eyes. For those ivory gates had opened upon no dark stone hiding-place or secret tunnel. They did not even reveal the afternoon sky outside, nor did they admit the shouts of her men still subduing the last of the defenders in the court below. Instead she was looking out upon a green woodland over which brooded a violet day like no day she had ever seen before. In paralyzed amazement she looked down, seeing not the bloody flags of the courtyard far below, but a mossy carpet at a level with the floor. And on that moss she saw the mark of blood-stained feet. This window might be a magic one, opening into strange lands, but through it had gone the man she swore to kill, and where he fled she must follow.

She lifted her eyes from the tracked moss and stared out again through the dimness under the trees. It was a lovelier land than anything seen even in dreams; so lovely that it made her heart ache with its strange, unearthly enchantment—green woodland hushed and brooding in the hushed violet day. There was a promise of peace there, and forgetfulness and rest. Suddenly the harsh, shouting, noisy world behind her seemed very far away and chill. She moved forward and laid her hand upon the ivory shutters, staring out.

The shuffle of the scared men behind her awakened Jirel from the enchantment that had gripped her. She turned. The dreamy magic of the woodland loosed its hold as she faced the men again, but its memory lingered. She shook her red head a little, meeting their fearful eyes. She nodded toward the open window.

"Giraud has gone out there," she said. "Give me your dagger, Giles. This sword is too heavy to carry far."

"But lady—Lady Jirel—dear lady—you can't go out there—Saint Guilda save us! Lady Jirel!"

Jirel's crisp voice cut short the babble of protest.

"Your dagger, Giles. I've sworn to slay Giraud, and slay him I shall, in whatever land he hides. Giles!"

A man-at-arms shuffled forward with averted face, handing her his dagger. She gave him the sword she carried and thrust the long-bladed knife into her belt. She turned again to the window. Green and cool and lovely, the woodland lay waiting. She thought as she set her knee upon the sill that she must have explored this violet calm even had her oath not driven her; for there was an enchantment about the place that drew her irresistibly. She pulled up her other knee and jumped lightly. The mossy ground received her without a jar.

For a few moments Jirel stood very still, watching, listening. Bird songs trilled intermittently about her, and breezes stirred the leaves. From very far away she thought she caught the echoes of a song when the wind blew, and there was something subtly irritating about its simple melody that seemed to seesaw endlessly up and down on two notes. She was glad when the wind died and the song no longer shrilled in her ears.

It occurred to her that before she ventured far she must mark the window she had entered by, and she turned curiously, wondering how it looked from this side. What she saw sent an inexplicable little chill down her back. Behind her lay a heap of moldering ruins, moss-grown, crumbling into decay. Fire had blackened the stones in ages past. She could see that it must have been a castle, for the original lines of it were not yet quite lost. Only one low wall remained standing now, and in it opened the window through which she had come. There was something hauntingly familiar about the lines of those moldering stones, and she turned away with a vague unease, not quite understanding why. A little path wound away under the low-hanging trees, and she followed it slowly, eyes alert for signs that Giraud had passed this way. Birds trilled drowsily in the leaves overhead, queer, unrecognizable songs like the music of no birds she knew. The violet light was calm and sweet about her.

She had gone on in the bird-haunted quiet for many

minutes before she caught the first hint of anything at
odds with the perfect peace about her. A whiff of woodsmoke drifted to her nostrils on a vagrant breeze. When
she rounded the next bend of the path she saw what had
caused it. A tree lay across the way in a smother of shaking leaves and branches. She knew that she must skirt it,
for the branches were too tangled to penetrate, and she
turned out of the path, following the trunk toward
its broken base.

She had gone only a few steps before the sound of a
curious sobbing came to her ears. It was the gasp of
choked breathing, and she had heard sounds like that too
often before not to know that she approached death in
some form or another. She laid her hand on her knife-hilt
and crept forward softly.

The tree trunk had been severed as if by a blast of
heat, for the stump was charred black and still smoking.
Beyond the stump a queer tableau was being enacted, and
she stopped quite still, staring through the leaves.

Upon the moss a naked girl was lying, gasping her life
out behind the hands in which her face was buried. There
was no mistaking the death-sound in that failing breath,
although her body was unmarked. Hair of a strange
green-gold pallor streamed over her bare white body, and
by the fragility and tenuosity of that body Jirel knew that
she could not be wholly human.

Above the dying girl a tall woman stood. And that
woman was a magnet for Jirel's fascinated eyes. She was
generously curved, sleepy-eyed. Black hair bound her
head sleekly, and her skin was like rich, dark, creamy
velvet. A violet robe wrapped her carelessly, leaving arms
and one curved shoulder bare, and her girdle was a snake
of something like purple glass. It might have been carved
from some vast jewel, save for its size and unbroken clarity. Her feet were thrust bare into silver sandals. But it
was her face that held Jirel's yellow gaze.

The sleepy eyes under heavily drooping lids were purple as gems, and the darkly crimson mouth curled in a
smile so hateful that fury rushed up in Jirel's heart as she
watched. That lazy purple gaze dwelt aloofly upon the

gasping girl on the moss. The woman was saying in a voice as rich and deep as thick-piled velvet,

"—nor will any other of the dryad folk presume to work forbidden magic in my woodlands for a long, long while to come. Your fate shall be a deadly example to them, Irsla. You dared too greatly. None who defy Jarisme live. Hear me, Irsla!"

The sobbing breath had slowed as the woman spoke, as if life were slipping fast from the dryad-girl on the moss; and as she realized it the speaker's arm lifted and a finger of white fire leaped from her outstretched hand, stabbing the white body at her feet. And the girl Irsla started like one shocked back into life.

"Hear me out, dryad! Let your end be a warning to—"

The girl's quickened breath slowed again as the white brilliance left her, and again the woman's hand rose, again the light-blade stabbed. From behind her shielding hands the dryad gasped,

"Oh, mercy, mercy, Jarisme! Let me die!"

"When I have finished. Not before. Life and death are mine to command here, and I am not yet done with you. Your stolen magic—"

She paused, for Irsla had slumped once more upon the moss, breath scarcely stirring her. As Jarisme's light-dealing hand rose for the third time Jirel leapt forward. Partly it was intuitive hatred of the lazy-eyed woman, partly revolt at this cat-and-mouse play with a dying girl for victim. She swung her arm in an arc that cleared the branches from her path, and called out in her clear, strong voice.

"Have done, woman! Let her die in peace."

Slowly Jarisme's purple eyes rose. They met Jirel's hot yellow glare. Almost physical impact was in that first meeting of their eyes, and hatred flashed between them instantly, like the flash of blades—the instinctive hatred of total opposites, born enemies. Each stiffened subtly, as cats do in the instant before combat. But Jirel thought she saw in the purple gaze, behind all its kindling anger, a faint disquiet, a nameless uncertainty.

"Who are you?" asked Jarisme, very softly, very dangerously.

Something in that unsureness behind her angry eyes
prompted Jirel to answer boldly,

"Jirel of Joiry. I seek the wizard Giraud, who fled me
here. Stop tormenting that wretched girl and tell me where
to find him. I can make it worth your while."

Her tone was imperiously mandatory, and behind
Jarisme's drooping lips an answering flare of anger
lighted, almost drowning out that faint unease.

"You do not know me," she observed, her voice very
gentle. "I am the sorceress Jarisme, and high ruler over
all this land. Did you think to buy me, then, earth-
woman?"

Jirel smiled her sweetest, most poisonous smile.

"You will forgive me," she purred. "At the first glance
at you I did not think your price could be high. . . ."

A petty malice had inspired the speech, and Jirel was
sorry as it left her lips, for she knew that the scorn
which blazed up in Jarisme's eyes was justified. The
sorceress made a contemptuous gesture of dismissal.

"I shall waste no more of my time here," she said. "Get
back to your little lands, Jirel of Joiry, and tempt me no
further."

The purple gaze rested briefly on the motionless dryad
at her feet, flicked Jirel's hot eyes with a glance of scorn
which yet did not wholly hide that curious uncertainty
in its depths. One hand slid behind her, oddly as if she
were seeking a door-latch in empty air. Then like a heat-
shimmer the air danced about her, and in an instant she
was gone.

Jirel blinked. Her ears had deceived her as well as her
eyes, she thought, for as the sorceress vanished a door
closed softly somewhere. Yet look though she would, the
green glade was empty, the violet air untroubled. No
Jarisme anywhere—no door. Jirel shrugged after a moment's bewilderment. She had met magic before.

A sound from the scarcely breathing girl upon the moss
distracted her, and she dropped to her knees beside the
dying dryad. There was no mark or wound upon her, yet
Jirel knew that death could be only a matter of moments.
And dimly she recalled that, so legend said, a tree-sprite

never survived the death of its tree. Gently she turned the girl over, wondering if she were beyond help.

At the feel of those gentle hands the dryad's lids quivered and rose. Brook-brown eyes looked up at Jirel, with green swimming in their deeps like leaf-reflections in a woodland pool.

"My thanks to you," faltered the girl in a ghostly murmur. "But get you back to your home now—before Jarisme's anger slays you."

Jirel shook her red head stubbornly.

"I must find Giraud first, and kill him, as I have sworn to do. But I will wait. Is there anything I can do?"

The green-reflecting eyes searched hers for a moment. The dryad must have read resolution there, for she shook her head a little.

"I must die—with my tree. But if you are determined—hear me. I owe you—a debt. There is a talisman—braided in my hair. When I—am dead—take it. It is Jarisme's sign. All her subjects wear them. It will guide you to her—and to Giraud. He is ever beside her. I know. I think it was her anger at you—that made her forget to take it from me, after she had dealt me my death. But why she did not slay you—I do not know. Jarisme is quick—to kill. No matter—listen now. If you must have Giraud—you must take a risk that no one here—has ever taken—before. Break this talisman—at Jarisme's feet. I do not know—what will happen then. Something—very terrible. It releases powers—even she can not control. It may—destroy you too. But—it is—a chance. May you—have—all good—"

The faltering voice failed. Jirel, bending her head, caught only meaningless murmurs that trailed away to nothing. The green-gold head dropped suddenly forward on her sustaining arm. Through the forest all about her went one long, quivering sigh, as if an intangible breeze ruffled the trees. Yet no leaves stirred.

Jirel bent and kissed the dryad's forehead, then laid her very gently back on the moss. And as she did so her hand in the masses of strangely colored hair came upon something sharp and hard. She remembered the talisman. It tingled in her fingers as she drew it out—an odd little

jagged crystal sparkling with curious aliveness from the
fire burning in its heart.

When she had risen to her feet, leaving the dead dryad
lying upon the moss which seemed so perfectly her couch,
she saw that the inner brilliance streaming in its wedge-
shaped pattern through the crystal was pointing a quivering apex forward and to the right. Irsla had said it would
guide her. Experimentally she twisted her hand to the left.
Yes, the shaking light shifted within the crystal, pointing
always toward the right, and Jarisme.

One last long glance she gave to the dryad on the moss.
Then she set off again down the path, the little magical
thing stinging her hand as she walked. And as she went
she wondered. This strong hatred which had flared so
instinctively between her and the sorceress was hot
enough to burn any trace of fear from her mind, and she
remembered that look of uncertainty in the purple gaze
that had shot such hatred at her. Why? Why had she not
been slain as Irsla was slain, for defiance of this queer
land's ruler?

For a while she paced unheedingly along under the
trees. Then abruptly the foliage ceased and a broad meadow lay before her, green in the clear, violet day. Beyond
the meadow the slim shaft of a tower rose dazzlingly
white, and toward it in steady radiance that magical
talisman pointed.

From very far away she thought she still caught the
echoes of that song when the wind blew, an irritating
monotony that made her ears ache. She was glad when
the wind died and the song no longer shrilled in her ears.

Out across the meadow she went. Far ahead she could
make out purple mountains like low clouds on the horizon, and here and there in the distances clumps of woodland dotted the meadows. She walked on more rapidly
now, for she was sure that the white tower housed
Jarisme, and with her Giraud. And she must have gone
more swiftly than she knew, for with almost magical
speed the shining shaft drew nearer.

She could see the arch of its doorway, bluely violet
within. The top of the shaft was battlemented, and she
caught splashes of color between the teeth of the stone
scarps, as if flowers were massed there and spilling blos-

soms against the whiteness of the tower. The singsong music was louder than ever, and much nearer. Jirel's heart beat a bit heavily as she advanced, wondering what sort of a sorceress this Jarisme might be, what dangers lay before her in the path of her vow's fulfillment. Now the white tower rose up over her, and she was crossing the little space before the door, peering in dubiously. All she could see was dimness and violet mist.

She laid her hand upon the dagger, took a deep breath and stepped boldly in under the arch. In the instant her feet left the solid earth she saw that this violet mist filled the whole shaft of the tower, that there was no floor. Emptiness engulfed her, and all reality ceased.

She was falling through clouds of violet blankness, but in no recognizable direction. It might have been up, down, or sidewise through space. Everything had vanished in the violet nothing. She knew an endless moment of vertigo and rushing motion; then the dizzy emptiness vanished in a breath and she was standing in a gasping surprise upon the roof of Jarisme's tower.

She knew where she was by the white battlements ringing her round, banked with strange blossoms in muted colors. In the center of the circular, marble-paved place a low couch, cushioned in glowing yellow, stood in the midst of a heap of furs. Two people sat side by side on the couch. One was Giraud. Black-robed, dark-visaged, he stared at Jirel with a flicker of disquiet in his small, dull eyes. He said nothing.

Jirel dismissed him with a glance, scarcely realizing his presence. For Jarisme had lowered from her lips a long, silver flute. Jirel realized that the queer, maddening music must have come from that gleaming length, for it no longer echoed in her ears. Jarisme was holding the instrument now in midair, regarding Jirel over it with a purple-eyed gaze that was somehow thoughtful and a little apprehensive, though anger glowed in it, too.

"So," she said richly, in her slow, deep voice. "For the second time you defy me."

At these words Giraud turned his head sharply and stared at the sorceress' impassive profile. She did not return his gaze, but after a moment he looked quickly

back at Jirel, and in his eyes too she saw that flicker of
alarm, and with it a sort of scared respect. It puzzled her,
and she did not like being puzzled. She said a little breath-
lessly,

"If you like, yes. Give me that skulking potion-brewer
beside you and set me down again outside this damned
tower of trickery. I came to kill your pet spellmonger
here for treachery done me in my own world by this
creature who dared not stay to face me."

Her peremptory words hung in the air like the echoes
of a gong. For a while no one spoke. Jarisme smiled
more subtly than before, an insolent, slow smile that made
Jirel's pulses hammer with the desire to smash it down
the woman's lush, creamy throat. At last Jarisme said, in
a voice as rich and deep as thick-piled velvet,

"Hot words, hot words, soldier-woman! Do you really
imagine that your earthly squabbles matter to Jarisme?"

"What matters to Jarisme is of little moment to me,"
Jirel said contemptuously. "All I want is this skulker here,
whom I have sworn to kill."

Jarisme's slow smile was maddening. "You demand it
of me—Jarisme?" she asked with soft incredulity. "Only
fools offend me, woman, and they but once. None com-
mands me. You will have to learn that."

Jirel smiled thinly. "At what price, then, do you value
your pet cur?"

Giraud half rose from the couch at that last insult, his
dark face darker with a surge of anger. Jarisme pushed
him back with a lazy hand.

"This is between your—friend—and me," she said. "I
do not think, soldier"—the appellation was the deadliest
of insults in the tone she used—"that any price you could
offer would interest me."

"And yet your interest is very easily caught." Jirel
flashed a contemptuous glance at Giraud, restive under
the woman's restraining hand.

Jarisme's rich pallor flushed a little. Her voice was
sharper as she said,

"Do not tempt me too far, earthling."

Jirel's yellow eyes defied her. "I am not afraid."

The sorceress' purple gaze surveyed her slowly. When

Jarisme spoke again a tinge of reluctant admiration lightened the slow scorn of her voice.

"No—you are not afraid. And a fool not to be. Fools annoy me, Jirel of Joiry."

She laid the flute down on her knee and hazily lifted a ringless hand. Anger was glowing in her eyes now, blotting out all trace of that little haunting fear. But Giraud caught the rising hand, bending, whispering urgently in her ear. Jirel caught a part of what he said, "—what happens to those who tamper with their own destiny—" And she saw the anger fade from the sorceress' face as apprehension brightened there again. Jarisme looked at Jirel with a long, hard look and shrugged her ample shoulders.

"Yes," she murmured. "Yes, Giraud. It is wisest so." And to Jirel, "Live, then, earthling. Find your way back to your own land if you can, but I warn you, do not trouble me again. I shall not stay my hand if our paths ever cross in the future."

She struck her soft, white palms together sharply. And at the sound the roof-top and the violet sky and the banked flowers at the parapets whirled around Jirel in dizzy confusion. From very far away she heard that clap of peremptory hands still echoing, but it seemed to her that the great, smokily colored blossoms were undergoing an inexplicable transformation. They quivered and spread and thrust upward from the edges of the tower to arch over her head. Her feet were pressing a mossy ground, and the sweet, earthy odors of a garden rose about her. Blinking, she stared around as the world slowly steadied.

She was no longer on the roof-top. As far as she could see through the tangled stems, great flowering plants sprang up in the gloaming of a strange, enchanted forest. She was completely submerged in greenery, and the illusion of under-water filled her eyes, for the violet light that filtered through the leaves was diffused and broken into a submarine dimness. Uncertainly she began to grope her way forward, staring about to see what sort of a miracle had enfolded her.

It was a bower in fairyland. She had come into a tropical garden of great, muted blooms and jungle silences. In the diffused light the flowers nodded sleepily among the leaves, hypnotically lovely, hypnotically soporific with their soft colors and drowsy, never-ending motion. The fragrance was overpowering. She went on slowly, treading moss that gave back no sound. Here under the canopy of leaves was a little separate world of color and silence and perfume. Dreamily she made her way among the flowers.

Their fragrance was so strongly sweet that it went to her head, and she walked in a waking dream. Because of this curious, scented trance in which she went she was never quite sure if she had actually seen that motion among the leaves, and looked closer, and made out a huge, incredible serpent of violet transparency, a giant replica of the snake that girdled Jarisme's waist, but miraculously alive, miraculously supple and gliding, miraculously twisting its soundless way among the blossoms and staring at her with impassive, purple eyes.

While it glided along beside her she had other strange visions too, and could never remember just what they were, or why she caught familiar traces in the tiny, laughing faces that peered at her from among the flowers, or half believed the wild, impossible things they whispered to her, their laughing mouths brushing her ears as they leaned down among the blossoms.

The branches began to thin at last, as she neared the edge of the enchanted place. She walked slowly, half conscious of the great transparent snake like a living jewel writhing along soundlessly at her side, her mind vaguely troubled in its dream by the fading remembrance of what those little, merry voices had told her. When she came to the very edge of the bowery jungle and broke out into clear daylight again she stopped in a daze, staring round in the brightening light as the perfumes slowly cleared from her head.

Sanity and realization returned to her at last. She shook her red head dizzily and looked round, half expecting, despite her returning clarity, to see the great serpent gliding across the grass. But there was nothing. Of course she had dreamed. Of course those little laughing voices had not told her that—that—she clutched after the vanishing tags of remembrance, and caught nothing. Ruefully she laughed and brushed away the clinging memories, looking round to see where she was.

She stood at the crest of a little hill. Below her the flower-fragrant jungle nodded, a little patch of enchanted greenery clothing the slopes of the hill. Beyond and below green meadows stretched away to a far-off line of forest which she thought she recognized as that in which she had first met Jarisme. But the white tower which had risen in the midst of the meadows was magically gone. Where it had stood, unbroken greenery lay under the violet clarity of the sky.

As she stared round in bewilderment a faint prickling stung her palm, and she glanced down, remembering the talisman clutched in her hand. The quivering light was streaming in a long wedge toward some point behind her. She turned. She was in the foothills of those purple mountains she had glimpsed from the edge of the woods. High and shimmering, they rose above her. And, hazily in the heat-waves that danced among their heights, she saw the tower.

Jirel groaned to herself. Those peaks were steep and rocky. Well, no help for it. She must climb. She growled a soldier's oath in her throat and turned wearily toward the rising slopes. They were rough and deeply slashed with ravines. Violet heat beat up from the reflecting rocks, and tiny, brilliantly colored things scuttled from her path—orange lizards and coral red scorpions and little snakes like bright blue jewels.

It seemed to her as she stumbled upward among the broken stones that the tower was climbing too. Time after time she gained upon it, and time after time when she lifted her eyes after a grueling struggle up steep ravines, that mocking flicker of whiteness shimmered still high and unattainable on some distant peak. It had the mistiness of unreality, and if her talisman's guide had not pointed steadily upward she would have thought it an illusion to lead her astray.

But after what seemed hours of struggle, there came the time when, glancing up, she saw the shaft rising on the topmost peak of all, white as snow against the clear violet sky. And after that it shifted no more. She took heart now, for at last she seemed to be gaining. Every laborious step carried her nearer that lofty shining upon the mountain's highest peak.

She paused after a while, looking up and wiping the moisture from her forehead where the red curls clung. As she stood there something among the rocks moved, and out from behind a boulder a long, slinking feline creature came. It was not like any beast she had ever seen before. Its shining pelt was fabulously golden, brocaded with queer patterns of darker gold, and down against its heavy jaws curved two fangs whiter than ivory. With a grace as gliding as water it paced down the ravine toward her.

Jirel's heart contracted. Somehow she found the knife-hilt in her hand, though she had no recollection of having drawn it. She was staring hard at the lovely and terrible cat, trying to understand the haunting familiarity about its eyes. They were purple, like jewels. Slowly recognition dawned. She had met that purple gaze before, insolent under sleepy lids. Jarisme's eyes. Yes, and the snake in her dream had watched her with a purple stare too. Jarisme?

She closed her hand tightly about the crystal, knowing that she must conceal from the sorceress her one potent weapon, waiting until the time came to turn it against its maker. She shifted her knife so that light glinted down the blade. They stood quite still for a moment, yellow-eyed woman and fabulous, purple-eyed cat, staring at each other with hostility eloquent in every line of each. Jirel clenched her knife tight, warily eyeing the steel-clawed paws on which the golden beast went so softly. They could have ripped her to ribbons before the blade struck home.

She saw a queer expression flicker across the somber purple gaze that met hers, and the beautiful cat crouched a little, tail jerking, lip twitched back to expose shining fangs. It was about to spring. For an interminable moment she waited for that hurtling golden death to launch itself upon her, tense, rigid, knife steady in her hand. . . .

It sprang. She dropped to one knee in the split second of its leaping, instinctively hiding the crystal, but thrusting up her dagger in defense. The great beast sailed easily over her head. As it hurtled past, a peal of derisive laughter rang in her ears, and she heard quite clearly the sound of a slamming door. She scrambled up and whirled in one motion, knife ready. The defile was quite empty in the violet day. There was no door anywhere. Jarisme had vanished.

A little shaken, Jirel sheathed her blade. She was not afraid. Anger burned out all trace of fear as she remembered the scorn in that ringing laugh. She took up her course again toward the tower, white and resolute, not looking back.

The tower was drawing near again. She toiled upward. Jarisme showed no further sign of her presence, but Jirel felt eyes upon her, purple eyes, scornful and sleepy. She could see the tower clearly, just above her at the crest of the highest peak, up to which a long arc of steps curved steeply. They were very old, these steps, so worn that many were little more than irregularities on the stone. Jirel wondered what feet had worn them so, to what door they had originally led.

She was panting when she reached the top and peered in under the arch of the door. To her surprise she found herself staring into a broad, semicircular hallway, whose walls were lined with innumerable doors. She remembered the violet nothingness into which she had stepped the last time she crossed the sill, and wondered as she thrust a tentative foot over it if the hall were an illusion and she were really about to plunge once more into that cloudy abyss of falling. But the floor was firm.

She stepped inside and paused, looking round in some bewilderment and wondering where to turn now. She could smell peril in the air. Almost she could taste the magic that hovered like a mist over the whole enchanted place. Little warning prickles ran down her back as she went forward very softly and pushed open one of those innumerable doors. Behind it a gallery stretched down miles of haze-shrouded extent. Arrow-straight it ran, the arches of the ceiling making an endless parade that melted into violet distance. And as she stood looking down the cloudy vista, something like a puff of smoke obscured her vision for an instant—smoke that eddied and billowed and rolled away from the shape of that golden cat which had vanished in the mountain ravine.

It paced slowly down the hall toward her, graceful and lovely, muscles rippling under the brocaded golden coat and purple eyes fixed upon her in a scornful stare. Jirel's hand went to the knife in her belt, hatred choking up in her throat as she met the purple eyes. But in the corridor a voice was echoing softly, Jarisme's voice, saying,

"Then it is war between us, Jirel of Joiry. For you have defied my mercy, and you must be punished. Your punishment I have chosen—the simplest, and the subtlest, and the most terrible of all punishments, the worst that could befall a human creature. Can you guess it? No? Then wonder a while, for I am not prepared yet to administer it fully . . . or shall I kill you now? Eh-h-h? . . ."

Th curious, long-drawn query melted into a purring snarl, and the great cat's lip lifted, a flare of murderous light flaming up in the purple eyes. It had been pacing nearer all the while that light voice had echoed in the air. Now its roar crescendoed into a crashing thunder that rang from the walls, and the steel springs of its golden body tightened for a leap straight at Jirel's throat. Scarcely a dozen paces away, she saw the brocaded beauty of it crouching, taut and poised, saw the powerful body quiver and tighten—and spring. In instinctive panic she leaped back and slammed the door in its face.

Derisive laughter belled through the air. A cloud of thin smoke eddied through the crack around the door and puffed in her face with all the insolence of a blow. Then the air was clear again. The red mist of murder swam before Jirel's eyes. Blind with anger, breath beating thickly in her throat, she snatched at the door again, ripping the dagger from her belt. Through that furious haze she glared down the corridor. It was empty. She closed the door a second time and leaned against it, trembling with anger, until the mist had cleared from her head and she could control her shaking hand well enough to replace the dagger.

When she had calmed a little she turned to scan the hall, wondering what to do next. And she saw that there was no escape now, even had she wished, for the door she had entered by was gone. All about her now closed the door-studded walls, enigmatic, imprisoning. And the very fact of their presence was an insult, suggesting that

Jarisme had feared she would flee if the entrance were left open. Jirel forced herself into calmness again. She was not afraid, but she knew herself in deadly peril.

She was revolving the sorceress' threat as she cast about for some indication to guide her next step. The simplest and subtlest and most terrible of punishments—what could it be? Jirel knew much of the ways of torture—her dungeons were as blood-stained as any of her neighbors'—but she knew too that Jarisme had not meant only the pain of the flesh. There was a subtler menace in her words. It would be a feminine vengeance, and more terrible than anything iron and fire could inflict. She knew that. She knew also that no door she could open now would lead to freedom, but she could not stay quiet, waiting. She glanced along the rows of dark, identical panels. Anything that magic could contrive might lie behind them. In the face of peril more deadly than death she could not resist the temptation to pull open the nearest one and peer within.

A gust of wind blew in her face and rattled the door. Dust was in that wind, and bitter cold. Through an inner grille of iron, locked across the opening, she saw a dazzle of whiteness like sun on snow in the instant before she slammed the door shut on the piercing gust. But the incident had whetted her curiosity. She moved along the wall and opened another.

This time she was looking through another locked grille into a dimness of gray smoke shot through with flame. The smell of burning rose in her nostrils, and she could hear faintly, as from vast distances, the sound of groans and the shivering echo of screams. Shuddering, she closed the door.

When she opened the next one she caught her breath and stared. Before her a thick crystal door separated her from bottomless space. She pressed her face to the cold glass and stared out and down. Nothingness met her gaze. Dark and silence and the blaze of unwinking stars. It was day outside the tower, but she looked into fathomless night. And as she stared, a long streak of light flashed across the blackness and faded. It was not a shooting star. By straining her eyes she could make out something like a thin sliver of silver flashing across the dark, its flaming tail fading behind it in the sky. And the sight made her ill with sudden vertigo. Bottomless void reeled around her, and she fell back into the hallway, slamming the door upon that terrifying glimpse of starry nothingness.

It was several minutes before she could bring herself to try the next door. When she did, swinging it open timorously, a familiar sweetness of flower perfume floated out and she found herself gazing through a grille of iron bars deep into that drowsy jungle of blossoms and scent and silence which she had crossed at the mountain's foot. A wave of remembrance washed over her. For an instant she could hear those tiny, laughing voices again, and she felt the presence of the great snake at her side, and the wild, mirth-ridden secrets of the little gay voices rang in her ears. Then she was awake again, and the memory vanished as dreams do, leaving nothing but tantalizing fragments of forgotten secrets drifting through her mind. She knew as she stared that she could step straight into that flowery fairyland again if the bars would open. But there was no escape from this magical place, though she might look through any number of opening doors into far lands and near.

She was beginning to understand the significance of the hall. It must be from here that Jarisme by her magical knowledge journeyed into other lands and times and worlds through the doors that opened between her domain and those strange, outland places. Perhaps she had sorcerer friends there, and paid them visits and brought back greater knowledge, stepping from world to world, from century to century, through her enchanted doorways. Jirel felt certain that one of these enigmatic openings would give upon that mountain pass where the golden cat with its scornful purple eyes had sprung at her, and vanished, and laughed backward as the door slammed upon it, and upon the woodland glade where the dryad died. But she knew that bars would close these places away even if she could find them.

She went on with her explorations. One door opened upon a steamy fern-forest of gigantic growths, out of whose deeps floated musky, reptilian odors, and the distant sound of beasts bellowing hollowly. And another upon a gray desert stretching flat and lifeless to the horizon, wan under the light of a dim red sun.

But at last she came to one that opened not into alien lands but upon a stairway winding down into solid rock whose walls showed the mark of the tools that had hollowed them. No sound came up the shaft of the stairs, and a gray light darkened down their silent reaches. Jirel peered in vain for some hint of what lay below. But at last, because inactivity had palled upon her and she knew that all ways were hopeless for escape, she entered the doorway and went slowly down the steps. It occurred to her that possibly she might find Jarisme below, engaged in some obscure magic in the lower regions, and she was eager to come to grips with her enemy.

The light darkened as she descended, until she was groping her way through obscurity round and round the curving stairs. When the steps ended at a depth she could not guess, she could tell that she had emerged into a low-roofed corridor only by feeling the walls and ceiling that met her exploring hands, for the thickest dark hid everything. She made her slow way along the stone hall, which wound and twisted and dipped at unexpected angles until she lost all sense of direction. But she knew she had gone a long way when she began to see the faint gleam of light ahead.

Presently she began to catch the faraway sound of a familiar song—Jarisme's monotonous little flute melody on two notes, and she was sure then that her intuition had been true, that the sorceress was down here somewhere. She drew her dagger in the gloom and went on more warily.

An arched opening ended the passage. Through the arch poured a blaze of dancing white luminance. Jirel paused, blinking and trying to make out what strange place she was entering. The room before her was filled with the baffling glitter and shimmer and mirage of reflecting surfaces so bewilderingly that she could not tell which was real and which mirror, and which dancing light. The brilliance dazzled in her face and dimmed into twilight and blazed again as the mirrors shifted. Little currents of dark shivered through the chaos and brightened into white sparkle once more. That monotonous music came to her through the quivering lights and reflections, now strongly, now faintly in the distance.

The whole place was a chaos of blaze and confusion. She could not know if the room were small or large, a cavern or a palace hall. Queer reflections danced through the dazzle of it. She could see her own image looking back at her from a dozen, a score, a hundred moving planes that grotesquely distorted her and then flickered out again, casting a blaze of light in her blinded eyes. Dizzily she blinked into the reeling wilderness of planes.

Then she saw Jarisme in her violet robe watching her from a hundred identical golden couches reflected upon a hundred surfaces. The figure held a flute to its lips, and the music pulsed from it in perfect time with the pulsing of the sorceress' swelling white throat. Jirel stared round in confusion at the myriad Jarismes all piping the interminable monotones. A hundred sensual, dreamy faces turned to her, a hundred white arms dropped as the flute left a hundred red mouths that Jarisme might smile ironic welcome a hundredfold more scornful for its multiplicity.

When the music ceased, all the flashing dazzle suddenly stilled. Jirel blinked as the chaos resolved itself into shining order, the hundred Jarismes merging into one sleepy-eyed woman lounging upon her golden couch in a vast crystal-walled chamber shaped like the semicircular half of a great, round, domed room. Behind the couch a veil of violet mist hung like a curtain shutting off what would have formed the other half of the circular room.

"Enter," said the sorceress with the graciousness of one who knows herself in full command of the situation. "I thought you might find the way here. I am preparing a ceremony which will concern you intimately. Perhaps you would like to watch? This is to be an experiment, and for that reason a greater honor is to be yours than you can ever have known before; for the company I am assembling to watch your punishment is a more distinguished one than you could understand. Come here, inside the circle."

Jirel advanced, dagger still clenched in one hand, the other closed about her bit of broken crystal. She saw now that the couch stood in the center of a ring engraved in the floor with curious, cabalistic symbols. Beyond it the cloudy violet curtain swayed and eddied within itself, a vast, billowing wall of mist. Dubiously she stepped over the circle and stood eyeing Jarisme, her yellow gaze hot with rigidly curbed emotion. Jarisme smiled and lifted the flute to her lips again.

As the irritating two notes began their seesawing tune Jirel saw something amazing happen. She knew then that the flute was a magic one, and the song magical too. The notes took on a form that overstepped the boundaries of the aural and partook in some inexplicable way of all the other senses too. She could feel them, taste them, smell them, see them. In a queer way they were visible, pouring in twos from the flute and dashing outward like little needles of light. The walls reflected them, and those reflections became swifter and brighter and more numerous until the air was full of flying slivers of silvery brilliance, until shimmers began to dance among them and over them, and that bewildering shift of mirrored planes started up once more. Again reflections crossed and dazzled and multiplied in the shining air as the flute poured out its flashing double notes.

Jirel forgot the sorceress beside her, the music that grated on her ears, even her own peril, in watching the pictures that shimmered and vanished in the mirrored surfaces. She saw flashes of scenes she had glimpsed through the doors of Jarisme's hallway. She saw stranger places than that, passing in instant-brief snatches over the silvery planes. She saw jagged black mountains with purple dawns rising behind them and stars in unknown figures across the dark skies; she saw gray seas flat and motionless beneath gray clouds; she saw smooth meadows rolling horizonward under the glare of double suns. All these and many more awoke to the magic of Jarisme's flute, and melted again to give way to others.

Jirel had the strange fancy, as the music went on, that it was audible in those lands whose brief pictures were flickering across the background of its visible notes. It seemed to be piercing immeasurable distances, ringing across the cloudy seas, echoing under the double suns, calling insistently in strange lands and far, unknown places, over deserts and mountains that man's feet had

never trod, reaching other worlds and other times and
crying its two-toned monotony through the darkness of
interstellar space. All of this, to Jirel, was no more than a
vague realization that it must be so. It meant nothing to
her, whose world was a flat plane arched by the heaven-
pierced bowl of the sky. Magic, she told herself, and gave
up trying to understand.

Presently the tempo of the fluting changed. The same
two notes still shrilled endlessly up and down, but it was
no longer a clarion call ringing across borderlands into
strange worlds. Now it was slower, statelier. And the
notes of visible silver that had darted crazily against the
crystal walls and reflected back again took on an order
that ranked them into one shining plane. Upon that plane
Jirel saw the outlines of a familiar scene gradually take
shape. The great door-lined hall above mirrored itself in
faithful replica before her eyes. The music went on
changelessly.

Then, as she watched, one of those innumerable doors
quivered. She held her breath. Slowly it swung open upon
that gray desert under the red sun which she had seen
before she closed it quickly away behind concealing panels. Again as she looked, that sense of utter desolation
and weariness and despair came over her, so uncannily
dreary was the scene. Now the door stood wide, its locked
grille no longer closing it, and as the music went on she
could see a dazzle like a jagged twist of lightning begin to
shimmer in its aperture. The gleam strengthened. She
saw it quiver once, twice, then sweep forward with blinding speed through the open doorway. And as she tried to
follow it with her eyes another moving door distracted
her.

This time the steamy fern-forest was revealed as the
panels swung back. But upon the threshold sprawled
something so frightful that Jirel's free hand flew to her
lips and a scream beat up in her throat. It was black—
shapeless and black and slimy. And it was alive. Like a
heap of putrescently shining jelly it heaved itself over the
door-sill and began to flow across the floor, inching its
way along like a vast blind ameba. But she knew without
being told that it was horribly wise, horribly old. Behind
it a black trail of slime smeared the floor.

Jirel shuddered and turned her eyes away. Another door was swinging open. Through it she saw a place she had not chanced upon before, a country of bare red rock strewn jaggedly under a sky so darkly blue that it might have been black, with stars glimmering in it more clearly than stars of earth. Across this red, broken desert a figure came striding that she knew could be only a figment of magic, so tall it was, so spidery-thin, so grotesquely human despite its bulbous head and vast chest. She could not see it clearly, for about it like a robe it clutched a veil of blinding light. On those incredibly long, thin legs it stepped across the door-sill, drew its dazzling garment closer about it, and strode forward. As it neared, the light was so blinding that she could not look upon it. Her averted eyes caught the motion of a fourth door.

This time she saw that flowery ravine again, dim in its underwater illusion of diffused light. And out from among the flowers writhed a great serpent-creature, not of the transparent crystal she had seen in her dream, but iridescently scaled. Nor was it entirely serpent, for from the thickened neck sprang a head which could not be called wholly unhuman. The thing carried itself as proudly as a cobra, and as it glided across the threshold its single, many-faceted eye caught Jirel's in the reflection. The eye flashed once, dizzyingly, and she reeled back in sick shock, the violence of that glance burning through her veins like fire. When she regained control of herself many other doors were standing open upon scenes both familiar and strange. During her daze other denizens of those strange worlds must have entered at the call of the magic flute.

She was just in time to see an utterly indescribable thing flutter into the hall from a world which so violated her eyes that she got no more than a glimpse of it as she flung up outraged hands to shut it out. She did not lower that shield until Jarisme's amused voice said in an undertone, "Behold your audience, Jirel of Joiry," and she realized that the music had ceased and a vast silence was pressing against her ears. Then she looked out, and drew a long breath. She was beyond surprise and shock now, and she stared with the dazed incredulity of one who knows herself in a nightmare.

Ranged outside the circle that enclosed the two women sat what was surely the strangest company ever assembled. They were grouped with a queer irregularity which, though meaningless to Jirel, yet gave the impression of definite purpose and design. It had a symmetry so strongly marked that even though it fell outside her range of comprehension she could not but feel the rightness of it.

The light-robed dweller in the red barrens sat there, and the great black blob of shapeless jelly heaved gently on the crystal floor. She saw others she had watched enter, and many more. One was a female creature whose robe of peacock iridescence sprang from her shoulders in great drooping wings and folded round her like a bat's leathery cloak. And her neighbor was a fat gray slug of monster size, palpitating endlessly. One of the crowd looked exactly like a tall white lily swaying on a stalk of silver pallor, but from its chalice poured a light so ominously tinted that she shuddered and turned her eyes away.

Jarisme had risen from her couch. Very tall and regal in her violet robe, she rose against the back-drop of mist which veiled the other half of the room. As she lifted her arms, the incredible company turned to her with an eager expectancy. Jirel shuddered. Then Jarisme's flute spoke softly. It was a different sort of music from the clarion that called them together, from the stately melody which welcomed them through the opening doors. But it harped still on the two seesawing notes, with low, rippling sounds so different from the other two that Jirel marveled at the range of the sorceress' ability on the two notes.

For a few moments as the song went on, nothing happened. Then a motion behind Jarisme caught Jirel's eye. The curtain of violet mist was swaying. The music beat at it and it quivered to the tune. It shook within itself, and paled and thinned, and from behind it a light began to glow. Then on a last low monotone it dissipated wholly and Jirel was staring at a vast globe of quivering light which loomed up under the stupendous arch that soared outward to form the second half of the chamber.

As the last clouds faded she saw that the thing was a huge crystal sphere, rising upon the coils of a translucent purple base in the shape of a serpent. And in the heart of the globe burned a still flame, living, animate, instinct with a life so alien that Jirel stared in utter bewilderment. It was a thing she knew to be alive—yet she knew it could *not* be alive. But she recognized even in her daze of incomprehension its relation to the tiny fragment of crystal she clutched in her hand. In that too the still flame burned. It stung her hand faintly in reminder that she possessed a weapon which could destroy Jarisme, though it might destroy its wielder in the process. The thought gave her a sort of desperate courage.

Jarisme was ignoring her now. She had turned to face the great globe with lifted arms and shining head thrown back. And from her lips a piercingly sweet sound fluted, midway between hum and whistle. Jirel had the wild fancy that she could see that sound arrowing straight into the heart of the vast sphere bulking so high over them all. And in the heart of that still, living flame a little glow of red began to quiver.

Through the trembling air shrilled a second sound. From the corner of her eye Jirel could see that a dark figure had moved forward into the circle and fallen to its knees at the sorceress' side. She knew it for Giraud. Like two blades the notes quivered in the utter hush that lay upon the assembly, and in the globe that red glow deepened.

One by one, other voices joined the chorus, queer, uncanny sounds some of them, from throats not shaped for speech. No two voices blended. The chorus was one of single, unrelated notes. And as each voice struck the globe, the fire burned more crimson, until its still pallor had flushed wholly into red. High above the rest soared Jarisme's knife-keen fluting. She lifted her arms higher, and the voices rose in answer. She lowered them, and the blade-like music swooped down an almost visible arc to a lower key. Jirel felt that she could all but see the notes spearing straight from each singer into the vast sphere that dwarfed them all. There was no melody in it, but a sharply definite pattern as alien and unmistakable as the symmetry of their grouping in the room. And as Jarisme's arms rose, lifting the voices higher, the flame burned more deeply red, and paled again as the voices fell.

Three times that stately, violet-robed figure gestured with lifted arms, and three times the living flame deepened and paled. Then Jarisme's voice soared in a high, triumphant cry and she whirled with spread arms, facing the company. In one caught breath, all voices ceased. Silence fell upon them like a blow. Jarisme was no longer priestess, but goddess, as she fronted them in that dead stillness with exultant face and blazing eyes. And in one motion they bowed before her as corn bows under wind. Alien things, shapeless monsters, faceless, eyeless, unrecognizable creatures from unknowable dimensions, abased themselves to the crystal floor before the splendor of light in Jarisme's eyes. For a moment of utter silence the tableau held. Then the sorceress' arms fell.

Ripplingly the company rose. Beyond Jarisme the vast globe had paled again into that living, quiet flame of golden pallor. Immense, brooding, alive, it loomed up above them. Into the strained stillness Jarisme's low voice broke. She was speaking in Jirel's native tongue, but the air, as she went on, quivered thickly with something like waves of sound that were pitched for other organs than human ears. Every word that left her lips made another wave through the thickened air. The assembly shimmered before Jirel's eyes in that broken clarity as a meadow quivers under heat waves.

"Worshippers of the Light," said Jarisme sweetly, "be welcomed from your far dwellings into the presence of the Flame. We who serve it have called you to the worship, but before you return, another sort of ceremony is to be held, which we have felt will interest you all. For we have called it truly the simplest and subtlest and most terrible of all punishments for a human creature.

"It is our purpose to attempt a reversal of this woman's physical and mental self in such a way as to cause her body to become rigidly motionless while her mind—her soul—looks eternally backward along the path it has traveled. You who are human, or have known humanity, will understand what deadly torture that can be. For no human creature, by the laws that govern it, can have led a life whose intimate review is anything but pain. To be frozen into eternal reflections, reviewing all the futility and pain of life, all the pain that thoughtless or intentional acts have caused others, all the spreading consequences of every act—that, to a human being, would be the most dreadful of all torments."

In the silence that fell as her voice ceased, Giraud laid a hand on Jarisme's arm. Jirel saw terror in his eyes.

"Remember," he uttered, "remember, for those who tamper with their known destiny a more fearful thing may come than—"

Jarisme shrugged off the restraining hand impatiently. She turned to Jirel.

"Know, earthling," she said in a queerly strained voice, "that in the books of the future it is written that Jarisme the Sorceress must die at the hands of the one human creature who defies her thrice—and that human creature a woman. Twice I have been weak, and spared you. Once in the forest, once on the roof-top, you cast your puny defiance in my face, and I stayed my hand for fear of what is written. But the third time shall not come. Though you are my appointed slayer, you shall not slay. With my own magic I break Fate's sequence, now, and we shall see!"

In the blaze of her purple eyes Jirel saw that the moment had come. She braced herself, fingers closing about the fragment of crystal in her hand uncertainly as she hesitated, wondering if the time had come for the breaking of her talisman at the sorceress' feet. She hesitated too long, though her waiting was only a split second in duration. For Jarisme's magic was more supremely simple than Jirel could have guessed. The sorceress turned a blazing purple gaze upon her and sharply snapped her plump fingers in the earthwoman's face.

At the sound Jirel's whole world turned inside out about her. It was the sheerest physical agony. Everything vanished as that terrible shift took place. She felt her own body being jerked inexplicably around in a reversal like nothing that any living creature could ever have experienced before. It was a backward-facing in a direction which could have had no existence until that instant. She felt the newness in the second before sight came to her— a breathless, soundless, new-born *now* in which she was the first dweller, created simultaneously with the new plane of being. Then sight broke upon her consciousness.

The thing spread out before her was so stupendous

that she would have screamed if she had possessed an animate body. All life was open to her gaze. The sight was too immeasurable for her to grasp it fully—too vast for her human consciousness to look upon at all save in flashing shutter-glimpses without relation or significance. Motion and immobility existed simultaneously in the thing before her. Endless activity shuttling to and fro—yet the whole vast panorama was frozen in a timeless calm through which a mighty pattern ran whose very immensity was enough to strike terror into her soul. Threaded through it the backward trail of her own life stretched. As she gazed upon it such floods of conflicting emotion washed over her that she could not see anything clearly, but she was fiercely insisting to her inner consciousness that she would not—*would not*—look back, dared not, could not—and all the while her sight was running past days and weeks along the path which led inexorably toward the one scene she could not bear to think of.

Very remotely, as her conscious sight retraced the backward way, she was aware of overlapping planes of existence in the stretch of limitless activity before her. Shapes other than human, scenes that had no meaning to her, quivered and shifted and boiled with changing lives —yet lay motionless in the mighty pattern. She scarcely heeded them. For her, of all that panoramic impossibility one scene alone had meaning—the one scene toward which her sight was racing now, do what she would to stop it—the one scene that she knew she could never bear to see again.

Yet when her sight reached that place the pain did not begin at once. She gazed almost calmly upon that little interval of darkness and flaring light, the glare of torches shining upon a girl's bent red head and on a man's long body sprawled motionless upon flagstones. In the deepest stillness she stared. She felt no urge to look farther, on beyond the scene into the past. This was the climax, the center of all her life—this torch-lit moment on the flagstones. Vividly she was back again in the past, felt the hardness of the cold flags against her knees, and the numbness of her heart as she stared down into a dead man's face. Timelessly she dwelt upon that long-ago heartbreak, and within her something swelled unbearably.

That something was a mounting emotion too great to have name, too complexly blending agony and grief and hatred and love—and rebellion; so strong that all the rest of the stupendous thing before her was blotted out and the gathering storm of what seethed in her innermost consciousness. She was aware of nothing but that overwhelming emotion. And it was boiling into one great unbearable explosion of violence in which rage took precedence over all. Rage at life for permitting such pain to be. Rage at Jarisme for forcing her into memory. Such rage that everything shook before it, and melted and ran together in a heat of rebellion, and—something snapped. The panorama reeled and shivered and collapsed into the dark of semi-oblivion.

Through the clouds of her half-consciousness the agony of change stabbed at her. Half understanding, she welcomed it, though the piercing anguish of that reversal was so strong it dragged her out of her daze again and wrung her anew in the grinding pain of that change which defied all natural laws. In heedless impatience she waited for the torture to pass. Exultation was welling up in her, for she knew that her own violence had melted the spell by which Jarisme held her. She knew what she must do when she stood free again, and conscious power flowed intoxicatingly through her.

She opened her eyes. She was standing rigidly before the great fire-quickened globe. The amazing company was grouped around her intently, and Jarisme, facing her, had taken one angry, incredulous step forward as she saw her own spell break. Upon that tableau Jirel's hot yellow eyes opened, and she laughed in grim exultation and swung up her arm. Violet light glinted upon crystal.

In the instant Jarisme saw what she intended, convulsive terror wiped all other expression from her face. A cry of mingled inarticulatenesses thundered up from the transfixed crowd. Giraud started forward from among them, frantic hands clawing out toward her.

"No, no!" shrieked Jarisme. "Wait!"

It was too late. The crystal dashed itself from Jirel's downswinging arm, the light in it blazing. With a splintering crash it struck the floor at the sorceress' sandaled feet and flew into shining fragments.

193

For an instant nothing happened. Jirel held her breath, waiting. Giraud had flung himself flat on the shining floor, reaching out for her in a last effort. His hands had flown out to seize her, and found only her ankles. He clung to them now with a paralyzed grip, his face hidden between his arms. Jarisme cowered motionless, arms clasped about her head as if she were trying to hide. The motley throng of watchers was rigid in fatalistic quiet. In tense silence they waited.

Then in the great globe above them the pale flame flickered. Jarisme's gaspingly caught breath sounded loud in the utter quiet. Again the flame shook. And again. Then abruptly it went out. Darkness stunned them for a moment; then a low muttering roar rumbled up out of the stillness, louder and deeper and stronger until it pressed unbearably upon Jirel's ears and her head was one great aching surge of sound. Above that roar a sharply crackling noise broke, and the crystal walls of the room trembled, reeled dizzily—split open in long jagged rents through which the violet day poured in thin fingers of light. Overhead the shattering sound of falling walls roared loud. Jarisme's magic tower was crumbling all around them. Through the long, shivering cracks in the walls the pale violet day poured more strongly, serene in the chaos.

In that clear light Jirel saw a motion among the throng. Jarisme had risen to her full height. She saw the sleek black head go up in an odd, defiant, desperate poise, and above the soul-shaking tumult she heard the sorceress' voice scream,

"Urda! Urda-sla!"

In the midst of the roar of the falling walls for the briefest instant a deathly silence dropped. And out of that silence, like an answer to the sorceress' cry, came a Noise, an indescribable, intolerable loudness like the crack of cyclopean thunder. And suddenly in the sky above them, visible through the crumbling crystal walls, a long black wedge opened. It was like a strip of darkest midnight splitting the violet day, a midnight through which stars shone unbearably near, unbearably bright.

Jirel stared up in dumb surprise at that streak of starry night cleaving the daylit sky. Jarisme stood rigid,

arms outstretched, defiantly fronting the thunderous dark
whose apex was drawing nearer and nearer, driving
downward like a vast celestial spear. She did not flinch
as it reached toward the tower. Jirel saw the darkness
sweep forward like a racing shadow. Then it was upon
them, and the earth shuddered under her feet, and from
very far away she heard Jarisme scream.

When consciousness returned to her, she sat up painfully and stared around. She lay upon green grass, bruised
and aching, but unharmed. The violet day was serene and
unbroken once more. The purple peaks had vanished. No
longer was she high among mountains. Instead, the green
meadow where she had first seen Jarisme's tower
stretched about her. In its dissolution it must have returned to its original site, flashing back along the magical
ways it had traveled as the sorceress' magic was broken.
For the tower too was gone. A little distance away she
saw a heap of marble blocks outlining a rough circle,
where that white shaft had risen. But the stones were
weathered and cracked like the old, old stones of an ancient ruin.

She had been staring at this for many minutes, trying
to focus her bewildered mind upon its significance, before the sound of groaning which had been going on for
some time impressed itself on her brain. She turned. A
little way off, Giraud lay in a tangle of torn black robes.
Of Jarisme and the rest she saw no sign. Painfully she got
to her feet and staggered to the wizard, turning him over
with a disdainful toe. He opened his eyes and stared at
her with a cloudy gaze into which recognition and realization slowly crept.

"Are you hurt?" she demanded.

He pulled himself to a sitting position and flexed his
limbs experimentally. Finally he shook his head, more in
answer to his own investigation than to her query, and
got slowly to his feet. Jirel's eyes sought the weapon at
his hip.

"I am going to kill you now," she said calmly. "Draw
your sword, wizard."

The little dull eyes flashed up to her face. He stared.
Whatever he saw in the yellow gaze must have satisfied

him that she meant what she said, but he did not draw,
nor did he fall back. A tight little smile drew his mouth
askew, and he lifted his black-robed arms. Jirel saw them
rise, and her gaze followed the gesture automatically. Up
they went, up. And then in the queerest fashion she lost
all control of her own eyes, so that they followed some
invisible upward line which drew her on and on skyward
until she was rigidly staring at a fixed point of invisibility
at the spot where the lines of Giraud's arms would have
crossed, were they extended to a measureless distance.
Somehow she actually saw that point, and could not look
away. Gripped in the magic of those lifted arms, she
stood rigid, not even realizing what had happened, unable even to think in the moveless magic of Giraud.

His little mocking chuckle reached her from immeasur-
ably far away.

"Kill me?" he was laughing thickly. "Kill me, Giraud?
Why, it was you who saved me, Joiry! Why else should
I have clung to your ankles so tightly? For I knew that
when the Light died, the only one who could hope to
live would be the one who slew it—nor was that a certainty, either. But I took the risk, and well I did, or I
would be with Jarisme now in the outer dark whence she
called up her no-god of the void to save her from oblivion.
I warned her what would happen if she tampered with
Fate. And I would rather—yes, much rather—be here,
in this pleasant violet land which I shall rule alone now.
Thanks to you, Joiry! Kill me, eh? I think not!"

That thick, mocking chuckle reached her remotely,
penetrated her magic-stilled mind. It echoed round and
round there, for a long while, before she realized what it
meant. But at last she remembered, and her mind woke
a little from its inertia, and such anger swept over her
that its heat was an actual pain. Giraud, the runaway
sorcerer, laughing at Joiry! Holding Jirel of Joiry in his
spell! Mocking her! Blindly she wrenched at the bonds of
magic, blindly urged her body forward. She could see
nothing but that non-existent point where the lifted arms
would have crossed, in measureless distances, but she felt
the dagger-hilt in her hand, and she lunged forward
through invisibility, and did not even know when the
blade sank home.

Sight returned to her then in a stunning flood. She rubbed dazed eyes and shook herself and stared round the green meadow in the violet day uncomprehendingly, for her mind was not yet fully awake. Not until she looked down did she remember.

Giraud lay there. The black robes were furled like wings over his quiet body, but red in a thick flood was spreading on the grass, and from the tangled garments her dagger-hilt stood up. Jirel stared down at him, emotionless, her whole body still almost asleep from the power of the dead man's magic. She could not even feel triumph. She pulled the blade free automatically and wiped it on his robes. Then she sat down beside the body and rested her head in her hands, forcing herself to awaken.

After a long while she looked up again, the old hot light rising in her eyes, life flushing back into her face once more. Shaking off the last shreds of the spell, she got to her feet, sheathing the dagger. About her the violet-misted meadows were very still. No living creature moved anywhere in sight. The trees were motionless in the unstirring air. And beyond the ruins of the marble tower she saw the opening in the woods out of which her path had come, very long ago.

Jirel squared her shoulders and turned her back upon her vow fulfilled, and without a backward glance set off across the grass toward the tree-hid ruins which held the gate to home.

DAVID H. KELLER
(1880–1966)

David H. Keller, noted American physician and popular author of science fiction and fantasy literature, was born and reared in Philadelphia, Pennsylvania. After graduating from the University of Pennsylvania Medical School, he served as a country doctor for approximately ten years. He then turned to psychiatry, which he practiced in a number of state mental institutions for roughly three decades. Most of his retirement years were spent at Underwood, the Keller family's eighteenth-century ancestral home located in South Stroudsburg, Pennsylvania. He died on July 13, 1966, at the age of eighty-six.

During Keller's long and productive life he wrote approximately seven hundred articles and several books on various medical subjects. However, the byline David H. Keller, M.D., also became well known in circles outside the medical profession. Always interested in writing for the sheer fun of it, Keller began dabbling in science fiction in his early teens, but it was not until the age of forty-seven that he actually sold one of his works. His story, "The Revolt of the Pedestrians," was accepted by Hugo Gernsback and subsequently published in the February, 1928, issue of *Amazing Stories*. The tale was very well received, and thereafter Keller became a regular contributor to *Amazing Stories, Science Wonder Stories, Weird Tales,* and a wide assortment of fan magazines. Indeed, in only a few years after the publication of "Revolt," he became one of America's most popular writers of science fiction and weird tales. Editors clamored for his stories, and devoted fans consistently placed his name first on various popularity polls. In addition, the publication, shortly before World War II, of some of his fiction in the French periodical *Les Primaires* helped Keller establish a popularity in France perhaps even greater than that in his own country.

Although most of Keller's fiction was remarkably well received, especially popular were his "Taine of San Francisco" (Keller's version of Sherlock Holmes) and "Overlord of Cornwall" stories. Perhaps his most famous story is "The Thing in the Cellar" (*Weird Tales*, March, 1932) which has seen numerous reprintings and translations. Some commentators, as a matter of fact, view this psychological masterpiece as one of the greatest horror stories ever written. Besides important short-story collections such as *Life Everlasting and Other Tales of Science, Fantasy and Horror* (1949) and *Tales from Underwood* (1952), Keller has published poetry (*Songs of a Spanish Lover,* 1924) and several novels, including *The Devil and the Doctor* (1940) and *The Eternal Conflict* (1949). Today, he is widely recognized as one of the important early pioneers in the writing of psychological science-fiction and fantasy stories.

"The Thirty and One" first appeared in the November, 1938, issue of *Marvel Science Stories*. A part of the "Overlord of Cornwall" series, it is an intriguing tale which exhibits some of the finest aspects of Keller's distinct prose style: lucidity, remarkable economy, meticulous diction, sardonic wit, whimsical humor, and a subtle undercurrent of mystery and dark foreboding. Especially interesting, though, is Keller's delineation of the central character, Lady Angelica, since she receives a decidedly different treatment from other Keller female protagonists. While most are depicted as rather treacherous, domineering, and emasculating vampire-women, the Lady Angelica (as the name implies) is an admirably strong and noble person who exhibits a good deal of generosity and compassion. Independent and strong-willed she is, but her self-sacrificing actions are a far cry from the destructive machinations of the unpleasant female protagonists in such stories as "The Golden Bough," "Bindings de Luxe," and "A Piece of Linoleum."

Noteworthy, too, is Keller's sustained use of foreshadowing. Although to some readers the ending of "The

Thirty and One" may seem a bit contrived, the consistent use of foreshadowing makes it clear that this is the denouement that Keller has planned all along. And what are we to make of his conclusion? Interpretations will no doubt vary from reader to reader, but one thing remains clear—even the most wonderful of man's scientific creations cannot control the inexorable hand of destiny. No, not even the marvelous elixir of synthesis.

∽ The Thirty and One ઐ

David H. Keller

Cecil, OverLord of Walling, in the Dark Forest, mused by the fire. The blind Singer of Songs had sung the sagas of ancient times, had waited long for praise and then, disquieted, had left the banquet hall guided by his dog. The Juggler had merely tossed his golden balls into the air till they seemed a glistening cascade, but still the OverLord had mused, unseeing. The wise Homunculus had crouched at his feet uttering words of wisdom and telling tales of Gobi and the buried city of Ankor. But nothing could rouse the OverLord from his meditations.

At last, he stood up and struck the silver bell with a hammer of gold. Serving men answered the call.

"Send me the Lady Angelica and the Lord Gustro," he commanded, and then once again sat down with chin in hand, waiting.

At last, the two came in answer to his summons. The Lady was his only daugher, as fair and as wise a Lady as there was in all Walling. Lord Gustro, some day, would be her husband, and help her rule in the Dark Forest. Meantime, he perfected himself in the use of the broadsword, lute, the hunting with the falcon, and the study of books. He was six feet tall, twenty years old, and had in him the makings of a man.

The three sat around the fire, two waiting to hear the one talk, the one waiting till he knew just how to say what had to be said. At last, Cecil began to talk:

"You no doubt know what is on my mind. For years I have tried to give happiness and peace and prosperity to the simple folk of our land of Walling. We were well situated in a valley surrounded by lofty, impassable forests. Only one mountain pass connected us with the great, cruel, and almost unknown world around us. Into that world, we sent in springtime, summer, and fall, our caravans of mules laden with grain, olives, wine, and uncut stones. From that world, we brought salt, weapons, bales of woolen and silken goods, for our needs. No one tried to molest us, for we had nothing much that they coveted. Perhaps safety made us grow soft, sleepy, and unprepared for danger.

"But it has come. We might have known there were things in that outer world we knew not of and therefore could not even dream of. But this spring, our first caravan winding over the mountains found, at the boundaries of the Dark Forest, a Castle blocking their way. Their mules were not birds and could not fly over; they were not mules and could not burrow under. And the lads with the mules were not warriors and could not break their way through. So they came back, unmolested, 'tis true, but with their goods unsold and unbartered.

"Now, I do not think that Castle was built by magic. I have personally looked at it, and it seems nothing but stone and mortar. And it is not held by an army of fighting men, for all we can hear is that one man holds it. But what a man! Half again as tall as our finest lad, and skilled in the use of weapons. I tried him out. One at a time, I sent to him John of the flying ax, and Herman who had no equal with the double-edged sword, and Rubin who could split a willow wand at two hundred paces with his steel-tipped arrow. These three men lie, worm food, in the ravine below the castle. And meantime, our country is strangulated as far as trade is concerned. We have cattle in the meadow, and wood in the forest, and grain in the bin, but we have no salt, no clothes to cover us from the cold, no finery for our women, or weapons for our men. And we never will have these as long as this castle and this man block our caravans."

"We can capture the Castle and kill the giant!" cried Lord Gustro, with the impetuosity of youth.

"How?" asked the OverLord. "Did I not tell you that the path is narrow? You know that. On one side, the mountains tower lofty as the flight of the bird and smooth as a woman's skin. On the other side, is the Valley of the Dæmons, and no one has ever fallen into it and come back alive. The only path is just wide enough for one man-led mule, and that path now leads through the castle. If we could send an army, 'twould be different. But only one man at a time can we send, and there is no man equal to successful combat with this giant."

The Lady Angelica smiled as she whispered, "We may conquer him through chicanery. For example, I have seen this hall filled with fighting men and fair ladies almost put into an endless sleep by gazing at the golden balls flying through the air and back into the clever hands of the Juggler. And the Blind Singer of Songs can make anyone forget all except the music of his tales. And our Homunculus is very wise."

The OverLord shook his head. "Not thus will the question be answered. This madman wants one thing, and that one thing means everything in the lastward, as far as our land and people are concerned. Perhaps you have guessed. I will give you the demand ere you ask the question. Our Lady's hand in marriage, and thus, when I die, he becomes the OverLord of Walling."

Lady Angelica looked over at Lord Gustro. He looked at the OverLord's daughter. At last, he said:

"Better to eat our grain and eat our olives and drink our wine. Better that our men wear bearskins and our women cover themselves with the skins of deer. It would be best for them to wear shoes of wood than pantufles of unicorn skin brought from Araby. It were a sweeter fate for them to perfume their bodies with crushed violets and may-flowers from our forest than to smell sweet with perfumes from the trees of the unknown Island of the East. This price is too heavy. Let us live as our fathers and fathers' fathers lived, even climb trees like the monkey folk, than trust to such an OverLord. Besides, I love the Lady Angelica."

The Lady smiled her thanks. "I still am thinking of the use of intelligence overcoming brawn. Have we no wisdom left in Walling, besides the fair, faint, dreams of weak woman?"

"I will send for the Homunculus," her father answered. "He may know the answer to that question."

The little man came in. He was a man not born of woman, but grown for seven years in a glass bottle, during all of which time he read books held before him by wise men, and was nourished with drops of wine and tiny balls of Asphodel paste. He listened to the problem gravely, though at times he seemed asleep. At last, he said one word.

"Synthesis."

Cecil reached over and, picking him up, placed him on one knee.

"Have pity on us, Wise Man. We are but simple folk and know but simple words. What is the meaning of this sage word?"

"I know not," was the peculiar answer. " 'Tis but a word that came to me out of the past. It has a sweet sound and methinks may have a meaning. Let me think. I recall now! It was when I was in the glass bottle that a wise man came and held before my eyes an illuminated parchment. On it was written in words of gold, this word and its meaning.

"Synthesis. All things are one and one thing is all."

"Which makes it all the harder for me," sighed the OverLord of Walling.

The Lady Angelica left her seat and came over to her father. She sank upon the bearskin at his feet and took the little hand of the dwarf in hers.

"Tell me, my dear Homunculus, what wise man 'twas who thus gave you the message on the illuminated parchment?"

"It was a very wise man and a very old man who lives by himself in a cave by the babbling brook, and yearly the simple folk take him bread and meat and wine, but for years no one has seen him. And perhaps he lives and perhaps he is dead, for all I know is that the food disappears. But perhaps the birds think that it is for them now that he lies sightless and thoughtless on his stone bed these many years."

"This is something we will find out for ourselves. Lord Gustro, order some horses, and the four of us will go to this man's cave. Three horses for us, my Lord, and an ambling pad for our little friend so naught of harm will befall him."

The four came to the cave, and the four entered it. A

light burned at the far end, and there was the wise man, very old and with nought but his eyes telling of the intelligence that never ages. On the table before him in a tangled confusion, were glasses and earthenware, and crucibles, and one each of astrolabe, alembic, and hourglass through which silver sands ran, and this was fixed with cunning machinery so that every day it tilted around and once more let the sand tell the passing of the twenty-and-four hours. There were books covered with mildewed leather and locked with iron padlocks and spider webs. Hung from the wet ceiling was a representation of the sun with the planets revolving eternally around that fair orb, but the pitted moon alternated with light and shadows.

And the wise man read from a book written in letters made by those long dead, and now and then he ate a crust of bread or sipped wine from a ram's horn, but never did he stop reading. When they touched him on the shoulder to attract his attention, he shook them off, murmuring, "By the Seven Sacred Caterpillars! Let me finish this page, for what a pity were I to die without knowing what this man wrote some thousand years ago in Ankor."

But at last he finished the page and sat blinking at them with his wise eyes sunk deep into a mummy face while his body shook with the decrepitude of age. And Cecil asked him:

"What is the meaning of the word, 'synthesis'?"

" 'Tis a dream of mine which only now I find the waking meaning of."

"Tell the dream," the OverLord commanded.

" 'Tis but a dream. Suppose there were thirty wise men learned in all wisdom obtained from the reading of ancient books on alchemy and magic and histories and philosophy. These men knew of animals and jewels such as margarites and chrysoberyls, and of all plants such as dittany which cures wounds, and mandragora which compelleth sleep (though why men should want to sleep, when there is so much to read and profit by the reading, I do not know). But these men are old and some day will die. So, I would take these thirty old men and one young man and have them drink a wine that I have distilled these many years, and by synthesis there would be only one body—that of the young man—but in that man's brain would be all the subtle and ancient wisdom of the thirty savants, and thus we would do century after century so no wisdom would be lost to the world."

The Lady Angelica leaned over his shoulder. "And have you made this wine?" she asked.

"Yes, and now I am working on its opposite, for why place thirty bodies into one unless you know the art of once again separating this one body into the original thirty. But that is hard. For any fool can pour the wine from thirty bottles into a single jar, but who is wise enough to separate them and restore them to their original bottles?"

"Have you tried this wine of synthetic magic?" asked the OverLord.

"Partly. I took a crow and a canary-bird and had them drink of it, and now, in yonder wicker cage, a yellow crow sits and nightly fills my cave with song as though it came from the lutes and citherns of faerie-land."

"Now, that is my thought," cried the Lady Angelica. "We will take the best and bravest fighters of our land, and the sweetest singer of songs, and the best juggler of golden balls, thirty of them, and I, myself, will drink of this wine of synthesis. Thus the thirty will pass into my body, and I will go and visit the Giant. In his hall, I will drink of the other wine, and there will be thirty to fight against the one. They will overcome him and slay him. Then I will drink again of the vital wine, and in my body I will carry the thirty conquerors back to Walling. Once there, I will again drink, and the thirty men will leave my body, being liberated by the wonder-wine. Some may be dead and others wounded, but I will be safe and our enemy killed. Have you enough of it—of both kinds?

The old man looked puzzled.

"I have a flagon of the wine of synthesis. Of the other, to change the synthesized back into their original bodies, only enough for one experiment, and mayhap a few drops more."

"Try those drops on that yellow bird," commanded Cecil.

The old man poured from a bottle of pure gold, graven with a worm that eternally renewed his youth by swallowing his tail, a few drops of a colorless liquid, and offered it to the yellow bird in the wicker cage. This the bird drank greedily, and of a sudden there were two birds, a black crow and a yellow canary, and ere the canary could pipe a song the crow pounced on it and killed it.

"It works," croaked the old man. "It works."

"Can you make more of the second elixir?" asked Lord Gustro.

"What I do once I can do twice," proudly said the ancient.

"Then start and make more, and while you are doing it, we will take the golden bottle and the flagon and see what can be done to save the simple folk of our dark forests, though this is an adventure that I think little of, for 'tis fraught with danger for a woman I love." Thus spake the OverLord.

And with the elixirs in a safe place, they rode away from the cave of the old man. But Lord Gustro took the OverLord aside and said:

"I ask a favor. Allow me to be one of these thirty men."

Cecil shook his head. "No. And once again and forever, NO! In the doing of this, I stand to lose the apple of my eye, and if she comes not back to me, I shall die of grief, and then you, and you alone, will be left to care for my simple folk. If a man has but two arrows and shoots one into the air, then he were wise to keep the other in his quiver against the day of need."

The Lady Angelica laughed as she suspected the reason of their whispering.

"I will come back," she said laughingly, "for the old man was very wise. Did you not see how the yellow bird divided into two, and the crow killed the canary?"

But the Homunculus, held in Lord Cecil's arms, started to cry.

"What wouldst thou?" asked the kindly OverLord.

"I would be back in my bottle again," sobbed the little one. And he sobbed till he went to sleep, soothed by the rocking canter of the war horse.

Two evenings later, a concourse of brave men met in the banquet hall. There were great, silent, men, skilled in the use of mace, byrnies, and baldricks, who could slay with sword, spear and double-bitted battle-ax. The Juggler was there, and a Singer of Songs, and a Reader of Books, very young but very wise. And a man was there with sparkling eyes who could by his glance put men to death-sleep and waken them with a snap of the thumb and finger. And to these were added the OverLord and Lord Gustro and the trembling Homunculus, and on her throne sat the Lady Angelica, very beautiful and very happy because of the great adventure she had a part to play in. In her hand was a golden goblet, and in the hands of the thirty men, crystal glasses, and the thirty and one drinking vessels were filled with the wine of synthesis, for half of the flagon was poured out. But the flagon, half-filled, and the golden drug viand, the Lady Angelica hid beneath her shimmering robe. Outside, a lady's horse, decked with diamond-studded harness, neighed uneasy in the moonlight,

Lord Cecil explained the adventure, and all the thirty men sat very still and solemn, for never had they heard the like before, for they none feared a simple death, but this dissolution was a thing that made even the bravest wonder what the end would be. Yet, when the time came and the command was given, they one and all drained their vessels, and even as the Lady drank her wine, they drank to the last drop.

Then there was silence broken only by the shrill cry of a hoot owl, complaining to the moon concerning the doings of the night folk in the Dark Forest. The little Homunculus hid his face in the shoulder of the OverLord, but Cecil and Lord Gustro looked straight ahead of them over the banquet table to see what was to be seen.

The thirty men seemed to shiver and then grow smaller in a mist that covered them, and finally only empty places were left at the banquet table, and empty glasses. Only the two men and the Lady Angelica and the shivering Homunculus were left. The Lady laughed.

"It worked," she cried. "I look the same, but I feel different, for in me are the potential bodies of the thirty brave men who will overcome the Giant and bring peace to the land. And now I will give you the kiss of hail and farewell, and will venture forth on my waiting horse." Kissing her father on the mouth and her lover on the cheek and the little one on the top of his curly-haired

head, she ran bravely out of the room. Through the stillness they could hear her horse's hooves, silver-shod,
pounding on the stones of the courtyard.

"I am afraid," shivered the little one. "I have all wisdom, but I am afraid as to this adventure and its ending."

Lord Cecil comforted him. "You are afraid because
you are so very wise. Lord Gustro and I would like to
fear, but we are too foolish to do so. Can I do anything to
comfort you, little friend of mine?"

"I wish I were back in my bottle," sobbed the
Homunculus, "but that cannot be because the bottle was
broken when I was taken from it, for the mouth of it was
very narrow, and a bottle once broken cannot be made
whole again."

All that night, Lord Cecil rocked him to sleep, singing
to him lullabies, while Lord Gustro sat wakeful before the fire biting his finger nails, and wondering what
the ending would be.

Late that night, the Lady Angelica arrived at the gate
of the Giant's Castle, and blew her wreathed horn. The
Giant dropped the iron-studded gate, and curiously peered
at the lady on the horse.

"I am the Lady Angelica," said the Lady, "and I have
come to be your bride if only you will give free passage to
our caravans so we can commerce with the great world
outside. When my father dies, you will be OverLord of
the land, and perchance I will come to love you for you
are a fine figure of a man, and I have heard much of
you."

The Giant towered over the head of her horse. He
placed his hand around her waist and plucked her from
the horse and carried her to his banquet hall and sat her
down at one end of the table. Laughing in a somewhat
silly manner, he walked around the room and lit pine
torches and tall candles till at last the whole room was
lighted. He poured a large glass of wine for the Lady and
a much larger glass for himself. He seated himself at the
other end of the table, and laughed again as he cried:

"It all is as I dreamed. But who would have thought
that the noble Lord Cecil and the brave Lord Gustro
would have been so craven! Let's drink to our wedding,
and then to the bridal chamber."

And he drank his drink in one swallow. But the Lady Angelica took from under her gown a golden flask and raising it, she cried:

"I drink to you and your future, whatever it may be." And she drained the golden flask and sat very still. A mist filled the room and swirled widdershams in thirty pillars around the long oak table. When it cleared, there were thirty men between the Giant and the Lady.

The Juggler took his golden balls, and the man with the dazzling eyes looked hard on the Giant, and the Student took from his robe a Book and read the wise sayings of dead Gods backwards, while the Singer of Songs plucked his harp strings and sang of the brave deeds of brave men long dead. But the fighting men rushed forward, and on all sides started the battle. The Giant jumped back, picked a mace from the wall, and fought as never man fought before. He had two things in mind: to kill, and to reach the smiling Lady and strangle her with bare hands for the thing she had done to him. But ever between him and the Lady was a wall of men who, with steel and song and dazzling eyes, formed a living wall that could be bent and crushed but never broken.

For centuries after, in the halls of Walling, the blind singers of songs told of that fight while the simple folk sat silent and listened to the tale. No doubt as the tale passed from one singer, aged, to the next singer, young, it became ornamented and embroidered and fabricated into something somewhat different from what really happened that night. But even the bare truth-telling at first hand, as told in parts, at different times, by the Lady Angelica, was a great enough tale. For men fought and bled and died in that hall. Finally, the Giant, dying, broke through and almost reached the Lady, but then the Song Man tripped him with his harp, and the Wise Man threw his heavy tome in his face, and the Juggler shattered his three golden balls against the Giant's forehead, and, at the lastward, the glittering eyes of the Sleep-Maker fastened on the dying eyes of the Giant and sent him on his last sleep.

The Lady Angelica looked around the shattered hall and at the thirty men who had all done their part, and she said softly:

"These be brave men, and they have done what was necessary for the good of their country and for the honor of our land. I cannot forsake them or leave them hopeless."

She took the rest of the wine of synthesis and drank part, and to every man she gave a drink, even the dead men whose mouths she had to gently open to wipe the blood from the gritted teeth, ere she could pour the wine into their breathless mouths. And she went back to her seat, and sitting there, she waited.

The mist again filled the hall and covered the dead and dying and those who were not hurt badly but panted from the fury of the battle. When the mist cleared, only the Lady Angelica was left there, for all the thirty had returned to her body through the magic of the synthesizing wine.

And the Lady said to herself:

"I feel old and in many ways different, and my strength has gone from me. I am glad there is no mirror to show me my whitened hair and bloodless cheeks, for the men who have come back unto me were dead men, and those not dead were badly hurt. I must get back to my horse before I fall into a faint of death."

She tried to walk out, but, stumbling, fell. On hands and knees, she crawled to where her horse waited for her. She pulled herself up into the saddle, and with her girdle she tied herself there, and then told the horse to go home. But she lay across the saddle like a dead woman.

The horse brought her back. Ladies in waiting took her to bed, and washed her withered limbs, and gave her warm drinks, and covered her wasted body with coverlets of lamb's wool. The wise physicians mixed healing drinks for her, and finally she recovered sufficiently to tell her father and her lover the story of the battle of the thirty against the Giant, how he was dead and the land safe.

"Now go to the old man and get the other elixir," she whispered, "and when it works have the dead buried with honor and the wounded gently and wisely cared for. Then we will come to the end of the adventure, and it will be one that the Singers of Songs will tell of for many winter evenings to the simple folk of Walling."

"You stay with her, Lord Gustro," commanded the

OverLord, "and I will take the wise Homunculus in my arms and gallop to the cave and secure the elixir. When I return we will have her drink it, and once again she will be whole and young again. Then I will have you two lovers marry, for I am not as young as I was, and I want to live to see the throne secure, and, the Gods willing, grandchildren running around the castle."

Lord Gustro sat down by his Lady's bed, and he took her wasted hand in his warm one. He placed a kiss on her white lips with his red warm ones, and he whispered: "No matter what happens and no matter what the end of the adventure, I will always love you, Heart-of-mine." And the Lady Angelica smiled on him, and went to sleep.

Through the Dark Forest galloped Cecil, OverLord of Walling, with the little wise man in his arms. He flung himself off his war horse, and ran quickly into the cave.

"Have you finished the elixir?" he cried.

The old man looked up, as though in doubt as to what the question was. He was breathing heavily now, and little drops of sweat rolled down his leathered face.

"Oh! Yes! I remember now. The elixir that would save the Lady, and take from her the bodies of the men we placed in her by virtue of our synthetic magic. I remember now! I have been working on it. In a few more minutes, it will be finished."

And dropping forward on the oak table, he died. In falling, a withered hand struck a golden flask and overturned it on the floor. Liquid amber ran over the dust of ages. A cockroach came and drank of it, and suddenly died.

"I am afraid," moaned the little Homunculus. "I wish I were back in my bottle."

But Cecil, OverLord of Walling, did not know how to comfort him.

URSULA K. LE GUIN
(1929–   )

Ursula K. Le Guin, author of numerous award-winning works of science fiction and fantasy literature, has, in little more than ten years, established herself as one of America's finest writers. Born in Berkeley, California, the daughter of anthropologist A. L. Kroeber and writer Theodora Kroeber, she received her B.A. from Radcliffe College in 1951 and her M.A. from Columbia University in 1952. A year later, while studying in Paris on a Fulbright Fellowship, she met and married Charles A. Le Guin, an historian. Since the mid 1960s Le Guin has not only maintained a remarkably prolific and brilliant literary career, but has also participated in numerous professional activities and conventions, as well as serving as leader of various writing workshops, including the University of Washington's Science Fiction Writer's Workshop. The Le Guins now live in Portland, Oregon, with their three children.

Although Le Guin has remarked that she has been writing science fiction and fantasy literature since the age of six, the success of her professional literary career was not assured until 1966, when her first novel, *Rocannon's World,* was published. This science fiction work was followed by a number of others in the same genre: *Planet of Exile* (1966), *City of Illusions* (1967), *The Left Hand of Darkness* (1969), *The Lathe of Heaven* (1971), and, most recently, *The Dispossessed* (1974). Illustrative of the high quality of her writing is the fact that *The Left Hand of Darkness* and *The Dispossessed* each received both the Hugo and Nebula awards, the highest honors that can be bestowed upon a sf author. Her short fiction has fared equally well, with "The Day Before the Revolution" (1974) receiving both the Nebula and Jupiter awards, and "The Ones Who Walk Away From Omelas" (1973) earning a Hugo. In the realm of fantasy literature, Le Guin has published the popular and critically acclaimed *Earthsea Trilogy*, which consists of *A Wizard of Earthsea* (1968—ALA Notable Book), *The Tombs of Atuan* (1971—Newberry Honor Book), and *The Farthest Shore* (1972—National Book Award in children's literature). Recently, she has published a collection of short stories (containing both sf and fantasy) entitled *The Wind's Twelve Quarters* (1975), a novel, *The Word for World Is Forest* (1976), a novelette, *Very Far Away from Anywhere Else* (1976), and *Wild Angels* (1975), a collection of poetry. As might be expected, in the past few years more and more scholarly articles and books have been published about Le Guin's work, including a special Le Guin issue of *Science Fiction Studies* (November, 1975) and George Edgar Slusser's *The Farthest Shores of Ursula Le Guin* (1976).

In her preface to "April in Paris," which appears in *The Wind's Twelve Quarters*, Ursula Le Guin states that: "This is the first story I ever got paid for; the second story I ever got published; and maybe the thirtieth or fortieth story I ever wrote." It is obviously a rather special story to Le Guin, and a special one to us as well. Like Barry Pain, whose story "The Glass of Supreme Moments," appears earlier in this volume, Le Guin has the knack of blending realism and fantasy with extraordinary effect. She manages to create a unique tone and atmosphere in this high fantasy by involving the painfully believable Professor Barry Pennywither from Munson College, Indiana, in the black magic of Jehan Lenoir.

This is essentially a humorous story, full of Le Guin's delightful brand of sly wit and biting irony. But it displays a serious side as well, because ultimately this is a story about loneliness. As it is Le Guin's clever but compassionate and understanding treatment of the suffering experienced by the social misfits, the "different" of any society, that makes the story so meaningful and moving. The reader cannot help but rejoice with the two very strange, but contented, couples who stroll happily on the banks of the river Seine at the conclusion of this tale.

❦ April in Paris ❧

Ursula K. Le Guin

Professor Barry Pennywither sat in a cold, shadowy garret and stared at the table in front of him, on which lay a book and a breadcrust. The bread had been his dinner, the book had been his lifework. Both were dry. Dr. Pennywither sighed, and then shivered. Though the lower-floor apartments of the old house were quite elegant, the heat was turned off on April 1st, come what may; it was now April 2nd and sleeting. If Dr. Pennywither raised his head a little he could see from his window the two square towers of Notre Dame de Paris, vague and soaring in the dusk, almost near enough to touch: for the Island of Saint-Louis, where he lived, is like a little barge being towed downstream behind the Island of the City, where Notre Dame stands. But he did not raise his head. He was too cold.

The great towers sank into darkness. Dr. Pennywither sank into gloom. He stared with loathing at his book. It had won him a year in Paris—publish or perish, said the Dean of Faculties, and he had published, and been rewarded with a year's leave from teaching, without pay. Munson College could not afford to pay unteaching teachers. So on his scraped-up savings he had come back to Paris, to live again as a student in a garret, to read fifteenth-century manuscripts at the Library, to see the chestnuts flower along the avenues. But it hadn't worked. He was forty, too old for lonely garrets. The sleet would blight the budding chestnut flowers. And he was sick of his work. Who cared about his theory, the Pennywither Theory, concerning the mysterious disappearance of the poet François Villon in 1463? Nobody. For after all his

Theory about poor Villon, the greatest juvenile delinquent of all time, was only a theory and could never be proved, not across the gulf of five hundred years. Nothing could be proved. And besides, what did it matter if Villon died on Montfaucon gallows or (as Pennywither thought) in a Lyons brothel on the way to Italy? Nobody cared. Nobody else loved Villon enough. Nobody loved Dr. Pennywither, either; not even Dr. Pennywither. Why should he? An unsocial, unmarried, underpaid pedant, sitting here alone in an unheated attic in an unrestored tenement trying to write another unreadable book. "I'm unrealistic," he said aloud with another sigh and another shiver. He got up and took the blanket off his bed, wrapped himself in it, sat down thus bundled at the table, and tried to light a Gauloise Bleue. His lighter snapped vainly. He sighed once more, got up, fetched a can of vile-smelling French lighter fluid, sat down, rewrapped his cocoon, filled the lighter, and snapped it. The fluid had spilled around a good bit. The lighter lit, so did Dr. Pennywither, from the wrists down. "Oh hell!" he cried, blue flames leaping from his knuckles, and jumped up batting his arms wildly, shouting "Hell!" and raging against Destiny. Nothing ever went right. What was the use? It was then 8:12 on the night of April 2nd, 1961.

A man sat hunched at a table in a cold, high room. Through the window behind him the two square towers of Notre Dame loomed in the Spring dusk. In front of him on the table lay a hunk of cheese and a huge, iron-latched, handwritten book. The book was called (in Latin) *On the Primacy of the Element Fire over the Other Three Elements*. It's author stared at it with loathing. Nearby on a small iron stove a small alembic simmered. Jehan Lenoir mechanically inched his chair nearer the stove now and then, for warmth, but his thoughts were on deeper problems. "Hell!" he said finally (in Late Mediaeval French), slammed the book shut, and got up. What if his theory was wrong? What if water were the primal element? How could you prove these things? There must be some way—some method—so that one could be sure, absolutely sure, of one single fact! But each fact led into others, a monstrous tangle, and the Authorities conflicted, and anyway no one would read his book, not even the wretched pedants at the Sorbonne. They smelled heresy. What was the use? What good this life spent in poverty and alone, when he had learned nothing, merely guessed and theoerized? He strode about the garret, raging, and then stood still. "All right!" he said to Destiny. "Very good! You've given me nothing, so I'll take what I want!" He went to one of the stacks of books that covered most of the floor-space, yanked out a bottom volume (scarring the leather and bruising his knuckles when the overlying folios avalanched), slapped it on the table and began to study one page of it. Then, still with a set cold look of rebellion, he got things ready: sulfur, silver, chalk. . . . Though the room was dusty and littered, his little workbench was neatly and handily arranged. He was soon ready. Then he paused. "This is ridiculous," he muttered, glancing out the window into the darkness where now one could only guess at the two square towers. A watchman passed below calling out the hour, eight o'clock of a cold clear night. It was so still he could hear the lapping of the Seine. He shrugged, frowned, took up the chalk and drew a neat pentagram on the floor near his table, then took up the book and began to read in a clear but self-conscious voice: "Haere, haere, audi me . . . " It was a long spell, and mostly nonsense. His voice sank. He stood bored and embarrassed. He hurried through the last words, shut the book, and then fell backwards against the door, gap-mouthed, staring at the enormous shapeless figure that stood within the pentagram, lit only by the blue flicker of its waving, fiery claws.

Barry Pennywither finally got control of himself and put out the fire by burying his hands in the folds of the blanket wrapped around him. Unburned but upset, he sat down again. He looked at his book. Then he stared at it. It was no longer thin and grey and titled *The Last Years of Villon: an Investigation of Possibilities*. It was thick and brown and titled *Incantatoria Magna*. On his table? A priceless manuscript dating from 1407 of which the only extant undamaged copy was in the Ambrosian Library in Milan. He looked slowly around. His mouth dropped slowly open. He observed a stove, a chemist's workbench, two or three dozen heaps of unbelievable leatherbound books, the window, the door. His window, his door. But crouching against his door was a little creature, black and shapeless, from which came a dry rattling sound.

Barry Pennywither was not a very brave man, but he was rational. He thought he had lost his mind, and so he said quite steadily, "Are you the Devil?"

The creature shuddered and rattled.

Experimentally, with a glance at invisible Notre Dame, the professor made the sign of the Cross.

At this the creature twitched; not a flinch, a twitch. Then it said something, feebly, but in perfectly good English—no, in perfectly good French—no, in rather odd French: "Mais vous estes de Dieu," it said.

Barry got up and peered at it. "Who are you?" he demanded, and it lifted up a quite human face and answered meekly, "Jehan Lenoir."

"What are you doing in my room?"

There was a pause. Lenoir got up from his knees and stood straight, all five foot two of him. "This is *my* room," he said at last, though very politely.

Barry looked around at the books and alembics. There was another pause. "Then how did I get here?"

"I brought you."

"Are you a doctor?"

Lenoir nodded, with pride. His whole air had changed. "Yes, I'm a doctor," he said. "Yes, I brought you here. If Nature will yield me no knowledge, then I can conquer Nature herself, I can work a miracle! To the Devil with science, then. I was a scientist—" he glared at Barry. "No longer! They call me a fool, a heretic, well by God I'm worse! I'm a sorcerer, a black magician, Jehan the Black! Magic works, does it? Then science is a waste of time. Ha!" he said, but he did not really look triumphant. "I wish it hadn't worked," he said more quietly, pacing up and down between folios.

"So do I," said the guest.

"Who are you?" Lenoir looked up challengingly at Barry, though there was nearly a foot difference in their heights.

"Barry A. Pennywither. I'm a professor of French at

Munson College, Indiana, on leave in Paris to pursue my studies of Late Mediaeval Fr—" He stopped. He had just realized what kind of accent Lenoir had. "What year is this? What century? Please, Dr. Lenoir—" The Frenchman looked confused. The meanings of words change, as well as their pronunciations. "Who rules this country?" Barry shouted.

Lenoir gave a shrug, a French shrug (some things never change). "Louis is king," he said. "Louis the Eleventh. The dirty old spider."

They stood staring at each other like wooden Indians for some time. Lenoir spoke first. "Then you're a man?"

"Yes. Look, Lenoir, I think you—your spell—you must have muffed it a bit."

"Evidently," said the alchemist. "Are you French?"

"No."

"Are you English?" Lenoir glared. "Are you a filthy Goddam?"

"No. No. I'm from America. I'm from the—from your future. From the twentieth century A.D." Barry blushed. It sounded silly, and he was a modest man. But he knew this was no illusion. The room he stood in, his room, was new. Not five centuries old. Unswept, but new. And the copy of Albertus Magnus by his knee was new, bound in soft supple calfskin, the gold lettering gleaming. And there stood Lenoir in his black gown, not in costume, at home. . . .

"Please sit down, sir," Lenoir was saying. And he added with the fine though absent courtesy of the poor scholar, "Are you tired from the journey? I have bread and cheese, if you'll honor me by sharing it."

They sat at the table munching bread and cheese. At first Lenoir tried to explain why he had tried black magic. "I was fed up," he said. "Fed up! I've slaved in solitude since I was twenty, for what? For knowledge. To learn some of Nature's secrets. They are not to be learned." He drove his knife half an inch into the table, and Barry jumped. Lenoir was a thin little fellow, but evidently a passionate one. It was a fine face, though pale and lean: intelligent, alert, vivid. Barry was reminded of the face of a famous atomic physicist, seen in newspaper pictures up until 1953. Somehow this likeness prompted him to say, "Some are, Lenoir; we've learned a good bit, here and there. . . ."

"What?" said the alchemist, skeptical but curious.

"Well, I'm no scientist—"

"Can you make gold?" He grinned as he asked.

"No, I don't think so, but they do make diamonds."

"How?"

"Carbon—coal, you know—under great heat and pressure, I believe. Coal and diamond are both carbon, you know, the same element."

"Element?"

"Now as I say, I'm no—"

"Which is the primal element?" Lenoir shouted, his eyes fiery, the knife poised in his hand.

"There are about a hundred elements," Barry said coldly, hiding his alarm.

Two hours later, having squeezed out of Barry every dribble of the remnants of his college chemistry course, Lenoir rushed out into the night and reappeared shortly with a bottle. "O my master," he cried, "to think I offered you only bread and cheese!" It was a pleasant burgundy, vintage 1477, a good year. After they had drunk a glass together Lenoir said, "If somehow I could repay you . . ."

"You can. Do you know the name of the poet François Villon?"

"Yes," Lenoir said with some surprise, "but he wrote only French trash, you know, not in Latin."

"Do you know how or when he died?"

"Oh, yes; hanged at Montfaucon here in '64 or '65, with a crew of no-goods like himself. Why?"

Two hours later the bottle was dry, their throats were dry, and the watchman had called three o'clock of a cold clear morning. "Jehan, I'm worn out," Barry said, "you'd better send me back." The alchemist was too polite, too grateful, and perhaps also too tired to argue. Barry stood stiffly inside the pentagram, a tall bony figure muffled in a brown blanket, smoking a Gauloise Bleue. "Adieu," Lenoir said sadly. "Au revoir," Barry replied. Lenoir began to read the spell backwards. The candle flickered, his voice softened. "Me audi, haere, haere," he read, sighed, and looked up. The pentagram was empty. The candle flickered. "But I learned so little!" Lenoir cried out to the empty room. Then he beat the open book with his fists and said, "And a friend like that—a real friend—" He smoked one of the cigarettes Barry had left him—he had taken to tobacco at once. He slept, sitting at his table, for a couple of hours. When he woke he brooded a while, relit his candle, smoked the other cigarette, then opened the *Incantatoria* and began to read aloud: "Haere, haere . . ."

"Oh, thank God," Barry said, stepping quickly out of the pentagram, and grasping Lenoir's hand. "Listen, I got back there—this room, this same room, Jehan! but old, horribly old, and empty, you weren't there—I thought, my God, what have I done? I'd sell my soul to get back there, to him—What can I do with what I've learned? Who'll believe it? How can I prove it? And who the devil could I tell it to anyhow? Who cares? I couldn't sleep, I sat and cried for an hour—"

"Will you stay?"

"Yes. Look, I brought these—in case you did invoke me." Sheepishly he exhibited eight packs of Gauloises, several books, and a gold watch. "It might fetch a price," he explained. "I knew paper francs wouldn't do much good."

At sight of the printed books Lenoir's eyes gleamed with curiosity, but he stood still. "My friend," he said, "you said you'd sell your soul . . . you know . . . so would I. Yet we haven't. How—after all—how did this happen? That we're both men. No devils. No pacts in blood. Two men who've lived in this room . . . "

"I don't know," said Barry. "We'll think that out later. Can I stay with you, Jehan?"

"Consider this your home," Lenoir said with a gracious gesture around the room, the stacks of books, the alembics, the candle growing pale. Outside the window, grey on grey, rose up the two great towers of Notre Dame. It was the dawn of April 3rd.

After breakfast (bread crusts and cheese rinds) they went out and climbed the south tower. The cathedral looked the same as always, though cleaner than in 1961, but the view was rather a shock to Barry. He looked down upon a little town. Two small islands covered with houses; on the right bank more houses crowded inside a fortified wall; on the left bank a few streets twisting around the college; and that was all. Pigeons chortled on the sun-warmed stone between gargoyles. Lenoir, who had seen the view before, was carving the date (in Roman numerals) on a parapet. "Let's celebrate," he said. "Let's go out into the country. I haven't been out of the city for two years. Let's go clear over there—" he pointed to a misty green hill on which a few huts and a windmill were just visible— "to Montmartre, eh? There are some good bars there, I'm told."

Their life soon settled into an easy routine. At first Barry was a little nervous in the crowded streets, but, in a spare black gown of Lenoir's, he was not noticed as outlandish except for his height. He was probably the tallest man in fifteenth-century France. Living standards were low and lice were unavoidable, but Barry had never valued comfort much; the only thing he really missed was coffee at breakfast. When they had bought a bed and a razor—Barry had forgotten his—and introduced him to the landlord as M. Barrie, a cousin of Lenoir's from the Auvergne, their housekeeping arrangements were complete. Barry's watch brought a tremendous price, four gold pieces, enough to live on for a year. They sold it as a wondrous new timepiece from Illyria, and the buyer, a Court chamberlain looking for a nice present to give the king, looked at the inscription—Hamilton Bros., New Haven, 1881—and nodded sagely. Unfortunately he was shut up in one of King Louis's cages for naughty courtiers at Tours before he had presented his gift, and the watch may still be there behind some brick in the ruins of Plessis; but this did not affect the two scholars. Mornings they wandered about sightseeing the Bastille and the churches, or visiting various minor poets in whom Barry was interested; after lunch they discussed electricity, the atomic theory, physiology, and other matters in which Lenoir was interested, and performed minor chemical and anatomical experiments, usually unsuccessfully; after supper they merely talked. Endless, easy talks that ranged over the centuries but always ended here, in the shadowy room with its window open to the Spring night, in their friendship. After two weeks they might have known each other all their lives. They were perfectly happy. They knew they would do nothing with what they had learned from each other. In 1961 how could Barry ever prove his knowledge of old Paris, in 1482 how could Lenoir ever prove the validity of the scientific method? It did not bother them. They had never really expected to be listened to. They had merely wanted to learn.

So they were happy for the first time in their lives; so happy, in fact, that certain desires always before subjugated to the desire for knowledge, began to awaken. "I don't suppose" Barry said one night across the table, "that you ever thought much about marrying?"

"Well, no," his friend answered, doubtfully. "That is, I'm in minor orders . . . and it seemed irrelevant. . . ."

"And expensive. Besides, in my time, no self-respecting woman would want to share my kind of life. American women are so damned poised and efficient and glamorous, terrifying creatures. . . ."

"And women here are little and dark, like beetles, with bad teeth," Lenoir said morosely.

They said no more about women that night. But the next night they did; and the next; and on the next, celebrating the successful dissection of the main nervous system of a pregnant frog, they drank two bottles of Montrachet '74 and got soused. "Let's invoke a woman, Jehan," Barry said in a lascivious bass, grinning like a gargoyle.

"What if I raised a devil this time?"

"Is there really much difference?"

They laughed wildly, and drew a pentagram. "Haere, haere" Lenoir began; when he got the hiccups, Barry took over. He read the last words. There was a rush of cold, marshy-smelling air, and in the pentagram stood a wild-eyed being with long black hair, stark naked, screaming.

"Woman, by God," said Barry.

"Is it?"

It was. "Here, take my cloak," Barry said, for the poor thing now stood gawping and shivering. He put the cloak over her shoulders. Mechanically she pulled it round her, muttering, "Gratias ago, domine."

"Latin!" Lenoir shouted. "A woman speaking Latin?" It took him longer to get over that shock than it did Bota to get over hers. She was, it seemed, a slave in the household of the Sub-Prefect of North Gaul, who lived on the smaller island of the muddy island town called Lutetia. She spoke Latin with a thick Celtic brogue, and did not even know who was emperor in Rome in her day. A real barbarian, Lenoir said with scorn. So she was, an ignorant, taciturn, humble barbarian with tangled hair, white skin, and clear grey eyes. She had been waked from a sound sleep. When they convinced her that she was not dreaming, she evidently assumed that this was some prank of her foreign and all-powerful master, the Sub-Prefect, and accepted the situation without further question. "Am I to serve you, my masters?" she inquired timidly but without sullenness, looking from one to the other.

"Not me," Lenoir growled, and added in French to Barry, "Go on; I'll sleep in the store-room." He departed.

Bota looked up at Barry. No Gauls, and few Romans, were so magnificently tall; no Gauls and no Romans ever spoke so kindly. "Your lamp" (it was a candle, but she had never seen a candle) "is nearly burnt out," she said. "Shall I blow it out?"

For an additional two sols a year the landlord let them use the store-room as a second bedroom, and Lenoir now slept alone again in the main room of the garret. He observed his friend's idyll with a brooding, unjealous interest. The professor and the slave-girl loved each other with delight and tenderness. Their pleasure over-lapped Lenoir in waves of protective joy. Bota had led a brutal life, treated always as a woman but never as a human. In one short week she bloomed, she came alive, evincing beneath her gentle passiveness a cheerful, clever nature. "You're turning out a regular Parisienne," he heard Barry accuse her one night (the attic walls were thin). She replied, "If you knew what it is for me not to be always defending myself, always afraid, always alone . . ."

Lenoir sat up on his cot and brooded. About midnight, when all was quiet, he rose and noiselessly prepared the pinches of sulfur and silver, drew the pentagram, opened the book. Very softly he read the spell. His face was apprehensive.

In the pentagram appeared a small white dog. It cowered and hung its tail, then came shyly forward, sniffed Lenoir's hand, looked up at him with liquid eyes and gave a modest, pleading whine. A lost puppy . . . Lenoir stroked it. It licked his hands and jumped all over him, wild with relief. On its white leather collar was a silver plaque engraved, "Jolie. Dupont, 36 rue de Seine, Paris VIe."

Jolie went to sleep, after gnawing a crust, curled up under Lenoir's chair. And the alchemist opened the book again and read, still softly, but this time without self-consciousness, without fear, knowing what would happen.

Emerging from his store-room bedroom-honeymoon in the morning, Barry stopped short in the doorway. Lenoir was sitting up in bed, petting a white puppy, and deep in conversation with the person sitting on the foot of the bed, a tall red-haired woman dressed in silver. The puppy barked. Lenoir said, "Good morning!" The woman smiled wondrously.

"Jumping Jesus," Barry muttered (in English). Then he said, "Good morning. When are you from?" The effect was Rita Hayworth, sublimated—Hayworth plus the Mona Lisa, perhaps?

"From Altair, about seven thousand years from now," she said, smiling still more wondrously. Her French accent was worse than that of a football-scholarship freshman. "I'm an archaeologist. I was excavating the ruins of Paris III. I'm sorry I speak the language so badly; of course we know it only from inscriptions."

"From Altair? The star? But you're human—I think—"

"Our planet was colonized from Earth about four thousand years ago—that is, three thousand years from now." She laughed, most wondrously, and glanced at Lenoir. "Jehan explained it all to me, but I still get confused."

"It was a dangerous thing to try it again, Jehan!" Barry accused him. "We've been awfully lucky, you know."

"No," said the Frenchman. "Not lucky."

"But after all it's black magic you're playing with—Listen—I don't know your name, madame."

"Kislk," she said.

"Listen, Kislk," Barry said without even a stumble, "your science must be fantastically advanced—is there any magic? Does it exist? Can the laws of Nature really be broken, as we seem to be doing?"

"I've never seen nor heard of an authenticated case of magic."

"Then what goes on?" Barry roared. "Why does that stupid old spell work for Jehan, for us, that one spell, and here, nowhere else, for nobody else, in five—no, eight—no, fifteen thousand years of recorded history? Why? Why? And where did that damn puppy come from?"

"The puppy was lost," Lenoir said, his dark face grave. "Somewhere near this house, on the Ile Saint-Louis."

"And I was sorting potsherds," Kislk said, also gravely, "in a house-site, Island 2, Pit 4, Section D. A lovely Spring day, and I hated it. Loathed it. The day, the work, the people around me." Again she looked at the gaunt little alchemist, a long, quiet look. "I tried to explain it to Jehan last night. We have improved the race, you see. We're all very tall, healthy, and beautiful. No fillings in our teeth. All skulls from Early America have fillings in the teeth. . . . Some of us are brown, some white, some gold-skinned. But all beautiful, and healthy, and well-adjusted, and aggressive, and successful. Our professions and degree of success are preplanned for us in the State Pre-School Homes. But there's an occasional genetic flaw. Me, for instance. I was trained as an archaeologist because the Teachers saw that I really didn't like people, live people. People bored me. All like me on the outside, all alien to me on the inside. When everything's alike, which place is home? . . . But now I've seen an unhygienic room with insufficient heating. Now I've seen a cathedral not in ruins. Now I've met a living man who's shorter than me, with bad teeth and a short temper. Now I'm home, I'm where I can be myself, I'm no longer alone!"

"Alone," Lenoir said gently to Barry. "Loneliness, eh?

228

Loneliness is the spell, loneliness is stronger. . . . Really it doesn't seem unnatural."

Bota was peering round the doorway, her face flushed between the black tangles of her hair. She smiled shyly and said a polite Latin good-morning to the newcomer.

"Kislk doesn't know Latin," Lenoir said with immense satisfaction. "We must teach Bota some French. French is the language of love, anyway, eh? Come along, let's go out and buy some bread. I'm hungry."

Kislk hid her silver tunic under the useful and anonymous cloak, while Lenoir pulled on his moth-eaten black gown. Bota combed her hair, while Barry thoughtfully scratched a louse-bite on his neck. Then they set forth to get breakfast. The alchemist and the interstellar archaeologist went first, speaking French; the Gaulish slave and the professor from Indiana followed, speaking Latin, and holding hands. The narrow streets were crowded, bright with sunshine. Above them Notre Dame reared its two square towers against the sky. Beside them the Seine rippled softly. It was April in Paris, and on the banks of the river the chestnuts were in bloom.

JOAN AIKEN
(1924–   )

"It is so much more fun inventing the word for it than doing the job! I think that is the main reason why I love writing. . . . It is so much better inventing a whole new world *just* the way you want it—than doing the jobs that are waiting to be done. . . . The very thought of all those awful little jobs is enough to make one sit down and write 'Once upon a time—.' " This is how Joan Aiken, English novelist, short-story writer, and author of children's books, rather playfully explains her motivation for writing in a recent issue of *Cricket: The Magazine for Children* (March, 1977). Considering the entertainment and pleasure she has brought to countless readers of every age over the past quarter of a century, we are thankful for the existence of those "awful little jobs."

Born September 4, 1924, in Rye, Sussex, the daughter of the distinguished poet Conrad Potter Aiken and Jessie (MacDonald) Aiken, Joan Aiken received her higher education at Wychwood School, Oxford (1936–41). After completing her work there, she joined the British Broadcasting Corporation for a one-year stint, and then moved on to the United Nations London Information Office, where she served as a research assistant in the Library (1943–49). It was here that she met and fell in love with Ronald George Brown, a press officer in the Information Office. They were married on July 7, 1945, but only ten years later, Brown died of lung cancer; the young widow was left to care for two small children. Shortly after her husband's death, Aiken found employment with *Argosy Magazine* (1955–60). In 1961 she joined the J. Walter Thompson Advertising Agency, but that same year decided to take her chances as a free-lance writer. Since then she has established herself as one of the finest, and most prolific, English writers of the twentieth century.

In a brief autobiographical statement in *Contemporary Authors* Aiken explains: "I always intended to be a writer; when I was five I went to the village store and spent two shillings (a huge sum then) on a large, thick writing-block in which to write poems, stories, and thoughts, as they occurred. It lasted for years . . . and when it was finished I bought another and then another." Although she published a short story as early as 1941, when she was just seventeen years old, her first major publication was *All You've Ever Wanted* (1953), a collection of children's short stories. Among her many other short-story collections are *A Necklace of Raindrops, and Other Stories* (1968), *Smoke From Cromwell's Time, and Other Stories* (1970), and *A Harp of Fishbones, and Other Stories* (1972). Her most popular novels include *The Wolves of Willoughby Chase* (1962), which earned the Lewis Carroll Award; *The Whispering Mountain* (1968), which received the *Manchester Guardian* Award and was runner-up for the Carnegie Award; *Night Fall* (1972), winner of the Mystery Writers of America Award; and *Midnight Is a Place* (1974), which prompted Timothy Foote to write ". . . the author proves once again that she writes about children in distress better than anyone since Dickens." (*Time,* 23 Dec. 1974). Besides her novels and short stories, Aiken has written poetry and a child's play, *Winterthing* (1972). She currently makes her home in Sussex, England, where she enjoys reading, painting, cooking, gardening, and listening to classical music, especially Handel and Purcell.

Not long ago Aiken wrote: "Thinking back over my children's books and my adult thrillers (if thrillers are adult) I honestly can't recall any difference at all in the actual writing process. . . . If ever I find myself writing anything . . . with less than the total care and skill I can command, I shall take this as a sign that I have written enough, and shall turn to some other profession." (*Contemporary Authors,* 1974). This literary philosophy, reminiscent of the attitude of other fantasists such as

C. S. Lewis and J. R. R. Tolkien, serves to remind us of the major strength and significance of "A Harp of Fishbones" and other quality fantasy works: All exhibit a universality which allows readers of all ages to enjoy, and profit from, them.

"A Harp of Fishbones" is a delightful fairy tale which clearly exhibits Aiken's consummate craftsmanship. The plot is energetic, tightly woven, and filled with surprises (note the ending); the characterization is handled with a deft and careful touch; the secondary world is convincingly described, with an admirable inner consistency; and the themes are concretely illustrated through the actions of the characters. Aiken is a marvelous scene writer, and although many of the scenes in this story are vividly drawn, the episode featuring Nerryn's successful breaking of the mountain goddesses's spell is especially moving and memorable. Those familiar with Lewis's Narnian Chronicles will immediately be reminded of Chapter XVI of *The Lion, The Witch, and The Wardrobe*, where Aslan breathes life into the multitude of creatures turned into lifeless statues by the malevolent White Witch. Both scenes, with their strong archetypal underpinnings, illustrate the power of high fantasy to elicit a sense of awe and wonder.

◄§ A Harp of Fishbones §►

Joan Aiken

Little Nerryn lived in the half-ruined mill at the upper end of the village, where the stream ran out of the forest. The old miller's name was Timorash, but she called him uncle. Her own father and mother were dead, long before she could remember. Timorash was no real kin, nor was he particularly kind to her; he was a lazy old man. He never troubled to grow corn as the other people in the village did, little patches in the clearing below the village before the forest began again. When people brought him corn to grind he took one-fifth of it as his fee and this, with wild plums which Nerryn gathered and dried, and carp from the deep millpool, kept him and the child fed through the short bright summers and the long silent winters.

Nerryn learned to do the cooking when she was seven or eight; she toasted fish on sticks over the fire and baked cakes of bread on a flat stone; Timorash beat her if the food was burnt, but it mostly was, just the same, because so often half her mind would be elsewhere, listening to the bell-like call of a bird or pondering about what made the difference between the stream's voice in winter and in summer. When she was little older Timorash taught her how to work the mill, opening the sluice-gate so that the green, clear mountain water could hurl down against the great wooden paddle-wheel. Nerryn liked this much better, since she already spent hours watching the stream endlessly pouring and plaiting down its narrow passage. Old Timorash had hoped that now he would be able to give up work altogether and lie in the sun all day, or crouch by the fire, slowly adding one stick after another and dreaming about barley wine. But Nerryn forgot to take flour in

payment from the villagers, who were in no hurry to remind her, so the old man angrily decided that this plan
would not answer, and sent her out to work.

First she worked for one household, then for another.

The people of the village had come from the plains;
they were surly, big-boned, and lank, with tow-coloured
hair and pale eyes; even the children seldom spoke. Little
Nerryn sometimes wondered, looking at her reflection
in the millpool, how it was that she should be so different
from them, small and brown-skinned with dark hair like a
bird's feathers and hazelnut eyes. But it was no use asking
questions of old Timorash, who never answered except by
grunting or throwing a clod of earth at her. Another difference was that she loved to chatter, and this was perhaps
the main reason why the people she worked for soon sent
her packing.

There were other reasons too, for, though Nerryn was
willing enough to work, things often distracted her.

"She let the bread burn while she ran outside to listen to
a curlew," said one.

"When she was helping me cut the hay she asked so
many questions that my ears have ached for three days,"
complained another.

"Instead of scaring off the birds from my corn-patch she
sat with her chin on her fists, watching them gobble down
half a winter's supply and whistling to them!" grumbled
a third.

Nobody would keep her more than a few days, and she
had plenty of beatings, especially from Timorash, who had
hoped that her earnings would pay for a keg of barley
wine. Once in his life he had had a whole keg, and he still
felt angry when he remembered that it was finished.

At last Nerryn went to work for an old woman who
lived in a tumbledown hut at the bottom of the street. Her
name was Saroon and she was by far the oldest in the village, so withered and wrinkled that most people thought
she was a witch; besides, she knew when it was going to
rain and as the only person in the place who did not fear
to venture a little way into the forest. But she was growing
weak now, and stiff, and wanted somebody to help dig her
corn-patch and cut wood. Nevertheless she hardly seemed
to welcome help when it came. As Nerryn moved about

at the tasks she was set, the old woman's little red-rimmed eyes followed her suspiciously; she hobbled round the hut watching through cracks, grumbling and chuntering to herself, never losing sight of the girl for a moment, like some cross-grained old animal that sees a stranger near its burrow.

On the fourth day she said,

"You're singing, girl."

"I—I'm sorry," Nerryn stammered. "I didn't mean to —I wasn't thinking. Don't beat me, please."

"Humph," said the old woman, but she did not beat Nerryn that time. And next day, watching through the window-hole while Nerryn chopped wood, she said,

"You're not singing."

Nerryn jumped. She had not known the old woman was so near.

"I thought you didn't like me to," she faltered.

"I didn't say so, did I?"

Muttering, the old woman stumped off to the back of the hut and began to sort through a box of mildewy nuts. "As if I should care," Nerryn heard her grumble, "whether the girl sings or not!" But next day she put her head out of the door, while Nerryn hoed the corn patch, and said,

"Sing, child!"

Nerryn looked at her, doubtful and timid, to see if she really meant it, but she nodded her head energetically, till the tangled grey locks jounced on her shoulders, and repeated,

"Sing!"

So presently the clear, tiny thread of Nerryn's song began again as she sliced off the weeds; and old Saroon came out and sat on an upturned log beside the door, pounding roots for soup and mumbling to herself in time to the sound. And at the end of the week she did not dismiss the girl, as everyone else had done, though what she paid was so little that Timorash grumbled every time Nerryn brought it home. At this rate twenty years would go by before he had saved enough for a key of barley wine.

One day Saroon said,

"Your father used to sing."

This was the first time anyone had spoken of him.

236

"Oh," Nerryn cried, forgetting her fear of the old woman. "Tell me about him."

"Why should I?" old Saroon said sourly. "He never did anything for *me*." And she hobbled off to fetch a pot of water. But later she relented and said,

"His hair was the colour of ash buds, like yours. And he carried a harp."

"A harp, what is a harp?"

"Oh, don't pester, child. I'm busy."

But another day she said, "A harp is a thing to make music. His was a gold one, but it was broken."

"Gold, what is gold?"

"This," said the old woman, and she pulled out a small, thin disc which she wore on a cord of plaited grass round her neck.

"Why!" Nerryn exclaimed. "Everybody in the village has one of those except Timorash and me. I've often asked what they were but no one would answer."

"They are gold. When your father went off and left you and the harp with Timorash, the old man ground up the harp between the millstones. And he melted down the gold powder and made it into these little circles and sold them to everybody in the village, and bought a keg of barley wine. He told us they would bring good luck. But I have never had any good luck and that was a long time ago. And Timorash has long since drunk all his barley wine."

"Where did my father go?" asked Nerryn.

"Into the forest," the old woman snapped. "I could have told him he was in for trouble. I could have warned him. But he never asked *my* advice."

She sniffed, and set a pot of herbs boiling on the fire. And Nerryn could get no more out of her that day.

But little by little, as time passed, more came out.

"Your father came from over the mountains. High up yonder, he said, there was a great city, with houses and palaces and temples, and as many rich people as there are fish in the millpool. Best of all, there was always music playing in the streets and houses and in the temples. But then the goddess of the mountain became angry, and fire burst out of a crack in the hillside. And then a great cold came, so that people froze where they stood. Your father said he only just managed to escape with you by running very fast. Your mother had died in the fire."

"Where was he going?"

"The king of the city had ordered him to go for help."

"What sort of help?"

"Don't ask *me*," the old woman grumbled. "You'd think he'd have settled down here like a person of sense, and mended his harp. But no, on he must go, leaving you behind so that he could travel faster. He said he'd fetch you again on his way back. But of course he never did come back—one day I found his bones in the forest. The birds must have killed him."

"How do you *know* they were my father's bones?"

"Because of the tablet he carried. See, here it is, with his name on it, Heramon the harper."

"Tell me more about the harp!"

"It was shaped like this," the old woman said. They were washing clothes by the stream, and she drew with her finger in the mud. "Like this, and it had golden strings across, so. All but one of the strings had melted in the fire from the mountain. Even on just one string he could make very beautiful music, that would force you to stop whatever you were doing and listen. It is a pity he had to leave the harp behind. Timorash wanted it as payment for looking after you. If your father had taken the harp with him, perhaps he would have been able to reach the other side of the forest."

Nerryn thought about this story a great deal. For the next few weeks she did even less work than usual and was mostly to be found squatting with her chin on her fists by the side of the stream. Saroon beat her, but not very hard. Then one day Nerryn said,

"I shall make a harp."

"Hah!" sniffed the old woman. "You! What do you know of such things?"

After a few minutes she asked,

"What will you make it from?"

Nerryn said, "I shall make it of fishbones. Some of the biggest carp in the millpool have bones as thick as my wrist, and they are very strong."

"Timorash will never allow it."

"I shall wait till he is asleep, then."

So Nerryn waited till night, and then she took a chunk of rotten wood, which glows in the dark, and dived into the deep millpool, swimming down and down to the depths where the biggest carp lurk, among the mud and weeds and old sunken logs.

When they saw the glimmer of the wood through the water, all the fish came nosing and nibbling and swimming round Nerryn, curious to find if this thing which shone so strangely was good to eat. She waited as long as she could bear it, holding her breath, till a great barrel-shaped monster slid nudging right up against her; then, quick as a flash, she wrapped her arms round his slippery sides and fled up with a bursting heart to the surface.

Much to her surprise, old Saroon was there, waiting in the dark on the bank. But the old woman only said,

"You had better bring the carp to my hut. After all, you want no more than the bones, and it would be a pity to waste all that good meat. I can live on it for a week." So she cut the meat off the bones, which were coal-black but had a sheen on them like mother-of-pearl. Nerryn dried them by the fire, and then she joined together the three biggest, notching them to fit, and cementing them with a glue she made by boiling some of the smaller bones together. She used long, thin, strong bones for strings, joining them to the frame in the same manner.

All the time old Saroon watched closely. Sometimes she would say,

"That was not the way of it. Heramon's harp was wider," or "You are putting the strings too far apart. There should be more of them, and they should be tighter."

When at last it was done, she said,

"Now you must hang it in the sun to dry."

So for three days the harp hung drying in the sun and wind. At night Saroon took it into her hut and covered it with a cloth. On the fourth day she said,

"Now, play!"

Nerryn rubbed her finger across the strings, and they gave out a liquid murmur, like that of a stream running over pebbles, under a bridge. She plucked a string, and the noise was like that a drop of water makes, falling in a hollow place.

"That will be music," old Saroon said, nodding her

head, satisfied. "It is not quite the same as the sound from your father's harp, but it is music. Now you shall play me tunes every day, and I shall sit in the sun and listen."

"No," said Nerryn, "for if Timorash hears me playing he will take the harp away and break it or sell it. I shall go to my father's city and see if I can find any of his kin there."

At this old Saroon was very angry. "Here have I taken all these pains to help you, and what reward do I get for it? How much pleasure do you think I have, living among dolts in this dismal place? I was not born here, any more than you were. You could at least play to me at night, when Timorash is asleep."

"Well, I will play to you for seven nights," Nerryn said.

Each night old Saroon tried to persuade her not to go, and she tried harder as Nerryn became more skilful in playing, and drew from the fishbone harp a curious watery music, like the songs that birds sing when it is raining. But Nerryn would not be persuaded to stay, and when she saw this, on the seventh night, Saroon said,

"I suppose I shall have to tell you how to go through the forest. Otherwise you will certainly die, as your father did. When you go among the trees you will find that the grass underfoot is thick and strong and hairy, and the farther you go, the higher it grows, as high as your waist. And it is sticky and clings to you, so that you can only go forward slowly, one step at a time. Then, in the middle of the forest, perched in the branches, are vultures who will drop on you and peck you to death if you stand still for more than a minute."

"How do you know all this?" Nerryn said.

"I have tried many times to go through the forest, but it is too far for me; I grow tired and have to turn back. The vultures take no notice of me, I am too old and withered, but a tender young piece like you would be just what they fancy."

"Then what must I do?" Nerryn asked.

"You must play music on your harp till they fall asleep; then, while they sleep, cut the grass with your knife and go forward as fast as you can."

Nerryn said, "If I cut you enough fuel for a month, and catch you another carp, and gather you a bushed of nuts, will you give me your little gold circle, or my father's tablet?"

But this Saroon would not do. She did, though, break off the corner of the tablet which had Heramon the harper's name on it, and give that to Nerryn.

"But don't blame me," she said sourly, "if you find the city all burnt and frozen, with not a living soul to walk its streets."

"Oh, it will all have been rebuilt by this time," Nerryn said. "I shall find my father's people, or my mother's, and I shall come back for you, riding a white mule and leading another."

"Fairy tales!" old Saroon said angrily. "Be off with you, then. If you don't wish to stay I'm sure *I* don't want you idling about the place. All the work you've done this last week I could have done better myself in half an hour. Drat the woodsmoke! It gets in a body's eyes till they can't see a thing." And she hobbled into the hut, working her mouth sourly and rubbing her eyes with the back of her hand.

Nerryn ran into the forest, going cornerways up the mountain, so as not to pass too close to the mill where old Timorash lay sleeping in the sun.

Soon she had to slow down because the way was so steep. And the grass grew thicker and thicker, hairy, sticky, all twined and matted together, as high as her waist. Presently, as she hacked and cut at it with her bone knife, she heard a harsh croaking and flapping above her. She looked up, and saw two grey vultures perched on a branch, leaning forward to peer down at her. Their wings were twice the length of a man's arm and they had long, wrinkled, black, leathery necks and little fierce yellow eyes. As she stood, two more, then five, ten, twenty others came rousting through the branches, and all perched round about, craning down their long black necks, swaying back and forth, keeping balanced by the way they opened and shut their wings.

Nerryn felt very much afraid of them, but she unslung the harp from her back and began to play a soft, trickling tune, like rain falling on a deep pool. Very soon the vultures sank their necks down between their shoulders and closed their eyes. They sat perfectly still.

When she was certain they were asleep, Nerryn made haste to cut and slash at the grass. She was several hundred yards on her way before the vultures woke and came cawing and jostling through the branches to cluster again just overhead. Quickly she pulled the harp round and strummed on its fishbone strings until once again, lulled by the music, the vultures sank their heads between their grey wings and slept. Then she went back to cutting the grass, as fast as she could.

It was a long, tiring way. Soon she grew so weary that she could hardly push one foot ahead of the other, and it was hard to keep awake; once she only just roused in time when a vulture, swooping down, missed her with his beak and instead struck the harp on her back with a loud strange twang that set echoes scampering through the trees.

At last the forest began to thin and dwindle; here the tree-trunks and branches were all draped about with grey-green moss, like long dangling hanks of sheepswool. Moss grew on the rocky ground, too, in a thick carpet. When she reached this part, Nerryn could go on safely; the vultures rose in an angry flock and flew back with harsh croaks of disappointment, for they feared the trailing moss would wind round their wings and trap them.

As soon as she reached the edge of the trees Nerryn lay down in a deep tussock of moss and fell fast asleep.

She was so tired that she slept almost till nightfall, but then the cold woke her. It was bitter on the bare mountainside; the ground was all crisp with white frost, and when Nerryn started walking uphill she crunched through it, leaving deep black footprints. Unless she kept moving she knew that she would probably die of cold, so she climbed on, higher and higher; the stars came out, showing more frost-covered slopes ahead and all around, while the forest far below curled round the flank of the mountain like black fur.

Through the night she went on climbing and by sunrise she had reached the foot of a steep slope of ice-covered boulders. When she tried to climb over these she only slipped back again.

What shall I do now? Nerryn wondered. She stood blowing on her frozen fingers and thought, "I must go on or I shall die here of cold. I will play a tune on the harp to warm my fingers and my wits."

She unslung the harp. It was hard to play, for her fingers were almost numb and at first refused to obey but, while she had climbed the hill, a very sweet, lively tune had come into her head, and she struggled and struggled until her stubborn fingers found the right notes to play it. Once she played the tune—twice—and the stones on the slope above began to roll and shift. She played a third time and, with a thunderous roar, the whole pile broke loose and went sliding down the mountain-side. Nerryn was only just able to dart aside out of the way before the frozen mass careered past, sending up a smoking dust of ice.

Trembling a little, she went on up the hill, and now she came to a gate in a great wall, set about with towers. The gate stood open, and so she walked through.

"Surely this must be my father's city," she thought.

But when she stood inside the gate, her heart sank, and she remembered old Saroon's words. For the city that must once have been bright with gold and coloured stone and gay with music was all silent; not a soul walked the streets and the houses, under thick covering of frost, were burnt and blackened by fire.

And, what was still more frightening, when Nerryn looked through the doorways into the houses, she could see people standing or sitting or lying, frozen still like statues, as the cold had caught them while they worked, or slept, or sat at dinner.

"Where shall I go now?" she thought. "It would have been better to stay with Saroon in the forest. When night comes I shall only freeze to death in this place."

But still she went on, almost tiptoeing in the frosty silence of the city, looking into doorways and through gates, until she came to a building that was larger than any other, built with a high roof and many pillars of white marble. The fire had not touched it.

"This must be the temple," she thought, remembering the tale Saroon had told, and she walked between the pillars, which glittered like white candles in the light from the rising sun. Inside there was a vast hall, and many people standing frozen, just as they had been when they

243

came to pray for deliverance from their trouble. They had offerings with them, honey and cakes and white doves and lambs and precious ointment. At the back of the hall the people wore rough clothes of homespun cloth, but farther forward Nerryn saw wonderful robes, embroidered with gold and copper thread, made of rich materials, trimmed with fur and sparkling stones. And up in the very front, kneeling on the steps of the altar, was a man who was finer than all the rest and Nerryn thought he must have been the king himself. His hair and long beard were white, his cloak was purple, and on his head were three crowns, one gold, one copper, and one of ivory. Nerryn stole up to him and touched the fingers that held a gold staff, but they were ice-cold and still as marble, like all the rest.

A sadness came over her as she looked at the people and she thought, "What use to them are their fine robes now? Why did the goddess punish them? What did they do wrong?"

But there was no answer to her question.

"I had better leave this place before I am frozen as well," she thought. "The goddess may be angry with me too, for coming here. But first I will play for her on my harp, as I have not brought any offering."

So she took her harp and began to play. She played all the tunes she could remember, and last of all she played the one that had come into her head as she climbed the mountain.

At the noise of her playing, frost began to fall in white showers from the roof of the temple, and from the rafters and pillars and the clothes of the motionless people. Then the king sneezed. Then there was a stirring noise, like the sound of a winter stream when the ice begins to melt. Then someone laughed—a loud, clear laugh. And, just as, outside the town, the pile of frozen rocks had started to move and topple when Nerryn played, so now the whole gathering of people began to stretch themselves, and turn round, and look at one another, and smile. And as she went on playing they began to dance.

The dancing spread, out of the temple and down the streets. People in the houses stood up and danced. Still dancing, they fetched brooms and swept away the heaps of frost that kept falling from the rooftops with the sound of the music. They fetched old wooden pipes and tabors out of the cellars that had escaped the fire, so that when Nerryn stopped playing at last, quite tired out, the music still went on. All day and all night, for thirty days, the music lasted, until the houses were rebuilt, the streets clean, and not a speck of frost remained in the city.

But the king beckoned Nerryn aside when she stopped playing and they sat down on the steps of the temple.

"My child," he said, "where did you get that harp?"

"Sir, I made it out of fishbones after a picture of my father's harp that an old woman made for me."

"And what was your father's name, child, and where is he now?"

"Sir, he is dead in the forest, but here is a piece of a tablet with his name on it."

And Nerryn held out the little fragment with Heramon the harper's name written. When he saw it, great tears formed in the king's eyes and began to roll down his cheeks.

"Sir," Nerryn said, "what is the matter? Why do you weep?"

"I weep for my son Heramon, who is lost, and I weep for joy because my grandchild has returned to me."

Then the king embraced Nerryn and took her to his palace and had robes of fur and velvet put on her, and there was great happiness and much feasting. And the king told Nerryn how, many years ago, the goddess was angered because the people had grown so greedy for gold from her mountain that they spent their lives in digging and mining, day and night, and forgot to honour her with music, in her temple and in the streets, as they had been used to do. They made tools of gold, and plates and dishes and musical instruments; everything that could be was made of gold. So at last the goddess appeared among them, terrible with rage, and put a curse on them, of burning and freezing.

"Since you prefer gold, got by burrowing in the earth, to the music that should honour me," she said, "you may keep your golden toys and little good may they do you! Let your golden harps and trumpets be silent, your flutes and pipes be dumb! I shall not come among you again until I am summoned by notes from a harp that is not made of gold, nor of silver, nor any precious metal, a harp that has never touched the earth but came from deep water, a harp that no man has ever played."

Then fire burst out of the mountain, destroying houses and killing many people. The king ordered his son Heramon, who was the bravest man in the city, to cross the dangerous forest and seek far and wide until he should find the harp of which the goddess spoke. Before Heramon could depart a great cold had struck, freezing people where they stood; only just in time he caught up his little daughter from her cradle and carried her away with him.

"But now you are come back," the old king said, "you shall be queen after me, and we shall take care that the goddess is honoured with music every day, in the temple and in the streets. And we will order everything that is made of gold to be thrown into the mountain torrent, so that nobody ever again shall be tempted to worship gold before the goddess."

So this was done, the king himself being the first to throw away his golden crown and staff. The river carried all the golden things down through the forest until they came to rest in Timorash's millpool, and one day, when he was fishing for carp, he pulled out the crown. Overjoyed, he ground it to powder and sold it to his neighbours for barley wine. Then he returned to the pool, hoping for more gold, but by now he was so drunk that he fell in and was drowned among a clutter of golden spades and trumpets and goblets and pickaxes.

But long before this Nerryn, with her harp on her back and astride of a white mule with knives bound to its hoofs, had ridden down the mountain to fetch Saroon as she had promised. She passed the forest safely, playing music for the vultures while the mule cut its way through the long grass. Nobody in the village recognized her, so splendidly was she dressed in fur and scarlet.

But when she came to where Saroon's hut had stood, the ground was bare, nor was there any trace that a dwelling had ever been there. And when she asked for Saroon, nobody knew the name, and the whole village declared that such a person had never been there.

Amazed and sorrowful, Nerryn returned to her grandfather. But one day, not long after, when she was alone, praying in the temple of the goddess, she heard a voice that said,

"Sing, child!"

And Nerryn was greatly astonished, for she felt she had heard the voice before, though she could not think where.

While she looked about her, wondering, the voice said again,

"Sing!"

And then Nerryn understood, and she laughed, and, taking her harp, sang a song about chopping wood, and about digging, and fishing, and the birds of the forest, and how the stream's voice changes in summer and in winter. For now she knew who had helped her to make her harp of fishbones.

LLOYD ALEXANDER
(1924–   )

Lloyd Alexander's career has a good deal in common with the quests he describes in much of his writing. In Alexander's case, the quest has been for the right subject and the right audience. He has, indeed, discovered a number of "right subjects," including time-travelling cats and Celtic mythology. And, to the great delight of his readers, he has found his "right audience" in children—and in adults who are mature enough to enjoy good children's literature. As did C. S. Lewis, Alexander writes children's literature because he finds it the best medium in which to say what he has to say.

But, as with most quests, Alexander's success came only after much striving, for many years. Alexander was born in Philadelphia, where he still lives with his Parisian-born wife, Janine. He decided at age fifteen to become a writer—a poet. After high school, he found it necessary to get a job (he worked as a bank clerk), but he wrote in the evenings. He earned enough money to enter college, but stayed there only a short time, since the courses were teaching him what he had already learned on his own. Believing that experience would be a better teacher, he joined the army, where he spent three and a half years during World War II. He went to Wales, Germany, and France as a member of army intelligence and stayed on for a while after the war in Paris, where he married Janine and attended the University of Paris.

Equipped with these experiences, he returned to Philadelphia, where he again got a job and pursued his writing at night. Seven years and three unpublished novels later, he decided to write about his own experiences and had his first book published in 1955. He continued to write adult fiction for a number of years until finally discovering in the early 1960s that he was destined to be a children's writer. The result of his discovery was the delightful work *Time Cat* (1963).

Alexander had read the legend of King Arthur and his knights and other stories from Celtic myth as a youth, and he had found Wales an enchanting and ancient land, but these interests didn't find expression in his writing until he reread Welsh legends while working on *Time Cat*. These readings, which included that storehouse of Celtic mythology, the *Mabinogion,* furnished Alexander with the incentive and a wealth of material for his most important work, the five books that make up the Prydain Cycle: *The Book of Three* (1964), *The Black Cauldron* (1965), *The Castle of Llyr* (1966), *Taran Wanderer* (1967), and *The High King* (1969). Among the numerous prizes these books received was the 1969 Newberry Award, for *The High King*. Literally because of popular demand, Alexander composed a number of stories related to the cycle. These appeared in 1973 as *The Foundling and Other Tales of Prydain.*

Alexander remains a prolific writer. In addition to writing several children's books (unrelated to Prydain) in the past four years, he also has published articles and stories in magazines. He has been on the editorial board of the excellent children's monthly *Cricket* since its inception in 1973. Indeed, one gets the distinct impression that even though Alexander seems to have achieved his quest, he is not going to rest or even slow down. Were we to ask him why, he would perhaps remind us of Gwydion's words to Taran after Taran had accomplished his quest: "That was the easiest of your tasks, only a beginning, not an ending" (*The High King*).

Like many good fantasy stories, "The Smith, the Weaver, and the Harper," while readily understood and enjoyed by children, can be even more fully appreciated by adults. Adults, one might add, need to be reminded of its theme even more than children do. This tale, from *The Foundling and Other Tales of Prydain,* draws its inspiration, as well as the figure of Arawn, from the *Mabinogion.* It remains true to its source in presenting Arawn as an imposing and dreaded figure. But, by associating the human characteristic of greed with this Celtic Lord of Death, Alexander gains a striking and unique effect. One can succumb to Death while yet remaining alive.

⊷ The Smith, the Weaver, ⊱ and the Harper

Lloyd Alexander

There was a time in Prydain when craftsmen were so skillful their very tools held the secrets of their crafts. Of these, the hammer of Iscovan the smith could work any metal into whatever shape its owner wished. The shuttle of Follin the weaver could weave quicker than the eye could see, with never a knot or a tangle. The harp of Menwy the bard sounded airs of such beauty it lifted the hearts of all who heard it.

But Arawn, Lord of Death, coveted these things and set out to gain them for himself, to lock them deep in his treasure house, so no man might ever have use of them.

And so it was that one day, working at his anvil, Iscovan saw a tall man standing in his doorway. The stranger was arrayed as a war-leader, sword at side, shield over shoulder; he wore a coat of mail whose links were so cleverly wrought and burnished it seemed smooth as satin and glittering as gold.

"Blacksmith," said the tall man, "the rowel of my spur is broken. Can you mend it?"

"There's no metal in all this world I can't mend, or shape, or temper," Iscovan answered. "A broken spur? A trifle! Here, put it on my anvil. With this hammer of mine I'll have it done in three strokes."

"You have a fair hammer," the warrior said, "but I doubt it can work metal such as this."

"Think you so?" cried Iscovan, stung by these words. "Well, now, see for yourself."

So saying, he laid the spur on his anvil, picked up his

hammer, and began pounding away with all the strength of his burly arms.

At last, out of breath, his brow smudged and streaming, he stopped and frowned at the spur. It showed not the least mark from his battering.

Iscovan pumped the bellows of his forge, picked up the spur with his tongs, and thrust it into his furnace. There, heating it white-hot, once again he set it on his anvil, and hammered as hard as he was able, to no avail.

"Trouble yourself no more," the stranger told the puzzled blacksmith. "In my country, armorers shape metal harder than any you know. If you would do likewise, you must use a hammer like theirs."

With that, he reached into a leather sack hanging from his belt and took out a little golden hammer, which he handed to the smith.

"That toy?" Iscovan burst out. "Make sport of me and you'll have more than a broken spur to mend!"

"Try it, nevertheless," replied the stranger.

Laughing scornfully, the smith gripped the hammer and struck with all his force, sure the implement would break in his hand. Instead, sparks shot up, there came a roar of thunder, and his anvil split nearly in two. However, after that single blow, the spur was good as new.

Iscovan's jaw dropped and he stared at the tall man, who said:

"My thanks to you, blacksmith. Now let me take my hammer and go my way."

"Wait," said Iscovan, clutching the tool. "Tell me, first, how I might get a hammer like yours."

"In my realm, these are treasured highly," replied the stranger. "You have only seen the smallest part of its worth. With such a hammer a smith can forge weapons that lose neither point nor edge, shields that never split, coats of mail no sword can pierce. Thus arrayed, even a handful of warriors could master a kingdom."

"Tell me nothing of arms and armor," Iscovan replied. "I'm no swordsmith, my skill is with plow-irons, rakes, and hoes. But, one way or another, I must have that hammer."

Now Iscovan had always been a peaceful man; but even as he spoke these words, his head began spinning with secret thoughts. The stranger's voice seemed to fan embers in his mind until they glowed hotter than his forge. And Iscovan said to himself, "If this man speaks the truth, and no sword or spear can harm them, indeed a handful of warriors could master a kingdom, for who could stand against them? But the smith who had the secret—he would be master of all! And why not I instead of another?"

The stranger, who meantime had been watching Iscovan narrowly, said:

"Blacksmith, you have done me a favor and by rights I owe a favor to you. So, I shall give you this hammer. But for the sake of a fair bargain, give me yours in its place."

Iscovan hesitated, picking up his old hammer and looking fondly at it. The handle was worn smooth by long use, the iron head was nicked and dented; yet this hammer knew its craft as deeply as Iscovan himself, for it had taken to itself the skill of all smiths. It had well served Iscovan and brought him the honor of his workmanship. Nevertheless, considering what new power lay within his grasp, Iscovan nodded and said:

"Done. So be it."

The stranger took Iscovan's iron hammer, leaving the gold one in the hands of the smith, and without another word strode from the forge.

No sooner had the stranger gone than Iscovan, with a triumphant cry, raised the hammer and gave his anvil a ringing blow. But even as he did, the hammer crumbled in his hand. The bright gold had turned to lead.

Bewildered, Iscovan stared at the useless tool, then ran from the forge, shouting for his own hammer back again. Of the stranger, however, there was no trace.

And from that time on, Iscovan drudged at his forge, never to find a hammer the equal of the one he had bartered away.

On another day, Follin the weaver was busy at his loom when a short, thickset man, ruddy-cheeked and quick-eyed, came into his weaving shed. Follin stopped plying his shuttle, which had been darting back and forth among the threads like a fish in water.

"Good greeting to you," said the stranger, clad in garments finer than any the weaver had ever seen. His heavy cloak was of cloth of gold, embroidered in curious patterns. "My cloak is worn and shabby. Will you weave another for me?"

"I don't know where you're from," returned Follin, dazzled at the traveler's apparel, "but surely it's a rich realm if you call that handsome cloak shabby."

"It serves well enough to wear on a journey, to be stained and spattered," returned the traveler. "But in my country this is no better than a castoff. Even a beggar would scorn it."

Follin, meanwhile, had climbed down from his bench at the loom. He could not take his eyes from the stranger's cloak, and when he ventured to rub the hem between his thumb and fingers, he grew still more amazed. The cloth, although purest gold, was lighter than thistledown and softer than lamb's wool.

"I can weave nothing like this," Follin stammered. "I have no thread to match it, and the work is beyond even my skill."

"It would be a simple matter," said the traveler, "if you had the means." He reached into a leather sack he carried at his belt. "Here, try this shuttle instead of yours."

Doubtfully, Follin took the shuttle, which looked as if it had never been used, while his own was worn and polished and comfortable to his hand. Nevertheless, at the stranger's bidding, Follin threw the shuttle across the threads already on his loom.

That same instant, the shuttle began flying back and forth even faster than his old one. In moments, before the weaver's eyes, shimmering cloth of gold appeared and grew so quickly the loom soon held enough for a cloak.

"Weaver, my thanks to you," said the stranger, gesturing for Follin to take the new cloth off the loom. "What reward shall you ask?"

Follin was to dumbfounded to do more than wag his head and gape at the work of the wondrous shuttle. And so the traveler continued:

"You have done me a favor. Now I shall do one for you. Keep the shuttle. Use it as it may best profit you."

"What?" cried Follin, scarcely believing his ears. "You mean to give me such a treasure?"

"Treasure it may be to you," replied the stranger, "not to me. In my country, such implements are commonplace. Nevertheless," he went on, "for the sake of a fair bargain, give me your shuttle in trade and you shall have this one."

Now Follin had never been a greedy man. But the traveler's words were like thin fingers plucking at the warp and weft of his thoughts. He had used his old shuttle all his life, and knew it to be filled with the wisdom and pride of his workmanship. Even so, he told himself, no man in his wits could turn down such an exchange. Instead of cloth, he could weave all the gold he wanted. And so he said:

"Done. So be it."

He handed his old shuttle to the traveler, who popped it into the leather sack and, without another word, left the weaving shed.

No sooner had the stranger gone out the door than Follin, trembling in excitement, leaped onto his bench and set about weaving as fast as he could. He laughed with glee and his eyes glittered at the treasure that would be his.

"I'll weave myself a fortune!" he cried. "And when I've spent that, I'll weave myself another! And another! I'll be the richest man in all the land. I'll dine from gold plates, I'll drink from gold cups!"

Suddenly the flying shuttle stopped, split asunder, and fell in pieces to the ground. On the loom the gleaming threads turned, in that instant, to cobwebs and tore apart in shreds before Follin's eyes.

Distraught at the cheat, bewailing the loss of his shuttle, Follin ran from the weaving shed. But the traveler had gone.

And from that time on, Follin drudged at his loom, never to find a shuttle the equal of the one he had bartered away.

On another day, Menwy the bard was sitting under a tree, tuning his harp, when a lean-faced man, cloaked in gray and mounted on a pale horse, reined up and called to him:

"Harper, my instrument lacks a string. Can you spare me one of yours?"

Menwy noticed the rider carried at his saddle bow a golden harp, the fairest he had ever seen. He got to his feet and strode up to the horseman to admire the instrument more closely.

"Alas, friend," said Menwy, "I have no strings to match yours. Mine are of the common kind, but yours are spun of gold and silver. If it plays as nobly as it looks, you should be proud of it."

"In my country," said the rider, "this would be deemed the meanest of instruments. But since it seems to please you, so you shall have it. For the sake of a fair bargain, though, give me yours in exchange."

"Now what a marvelous place the world is!" Menwy answered lightly. "Here's a fellow who rides out of nowhere, and asks nothing better than to do me a favor. And would I be so ungrateful as to turn it down? Come, friend, before there's any talk of trading this and that, let's hear a tune from that handsome harp of yours."

At this, the rider stiffened and raised a hand as if the bard had threatened him; but, recovering himself, he replied:

"Prove the instrument for yourself, harper. Take it in your hands, listen to its voice."

Menwy shook his head. "No need, friend. For I can tell you now, even though yours sang like a nightingale, I'd rather keep my own. I know its ways, and it knows mine."

The rider's eyes flickered for an instant. Then he replied:

"Harper, your fame has spread even as far as my realm. Scorn my gift as you will. But come with me and I swear you shall serve a king more powerful than any in Prydain. His bard you shall be, and you shall have a seat of honor by his throne."

"How could that be?" asked Menwy, smiling. "Already I serve a ruler greater than yours, for I serve my music."

Now Menwy was a poet and used to seeing around the edge of things. All this while, he had been watching the gray-cloaked horseman; and now as he looked closer, the rider and the golden harp seemed to change before his eyes. The frame of the instrument, which had appeared

257

so fair he saw to be wrought of dry bones, and the strings were serpents poised to strike.

Though Menwy was as brave as any man, the sight of the rider's true face behind its mask of flesh froze the harper's blood. Nevertheless, he did not turn away, nor did his glance waver as he replied:

"I see you for what you are, Lord of Death. And I fear you as all men do. For all that, you are a weak and pitiful king. You can destroy, but never build. You are less than the humblest creature, the frailest blade of grass. For these live, and every moment of their lives is a triumph over you. Your kingdom is dust; only the silent ending of things, never the beginnings."

At that, Menwy took his harp and began to play a joyful melody. Hearing it, the horseman's face tightened in rage; he drew his sword from its sheath and with all his might he struck at the bard.

But the blow missed its mark and instead struck the harp, shattering it to bits. Menwy, however, flung aside the pieces, threw back his head, and laughed in defiance, calling out:

"You fail, Death-Lord! You destroy the instrument, but not its music. With all your power you have gained only a broken shell."

In that moment, when the harp had been silenced, arose the songs of birds, the chiming of brooks, the humming of wind through grass and leaves; and all these voices took up the strands of melody, more beautiful than before.

And the Lord of Death fled in terror of life.

PATRICIA ANNE MCKILLIP
(1948–   )

Patricia McKillip, one of the youngest of contemporary writers of fantasy, is probably best known for her novel *The Forgotten Beasts of Eld* (nominated in 1974 for the Mythopoeic Award for fantasy), but she has written several other impressive works in the past five years. While she has received much critical attention, little has been written about her personally. When Joe R. Christopher reviewed *The Forgotten Beasts of Eld* in the April, 1975, *Mythprint,* he remarked that she was not listed in *Contemporary Authors* or *Biography Index.* She has since appeared in the former work, but only in a four-line notice. Nor is she mentioned, as she ought to be, in any of the collections devoted to adult or children's writers.

McKillip was born in Salem, Oregon, the daughter of Wayne T. and Helen (Roth) McKillip. Because her father was in the Air Force, the family moved frequently, and she has lived in Arizona, California, and England. While in England, at the age of fourteen, she wrote her first story, a thirty-page fairytale. She was living at the time in a large, 300-year-old house that overlooked an old church and graveyard. This later became the setting for her first fantasy novel, *The House on Parchment Street* (1973). Back in California a few years later, McKillip went to the College of Notre Dame in Belmont and then to San Jose State, where she received her B.A. in 1971 and M.A. in 1973 in English. She had thought at one time about a career as a concert pianist, but decided on writing instead. She is single and now lives in San Francisco. In a letter to us, McKillip comments that "besides writing, I enjoy music, water in any form, travelling, and reading everything from P. G. Wodehouse to Erica Jong."

In addition to the two works already mentioned, McKillip has written: *The Throme of the Erril of Sherill* (1973), chapters two and three of which form the excerpt included here; *Night Gift* (1976); and *The Riddle Master of Hed* (1976), which is the first volume of a projected trilogy. Judging by the excellence of *Riddle Master*, McKillip's trilogy should take a place of honor alongside those of Le Guin (*Earthsea Trilogy*), C. S. Lewis (*Outer Space Trilogy*), and other masters of the genre.

The Throme of the Erril of Sherill, like *Forgotten Beasts* and *Riddle Master*, draws its background and inspiration from medieval legend and romance. All three are set in the secondary world of faërie and focus on the workings of magic. McKillip in particular delights in portraying exotic beasts, like Dracoberus, the dagon, in *The Throme*. She excels in descriptions of such creatures. Indeed, her ability as a stylist to create a vivid secondary world and its inhabitants is perhaps her greatest talent. Her lyrical prose in *The Throme* echoes for the reader the metrical romances and epics of an earlier time. According to McKillip, "much of the word-play in that [*The Throme*] was inspired by a course in Middle English I was taking at the time." The names of her characters and places are themselves phrases of poetry, evocative of olden days: Cnite Caerles, Earl Merle, Mirk-Well of Morg. Yet the characters who inhabit the "Kingdom of Everywhere" are very human and sympathetic ones, including Caerles, the hero. Caerles is on a quest in search of the Throme, a quest that, in the best tradition, turns out to be a spiritual quest as well as a physical one. Magnus Thrall, whose desires have been satiated by being King of Everywhere, yet finds himself dissatisfied. He refuses to give his daughter, Damsen, in marriage to Cnite Caerles unless Caerles can bring to him the fabled epic written by the Erril of Sherill. But the Throme—and all that it represents—was not written in his sort of kingdom. It is significant that only after freely giving away his bejeweled sword does Caerles discover a guiding light in his quest.

From The Throme of the Erril of Sherill

Patricia A. McKillip

And so the Cnite Caerles spent the night under a tree. He hated sleeping under trees. Trees whispered at night and dropped things on his face; trees wound underground and made hard knobs of their roots that gave lump in the back and crick in the neck. Trees let the sun too early in his eyes, and the sun would not go away. But worse than the sun was the Thing, that jumped out of nowhere onto the stomach of the Cnite Caerles.

"Oog," said Caerles and opened one eye. A child looked back at him, her hair in sweet, moist tendrils down her back, her finger in her mouth. The other eye of the Cnite Caerles opened. "Child," he said cheerlessly, "Why are you sitting on my stomach?"

"I have lost my dagon," said the child through her finger. Caerles looked at her motionlessly, unblinking in the sunlight.

"I, too, have lost something," he said finally. "I have lost my true heart's love, the well-spring of my deep heart's laughter, because I am sent on a hopeless quest from which I will never return. But that is no reason to go and sit on someone else's stomach."

"I want my dagon," said the child. She bounced up and down impatiently on the Cnite Caerles. Her eyes were blue as the tiny flowers that grew pointed like stars all around them. The Cnite reached out to still her, and she sat still, looking down at him, her eyes blue and fearless and certain as the true season's sky.

"Who are you?" said Caerles.

"I am Elfwyth. My dagon is Dracoberus."

261

"Did you call him?"

"I called and called and called. And called. Who are you?"

"I am the Cnite Caerles, and I do not think I like small girls. Perhaps Damsen will have only sons."

Elfwyth took her finger out of her mouth. "I do not think I like you," she said sternly. "And if you do not help me find my dagon I will bounce up and down and I will cry."

The Cnite Caerles lifted her in his strong arms and stood up and set her on the ground, where she came barely higher than his knee. He folded his arms and looked down at her. She folded her arms and looked back up at him. Then, sudden as a falling star, came a tear rilling from the curve of her eye down to the corner of her mouth. Another followed, and her blue eyes were flowers with hearts of rain.

"Oh, please," she sniffed. "Oh, please find my dagon. Then I will help you look for what you have lost. Oh, please."

"Oh, please," Caerles said weakly. "Do not cry. If you cry I will have to help you, for the love of the tears in my sweet Damsen's eyes."

"Oh, please find my dagon. I am lost and sorely sad without him, for I love him, and he loves me, and I will not go home without him."

Caerles gave a sigh sadder than the wind's sigh on moonless nights. "Oh, child," he said. "You are more annoying than a tripping tree root. What is a dagon?"

Elfwyth glanced up at him out of her still eyes. She sniffed. "It is a small animal. A little, little animal. And it has a little voice, and pretty eyes. You will not be afraid of it."

"I am afraid of nothing," Caerles said.

"And it will like you very much . . . if you find it while I am with you. It likes me most of all." She took the hand of the Cnite Caerles and turned him towards the morning sun. Flowers bent gently under her bare feet. "But it will like you, too, if you speak gently to it, I think. . . . It is my dagon, my Dracoberus, and it is a gift to me from seven—people. And then, if you find it, I will love you, too." She smiled up at him, raising her fair face like a flower opening, and Caerles gave once more the wisp and whisper of a sigh.

"Thank you," he said glumly, and lifted her up into his great curved saddle.

They followed the sun until noon.

At noon the sun was a soundless, rearing lion frightening their shadows into littleness, a huge, golden dragon that was never still, the coin-gold heart of a blazing flower. At noon, they stopped to drink at the ice-colored sliver of a sheer stream. Elfwyth danced with her bare feet into the heart of the stream, among the polished stones and speckled sand, and as she splashed under the full eye of noon there came a roar like the waking of seven beasts in new spring. The Cnite Caerles ran to her, and the stream water sank deep into his mouse-colored boots. He lifted the child, holding her all wet against him, and then her voice shrilled into his eye.

"Oh, my Dracoberus!"

There was a flash like the wink of lightning. A slender hound with violet eyes and fiery breath ran bellowing from the trees, and it was taller than Caerles' horse. Caerles stared motionless at its coming, while the child Elfwyth wriggled against him and his horse behind him reared and whimpered. Behind the hound rode seven men in seven colors, each with an eye ablaze on his breast, and a spear, ice-tipped, in his hand. Elfwyth twisted eagerly in the Cnite's arms.

"Oh, let me go—" she cried, and slithered like a fish into the water. She ran across the stream to the fiery hound and the sudden hiss of its breath over her head came at Caerles in a flood of flame. He sat down in the water. Seven men gathered at the water's edge. Seven spears formed a gleaming crescent above the Cnite's heart. Elfwyth hugged the neck of the whimpering hound. She kissed its violet eyes and turned her head.

"If you hurt the Cnite I will cry."

Caerles looked up at the still faces and fish nibbled at his fingers. He said between his teeth, "I do not like small girls."

"Go and kiss him thanks," Elfwyth said to the great, frolicking dagon.

"I do not want to be thanked," said the Cnite.

"You are afraid of my Dracoberus."

"Yes."

"You told me you were afraid of nothing!"

"Elfwyth, Elfwyth," said a man in scarlet, "it is not good for a small girl to mock a grown man. Who is this one?"

"I do not know. I found him beneath a tree and I bounced on him until he came with me to find my dagon."

The seven spears rose, flashing like birds. "We are the Seven Watchers of the child Elfwyth of the Erle Merle. We will bring you to him and thanks for his child, and you will be bedded in soft silk and washed in wine, if you but give us your name."

Caerles rose from the stream. "I am the Cnite Caerles, and I am questing for the Throme of the Erril of Sherill."

The Seven Watchers looked at one another. "It does not exist."

"I know, but I must find it. Will the Erle Merle help me? If not, I will bed myself in soft grass, having already washed."

The Seven Watchers turned their mounts. "The Erle Merle is wiser than an oak tree at twilight, wiser than the pale moon at moon rise. If he can help you, he will."

Caerles went with them, and Elfwyth rode the flaming dagon Dracoberus, and the barred gates of the Erle Merle opened without the touch of a hand to welcome them. The Erle Merle was a tall, thin wraith of bones and pale skin and hair like the spun gossamer of spider's web. His eyes flashed like jewels, now emerald, now amber, and they smiled as the child Elfwyth came to hug his knees.

"I have found my Dracoberus!" she shouted into his rich robe. "Now you must give that Cnite the Throme of the Sherill of Erril."

"Erril of Sherill," said the Erle Merle, and his eyes as he looked up flashed blue sapphire at Caerles. His hand strayed thoughtfully among the towzled curls of Elfwyth's head. "You are my wild child, and it was your Dracoberus and your Watchers and this Cnite who found you. Now go to him and give him your hand like a true lady and bring him gently into my house."

And that she did, gently.

When they had eaten much of thin, hot slices of rare

meats and golden-crusted breads and sweet wines and fruits, the Erle Merle sat back in his chair and looked first at Caerles and then at Elfwyth. Above his head was a huge, unwinking eye that the sun burnt gold, and all down the lengths of two sides of his hall lesser eyes watched, pools of violet, green, silver.

"I do not know where the Throme is," he said. "Or where it is not. I only know that it is not here." He tapped softly at the rim of his cup with the crescent moon of his curved nail, and his eyes went limpid grey. "I may have a suggestion, but it will lead to danger."

"There is a woman who weeps, waiting for me in Magnus Thrall's house," Caerles said. "I do not know that word danger."

"So." The Erle Merle's eyes winked like pure stars. "Then I suggest you look for the Throme of the Erril of Sherill at the Mirk-Well of Morg."

The Cnite Caerles stared into his emerald green eyes. He said in a voice two tones smaller, "But the Mirk-Well of Morg does not exist. It is a line in a song, a passage of a tale told to children by fire light. How can I go to a place that is not there?"

The Erle Merle looked back at him out of midnight eyes. "What better place to find a thing that does not exist?" he inquired, and Caerles sighed deeply from his heart's marrow.

"Then I will go there," he said.

The child Elfwyth bounced suddenly in her chair. "I will go with you," she cried, "and my Dracoberus will keep you from danger."

"A quest is no journey for a frail child," said the Erle Merle, and his voice was a wind's murmur in the still hall. "My child, a true lady would give thanks to a Cnite who had braved fire and water to please her. Good thanks would be to give him what he may need most."

Elfwyth looked at the Erle Merle. Her eyes grew round and heavy in the colored light from the watching windows, and her voice grew thin and quivered. "But he is afraid of my Dracoberus."

"I do not think he would be if you lent him your dagon to protect him from the glooms and harshnesses of the Mirk-Well."

"But he has a horse."

"I have a horse," said the Cnite Caerles quickly. "And I need no thanks."

The Erle Merle turned his face to Caerles and the glow of his eyes was of sweet, wine-drenched amethyst. "Thanks must be given," he answered softly, "and who will receive them if you do not?"

The child Elfwyth sat still as a drooping flower. Then she lifted her fair head and sat straight in her straight chair. "You will ride my Dracoberus," she said staunchly. "And he will protect you. And when you are done, you will ride him back to me. I will lend him to you in thanks, because you came with me in the morning light."

The Cnite Caerles achieved a smile. "I will ride him back to you safely," he said fairly, "and for the sake of my sweet Damsen, I thank you, for the protection of your Dracoberus against whatever dangers lie in the Mirk-Well of Morg, wherever they are, if they exist."

The child Elfwyth smiled back at him. She said anxiously, "Do not forget to bring him back to me."

"Oh, child," said Caerles from his deep heart. "There is no danger of that."

And that is how the Cnite Caerles left the hall of the Erle Merle by morning light, riding the violet-eyed, fire-voiced dagon Dracoberus instead of his true horse. He rode towards the path of the setting sun, where all darkness began, and the sun rode above him across the sky. At night, the eyes of Dracoberus glowed like violet stars, and his breath warmed the streaming air. He ate leaves from the trees and tender flowers newly opened, and he acquired a habit of licking the Cnite's face with his great, red, fiery tongue. He moved like a wind over plowed field and meadow, and at the end of the second dusk Caerles knew they were lost.

"Though," he said reasonably as he dismounted, "I cannot be lost when I am going nowhere." And he was surprised when instead of earth beneath his foot, he felt a nothingness that continued in a dazing rush. He landed asprawl on the damp . earth and found the violet stars looking at him from an unreasonable distance. "How," said the Cnite Caerles reasonably between his teeth, "can

I possibly get where I want to go when I cannot go any-where at all?"

The dagon whimpered down to him in sadness like a child, and Caerles could hear the thump of its great tail like a heart-beat on the earth above. Then of a sudden the burning violets vanished, and the Cnite heard a light Boy's voice in a lulling croon.

"Oh, I love you, I love you, I love you. . . ." And through his voice came the purry whine of the dagon and the thump-thump of its tail.

"Who is up there?" Caerles called. The voice was si-lent. A dark face peered over the edge of the earth.

"Who is down there?"

"I am the Cnite Caerles. Will you help me?"

The voice was silent again. The night was silent but for the little voices of secret things that no eye could see. The trees lifted their great black heads against the stars and the wind curled through them, sighing.

"Is this your thing up there? This beautiful purple and red and grey thing?"

"It is the dagon Dracoberus that I was riding. Am I in the Mirk-Well of Morg?"

"No. You are in my borebel pit. Are you sure you are not a borebel?"

"I am not a borebel," said Caerles. "I am the Cnite Caerles of Magnus Thrall, questing for the Damsen of the King. I am cold and dirty and sore and hungry and I do not like your borebel pit."

"Well," said the voice. "Well. I think if you were not a borebel you would not be down there. It is a pit only for borebels. There is a long-toothed, hoary-voiced, squinty-eyed borebel snuffling around my mother's house and I dug a pit to trap it. How do I know you are not a squinty-eyed borebel with a sweet voice to trick me?"

The Cnite Caerles closed his eyes. He opened them again and said patiently, "Do borebels ride dagons?"

"No. But I think you ate the Cnite who was riding this dagon, and now he belongs to no one. So I will take care of him, for he is more beautiful than anything I have ever seen and he loves me, too."

"I am not a borebel," said Caerles. "And that dagon was lent to me by the child of the Erle Merle to protect me from all danger with its swift speed and its flaming tongue, but I do not know what will protect me from a troublesome young Boy."

"Perhaps I will let you out," said the voice, "if you give me the dagon. Then I will have someone to sprawl on meadow-grass with, and explore deep caves, and dabble with in the river. If you give me the dagon, I will know you are not a borebel, for a borebel never gives anything to anyone."

"But I cannot give you Dracoberus because he does not belong to me."

"Then," said the voice cheerfully, "you must be a borebel. Do not worry about your dagon. I will love him well."

The Cnite Caerles sat down on the damp earth of the borebel pit. "Boy," he said wearily, "I am a Cnite on a quest for the love of a wheat-haired, wine-eyed lady who is waiting with love for me. You will have the dagon to love but who will there be to love that lady if you do not let me out of this pit?"

There was the sound above of shifting leaves. "Well," said the voice, and again, "Well." Then it said again cheerfully, "If you are truly a borebel, there is no lady and no love, so I will take your dagon. But do not worry. I will feed you."

The heads of the Boy and the dagon vanished, and the Cnite Caerles was left alone with the far-away stars and the whispers of trees and the walls of earth rising around him. "Oh my Damsen," he mourned softly to the memory of her, "will you still love a clumsy Cnite who falls into borebel pits?" And the Throme seemed as far from him as the star-worlds above.

Morning fell into the borebel pit onto Caerles' eyes, and he looked up and found a rope of sunlight up to the bright earth. He sat up and sighed for the ache in his bent bones and the thirst in his throat and the mud on his mouse-colored boots. Then he heard the whimper and frolick of the dagon and the high, sweet whistle of the Boy swooping like a bird's cry through the trees.

"Borebel," he called, "I have brought your breakfast. And then the dagon and I will run as far as the world's edge together, and shout louder than sound, and we will not come back until there is no more night. Borebel, borebel, I have brought bread and porridge and milk, oh borebel. . . ."

And as he called and whistled, a strange noise tangled in his whistling: a snickering, snuffling, snorting noise that came to the very edge of the borebel pit. And then of a sudden, it came down into the borebel pit, and the Cnite leaped out of its way. Across from him lay a tiny-eyed, long-toothed, bristle-hided borebel blinking its red eyes in astonishment.

"O Borebel," Caerles breathed, for the borebel, sitting, was as high as his chin. "Move gently, or I will kill you, and I did not set out to kill borebels."

The borebel snorted. Its eyes flamed suddenly blood-red with rage, and the Cnite drew his sword. The borebel stood up on its short-haired hind legs and the scream of its fury silenced the birds in the morning trees.

"O Borebel," said the Boy above them, and his voice quivered like a bow-string. "Look up."

The borebel looked up. The Boy dropped a great bowl of steaming porridge onto its squinty-eyed face.

The borebel danced and roared and splatted the porridge out of its red eyes and its long-toothed snout. The Boy dropped the end of a rope down the pit-edge to the Cnite. The dagon Dracoberus howled at the other end. Red flame singed the borebel's hide. Then the dagon pulled with its might and Caerles slithered out of the borebel pit.

He stood free above the mournful borebel, all covered with earth and tiny twigs and the frayed ends of leaves. The Boy looked up at him, shivering in the sunlight. He was bone-thin and brown, with scarred knees and elbows and his eyes were round as twin platters on a white table.

"You are not a borebel," he whispered. The dagon licked the Cnite's face with a swoop of its tongue, then lay on his feet and thumped its tail.

"Boy," began Caerles. Then he stopped, and his anger faded away in the sigh of his breath. "No. I am not a borebel."

"I wish—I wish you had been. But I knew you were not. Are you going to be very angry?"

"You saved my life," said the Cnite, "in spite of the

deep longing of your heart. I too have a deep longing for a special love. I cannot give you the dagon for a fearless-eyed child loves it, but I will give you, for your sacrifice, whatever else you may ask of me."

The Boy licked his mouth. "Then may I have—" He stopped and swallowed. "Then may I please have your sword?"

The Cnite Caerles was silent. Little winds came pluck-ing at him, springing away like teasing children. The great dagon rolled over and scratched its back on the bracken. He drew it finally from his belt and it flowed silver in the light and tiny jewels, red and white and green, winked in its hilt.

"It is yours," he said, "because you asked it of me. But why do you want it?"

"To kill borebels bravely with, when they come snuf-fling in my mother's garden. And then I will not have to dig any more pits."

Caerles gave him the sword. The Boy's eyes caressed it from pommel to tip and he smiled. "It is very beautiful. But not," he sighed, "as beautiful as the dagon beside me at night. And now, if you will come, my mother will give you some breakfast. And some water to wash with. . . ."

The Boy's mother shook the Boy for leaving the Cnite overnight in the borebel pit, and then she hugged him to her, winking and blinking, for his quick wits, and then she shook him again for his request of the sword. Then she filled a heaping bowl of porridge for the Cnite and listened to the tale of his search. Then she said,

"There is no such thing as the Mirk-Well of Morg."

"I know," Caerles said. "But you see I must find it."

The Boy's mother shook her head. "Mirk-Well of Morg is a tale for old men and babies, not for great Cnites. Now, if I were you, which I am not, being simple and stout and motherly, I would look in the Floral Wold at the World's End. Now, there is a place for a Throme of beauty. A dreamer dreamed the Floral Wold, and it ap-peared, somewhere beyond the sunrise. I would go there. But then I am only a poor old woman with only half my teeth, and the Throme most likely does not exist. But I would go there, to the Floral Wold, if I were a brave Cnite with a loving, weeping woman. Eat your porridge."

The Cnite Caerles ate his porridge. Then he said, "I do not know where to go. The Erle Merle said nothing of a Floral Wold, but I cannot go to the Mirk-Well of Morg without a sword."

"It does not exist," said the Boy's mother, "and it was wrong of the Boy to ask for your sword."

"He would not give me the dagon," the Boy argued contentedly; "I would have taken that instead."

The Boy's mother ticked her tongue. Then she bent down and lugged a worn chest out of a spider-woven corner. She opened the lid and it wailed with age. A glow came from the chest like the milk-white eye of a lost star. "This my mother gave me," she said, "and her mother to her. It is the guiding light to the Floral Wold, the candle that illumines dreams." She lifted the star from the chest. It pulsed, softly white at the end of a staff, now petaled like a flower, now pointed like crystal, and the far heart of it was ice-blue. The Boy's eyes grew wide, twin stars from the star-wand winking in them.

"Oh, it is beautiful," he sighed longingly, and his mother slapped his reaching hands.

"Greedy," she said, glowering. "Be content with the pure jewels in that sword." She gave the star to Caerles, and the longing came, too, into his voice.

"Oh, Lady," he said softly, "I am greedy, too, for that land where this grew. If it exists, then I think I will begin to believe that the Throme exists, too, somewhere beyond the sunrise, beyond the World's End."

SYLVIA TOWNSEND WARNER
(1893–1978)

Sylvia Townsend Warner, poet, novelist, short-story writer, and biographer, is one of England's most versatile and brilliant authors. Born at Harrow-on-the-Hill, Middlesex, the daughter of a schoolmaster, she was educated privately. Acquiring an interest in music very early in life, she spent an entire decade, from her early twenties through her early thirties, compiling, with three other editors, an impressive ten-volume work entitled *Tudor Church Music*. As might be expected, this rather definitive research project brought her widespread recognition as an expert on Renaissance music.

At the age of twenty-nine, Warner began writing poetry, and three years later, in 1925, she published her first collection, *The Espalier*. Although her writing career can be said to have begun with this warm and witty book of poems, her real breakthrough as an author came in 1926 with the fantasy novel *Lolly Willowes,* which had the distinction of being the initial selection of the American Book-of-the-Month Club. Following this popular work were other novels such as the rather philosophical *Mr. Fortune's Maggot* (1927), a Literary Guild selection; *The True Heart* (1929); *Summer Will Show* (1936); and *The Flint Anchor* (1954). Many commentators consider *The Corner That Held Them* (1948), a fascinating and informative novel about life in a medieval English convent, to be the finest of her endeavors in this genre. Her novels, like her poems, are characterized by a polished style and an urbane, whimsical wit. Her collections of short fiction include *A Garland of Straw* (1943), *The Museum of Cheats* (1947), *The Innocent and the Guilty*

(1971), and, most recently, *Kingdoms of Elfin* (1977), a collection of several delightful works of fantasy, most of which were originally published as a series in *The New Yorker*. Warner also gained considerable prestige and renown as a biographer. Although her work on a biography of one of her great admirers, T. F. Powys, was not completed, she published an extraordinarily fine biography of T. H. White (1968).

Although well into her eighties, this remarkable scholar, wit, and author extraordinaire continued to delight her many devoted readers with a steady flow of fine writing. Warner died May 1, 1978, in Dorset, England.

In a letter we recently received from Warner, she reacted to our inclusion of "Elphenor and Weasel" in this volume by stating that we had "picked a story [I myself] would have chosen for such an anthology." It is not difficult to understand why this tale is one of Warner's favorites. There is a gentleness, a delicacy, a charm, that is more apparent here than in most of her other Elfin Kingdom stories, which often stress the more sinister, cruel, and malevolent elements of faërie. Quite simply, this is a beautiful and touching love story.

But it is also a great deal more. Warner's particular fantasy formula calls for an interaction of Elfin beings and mortals that very effectively puts in bold relief the essential qualities of the human condition. This is certaintly true of "Elphenor and Weasel." We see, quite clearly, both the good, and the bad, of man's lot. The deceit, charlatanry, greed, suspicion, and religious hypocrisy are poignantly displayed during the course of the narrative; but so too is the "agreeably terminal" nature of our existence, and also its infinite variety. (Elphenor finds that "there [is] better entertainment in the mortal world. Mortals [pack] more variety into their brief lives —perhaps because they [know] them to be brief.") But perhaps above all else, this is a story about intolerance, and the alienation, suffering, bitterness, and loneliness resulting from it. Just as in our own world, the Kingdoms of Elfin discriminate against those of different colored skins and different beliefs. "Two Stranger Children"—what a world of sad meaning is in that Register of Burials epithet.

Elphenor and Weasel

Sylvia Townsend Warner

The ship had sailed barely three leagues from IJmuiden when the wind backed into the east and rose to gale force. If the captain had been an older man he would have returned to port. But he had a mistress in Lowestoft and was impatient to get to her; the following wind, the waves thwacking the stern of the boat as though it were the rump of a donkey and tearing on ahead, abetted his desires. By nightfall, the ship was wallowing broken-backed at the mercy of the storm. Her decks were awash and cluttered with shifting debris. As she lurched lower, Elphenor thrust the confidential letter inside his shirt, the wallet of mortal money deeper in his pocket, and gave his mind to keeping his wings undamaged by blows from ripped sails and the clutches of his fellow-passengers. Judging his moment, he took off just before the ship went down, and was alone with the wind.

His wings were insignificant: he flew by the force of the gale. If for a moment it slackened he dropped within earshot of the hissing waves, then was scooped up and hurled onward. In one of these descents he felt the letter, heavy with seals, fall out of his breast. It would be for-ever private now, and the world of Elfin unchanged by its contents. On a later descent, the wallet followed it. His clothes were torn to shreds, he was benumbed with cold, he was wet to the skin. If the wind had let him drown he would have drowned willingly, folded his use-less wings and heard the waves hiss over his head. The force of the gale enclosed him, he could hardly draw breath. There was no effort of flight; the effort lay in being powerlessly and violently and almost senselessly conveyed—a fragment of existence in the drive of the storm. Once or twice he was asleep till a slackening of the wind jolted him awake with the salt smell of the sea beneath him. Wakened more forcibly, he saw a vague glimmer on the face of the water and supposed it might be the light of dawn; but he could not turn his head. He saw the staggering flight of a gull, and thought there must be land not far off.

The growing light showed a tumult of breakers ahead, close on each other's heels, devouring each other's bulk. They roared, and a pebble beach screamed back at them, but the wind carried him over, and on over a dusky flat landscape that might be anywhere. So far, he had not been afraid. But when a billow of darkness reared up in front of him, and the noise of tossing trees swooped on his hearing, he was suddenly in panic, and clung to a bough like a drowning man. He had landed in a thick grove of ilex trees, planted as a windbreak. He squirmed into the shelter of their midst, and heard the wind go on without him.

Somehow, he must have fallen out of the tree without noticing. When he woke, a man with mustachios was looking down on him.

"I know what you are. You're a fairy. There were fairies all round my father's place in Suffolk. Thieving pests, they were, bad as gypsies. But I half liked them. They were company for me, being an only child. How did you get here?"

Elphenor realized that he was still wearing the visibility he had put on during the voyage as a measure against being jostled. It was too late to discard it—though the shift between visible and invisible is a press-button affair. He repressed his indignation at being classed with gypsies and explained how the ship from IJmuiden had sunk and the wind carried him on.

"From IJmuiden, you say? What happened to the rest of them?"

"They were drowned."

"Drowned? And my new assistant was on that ship! It's one calamity after another. Sim's hanged, and Jacob

Kats gets drowned. Seems as though my stars meant me to have you."

It seemed as though Elphenor's stars were of the same mind. To tease public opinion he had studied English as his second language; he was penniless, purposeless, breakfastless, and the wind had blown his shoes off. "If I could get you out of any difficulties—" he said.

"But I can't take you to Walsham Borealis looking like that. We'll go to old Bella, and she'll fit you out."

Dressed in secondhand clothes too large for him and filled with pork pie, Elphenor entered Walsham Borealis riding pillion behind Master Elisha Blackbone. By then he knew he was to be assistant to a quack in several arts, including medicine, necromancy, divination, and procuring.

Hitherto, Elphenor, nephew to the Master of Ceremonies at the Elfin Court of Zuy, had spent his days in making himself polite and, as far as in his tailor lay, ornamental. Now he had to make himself useful. After the cautious pleasures of Zuy everything in this new life, from observing the planets to analyzing specimens of urine, entertained him. It was all so agreeably terminal: one finished one thing and went on to another. When Master Blackbone's clients overlapped, Elphenor placated those kept waiting by building card houses, playing the mandora, and sympathetic conversation—in which he learned a great deal that was valuable to Master Blackbone in casting horoscopes.

For his part, Master Blackbone was delighted with an assistant who was so quick to learn, so free from prejudice, and, above all, a fairy. To employ a fairy was a step up in the world. In London practice every reputable necromancer kept a spiritual appurtenance—fairy, familiar, talking toad, airy consultant. When he had accumulated the money, he would set up in London, where there is always room for another marvel. For the present, he did not mention his assistant's origin, merely stating that he was the seventh son of a seventh son, on whom any gratuities would be well bestowed. Elphenor was on the footing of an apprentice; his keep and training were sufficent wages. A less generous master would have demanded the gratuities, but Master Blackbone had his eye on a golden future, and did not care to imperil it by more than a modest scriptural tithe.

With a fairy as an assistant, he branched out into larger developments of necromancy and took to raising the Devil as a favour. The midnight hour was essential and holy ground desirable—especially disused holy ground: ruined churches, disinhabited religious foundations. The necromancer and the favoured clients would ride under cover of night to Bromholm or St. Benet's in the marshes. Elphenor, flying invisibly and dressed for the part, accompanied them. At the Word of Power he became visible, pranced, menaced, and lashed his tail till the necromancer ordered him back to the pit. This was for moonlight nights. When there was no moon, he hovered invisibly, whispering blasphemies and guilty secrets. His blasphemies lacked unction; being a fairy he did not believe in God. But the guilty secrets curdled many a good man's blood. A conscience-stricken clothier from a neighbouring parish spread such scandals about the iniquities done in Walsham Borealis that Master Blackbone thought it wisest to make off before he and Elphenor were thrown into jail.

They packed his equipment—alembics, chart of the heavens, book of spells, skull, etc.—and were off before the first calm light of an April morning. As they travelled southward Elphenor counted windmills and church towers and found windmills slightly predominating. Church towers were more profitable, observed Master Blackbone. Millers were rogues and cheats, but wherever there was a church you could be sure of fools; if Elphenor were not a fairy and ignorant of Holy Writ he would know that fools are the portion appointed for the wise. But for the present they would lie a little low, shun the Devil, and keep to love philtres and salves for the itch, for which there is always a demand in spring. He talked on about the herbs they would need, and the henbane that grew round Needham in Suffolk, where he was born and played with fairies, and whither they were bound. "What were they like?" Elphenor asked. He did not suppose Master Blackbone's fairies were anything resplendent. Master Blackbone replied that they came out of a hill and were green. Searching his memory, he added that they smelled like elderflowers. At Zuy, elderflowers were used to flavour gooseberry jam—an inelegant conserve.

At Zuy, by now, the gardeners would be bringing the tubs of myrtle out of the conservatories, his uncle would be conducting ladies along the sanded walks to admire the hyacinths, and he would be forgotten; for in good society failures are smoothly forgotten, and as nothing had resulted from the confidential letter it would be assumed he had failed to deliver it. He would never be able to go back. He did not want to. There was better entertainment in the mortal world. Mortals packed more variety into their brief lives—perhaps because they knew them to be brief. There was always something going on and being taken seriously: love, hate, ambition, plotting, fear, and all the rest of it. He had more power as a quack's assistant then ever he would have attained to in Zuy. To have a great deal of power and no concern was the life for him.

Hog's grease was a regrettable interpolation in his career. Master Blackbone based his salves and ointments on hog's grease, which he bought in a crude state from pork butchers. It was Elphenor's task to clarify it before it was tinctured with juices expressed from herbs. Wash as he might, his hands remained greasy and the smell of grease hung in his nostrils. Even the rankest-smelling herbs were a welcome change, and a bundle of water peppermint threw him into a rapture. As Master Blackbone disliked stooping, most of the gathering fell to him.

It is a fallacy that henbane must be gathered at midnight. Sunlight raises its virtues (notably efficacious against toothache, insomnia, and lice), and to be at its best it should be gathered in the afternoon of a hot day. Elphenor was gathering it in a sloping meadow that faced south. He was working invisibly—Master Blackbone did not wish every Tom, Dick, and Harry to know what went into his preparations. Consequently, a lamb at play collided with him and knocked the basket out of his hand. As it stood astonished at this sudden shower of henbane, Elphenor seized it by the ear and cuffed it. Hearing her lamb bleat so piteously, its mother came charging to the rescue. She also collided with Elphenor and, being heavy with her winter fleece, sent him sprawling. He was still flat on his back when a girl appeared from nowhere, stooped over him, and slapped his face, hard and accurately. To assert his manly dignity he pulled her down on top of him—and saw that she was green.

She was a very pretty shade of green—a pure delicate tint, such as might have been cast on a white eggshell by the sun shining through the young foliage of a beech tree. Her hair, brows, and lashes were a darker shade; her lashes lay on her green cheek like a miniature fern frond. Her teeth were perfectly white. Her skin was so nearly transparent that the blue veins on her wrists and breasts showed through like some exquisitely marbled cheese.

As they lay in an interval of repose, she stroked the bruise beginning to show on his cheek with triumphant moans of compassion. Love did not heighten or diminish her colour. She remained precisely the same shade of green. The smell, of course, was that smell of elderflowers. It was strange to think that exactly like this she may have been one of the fairies who played with Elisha Blackbone in his bragged-of boyhood, forty, fifty years back. He pushed the speculation away, and began kissing her behind the ear, and behind the other ear, to make sure which was the more sensitive. But from that hour love struck root in him.

Eventually he asked her name. She told him it was Weasel. "I shall call you Mustela," he said, complying with the lover's imperative to rename the loved one; but in the main he called her Weasel. They sat up, and saw that time had gone on as usual, that dusk had fallen and the henbane begun to wilt.

When they parted, the sheep were circling gravely to the top of the hill, the small grassy hill of her tribe. He flew leisurely back, swinging the unfilled basket. The meagre show of henbane would be a pretext for going off on the morrow to a place where it grew more abundantly; he would have found such a place, but by then it was growing too dark for picking, and looking one way while flying another he had bruised his cheek against a low-growing bough. At Zuy this artless tale would not have supported a moment's scrutiny; but it would pass with a mortal, though it might be wise to substantiate it with a

280

request for the woundwort salve. For a mortal, Master Blackbone was capable of unexpected intuitions.

The intuitions had not extended to the reverence for age and learning which induced Elphenor to sleep on a pallet to the windward. Toward morning, he dreamed that he was at the foot of the ilex; but it was Weasel who was looking down at him, and if he did not move she would slap his face. He moved, and woke. Weasel lay asleep beside him. But at the same time they were under the ilex, for the waves crashed on the screaming pebble beach and were Master Blackbone's snores.

At Zuy the English Elfindom was spoken of with admiring reprehension: its magnificence, wastefulness, and misrule, its bravado and eccentricity. The eccentricity of being green and living under a hill was not included. A hill, yes. Antiquarians talked of hill dwellings, and found evidence of them in potsherds and beads. But never, at any time, green. The beauties of Zuy, all of them white as bolsters, would have swooned at the hypothesis. Repudiating the memory of past bolsters, he looked at Weasel, curled against him like a caterpillar in a rose leaf, green as spring, fresh as spring, and completely contemporary.

She stirred, opened her eyes, and laughed.

"Shush!"

Though invisible, she might not be inaudible, and her voice was ringing and assertive as a wren's. She had come so trustingly it would be the act of an ingrate to send her away. Not being an ingrate he went with her, leaving Master Blackbone to make what he would of an early-rising assistant. They breakfasted on wild strawberries and a hunk of bread he had had the presence of mind to take from the bread crock. It was not enough for Weasel, and when they came to a brook she twitched up a handful of minnows and ate them raw. Love is a hungry emotion, and by midday he wished he had not been so conventional about the minnows. As a tactful approach, he began questioning her about life in the hill, it's amenities, its daily routine. She suddenly became evasive: he would not like it; it was dull, old-fashioned, unsociable.

"All the same, I should like to visit it. I have never been inside a hill."

"No! You can't come. It's impossible. They'd set on you, you'd be driven out. *You're not green.*"

Etiquette.

"Don't you understand?"

"I was wondering what they would do to you if they found out where you woke this morning."

"Oh, that! They'd have to put up with it. Green folk don't draw green blood. But they'd tear *you* in pieces."

"It's the same where I come from. If I took you to Zuy, they might be rather politer, but they'd never forgive you for being green. But I won't take you, Weasel. We'll stay in Suffolk. And if it rains and rains and rains—"

"I don't mind rain—"

"We'll find a warm, dry badger sett."

They escaped into childishness and were happy again, with a sharpened happiness because for a moment they had so nearly touched despair.

As summer became midsummer, and the elder blossom outlasted the wild roses and faded in its turn till the only true elderflower scent came from her, and the next full moon had a broader face and shone on cocks of hay in silvery fields, they settled into an unhurried love and strolled from day to day as through a familiar landscape. By now they were seldom hungry, for there was a large crop of mushrooms, and Elphenor put more system into his attendances on Master Blackbone, breakfasting soundly and visibly while conveying mouthfuls to the invisible Weasel (it was for the breakfasts that they slept there). Being young and perfectly happy and pledged to love each other till the remote end of their days, they naturally talked of death and discussed how to contrive that neither should survive the other. Elphenor favoured being struck by lightning as they lay in each other's arms, but Weasel was terrified by thunder—she winced and covered her ears at the slightest rumble—and though he talked soothingly of the electric fluid and told her of recent experiments with amber and a couple of silk stockings, one black, one white, she refused to die by lightning stroke.

And Master Blackbone, scarcely able to believe his ears, madly casting horoscopes and invoking the goddess

Fortuna, increasingly tolerant of Elphenor's inattention, patiently compounding his salves unassisted, smiling on the disappearances from his larder, was day after day, night after night, more sure of his surmise—till convinced of his amazing good fortune he fell into the melancholy of not knowing what best to do about it, whether to grasp fame single-handed or call in the help of an expert and self-effacingly retire on the profits. He wrote a letter to an old friend. Elphenor was not entrusted with this letter, but he knew it had been written and was directed to London. Weasel was sure Master Blackbone was up to no good— she had detested him at first sight. They decided to keep a watch on him. But their watch was desultory, and the stranger was already sitting in Master Blackbone's lodging and conversing with him when they flew in and perched on a beam.

The stranger was a stout man with a careworn expression. Master Blackbone was talking in his best procuring voice.

"It's a Golconda, an absolute Golconda! A pair of them, young, in perfect condition. Any manager would snap at them. But I have kept it dark till now. I wanted you to have the first option."

"Thanks, I'm sure," said the stranger. "But it's taking a considerable chance."

"Oh no, it isn't. People would flock to see them. You could double the charges—in fact you should, for it's something unique—and there wouldn't be an empty seat in the house. Besides, it's a scientific rarity. You'd have all the illuminati. Nobs from the colleges. Ladies of fashion. Royal patronage."

The stranger said he didn't like buying pigs in pokes.

"But I give you my word. A brace of fairies—lovely, young, amorous fairies. Your fortune would be made."

"How much do you want?"

"Two-thirds of the takings. You can't say that's exorbitant. Not two-thirds of the profits, mind. Two-thirds of the takings and a written agreement."

The stranger repeated that he didn't like buying pigs in pokes, the more so when he had no warrant the pigs were within.

"Wait till tonight! They come every night and cuddle on

283

that pallet there. They trust me like a father. Wait till they're asleep and throw a net over them, and they're yours."

"But when I've got them to London, suppose they are awkward, and won't perform? People aren't going to pay for what they can't see. How can I be sure they'll be visible?"

Master Blackbone said there were ways and means, as with performing animals.

"Come, Weasel. We'll be off."

The voice was right overhead, loud and clear. Some cobwebs drifted down.

Elphenor and Weasel were too pleased with themselves to think beyond the moment. They had turned habitually toward their usual haunts and were dabbling their feet in the brook before it occurred to Elphenor that they had no reason to stay in the neighbourhood and good reason to go elsewhere. Weasel's relations would murder him because he was not green, Master Blackbone designed to sell them because they were fairies. Master Blackbone might have further designs: he was a necromancer, though a poor one; it would be prudent to get beyond his magic circle. Elphenor had congratulated himself on leaving prudence behind at Zuy. Now it reasserted itself and had its charm. Prudence had no charm whatever for Weasel; it was only by representing the move as reckless that he persuaded her to make it.

With the world before them, he flew up for a survey and caught sight of the sea, looking as if ships would not melt in its mouth—which rather weakened the effect of his previous narrative of the journey from IJmuiden to the ilexes. Following the coastline they came to Great Yarmouth, where they spent several weeks. It was ideal for their vagrant purposes, full of vigorous, cheerful people, with food to be had for the taking—hot pies and winkles in the marketplace, herring on the quayside where the fishing boats unloaded. The air was rough and cold, and he stole a pair of shipboy's trousers and a knitted muffler for Weasel from a marine store near the Custom House. He was sorry to leave this kind place. But Weasel showed such a strong inclination to go to sea, and found it so amusing to flaunt her trousers on the quayside and startle her admirers with her green face, that she was becoming notorious, and he was afraid Master Blackbone might hear of her. From Yarmouth they flew inland, steering their course by church towers. Where there is a church tower you can be sure of fools, Master Blackbone had said. True enough; but Elphenor tired of thieving—though it called for more skill in villages—and he thought he would try turning an honest penny, for a change. By now he was so coarsened and brown-handed that he could pass as a labouring man. In one place he sacked potatoes, in another baled reeds for thatching. At a village called Scottow, where the sexton had rheumatism, he dug a grave. Honest-pennying was no pleasure to Weasel, who had to hang about invisibly, passing the time with shrivelled blackberries. In these rustic places which had never seen a circus or an Indian peddler, her lovely green face would have brought stones rattling on their heels.

Winter came late that year and stealthily, but the nights were cold. Nights were never cold in Suffolk, she said. He knew this was due to the steady temperature under the hill, but hoping all the same she might be right he turned southward. He had earned more than enough to pay for a night at an inn. At Bury St. Edmunds he bought her a cloak with a deep hood, and telling her to pull the hood well forward and keep close to his heels he went at dusk to a respectable inn and hired the best bedroom they had. All went well, except that they seemed to look at him doubtfully. In his anxiety to control the situation he had reverted to his upper-class manner, which his clothes did not match with. The four-poster bed was so comfortable that he hired the room for a second night, telling the chambermaid his wife had a headache and must not be disturbed. It was certainly an elopement, she reported; even before she had left the room, the little gentleman had parted the bed curtains and climbed in beside the lady. After the second night there was no more money.

They left on foot, and continued to walk, for there was a shifting, drizzling fog which made it difficult to keep each other in sight if they flew. Once again they stole a dinner, but it was so inadequate that Elphenor decided to try begging. He was rehearsing a beggar's whine when they saw a ruddy glow through the fog and heard a ham-

mer ring on an anvil. Weasel as usual clapped her hands
to her ears; but when they came to a wayside forge the
warmth persuaded her to follow Elphenor, who went in
shivering ostentatiously and asked if he and his wife could
stand near the blaze: they would not get in the way, they
would not stay long. The blacksmith was shaping horse-
shoes. He nodded, and went on with his work. Elphenor
was preparing another whine when the blacksmith remarked it was no day to be out, and encouraged Weasel,
who stood in the doorway, to come nearer the fire.

"Poor soul, she could do with a little kindness," said
Elphenor. "And we haven't met with much of it today. We
passed an inn, farther back"—it was there they had stolen
the heel of a Suffolk cheese—"but they said they had no
room for us."

Weasel interrupted. "What's that black thing ahead,
that keeps on showing and going?"

The blacksmith pulled his forelock. "Madam. That's
the church."

They thanked him and went away, Elphenor thinking
he must learn to beg more feelingly. The blacksmith stood
looking after them. At this very time of year, too. He
wished he had not let slip the opportunity of a Hail Mary
not likely to come his way again.

The brief December day was closing when they came
to the church. The south porch, large as a room, was
sheltered from the wind, and they sat there, huddled in
Weasel's cloak. "We can't sleep here," Elphenor said. For
all that, he got up and tried the church door. It was
locked. He immediately determined to get in by a window. They flew round the church, fingering the cold
panes of glass, and had almost completed their round and
seen the great bulk of the tower threatening down on
them, when Weasel heard a clatter overhead. It came
from one of the clerestory windows, where a missing pane
had been replaced by a shutter. They wrenched the shutter open, and flew in, and circled downward through darkness, and stood on a flagstone pavement. Outlined against
a window was a tall structure with a peak. Fingering it,
they found it was wood, carved, and swelling out of a
stem like a goblet. A railed flight of steps half encircled
the stem. They mounted the steps and found themselves

in the goblet. It was an octagonal cupboard, minus a top
but carpeted. By curling round each other, there would be
room to lie down. The smell of wood gave them a sense of
security, and they spent the night in the pulpit.

He woke to the sound of Weasel laughing. Daylight
was streaming in, and Weasel was flitting about the roof,
laughing at the wooden figures that supported the cross-
beams—carved imitations of fairies, twelve foot high, with
outstretched turkey wings and gaunt faces, each uglier
than the last. "So that's what they think we're like," she
said. "And look at *her!*" She pointed to the fairy above
the pulpit, struggling with a trumpet.

Exploring at floor level, Elphenor read the Ten Com-
mandments, and found half a bottle of wine and some
lozenges. It would pass for a breakfast; later, he would
stroll into the village and see what could be got from
there. While he was being raised as the Devil at Walsham
Borealis, he had learned some facts about the Church of
England, one of them that the reigning monarch, sym-
bolically represented as a lion and a unicorn, is worshipped noisily on one day of the week and that for the
rest of the week churches are unmolested. There was
much to be said for spending the winter here. The building was windproof and weatherproof, Weasel was delighted with it, and, for himself, he found its loftiness and
spaciousness congenial, as though he were back in Zuy—
a Zuy improved by a total removal of its inhabitants. He
had opened a little door and discovered a winding stone
stairway behind it when his confidence in Church of England weekdays was shaken by the entrance of two women
with brooms and buckets. He beckoned to Weasel,
snatched her cloak from the pulpit, and preceded her up
the winding stairs, holding the bottle and the lozenges.
The steps were worn; there was a dead crow on one of
them. They groped their way up into darkness, then into
light; a window showed a landing and a door open on a
small room where some ropes dangled from the ceiling.
Weasel seized a rope and gave it a tug, and would have
tugged at it more energetically if Elphenor had not inter-
vened, promising that when the women had gone away
she could tug to her heart's content. Looking out of the
cobwebbed window, he saw the churchyard far below and

realized they must be a long way up the tower. But the steps wound on into another darkness and a dimmer lightness, and to another landing and another door open on another room. This room had louvred windows high up in the wall, and most of its floor space was taken up by a frame supporting eight bells, four of them upside down with their clappers lolling in their iron mouths. This was the bell chamber, he explained. The ropes went from the bells into the room below, which was the ringing chamber. There was a similar tower near Zuy; mortals thought highly of it, and his tutor had taken him to see it.

Weasel began to stroke one of the bells. As though she were caressing some savage sleeping animal, it presently responded with a noise between a soft growl and a purr. Elphenor stroked another. It answered at a different pitch, deeper and harsher, as though it were a more savage animal. But they were hungry. The bells could wait. The light from the louvred windows flickered between bright and sombre as the wind tossed the clouds. It was blowing up for a storm.

They would be out of the wind tonight and for many nights to come. January is a dying season, there would be graves to dig, and with luck and management, thought Elphenor, he might earn a livelihood and be a friend to sextons here and around. Weasel would spare crumbs from the bread he earned, scatter them for birds, catch the birds, pluck and eat them: she still preferred raw food, with the life still lively in it. On Sundays, she said, they would get their week's provisions; with everybody making a noise in church, stealing would be child's play. The pulpit would be the better for a pillow, and she could soon collect enough feathers for a pillow, for a feather mattress even: one can always twitch a pillowcase from the washing line. The wine had gone to their heads; they outbid each other with grand plans of how they would live in the church, and laughed them down, and imagined more. They would polish the wooden fairies' noses till they shone like drunkards' noses; they would grow watercresses in the font; Elphenor would tell the complete story of his life before they met. Let him begin now! Was he born with a hook nose and red hair? He began, obediently and prosily. Weasel clamped her eyes open, and suppressed yawns. He lost the thread of his narrative. Drowsy with wine, they fell asleep.

He woke to two appalling sounds. Weasel screaming with terror, a clash of metal. The bell ringers had come to practise their Christmas peal, and prefaced it by sounding all the bells at once. The echo was heavy on the air as they began to ring a set of changes, first the scale descending evenly to the whack of the tenor bell, then in patterned steps to the same battle-axe blow. The pattern altered; the tenor bell sounded midway, jolting an arbitrary finality into the regular measure of eight. With each change of position the tenor bell accumulated a more threatening insistency, and the other bells shifted round it like a baaing flock of sheep.

Weasel cowered in Elphenor's arms. She had no strength left to scream with; she could only tremble before the impact of the next flailing blow. He felt his senses coming adrift. The booming echo was a darkness on his sight through which he saw the bells in their frame heaving and evading, evading and heaving, under a dark sky. The implacable assault of the changing changes pursued him as the waves had pursued the boat from IJmuiden. But here there was no escape, for it was he who wallowed broken-backed at the mercy of the storm. Weasel lay in his arms like something at a distance. He felt his protectiveness, his compassion, ebbing away; he watched her with a bloodless, skeleton love. She still trembled, but in a disjointed way, as though she were falling to pieces.

He saw the lovely green fade out of her face. "My darling," he said, "death by lightning would have been easier." He could not hear himself speak.

The frost lasted on into mid-March. No one went to the bell chamber till the carpenter came to mend the louvres in April. The two bodies, one bowed over the other, had fallen into decay. No one could account for them, or for the curious weightless fragments of a substance rather like sheet gelatine which the wind had scattered over the floor. They were buried in the same grave. Because of their small stature and light bones they were entered in the Register of Burials as *Two Stranger Children*.

VERA CHAPMAN
(1898–   )

Vera Chapman, until recently, was known only to a relatively small circle: her family, acquaintances, and the members of the Tolkien Society. She founded the Tolkien Society in London in 1969 to provide a forum for discussing the works of J. R. R. Tolkien, who agreed to become the honorary president of the group in 1972. Apparently her activities in the society provided the stimulus for writing her own works, and she had her first book published in 1976. Several additional works have followed in quick succession; three of these ("The Three Damosels" triology: *The Green Knight, The King's Damosel,* and *King Arthur's Daughter*) have been published in this country by Avon Books. She wrote "Crusader Damosel" in 1977, specifically for the present volume, and we trust it will serve to further the reputation of this remarkable woman whose retirement years are proving indeed to be among her most active and fruitful.

Since Mrs. Chapman is a newcomer to the field, very little has been written about her. She has, however, graciously provided us with an autobiographical sketch.

I was born in 1898, in Bournemouth, Hampshire, England. I went to Oxford (Lady Margaret Hall) in 1918, and was one of the very first women to be granted full membership of Oxford University in 1919, to wear the gown, and to graduate in 1921. I married a clergyman of the Church of England in 1924, and my first married home was in Lourenço Marques, which was then Portuguese East Africa (Mozambique). I returned to England in 1925, and for many years lived in country vicarages. Shortly after the 1940 war, I worked in the Colonial Office as a student welfare officer. I have now been retired for many years. I live in a Council flat (apartment) in Camden Town, London, and I have two children and four grandchildren. My first novel, *The Green Knight*, was published in 1976, and was followed by *The King's Damosel* and *King Arthur's Daughter*, and in 1977 by *Judy and Julia*. The first three are published as "children's stories," but are really not intended for children; the fourth, *Judy and Julia*, really is a children's book.

Without having been asked about it specifically, Chapman comments, with characteristic straightforwardness and modesty, about being a new author in her seventies.

There are several reasons why I have not attained publication until so late in life: chiefly that although I always meant to write, I have had so many other things to do—and also that until recently, there has not been much opening for "fantasy" writing—I had to wait till the present interest in imaginative writing gave me a chance. I have certainly accumulated the proverbial "rejection slips enough to paper a room."

In speaking of the background to the present story and to her other books, she states that it "has been largely a matter of a lifetime of 'grasshopper' reading and 'fly-paper' memory. In other words I have read what I liked and remembered what interested me." Her reading and her memory have provided her with a sound historical base, as the present story shows. Among her readings, she lists Zoë Oldenbourg's *The Crusades* and Jack Lindsay's *The Crusaders*.

"Crusader Damosel" is a highly original blending of history, romance, and fantasy. The battle of the Horns of Hattin occurred in 1187, with Saladin leading the Muslims in a decisive victory over the Christians under King Guy of Jerusalem. As Chapman notes, it was the quarrel between King Guy and Count Raymond of Toulouse that led to the Christians' defeat, "from which the two great

Chivalric Orders never fully recovered." Using this event as background, Chapman unfolds for us the love story of Hugh and Adela, which presents a thematic counterpoint to the religiously motivated carnage. The fantasy element in the story melds the historical and romantic components. Hugh and Adela, who have exchanged furtive glances, meet only on the "Other Side of the Curtain," a land "beyond dreams." Their visionary experiences there reveal to them, especially to Adela, the tragic reality of the religious war. Reinforcing the delicately balanced plot lines is the finely tuned style. Chapman's style adjusts with facility to bring alive the authentic detail of the movements and battles of armies, to create the visionary exploits in the land "Beyond the Curtain," and to develop a convincing love story. And, finally, moving palpably through the entire story is the vibrant central figure, the Crusader Damosel.

◆§ Crusader Damosel §◆

Vera Chapman

When Adela learnt that her father was to go to the Holy
Land, taking her and her mother with him, she was delighted. Her mother, Dame Blanche, was less delighted,
but there was not much choice in the matter. Sir Brian
de Bassecourt, of Stoke Bassecourt in the county of Kent,
had been ordered by the Abbot to go on the Crusade, or
else build an expensive chantry for the abbey—for Sir
Brian had killed a monk. He hadn't really meant to kill
the monk, he said, but when he found him half way up
the stairs to Dame Blanche's bower, he had given him
a little push down, and—the man had broken his neck.
The Abbot acquitted him of wilful murder, but ordered
that he should either build a chantry or go on the Crusade. Sir Brian wasn't a rich man, so although the Crusade might cost a good deal of money, the chantry would
cost far more. Besides, there were advantages, as he
pointed out to Dame Blanche.

"Just think—we get all our sins forgiven, all of them—
yours too, and Adela's. And if we should die on the journey—"

Dame Blanche gave a shriek.

"*If* we should, we'd all go to heaven at once—no
Purgatory at all. Think of that!"

"I'd rather not think of that," said Dame Blanche.

"Don't, then, my dear—never mind. There's other
things. Almost everyone that goes out to Outremer comes
back with a fortune. There's plunder, and ransoms—
there's even lands and castles for the picking up. *And*
we'd be sure to find a husband for Adela, which is more
than we'll do here."

So Dame Blanche went about her preparations, tearfully at first, and later with zeal and fervour—and Adela watched the preparations with mounting excitement.

Adela was fifteen, and had never been outside Stoke Bassecourt, where they lived in a humdrum little farmhouse dignified by the name of Manor, which Duke William had bestowed on Sir Brian's great-grandfather. Adela had a fine Norman profile, jet-black hair, and blue eyes inherited from a Saxon grandmother. She was a bold girl, something of a tomboy, a good rider, and afraid of nothing she had met so far. But attractive as she was, she might as well go into a convent and be done with it, in that dull little corner. She'd never find a husband there.

So, after an overwhelming fuss and bother of preparation, they set out—Sir Brian in armour on his big charger, Dame Blanche in a mule litter, Adelaide on a palfrey. She had devised herself a dress like that invented by Queen Eleanor some seventy years before, when she and all her ladies went on the First Crusade with King Louis, before she became Queen of England. Well-cut leather breeches, discreetly covered by a long, voluminous divided skirt, so full and flowing that no one could see that the wearer sat easily astride on a man's saddle underneath all that brocade. There was also a light corselet of soft leather, shaped so as to enhance the figure very discreetly, and covered with a silken surcoat. In that outfit, with a hooded cape for the rain, Adela sat proudly and confidently on her pretty black mare.

The first rallying point was at Wrotham, for the Kentish levies. Here the Crusaders made their vows and "took the Cross—." Sir Brian had a bold red cross, made of two stripes of red cloth, stitched to his mantle, while he took the Crusader's Oath in the church.

Adela wanted to be enrolled as a Crusader too. She saw at least two imposing ladies going up and receiving the Cross. "Why can't I?" she asked Sir Brian. *"They* can."

"Oh, yes, my dear, they do let ladies take the Cross, but only if they bring their own retinue of fighting men, as those two ladies are doing. I'm afraid my small following is barely a quota for one—besides that, you are under age."

But the noble words of the Crusader's Oath stayed in

Adela's mind and haunted her. She wove daydreams about riding out to help King Guy to defend Jerusalem, with a long sword at her side, fighting to keep the heathen from regaining the Holy Sepulchre, the holiest spot on earth.

Somehow the milling crowd got across the Channel, and in the fields of France a long caravan formed, and slowly made its straggling way across Europe. It was an astonishing assembly— knights and noblemen with their soldiers, bands of volunteers from the country trudging with their bows, monks and clerics of every order, pilgrims, peddlers, hucksters and sutlers, wives and families of fighting men —and, of course, a number of dubious ladies who travelled with the wagons and were discreetly known as "baggage." Then there were smiths and cooks, with their furnaces and cauldrons, and flocks of sheep and herds of cattle to provide meat on the hoof—and Lord-knows-what besides. It was like a slowly moving town. Every day saw them strung out along the road, all in their accustomed order, with marshals riding up and down the line to keep them together. At night there could be the most astonishing variety of resting places. Sometimes they would reach a town or a castle, and then some of them at least (particularly the ladies, such as Adela and her mother) would be guests in comfort—or in more or less discomfort, as the luck was. Sometimes the company would halt in the open country, and make camp—everybody would pitch their tents, and once you got used to this and got organized, it wasn't bad at all. When a camp was made, it was a good opportunity to go up and down the lines and call on one's friends. Blanche did a good deal of visiting, with Adela beside her, rather overwhelmed with the newness of it all, and for the time being, diffident and a little withdrawn. Sir Brian brought young knights to their tent and presented them, ceremoniously, to Blanche and Adela. They were fine to look at, but Adela could find nothing to say to them.

Every morning began solemnly with Mass, either in the church of the town where they happened to be, or in a great pavilion set up with an altar and all the holy adornments—the knights and ladies devoutly kneeling on the grass outside. (But Dame Blanche took care to have a cushion.) It was one morning half way through France, when Mass was being celebrated in the pavilion, and all the company was ranged in order outside, that Adela looked over her right shoulder, and saw a phalanx of men, standing foursquare together, in straight rows. All were in armour, and over the armour a white tunic and a long white mantle, emblazoned with the red cross. Their helmets were round, and cut straight across the top, like round towers. Something grim and resolute marked these men out from the rest. Adela ran her eyes along their faces, such of them as she could see. Mostly bearded, greyish, lined, some of them scarred. But one—he was young, bright-eyed. Something about him said to Adela: "This is the one."

She had turned half round—very naughtily—and for the life of her she could not keep herself from fixing her eyes on his face. And he looked at her for one moment— dark brown his eyes were—and a flash of understanding passed between them. Then Dame Blanche was pinching Adela's arm quite painfully, and jerking her round. Adela returned to her devotions—but she hardly knew what she was doing.

At the end of Mass, Adela stole a discreet glimpse over her shoulder—but now the crowd in general turned to see the men in white mantles, frowning and aloof, marching away in disciplined ranks. She tried in vain to see the face she had noticed.

"Adela," her mother said, "you mustn't look at those men. Don't you know what they are? Those are the Knights Templars."

"Are they? Well, what's wrong with them?"

"Nothing *wrong* with them—but don't you understand, they mustn't look at women, or even let women look at them. They are under a vow of poverty, obedience, and— chastity. You keep your eyes away from them, my dear."

But Adela had looked once too often already.

The Templars, part of whose duty it was to protect pilgrims, and the relatives and dependents of Crusaders, on their way to the Holy Land, now constituted themselves a guard to the company. Strung out at intervals, they patrolled the borders of the road, as well as going ahead and also covering the rear. They changed their positions often —and so one day Adela saw that face again, and then

again, and found out from some of the servants that his
name was Hugo Des Moulins, and that in spite of his
French name, he was an English knight from Sussex. She
looked him in the face, but the first time he answered her
look with a kind of breathlessness, and the second time
with a frown of anxiety, almost of pain. She knew she
ought not to let her mind dwell on him, but how could
she help it? And as they continued on their way, and
reached Venice, and took ship (a dreadful passage it was)
to Acre, her case grew more and more desperate. Until at
last, at Acre, as soon as they were settled into their humble quarters in the great stony fortress, she felt she must
take action. So, as soon as she knew where that lady
would be quartered, she sought out the Abbess of Shaston.

The Abbess of Shaston was a remarkable woman. She
knew a wonderful great deal about a great many things—
people came to her to be cured of illnesses, and of heart-
aches—to resolve doubts, and points of law, and settle
quarrels; to seek love, or to be delivered from love; she
was sought by women who wished to have babies, and, it
was whispered, by those who did not. She could not be
called a midwife nor a leech, for such occupations would
be beneath the dignity of an Abbess; but it was thought
that she knew more than all the wise-women and all
the doctors together. She went back and forward to the
Holy Land as it pleased her, and it was said that she knew
the secrets of the Saracens as well as of the Christians.
She was certainly not a witch—nobody dared say such a
thing, for she had high connections. She obeyed no au-
thority lower than the Pope's—if his, seeing that she was
perhaps his cousin. She was extremely ugly, but very
stately. Adela sought her out, taking with her the little
jewel-box she always carried with her, containing such
modest jewelry as she possessed. She opened this, and
left it lying open before the Abbess.

"Put those things away, child," said the Abbess. "Now
tell me. You're in love, of course?"

So Adela told her.

"A Templar? That's difficult. Why did it have to be a
Templar, you silly girl? You know he can't marry you. Do
you want to be his paramour?"

Adela blushed. "Oh, but Templars don't have paramours."

"Don't they, then?—There's a lot you don't know about Templars.—But that wouldn't do for you, nor for him, I think. What do you want, then?"

"Can't a Templar ever be absolved from his vows?"

"Oh, yes, he can. The Pope can dispense his vow. I'd see it done myself—the Pope would do it for me." She spoke with airy assurance. "Only—the petition must come from him, not from anyone else. He himself must ask for it. Would he do that—for you?"

"He doesn't know me," said Adela with her eyes downcast.

"No.—Oh, but he does, though. He dreams of you."

"How—how on earth do you know?"

"Never mind how—but I know. You and he know each other quite well, on the Other Side of the Curtain. But that's no good for earthly matters."

"What do you mean—the Other Side of the Curtain?"

"The other side of life and being. Even beyond dreams. Out of the body. You and he meet together, night after night, while your dreams hang a misleading curtain before your mortal minds."

Adela felt as if a great window was opened before her, full of beauty and wonder.

"Oh, if only I could know—if only I could remember! Could you not send me through the Curtain in my waking mind, or make it so that I remembered?"

"My child, I believe I could. But you must attend and do exactly as I say."

So then she gave Adela certain instructions, and taught her certain words and certain signs. And once again she waved aside Adela's jewel-box.

So that night, Adela, lying on her bed wide awake, and having done all that the Abbess told her, felt herself rise out of her body, like slipping a hand out of a glove. She looked down at herself lying peacefully asleep on the bed, and then she stepped over herself, and was lightly out of doors and across the night and into a moonlit orchard, where Hugo was waiting for her.

"Welcome, my dear companion," he said, and clasped

both her hands, but did not kiss her. It was enough for her, so far—just to feel his happy fellowship.

"I knew you would come," he said. "You always do."

"Yes," she answered, feeling quite sure that they had known each other quite well for a long time. "But this time I shall know what I am doing, and remember it afterwards."

"I wish I did," he said. "I never remember anything when I am awake. I don't know even that I know you."

"What do you call me—here?" she asked.

"Why—Adal, I think," he answered.

"And am I a boy or a girl?"

"A boy, of course—no, a girl—oh, to be sure, I don't know." and he laughed in confusion. "But come on—the trumpets are sounding—we must ride against the infidel."

By his side was a horse, saddled and ready, and she got up behind him. It seemed that they were both armoured and accoutred in the Templars' armour, and she had a long sword by her side. She remembered the device on the Templars' seal—two knights riding on one horse.

They galloped out of the orchard, and it was daylight. Before them lay a wide plain, and far off a little compact city on a hill, which she knew must be Jerusalem. Behind them rode the squadron of the Templars, but she could not see them clearly because they were behind her. Suddenly, as they rode toward the City, there rose up before them a host of ugly little black men. They were ape-like and dusty-looking, their clothes black as well as their faces, and on their heads were small red turbans with golden crescents. They all looked alike, and all had horrible grinning faces, and sharp crooked swords.

"Oh, what are these?" exclaimed Adela.

"Paynims, Saracens—have no fear of them—charge for the Cross!" And he drew his sword and galloped into the thick of them. She drew her sword too, but passed it into her left hand so that, as he slashed on the right she could slash on the left. In the body which she now seemed to wave, her left arm was as good as her right.

They hewed at the little black men, who fought fiercely and shouted, but fell as they slashed them, without any blood—they seemed to be made of something like soft wood, or wax, and never bled, nor did their expressionless faces show any pain. More and more came up on them, but they hewed them all down, and rushed on through them with a fierce delight. Behind them came the other Crusaders but never overtook them. At one moment Hugo drew rein, and Adela was able to look behind them—there were a few of the Crusaders fallen, but over each one hovered a fine white-winged angel, just like those in the church paintings at home—gently drawing the man's soul out of his body, and carrying it upward.

The Holy City was nearer now, and shone with gold; on a pinnacle in the midst Our Lady stood, in a robe of blue, with the Holy Child in her arms. As the Crusaders fought their way towards the City through the tumbling black men, Our Lady smiled at Hugo and Adela and flung a handful of rose petals.

And then Adela was suddenly awake, and it was all a dream—or was it? The tips of her fingers smelt of roses.

There were galleries all round the great courtyard, and there Adela, her mother, and all the ladies of the company, were seated on the chairs to watch a spectacle. Down below, the courtyard was thronged with armed men. With pomp and pageantry, a procession entered below. Count Raymond himself, with all his peers, glittering with metal and coloured silks, and a tall swordsman by his side, and men with a brazier. Adela supposed the brazier was to keep Count Raymond warm out there.

Then were led in a long line of tall, dignified men, in long white robes and turbans. Their arms were tied, and the foot soldiers led them along. Their faces were sallow but pale, and their eyes dark, and all had beards, some black, some grey. They held themselves with sorrowful composure, and reminded Adela of pictures she had seen of Christian martyrs.

"Oh, who are these?" she asked.

"Paynims, child—Saracens, Mussulmans and heathens. These are the enemy."

"Oh—" But these were not in the least like the little black men in the dream.

The first was led before Count Raymond in his chair. Now, Adela thought, he will loose his bonds and set him free. The paynim man made a low obeisance—Count Raymond gave a sign to the man with the sword—the

301

sword fell, and the paynim's head toppled horribly to the ground. Indeed these were not like the little men who did not bleed. . . .

Another and another. . . . There were some whose hands were chopped off. . . .

"They don't feel anything, those paynims," said Dame Blanche. "They'd serve our own men the same if they caught them. Anyway they've refused baptism. Now this one will be a different punishment, look—"

"Let me go—I don't feel well," Adela said, shuddering, and escaped to her room, where she cried for hours.

It was some nights before she could get "through the Curtain" to Hugo again, but when she did, she told him about it, and all her horror and revulsion. And he looked serious and worried, and said, "How can we understand? All we know, when we are awake, is that we must obey and fight. But I know—I have felt it too."

But then the little black men crept up on them, and once again they had to fight their way through them. And this time they broke right through the Saracen army, and came to the golden walls of the Holy City—and the gates stood open, and they went in. There was nobody to be seen there—all stood deserted, all the houses of gold, with their windows of jewels—but from somewhere, high up, a sound of heavenly music and joyful singing filled the air. From every part of the city could be seen the pinnacle where Our Lady stood.

"Come," said Hugo, "we must seek the Sepulchre of the Lord," and they went on through the golden streets, but somewhere the ways diverged, and Adela looked round for Hugo and he was not there. She went on, calling for him, and found herself outside the City on the other side, looking back at the walls.

And there before her, but facing the City, was the host of the Saracens—those same tall, turbaned, white-robed men, with pale faces and dark beards. They were armed and on horses, and galloping, galloping towards the City. Out against them came a horde of little black men, just like those she had fought against with Hugo, just as ugly and just as wooden, but these had round red caps on their heads with silver crosses on them. And the Saracens charged into them, hewing and slicing off heads, arms and legs as before; and as before, the little black men fell without bleeding and with no sign of pain. Before the Saracens, as they fought, stood the Holy City, but on the pinnacle where Adela had seen Our Lady, was a tall tree full of flowers. Some of the Saracens fell, and over each one hovered a beautiful girl, with butterfly wings and clothed in rainbow silks, who drew out his soul and carried it aloft.

Two Saracens closed up beside her.

"Come, lady," they said, "we welcome you with all honour." They led her away from the battle, to a richly decorated tent where sat Saladin himself on silken cushions. He smiled and bade her welcome, and as she thought of the tall men slaughtered in the castle yard, her eyes filled with tears.

"Lady of the Giaours," he said, "if we all pitied our enemies, there would be no wars."

"And would not that be a good thing?" she said with the boldness of a dream.

"Ah, who knows? But we know that Allah made soldiers to fight. What else would they do?"

He made her sit on cushions by his side, and sip a strange sweet drink, and he told her a password which she was to remember. Over and over he said it—and she woke up saying it. In the moment of waking she wrote it down, in a sort of fashion, in such letters as she knew, just so that she should not forget it.

Everything was astir in the castle and town of Acre. "We shall have to move as soon as we can," said Sir Brian. "Get boats and be off to-morrow early. It isn't safe here. Saladin's forces are between us and Tiberias. We're cut off. Tiberias is besieged, with Count Raymond's wife and family in it. Some say the army is to march on Tiberias—some say not. I know what *we'll* do. Get packed."

So the rest of the day was full of bustle. But Adela, whose heart was heavy with foreboding, went to sleep early.

When she slipped out of her body, and went in search

303

of Hugo, she knew there was a difference. She did not find herself in the moonlit orchard—she was not in the magical world of visions, but hovering over and wandering through the real world, like a ghost, unseen. She was watching the army of the Crusaders on the march, through the night, the Templars leading. Hugo was there, on his horse, but not riding gallantly. They were none of them riding gallantly. They laboured through the night on tired horses, and drooped in their saddles. She heard them talking.

"Why on earth did we have to leave Sephoria? Plenty of water in Sephoria, and a good defensive position. But no—before we'd time even to water the horses—"

"And after marching all day—hardly time for a mouthful to drink, and God! I'm thirsty . . ."

"They say the Commanders quarrelled. Count Raymond, like a sensible man, said stay in Sephoria, with the water, and wait a bit—though, mind you, it's *his* wife and children who are in Tiberias. He said it was a trap to get us to move out. And King Godfrey listened to him, didn't he?"

"Yes, but then Count Gerard came in, and said Raymond was a traitor and had sold out to the Saracens. So King Guy got in a panic and ordered us to march on Tiberias at once, before we'd had any rest."

"What can you do, when your Commanders disagree? —Oh, what would I give for a drink. Never mind ale or wine—just water."

"If we can get through to Galilee, there's plenty of water."

"And all the Saracens between us and Galilee. The horses will flounder first."

"What's this place we're making for—the top of that hill?"

"They call it Hattin—the Horns of Hattin—the Horns of Hattin—"

She moved through the ranks and hovered over Hugo, trying to enter his mind. But all that came across to her was thirst, thirst, thirst—and the oppressive weight of his armour, the heat inside it, the weakness of the body that had sweated all day and was now drained dry. The grey-faced old Templars rode beside him, bidding him cheer up, for the more the suffering the greater the glory. He listened dull-eyed.

She woke, dry-throated, crying out, "Water, water—the Horns of Hattin, the Horns of Hattin . . ."

She knew what she had to do. Quietly she slipped out of bed and dressed in her riding breeches and corselet, but without the skirt, and threw a hooded mantle over her. Stealthily she slipped out to the horse-lines, found her own black mare, saddled her, and before she mounted, slung on her saddle two small casks full of water. It was as much as she could require the mare to carry.

The sentry at the door barred her way.

"Oh, please—" she said.

"Oh, a lady. By heaven, the Lady Adela—"

"Soldier," she said, "you know why people sometimes have reasons to slip out alone—"

Certainly he did—with half the Castle engaged in love-affairs.

"Surely—but *you*, Lady Adela—I'd never have thought *you*—"

In the dark he could not see her blush.

"All right, my lady—not a word from me. But take care of yourself, won't you?" He let her past.

Then she rode like the wind towards Tiberias.

From daybreak to noon she rode, and that noon was fiercely hot. It was July, and the grass was dry and the earth was splitting. Once in sheer exhaustion she dismounted, drank from a wayside spring and let the mare drink, and rested a short time. She could not have eaten if she had had food with her. Then she went on eastwards, and as she went she could smell burning grass. Nothing unusual in that—the grass caught fire very easily at that season. But now the smoke was denser—soon it was a choking smother. As she came up a hill, and saw Galilee below her, she also saw the battle. It raged fiercely over the plateau—the Horns of Hattin! The army of the Cross, fighting fiercely, fighting desperately against the vast, overwhelming army of the Saracens. As they fought, the smoke from the grass-fire, blowing away from the Saracens, covered the Crusaders in its stifling, throat-drying fog.

The foot-soldiers had broken and fled. Most of the horses lay exhausted on the ground, and the knights were falling one by one, or lying, helpless heaps of clashing metal, at their enemies' feet. This was no battle of little black bloodless men—far from it. Adela was spared nothing of the blood and horror.

Alone among the rest stood the Templars and the Hospitallers, grouped around the black-and-white banner, isolated in the field like the last sheaf to be reaped. They were laying about them fiercely, and Hugo was amongst them—but they were failing. As she watched she saw him fall.

Without a moment's hesitation she spurred forward, forcing the unwilling mare to face the smoke. But there was rough cliff in front of her, and a drop—no way down. She had to go round, and the only way she could go led her in a curve to the opposite side of the battlefield. She found herself dashing into the lines of the Saracens. Hands reached up to catch her bridle-reins.

"Oh, let me go!" she exclaimed, not at all sure if they understood her language. "I must get to him. I must save life—save life, do you understand?" The dark faces grinned, not comprehending. It seemed the battle was over—the Saracens were coming back from the field, leading prisoners.

Then Adela remembered the password she had learnt from Saladin in her dream, and spoke it.

The men fell back in astonishment, and let her through.

Down that grim hillside she went, the smoke still all about her. She tried to remember the place where she had seen Hugo fall by the black-and-white standard. The worst was having to pass the other men, wounded, dying, ghastly, who cried to her from the ground for water. Some of them were too parched to cry out. Some seemed to be unwounded—it was only the heat and the smoke and the drought that had killed them. But she could not spare any water at all. There were one or two with still enough strength to scramble to their feet and try to snatch the water-barrels. But she beat them off with her riding-whip

—they had not much strength after all and could not run after her.

And at last she found him.

He lay on a horrible heap of dead men, and he did not move. She dismounted, and dragged him aside to a clean patch of ground, and bathed his face, and trickled water into his mouth, and freed him from his armour—she had to take his dagger to cut its lacings, and even when she had unfastened it, the metal was still hot to the touch. She flung each piece away from him. He began to stir, opened his eyes, and then was able to swallow the water she held to his lips. She laid a wet kerchief over his nostrils against the smoke. And when at last he showed enough signs of life, she helped him on to her mare, and mounted behind him, holding him, and so rode slowly and carefully away from that dreadful place, once again like two Templars on one horse. She went boldly through the camp of the Saracens, and spoke that password. The Saracens buzzed and chattered in amazement, and some of them sent messengers to tell Saladin, but they let them through.

And after a long time they halted by the sweet shores of Galilee, and she laid him with his back propped against a sycamore tree, and let him drink again. And then he took notice of her at last.

"Adal," he said. "My good comrade. But I thought truly that we had been through Purgatory together, and were entering Paradise. But now I know that you are a woman."

"Are you glad or sorry?" she said.

"Oh, I'm glad, I'm glad!" he cried. "And yet—what am I saying? My vow—the Templars—"

Very gently she told him how the Templars and the Hospitallers lay on the battlefield. He crossed himself, and wept. Then he held out his arms to her as if she had been his mother.

"And now—but what shall we do, my love, what shall we do?"

"I know what we must do," she said. "We'll go to the Abbess of Shaston. She'll make everything right for us."

SUPERIOR
FANTASY AND SCIENCE FICTION
FROM AVON BOOKS

☐ A For Andromeda		
Fred Hoyle and John Elliot	23366	$1.25
☐ And All The Stars A Stage James Blish	27177	$1.25
☐ Cities In Flight James Blish	41616	$2.50
☐ Cryptozoic Brian Aldiss	33415	$1.25
☐ Doorways In The Sand Roger Zelazny	32086	$1.50
☐ Forgotten Beasts of Eld Patricia McKillip	42523	$1.75
☐ The Gray Prince Jack Vance	26799	$1.25
☐ The Investigation Stanislaw Lem	29314	$1.50
☐ The Lathe of Heaven Ursula K. LeGuin	38299	$1.50
☐ Macroscope Piers Anthony	36798	$1.95
☐ Memoirs Found In A Bathtub		
Stanislaw Lem	29959	$1.50
☐ Metal Monster A. Merritt	31294	$1.50
☐ Mindbridge Joe Haldeman	33605	$1.95
☐ Omnivore	40527	$1.75
☐ Orn Piers Anthony	40964	$1.75
☐ Ox Piers Anthony	29702	$1.50
☐ Pilgrimage Zenna Henderson	36681	$1.50
☐ Raum Carl Sherrell	33043	$1.50
☐ Seven Footprints to Satan A. Merritt	28209	$1.25
☐ Song for Lya and Other Stories		
George R. Martin	27581	$1.25
☐ Starship Brian W. Aldiss	22588	$1.25
☐ Sword of the Demon Richard A. Lupoff	37911	$1.75
☐ 334 Thomas M. Disch	42630	$2.25

Available at better bookstores everywhere, or order direct from the publisher.

AVON BOOKS, Mail Order Dept., 250 West 55th St., New York, N.Y. 10019

Please send me the books checked above. I enclose $_____(please include 25¢ per copy for postage and handling). Please use check or money order—sorry, no cash or COD's. Allow 4-6 weeks for delivery.

Mr/Mrs/Miss _____

Address _____

City_____ State/Zip_____

SSF 11-78